RESILIENCE

BOOK SEVEN IN THE CHRONICLES OF ALSEA

FLETCHER DELANCEY

HEARTSOME PUBLISHING

For the ones who don't fit in.
What makes you different may make you extraordinary.

CONTENTS

ACKNOWLEDGMENTS

For this book, my usual team had to be expanded. I threw quite a bit of biology in here and brought in two new consultants to check my work. Many thanks to Alma Tiwe, my biologist friend who might be even geekier than I am, and to Polly Rankin, whose years of experience as a fisheries biologist made her a reader I particularly wanted to impress. (She was! My ego had to be squished back to normal size.)

Rebecca Cheek gave me the benefit of her expertise as well, both in the life and physical sciences, and suggested making a gruesome scene even more gruesome, which I did gleefully. Saskia Goedhart made sure that the opening fight scene was properly choreographed and confirmed that yes, it really could happen that quickly. I picked a few military brains for questions such as who would service a shuttle and how big a shuttle bay should be; for that, my thanks go to Clifford Flesch, a US Navy veteran, and Maj. Chris Butler, USAF, Retired.

Dr. Ana Mozo gifted me with her time despite being terribly crunched for it herself, and offered a wheelbarrow of advice regarding the many medical scenes. There were a bunch, given that a major character in this book is a ship's chief surgeon.

Rick Taylor also lent his critical eye, particularly for the issue of character consistency. Karyn Aho continues to be my Prime Beta, the first stop for any manuscript, while she makes certain that my characters' psychological underpinnings are secure and believable.

On the editing side, Cheri Fuller played an excellent game of whack-a-mole: she would point out my repetitive word usage, and in correcting those problems, I'd promptly commit new offenses. We did get all the moles whacked, whereupon proofreader Lisa Shaw found a few gophers that had escaped. Those are now corralled as well.

Cover designer Dane Low did an amazing job in visualizing my alien, as if he peeked inside my head and drew what he saw there. This was achieved after a slight initial hiccup, when I mentioned bioluminescence and he drew something that looked like an alien on a glorious LSD trip. I'm sorry I couldn't use it, but I kept the file.

And thank goodness for my wonderful wife, Maria João Valente, who fell in love with a writer and somehow didn't regret it even after learning the down side: that writers can pour astonishing quantities of words into a document while having very little left to say aloud.

But I've got the words poured and printed now, and will hand them to you, the reader. Thank you for buying this book—and buckle up, because this one is a fast ride all the way to the end.

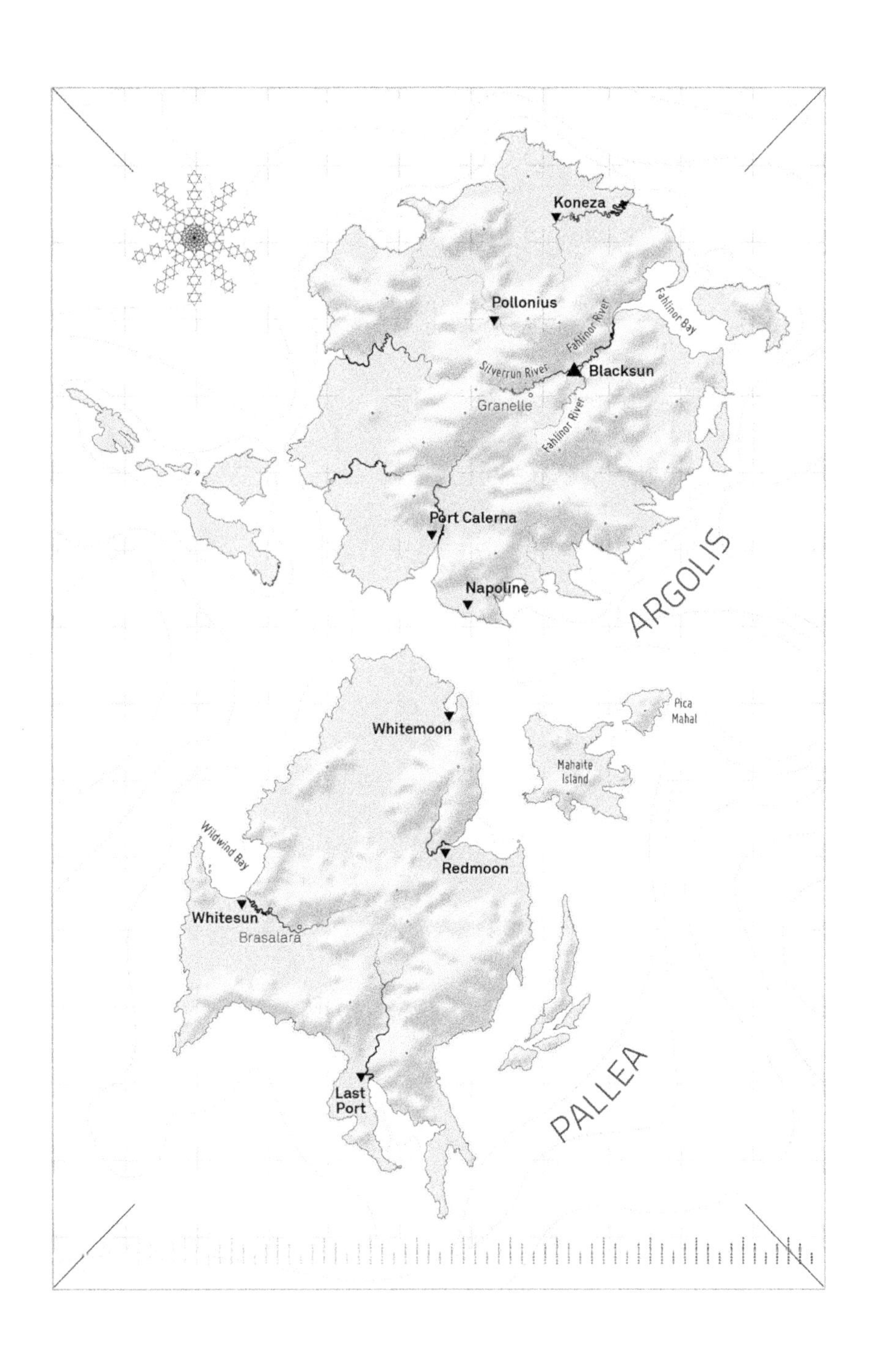
Koneza
Pollonius
Fahlinor Bay
Fahlinor River
Silverrun River
Blacksun
Granelle
Fahlinor River
Port Calerna
Napoline
ARGOLIS
Pica
Mahal
Whitemoon
Mahaite
Island
Wildwind Bay
Redmoon
Whitesun
Brasalara
Last
Port
PALLEA

PROLOGUE

"*I will represent Alsea to the best of my ability.*"

First Guard Rahel Sayana had said those words just eight days ago, before making her first trip into orbit. Looking at the groaning crew members strewn about the floor at her feet, she had the uncomfortable feeling that she'd already broken her promise.

And the day had started so well.

1

RAIN

The chime at her door came precisely on time, as always. One thing Rahel had learned about Dr. Lhyn Rivers was that she took her job seriously. Though not formally attached to the crew, she had been contracted to teach Rahel about Protectorate culture and the ship she was serving on. Every day, she appeared at the same time to begin a new tour.

"Good morning!" she said brightly when Rahel opened the door. Her hair was contained in its usual complicated braid, dark brown and silver blended together, and her vivid green eyes—too large for her face and one of the most alien things about her, even with the lack of facial ridges—were alert despite the early hour. "Ready for deck twenty-one?"

"Barely." Rahel stepped out, the door sliding closed behind her, and walked down the curving corridor beside her taller friend. "Dr. Wells kept me late last night with at least fifteen different scans. I'm glad to be done with it. Every time she put me in that omniphasic diagnostic bed, I was afraid she'd press the wrong button and send me shooting off the ship."

"Oh, that's right. Yesterday was your last compulsory day of testing. Congratulations on surviving a full week in the gentle hands of our chief surgeon."

Rahel let out a huff of laughter. "Her hands are the only gentle thing about her."

Dr. Wells had been a fixture during this first week aboard the *Phoenix*.

She was competent and intimidating in equal measure, and her temper was the stuff of legend. Rahel hadn't seen it yet, but she had heard stories.

"That's not true, you know." Lhyn angled over to a small alcove built into the bulkhead, its recessed lights shining on the yellow-flowered plant that filled it. "Dr. Wells is a kinder person than most people realize. It's a cultural constant that people present different public and private faces. Yet we still assume that what we see in public tells us all we need to know." She touched one of the flowers, which turned a deep blue beneath her finger, and added, "I love Filessian orchids."

"I like them because I can remember their name. The rest of these . . ." Rahel gestured at the corridor with its profusion of plants. Graceful arches marched along its length, bracketed by pillars housing broad-leaved vines that swept to the floor. More plants clung to the tops of the arches, some small and bushy, others with long, leathery leaves that reached for the ceiling. Along the sides of the corridor, each door was topped by a lintel crowded with greenery, and if that weren't enough, every few steps was an alcove featuring either a Filessian orchid or some equally spectacular flower. Between these were large mosaics of colored tiles, spotlit as if they were installations in an art gallery.

Rahel had never expected a warship to look like a place of worship. She felt immediately at home here, enjoying even the air she breathed. She had been prepared for sterile air, but the *Phoenix* had a subtle, woodsy scent, spiced with the fragrance of its many blooming plants.

"I can't imagine why you're having trouble remembering the names of a few hundred plant species along with the schematics of a Pulsar-class ship," Lhyn quipped.

"Ha. I was looking over the schematics for deck twenty last night and realized I'd already forgotten at least a quarter of what you showed me. How is it that you Gaians can install a lingual implant in my head so I can speak your language, but you can't program me with a map of this ship?"

She was teasing, of course, but Lhyn took her seriously.

"It's a different kind of learning. Language is a result of neural impulses that are translated to specific muscular movements of the tongue, cheeks, lips—"

"Lhyn."

". . . and jaw, but—hm?"

"That wasn't an actual question."

"Oh. Right. Sorry."

The burn of embarrassment hit Rahel's senses, and she shook her head at herself.

As a scholar, Lhyn was supremely confident. She was one of the Protectorate's most famous anthropologists, spoke thirty-eight languages fluently and fifteen more quite well, and could put details together with a speed and intuition that left Rahel breathless. But Lhyn had explained that studying cultures and moving through them were two different things. She might be a genius at one—and the fact that she would use that word to describe herself was a perfect example of her confidence—but that didn't translate to any facility at the other. It was one of the reasons she had chosen Alsea as her home: in a culture of empaths, her inability to blend in was an asset. Alseans valued a person whose words always matched her emotions.

"No need for apologies," Rahel said. "Besides, I'm only now getting used to my mouth saying words I don't know. I can't imagine how odd it would be to have my brain coming up with facts I don't know."

Lhyn smiled, all embarrassment gone. "Wouldn't it be *amazing?* To have limitless information at your fingertips? It's been tried, of course." She led Rahel down the corridor. "But the Protectorate outlawed the research."

"Why would they do that?"

"Every attempt to go from theoretical to experimental failed. The voluntary subjects couldn't cope with the information density."

It was a clean-sounding phrase, but Lhyn's sympathetic horror said otherwise.

"What does that mean?" Rahel asked.

"They burned out their brains. Overloaded the neural connections and—" Lhyn held her hands apart, then flipped them upward. "Fried them."

"Like the Voloth?" It was the only comparison she could think of, the invaders who had tried to conquer her home and were instead driven mad by Alsean high empaths.

"Not exactly. They didn't go insane, just catatonic." Lhyn stopped by the mosaic across the corridor from the lift, a brilliant rendering of a red waterfall cascading down a sheer cliff. "But as long as you're aboard a ship like the *Phoenix*, you have something close to limitless data. Go ahead, find out what this is."

It was one of the first and most valuable things Lhyn had showed her. Rahel was used to tapping an earcuff to activate it and make a call, but communication equipment on the *Phoenix* was more advanced. Now when she prepared to leave her quarters, she inserted a small, comfortable ear plug that not only allowed sound to pass through from the outside, but also enhanced it. The internal com linked to the ship's computer, which constantly tracked her location and listened for any requests.

Best of all, she and the computer could converse in High Alsean, a welcome bit of familiarity in this alien place. She could even choose among several different voices for their conversations, though after trying them all, she had settled on the same one that the computer used for its external communication.

"Phoenix," she said, "what is the mosaic at my location supposed to be?"

The feminine voice spoke flawless High Alsean inside her head. *"The Firefall of Allendohan, a waterfall four hundred and twelve meters in height. It flows over a cliff face composed of quartzite and iron oxide, giving the rock a red tint. At sunset, the angle of illumination increases the reflection of red wavelengths. During these times, lasting from five to thirty-five minutes, the waterfall appears to be in flames."*

"Have you seen it?" Rahel asked. Allendohan was Lhyn's home planet.

"Yes, it's spectacular. It's on the opposite side of the planet from where I grew up, though. I only saw it twice. The irony is that this artist isn't from Allendohan. I had no idea the Firefall was so famous until I left home."

"There's a philosophical truth in there somewhere."

Lhyn chuckled as they crossed to the lift, which chirped in recognition of their arrival and opened its doors. "Probably, but I'm a linguist, not a philosopher," she said. "Deck twenty-one, hydroponics."

The lift's lighting took on a slightly blue cast, the only indication that they were now hurtling through the ship.

"You're also an anthropologist," Rahel said. "I don't see how you can do that without being at least something of a philosopher."

"Don't tell. I keep that out of my articles."

The lighting returned to normal and the doors opened, revealing a vast bay four decks high.

Rahel stepped out, marveling at the size of this place. It was filled with tall, tiered racks of plants in orderly rows stretching from one side to the other, beneath a forest of trees that brushed the ceiling. From the trees hung even more plants, fantastical shapes that twisted and curled and adorned themselves with blooms and fruits unlike anything on Alsea. Fleet personnel wearing the uniform of the botanics section busied themselves among the racks and wove through a bewildering maze of pipes with varying diameters and orientations. The air was heavy and moist, full of the scent of growing things, and she could hear pressurized water hissing as it was released somewhere out of sight.

"Great Mother," she blurted. "Has Salomen seen this?"

"It's one of the first things I showed her." Lhyn's enjoyment was on her face as well as her emotions as she gazed around the cavernous bay. "She didn't want to leave."

"Are you speaking of Bondlancer Opah? Aye, she was a treasure. It's not often we get a world leader in our little corner of the ship." A slender, black-haired man rose from a crouch at the end of the nearest rack, tossed a few dead leaves into the bin beside him, and dusted off his hands. Holding one out to Rahel, he said, "And now I get a new celebrity. Masaru Shigeo, chief of botanics. You must be Rahel Sayana."

Rahel would never get used to the Fleet custom of grasping hands, much less the odd up-and-down motion that seemed to vary every time she met someone new. Some people did the motion once, others twice, a few three times, and two had done it repetitively as they spoke to her, as if they'd forgotten what their hands were doing. Sometimes her hand was held gingerly, as if she had a contagious disease; other times she found herself in some sort of unspoken contest to prove who had the superior strength. She found no pattern to the ritual, nor any way to predict how the next one would be conducted. Lhyn said a wealth of information could be learned about the other person from the way they shook hands, but Rahel much preferred the Alsean way: a simple meeting of the palms, held vertically at shoulder level, allowing a transfer of emotions through the skin contact.

But the Gaians were sonsales, unable to sense emotions even through physical touch, so she accepted Shigeo's hand.

He moved her arm up and down twice, using a crisp, economical motion, then released her with a slight smile. “Not used to shaking hands, eh?”

“It’s . . . different,” Rahel allowed. She turned to Lhyn. “Why do you call it shaking? Shaking is this.” She held up a hand and shook it vigorously, then stopped when both Lhyn and Shigeo burst out laughing. “What? I know that’s the right word.” Her language chip didn’t make mistakes in terminology.

“It’s the right word.” Lhyn was still chuckling. “Just the wrong application. And you’re right, that doesn’t describe it. I’ll have to look up the etymology.”

“In some instances, we should call it jerking,” Shigeo said.

“Shippers, yes. I try to avoid those. Then there’s pulling.”

“Or sublimated fighting,” he offered.

“Oh, good one. Or sublimated seduction.”

“I don’t get those very often, more’s the pity.”

“How do you sublimate seduction in a handshake?” Rahel asked.

With his dark brown eyes twinkling, Shigeo held out his hand and waited patiently until she accepted it. Gently, he enclosed her hand and held it still.

“Rahel Sayana, it is a great pleasure,” he murmured in a deeper voice than she had yet heard from him. She watched in confusion as he executed a graceful bow. “I’ve waited a long time to meet the first Alsean space explorer,” he said to her hand, then looked up through his long lashes. “It was worth the wait.”

He straightened, letting his fingers slowly slide along hers until they slipped away.

“I don’t understand,” Rahel said. “That wasn’t seductive at all.”

As Lhyn laughed, Shigeo thumped a hand over his heart and staggered back a step. “I’m wounded.”

“That’s what you get for trying physical seduction on an empath.” Lhyn’s amusement rolled off her skin, wrapping around Rahel with bubbly warmth. “She can sense that you’re not attracted.”

He straightened and flashed white, even teeth in an easy grin. “It’s true, I usually prefer less intimidating women. You look like you could toss me over that rack.”

"She probably could," Lhyn said before Rahel could respond. "Alseans have denser musculature than we do. She's even stronger than she looks."

Shigeo raised his eyebrows—a motion that always seemed strange on these Gaians with their lack of forehead ridges—and looked Rahel up and down. "That will appeal to some for sure. Be careful," he added, his emotions growing abruptly heavier. "There are people aboard this ship who will want to bed you for the challenge and bragging rights."

"They won't have much luck," Rahel said. "I'm asexual." The word sounded harsh to her ear, an inadequate translation of the Alsean *sansara.*

His emotions lightened once more. "In that case, I look forward to hearing about all the failed score-counters. Shall we start your tour?" He swept a hand out, indicating the open space behind him. "I don't know why Lhyn waited this long to bring you to the most critical part of the ship, but the important thing is that you're finally here. Let me show you the lungs of the *Phoenix.*"

The tour lasted two hours, and Rahel enjoyed every bit of it. She had met so many aliens over the last eight days that only a few of the names and faces stood out, but Shigeo easily rose to the top level. Like Lhyn, he showed no discomfort at her ability to sense his emotions, probably because he had so little to hide.

He was small, his head barely rising past her shoulder, but he commanded quiet authority in his domain. His occasional orders to the botanists were often phrased as suggestions or requests, yet were obeyed without question. Most of his subordinates felt an ease in his presence that was almost visible to Rahel's empathic senses.

But there were a few exceptions.

"She doesn't like me, does she?" Shigeo asked as they moved past one such exception.

"Shigeo," Lhyn said in a warning tone.

"No. She's envious of you." Rahel glanced at Lhyn, who was shaking her head. "Or of something about you. But she respects you."

Shigeo stopped walking and looked at her with a slight smile. "What a temptation you are."

"A temptation you already flunked," Lhyn retorted. "I know I'm not imagining our conversation yesterday."

Rahel looked between them. "I'm not supposed to tell you what I sense?"

"You're not supposed to be put in that position." Lhyn folded her arms across her chest, glaring down at Shigeo though Rahel could feel no heat in it. "He can spout the scientific names of three thousand plant species, but he can't remember what I told him twenty-four hours ago."

"And you think Captain Serrado won't put her in exactly that position?" Shigeo's calm was undisturbed, though Lhyn was now exuding true irritation. "What else is an empath here for?"

"I thought I was here to be the first Alsean space explorer."

"You are," Lhyn said firmly.

"And to serve Fleet in whatever capacity it needs and that you're capable of providing." Shigeo motioned them toward a panel on the wall. "We've reached the end of our tour."

"You're an asshead, Shigeo." Lhyn's irritation had subsided into grudging acceptance.

"I'm practical. Now then, Rahel, would you like to do the honors? It's time for the rain cycle." He opened the panel, exposing a colorful array of controls, and pointed toward a large green square adorned with an image of a water drop. "Press that and watch the magic."

Nothing in his or Lhyn's emotions suggested a need for caution, so Rahel pressed the button.

A loud horn sounded through the bay, inspiring an instant reaction in the throng of botanists. Within moments, most had moved to stand beneath the overhang that ran around all four bulkheads. The few who remained amongst the plants were shrugging on clothing similar to an Alsean rain cloak.

The horn blew again, two notes this time. A quieter sound accompanied movement overhead, and Rahel looked up to see the pipes now bristling with silver disks lining each side. With a hiss, the disks began to spin, spraying water that drifted down in a fine mist. The hiss grew in volume, the mist thickened, and soon it really was raining, a deluge of water that reminded her of spring rainstorms in her home city of Whitesun.

She stared around, caught up in the magic, for that was indeed the right descriptor. Never had she imagined seeing rain on a starship.

"Some of our plants derive nutrients through their leaves." Shigeo spoke loudly to be heard over the falling water. "All of them benefit from having their leaves washed occasionally. I swear that after a rain cycle, I can feel them sighing in happiness." He glanced over with a smile. "I wish I had your empathy to feel it for real."

"I can't sense plants," Rahel said. "But you're probably right." She took a deep breath of air, weighted with the clean scent of wet leaves and the heady perfume of bruised blossoms, then held out her hand to feel the raindrops spattering against her skin.

Now she understood the grated flooring. The water fell right through it, gurgling into a collection system that filtered and recycled it. She was going to study the schematics on this bay the moment she got back to her quarters.

For fifteen minutes, they watched the rain and discussed the systems. Rahel learned that the bay was divided into zones, each with different types and lengths of rain cycles for the needs of different plant species. Only occasionally did the entire bay get doused, and Shigeo had delayed it by one day so she could see it.

It was with great reluctance that she followed his instructions to shut off the cycle. She had seen technology that qualified as miraculous on her tours of this ship, but nothing had felt as magical as a simple rain—or as close to home.

Lhyn thanked Shigeo for his time and escorted Rahel through another section of the deck, but her descriptions and explanations fell on largely deaf ears. Rahel's mind was still in the hydroponics bay, leaving her too distracted to take in the details.

"Time for a break," Lhyn announced, tapping the control of a door that featured a thicket of hairy-leaved plants atop its lintel.

Though Rahel had never seen the room beyond, its cushioned mats and the sharp scent of hard-working Gaian bodies was familiar. She had already used a similar training room near her quarters several times.

"Why don't you wear yourself out going through your forms and I'll pick you up in an hour for lunch? The showers are through there." Lhyn pointed.

"Was I that obvious?"

"Oh, sister," Lhyn said in High Alscan, using the affectionate address she had picked up in Whitesun. "I don't need empathy when I have eyes. See you in an hour."

2

RESPECT

Rahel would have preferred her own workout clothes, but like the training room on her deck, this one had a stock of close-fitting, stretchy clothing in standard sizes. She changed swiftly and hung her uniform on the rod that ran the length of the dressing room. At least twenty other uniforms hung there as well, representing every section on the *Phoenix*. Hers stood out starkly with its Alsean style and the dark green color blocks of the Bondlancer's Guard. In her opinion, it was much more attractive.

Stave grip in hand, she walked barefoot to the center of an empty mat. Thirteen crew members were using the room's equipment or practicing their own disciplines on other mats, and she wondered about the discrepancy in numbers. A quick glance around revealed another door across from the changing room—a secondary training area, she guessed.

Her empathic senses were awash with the curiosity emanating from so many sonsales aliens, along with the usual spikes of nervousness. No matter how much she smiled or tried to appear unthreatening, the mere fact of her empathy was enough to engender fear in some Gaians.

"They're not used to the possibility of their emotions being read," Lhyn had explained on her first day. "That's going to scare some of them."

"I don't *want* to read their emotions." Rahel had only been aboard for six hours, but she was already tired of fending off the unwanted broadcasts of everyone around her.

"They'll figure that out at some point. Then they'll calm down."

But Lhyn hadn't said how long that would take. It had been eight days and Rahel still sensed the fear every time she walked through the corridors or met a new group of Gaians.

Only one crew member in this room looked at her directly. Stocky and well muscled, with short brown hair and a square jaw, she emanated calm competence. Though her workout clothing gave no hint of her specialty, she was obviously a warrior. That competence had a deadly shadow behind it.

The other woman nodded once, a greeting of like to like, and went back to what appeared to be resistance training on the complicated machine she was using.

Rahel closed her eyes and raised her blocks, pushing away the emotions in the room until a blessed silence descended on her senses. After several long, slow breaths, she opened her eyes again and pressed the golden stave grip in her hand.

The metal segments shot out of each end, telescoping instantly into a solid weapon. She swung it through two sets of slow-paced initial forms, warming up her muscles, then launched into the far more strenuous combat forms. The exertion settled her body and began to clear her head, draining some of the tension that had built up since she came aboard.

She was physically safe here, free of concerns about hiding or being detained and punished for past crimes. Her honor was restored, and she was living out her dreams.

Yet every night, she fell into bed exhausted by the unending assault of emotions against her senses. Before coming here, she had worked with a tutor to improve her blocks, but she had not learned to hold them up all day long. It was more tiring than the dance of combat, because a fight eventually ended. This never would. She shared a ship with a crew of one thousand two hundred and sixty-five—a floating city in space, Lhyn called it—and not one of them could front their emotions.

Never again would she envy high empaths for their greater ability to sense emotion. These days she almost wished she were a low empath, needing physical touch to know what others felt. Not even in sleep could she escape the onslaught. Her nearest neighbors in the crew quarters were within range, and there was regular traffic in the corridor outside. Her dreams were troubled and her sleep restless, and every day she woke feeling edgier, slower, and less controlled than the day before.

Fortunately, none of that had shown up on Dr. Wells's tests, and Rahel was not about to volunteer the information. Better to keep working on her stamina.

Body and mind are connected, she thought as she began another set of combat forms. *To train one is to train the other.* As a young warrior just learning how to use her body, she had never paid much attention to the second half of that quote. Now she thought it might be a great deal more important.

The door opposite the changing room slid open and seven laughing crew members jostled through. Rahel ignored them as she whirled and brought her stave up in a block against an imaginary opponent.

"Hey, look at that! It's the Alsean!"

She pulled back and whipped the stave down, letting one end hit the mat before using the rebound to flip it upward. Spinning again, she ducked under the likely return blow before straightening up and twisting her torso to drive the stave through a sharp backward thrust.

"Fancy," another voice snickered. "But useless."

"No kidding. What was Captain Serrado thinking when she brought that on board?"

"Hey. Alsean. Don't be rude."

Rahel planted the end of her stave in the mat and looked at the hecklers. "I don't think I'm the one being rude."

"She speaks!" A tall male, apparently the leader of the group, grinned widely. "Then you can tell us why Serrado took you on. What are you supposed to do with that little stick?"

A shorter woman waved an energy weapon. "You're still fighting with sticks and swords," she sneered. "Out here in the galaxy, we use real weapons."

"Yeah," said the leader. "Let's see you stop this with your stick." He raised his own weapon and fired.

Rahel was so shocked by the aggressive act in this supposedly safe environment that she stood there dumbly as a green laser hit her in the torso.

Nothing happened. There was no pain, nor even any heat. She stared down at herself, her empathic shields shattered by the surprise, as the others roared with laughter. Dislike, condescension, and fear battered against her senses.

"Some warrior!" one of them called, and the others laughed louder.

"What's the matter, you need more advance warning?" the first woman asked. "Here, try it again." She raised her weapon, gleeful aggression pouring off her in a toxic cloud.

Rahel had no way of knowing whether this weapon was as harmless as the first. From her first days of training with a molecular disruptor, she had been taught to never point it at another person unless she meant to maim or kill.

Her reaction was built on a lifetime of warrior training, the stave whipping out to crack against the woman's wrist. With a shriek of pain, the woman dropped her weapon.

"Aah!" she cried. "You broke my fucking wrist!"

"Sucking Seeders, you really are a barbarian," the leader snarled. He flung down his weapon and charged.

Had he given her time, Rahel would have explained her reasoning. If it had been a mistake, she would have apologized.

But he gave her no time, and his five uninjured friends were right behind him, their violent intent obvious even to a sonsales.

Rahel took out the leader with a blow to the side of his knee, dropping him like a sack to the mat. She flipped the stave back and half over her shoulder, then drove it forward, breaking the nose of the next closest attacker. That slowed the others long enough for her to whirl around and slam her stave into the jaw of the big woman trying to flank her, then spin back and let the force of her turn fuel a strike against the ankle of another.

The remaining two stopped their approach, watching her warily as they tried to work together to bring her down. She should have stepped back and given them a chance to end the fight, but the blood sang in her ears and eight days of emotional exhaustion broke through her restraint. She ceased fighting defensively and went after them with fire in her heart.

The first tried to block her strike with his forearms, a good strategy in hand-to-hand combat but painful in a stave fight. He howled as the metal cracked against his elbows, then bent double with a whine. Still in motion, Rahel didn't look at the final opponent while swinging her stave upward. At the last moment, she realized the woman was holding up her hands in surrender, but by then it was too late to pull the blow. It crashed against her ribs and sent her sprawling.

Rahel settled back into the ready position, stave held diagonally across her torso, and scanned the room for further dangers.

"Well," said the warrior woman with the short brown hair, "*that* was impressive. And well deserved, I'd say." She was standing close by, having left her machine behind.

Rahel sank more deeply into her position, leg muscles tensed to spring, until her mind cleared enough to sense the lack of aggression. In fact, this woman seemed oddly pleased.

"Pearson has bricks for brains," she continued. "His buddies might think twice about following him after this." She held out a hand. "Warrant Officer Roris, weapons specialist. Glad to meet you."

Rahel looked around the silent room. Every other crew member was staring at her with wide eyes, exuding astonishment and a surprising level of respect, but no danger. Six of her attackers lay groaning on the mat, while the first woman had collapsed onto a bench, holding her wrist in stupefied shock.

She had promised to represent Alsea.

She was reasonably certain that damaging seven crew members was not considered adequate representation. Captain Serrado was going to be furious.

Accepting Roris's hand, she said, "First Guard Rahel Sayana. Though you probably don't need to remember my name. I don't think I'll be here long enough for that."

3

EXPECTATIONS

Captain Ekatya Serrado read the report off her display. "Displaced patella. Fractured jaw. Two broken carpals." She looked up at the other occupant of her office, standing stiffly erect with her gaze fixed on the wall above Ekatya's head. "Broken fibula. Was that just to balance it out? Break the wrist of one and the ankle of another?"

Rahel Sayana flinched but did not shift her gaze. "No, Captain."

Ekatya waited, then went back to the report. "Displaced nasal cartilage; well, at least that's one bone you didn't break. Oh, wait. Hairline fractures in both ulnas of another victim, and you wrapped it up with three cracked ribs."

She blanked the display, leaving it transparent, and leaned back in her chair. "I haven't seen a non-combat injury list like this since three of my weapons teams got into a bar fight on Erebderis Station. I hope your excuse is better than theirs."

"I have no excuse, Captain."

"None at all? You attacked without provocation?"

It wasn't as easy to read Rahel's facial expressions as it would have been with a Gaian crew member. The three ridges fanning across her forehead —one drawing a vertical line, the other two arcing toward her temples and vanishing under auburn hair—disguised many of the minute muscular cues that would otherwise give a clue to her thoughts. Sharp cheekbone ridges lent a gravity to her expression even when she smiled.

Fortunately, Ekatya had a great deal of experience in reading Alseans, given her close friendship with both the Lancer and Bondlancer of Alsea. She looked into those slanted amber eyes and saw resignation. Rahel had already assumed her fate.

Time for her first real lesson in Fleet standards, then.

"First Guard, I asked you a question. I'd appreciate the courtesy of an answer."

Rahel drew herself impossibly straighter. "I did strike first."

"I didn't ask if you struck first. I asked if you struck without provocation."

The first crack appeared. "I, um. I thought there was provocation. But now I know they weren't threatening me. At first, I mean."

Ekatya knew exactly how she had learned that. Dr. Wells had been none too pleased to find seven injured crew members pouring into her medbay lobby. The lecture she had unleashed on Rahel was already making its way around the gossip circuit.

What Rahel didn't know was that after Dr. Wells had spoken to Warrant Officer Roris—who had made the initial call to medical—she had then come to Ekatya's office and launched into another tirade, pointing out that bullying was a Class Three offense and if she weren't bound by her oath, she would have tossed the injured crew members into the nearest waste reclamation tank. "If they're going to behave like little shits, they ought to swim with it," she had snapped, before turning on her heel and exiting without waiting for dismissal.

"They weren't threatening you at first," Ekatya repeated. "Which implies they threatened you later. But I don't want implications. I want facts." She rested her forearms on the desk and interlaced her fingers. "You're a First Guard. If you'd had a normal career in the Alsean Defense Force, you'd probably have fifty or more Guards under your supervision now. Tell me, what would you do if a Guard in your command wouldn't tell you the truth about what happened in a fight? If she made you guess about the chain of events?"

For the first time, Rahel met her eyes. "I'd make sure that Guard—" She stopped, her bearing softening as the realization hit. "Knew who was in charge and what my expectations were," she finished weakly.

Ekatya nodded. "Have I made my expectations clear?"

"You want the facts."

"All of them," Ekatya clarified. "Now sit down and tell me what happened."

She had to give Rahel credit: her account did not vary from that of Warrant Officer Roris except where it filled in the gaps. Roris had seen the fight purely from a physical perspective, but Rahel had *felt* the aggression and threat. Ekatya could only imagine how powerful that must have been, particularly for an Alsean with a grand total of eight days in an alien culture.

"I apologize, Captain," Rahel concluded. "I know this wasn't what you hoped for."

"You're right. I hoped my crew members would have better ethics than to bully the newest arrival. And better sense than to attack an Alsean warrior with an extended stave in her hand."

Rahel stared at her with wide eyes. "You're not—"

"I'm not sending you back to Alsea, no." Ekatya watched her erect posture go loose and added, "That doesn't mean you'll escape punishment. You continued the fight after the threat was removed. That's no more acceptable here than it would be on Alsea. We don't have empathic Alsean healers here. We can't heal bones in one day. You've put seven members of this crew out of commission for several duty shifts, and that's a loss to ship's readiness."

"I understand."

"But," Ekatya lifted a finger, "I'm also aware that you could have caused much more damage than you did. You targeted non-vital areas, and you hit each of them once. Just enough to put them down." She looked at the broad-shouldered, powerfully built woman across from her and marveled at the idiocy of those troopers. They had just finished a virtual reality weapons training—which was, in part, about distinguishing threats—and promptly failed a real-life application.

She knew about the unsavory gossip regarding her acceptance of Rahel on the crew. Theories varied from "political stunt" to "empathic spy for the captain" to "personal favor to the Lancer of Alsea," the last accompanied by distasteful speculation as to why that favor might be owed. In truth, Rahel had done her a favor by so quickly establishing that she was a skilled soldier and not to be trifled with. It would probably take less than two days for word to reach every member of the crew.

"I'm assigning you to the medbay cleaning detail for the next seven days," she said. "You'll continue your tours and training with Dr. Rivers, but when you're not with her, you'll report to Dr. Wells."

"Yes, Captain." By the look on Rahel's face, this was one step up from damnation. "Shall I start now?"

"In a moment. Rahel," she said deliberately, signifying that this was no longer a dressing down, "I wish I could tell you that every member of my crew is as open-minded as my section chiefs. I didn't choose my chiefs solely for their skill and experience. I also wanted to be sure they would fit with my ideals. But they chose their own officers, and those officers chose staff, and some of my crew were assigned here by Fleet. Most of them are everything I could hope for. But not all."

"You can't take responsibility for everyone."

"I *do* take responsibility—for their actions. What I can't do is regulate how they think. You shouldn't have to feel prejudice and fear, but you will. I know you'll never cause empathic harm. I've made sure this crew knows that as a mid empath, you're not even capable of it. That doesn't mean they all believe me. There's a political faction in the Protectorate . . ." She hesitated. Every time she spoke of this, the rage came with it, and she did not want Rahel to sense that.

"The Defenders of the Protectorate. Lhyn told me about them."

"She told you everything?"

"Not verbally. I wondered why she would react that way about a political faction, even if they're against everything she stands for. Then I looked them up on the newscoms." Rahel's expression darkened. "Now I know why she understands things that someone like her shouldn't have to know about."

Ekatya nodded, not trusting her voice or emotions if she said anything else on the topic of Lhyn's torture. "Then you know why some of this crew won't trust you. And even those who know you're safe might still be uncomfortable knowing you can sense them. You're the first of your kind, a pioneer. It won't be easy."

"I know."

"But Salomen chose you. I hold your oath by proxy, and that means I chose you, too, just like I chose my section chiefs. I'm holding you to a higher standard. Do you understand?"

"Yes, Captain." Even sitting, Rahel somehow grew taller. "I'll do my best."

"Try to do it without breaking any more bones, all right?"

"Yes, Captain."

"Good. Dr. Wells is waiting for you. You're dismissed."

Rahel stood up and held a fist over her heart while quickly lowering her head. "Thank you."

The Alsean salute took some getting used to, Ekatya mused. She watched her newest officer stride for the door and said, "You should know one more thing. When those seven get out of the medbay, they're assigned to a cleaning detail, too. For fourteen days."

Rahel's mouth quirked in a tiny smile, as if she were afraid to let it show. She nodded again and vanished out the door.

Ekatya reactivated her screen and called Dr. Wells on the intraship com. As soon as the doctor appeared, she said, "Rahel Sayana is on her way. I'm impressed; she's already scared to death of you."

"Not quite what I was striving for," Wells said ruefully. "Did you decide on the sentence for the bullies?"

"Mm-hm. One of my section chiefs gave me the idea. If they're going to behave like little shits, they ought to work with it, don't you think?"

An approving smirk lit her face. "You assigned them to waste reclamation?"

"Two weeks of it. On the night shift."

"Does Rahel know that?"

"She knows their sentence is twice as long as hers, but not what they're doing. I left that for you to share when the time is right."

"You're more of a psychologist than I gave you credit for, Captain."

"Didn't you know that's in the job description?" Ekatya signed off and leaned back in her chair, thinking of Rahel's expression when she mentioned learning about Lhyn's story.

The security footage from the training room had been impressive, to say the least. Rahel's reflexes were lightning fast; she had gone through six opponents as if they were standing still. The entire fight had taken less than twenty seconds.

Apparently, Alseans weren't merely stronger than Gaians. They were faster, too, or at least the highly trained warriors were. Which meant she had an experienced, hypercompetent warrior on her ship who already felt protective of Lhyn—and could sense threats.

Once Rahel was through her punishment week, Ekatya knew what her next assignment would be.

4

CHASES AND BRACES

By the end of her first shift on cleaning detail, Rahel concluded that Captain Serrado was either a brilliant commander or an evil one. Now that she knew what this punishment entailed, she would gladly have chosen the brig instead.

Dr. Wells had greeted her without a trace of the earlier anger and turned her over to a subordinate, who led her to a lower deck. There she was introduced to the horrors of medical laundry, stained with fluids and occasional solids that she did not want to think about. The *Phoenix* had rendezvoused with a passenger ship that had experienced a gastrointestinal virus outbreak, and the medbay was full of patients in varying states of distress.

Sheets, towels, medshirts, trousers, and cleaning cloths all made their way down through the recycle chutes located in every treatment room. Most of the process was automated, as the materials traveled from the collection bins into either the sterilization equipment or the incinerator, but now and again some offending material got stuck or went the wrong way. This would stall the system, requiring a worker to pull the material and send it on. Rahel quickly learned that the pieces needing manual handling were invariably the most disgusting ones.

From there, she was sent up three decks to clean a surgical bay, which made dirty laundry seem appetizing. Thankfully, the nurse in charge took care of the used instruments. Though Rahel was no stranger to blood, seeing it on those shining implements gave her stomach a turn she would never admit to.

Her job was collecting the medical waste that littered the room and bagging it for later disposal. As the two of them worked, the nurse explained that he had already engaged the full-room decontamination process, rendering the waste largely inert. Care still had to be taken, of course, and incineration remained the best method of disposal. The incinerator Rahel had heard of in the laundry was really a diverted flow from the surf engines. Directed through a special processing chamber, the extreme heat quickly reduced waste to sterile ash, which was then repurposed as an ingredient in matter printer base material.

Bagging medical waste was disgusting, but Rahel enjoyed the final step of the cleaning. The nurse led her through the door, locked it, and activated the decontamination process for the second and final time. They watched through the window as planes of blue light swept every surface in the room.

Worst of all the assignments was when she learned how to change linens in the occupied treatment rooms, accompanied by a nurse who dealt with the patient while Rahel stripped the sheets. She saw more of these patients than she ever wanted to, but more than that, she felt them. Something about being sick or injured magnified Gaian emotions, and her blocks were insufficient at such close range. She had a splitting headache by the end of her shift and wasted no time getting out—but was stopped at the brink of freedom by Dr. Wells.

Rarely had Rahel encountered a person with a more deceptive exterior. Dr. Wells looked unassuming, with her average height and small bone structure. Her eyes were nearly as green as Lhyn's but slanted like Rahel's, and her cheekbones were so pronounced that they seemed more Alsean than Gaian. She wore her light brown hair in an exotic twist at the back of her head, improbably held in place with two wooden sticks. Her slim stature and delicate features made her seem fragile, but when she growled with that thundercloud on her face, everyone in the medbay cowered.

The thundercloud was nowhere to be seen now. "How are you doing?" she asked.

"I'm fine."

Dr. Wells raised a skeptical eyebrow. "I wouldn't ask if I didn't want to know. It's been a difficult day for you. How are you? Any empathic effects?"

The anger came out of nowhere. Dr. Wells had been instrumental in making this a difficult day for her, and suddenly she was solicitous? Her concern was sincere, but in this moment Rahel did not care. Not even in her long-ago trainee days had she been so publicly humiliated as she was by this morning's lecture in the middle of the lobby. Alsean instructors expected mistakes and helped their students learn from them. They did not destroy any peer respect the student had worked so hard to earn.

"I'm fine," she repeated. "Is there another test you want to put me through, or may I go now?"

Dr. Wells eyed her, then deflated as she shook her head. "No tests. I'll see you tomorrow."

"Not if I see you first," Rahel muttered under her breath as she left.

For the next three days, she lived for her morning tours and training with Lhyn, suffered through her punishment shifts, and avoided Dr. Wells and her intrusive inquiries whenever possible.

But she couldn't avoid the emotions. They pounded against her until her blocks inevitably failed and the headache built. It reached a crescendo at the end of her shift, subsided to a barely tolerable level by the next morning, and built again on her next punishment shift. Every day, the crescendo was higher.

On the morning of the fifth day, Lhyn took her to meet Commander Przepyszny, the section chief for operations. He was quite tall, though not as tall as Lhyn, and had the beginnings of a soft belly pressing against his tool belt. His dark skin and high forehead complemented the thick, kinky silver hair that stood straight up for the length of a finger and ended at a perfectly level cut.

"Call me Zeppy," he said, shaking her hand with crushing strength. Though others had attempted that as a means of establishing superiority, his emotional signature held no such intentions. He simply had that strong a grip and didn't realize it.

"Zeppy?" Rahel held her hand behind her back and flexed it, working out the cramp.

"Nobody can pronounce my last name and I can't be bothered to teach everyone."

"Plus it's a good description for him," Lhyn put in. "Or it would be if he replaced the e with an i." She gave Rahel an expectant look.

This was a test, then. A lingual implant worked only for hearing and speaking; it did nothing for the written language. Every day after their morning tour, Lhyn drilled her in the Common alphabet and the words most often used in schematics and signage. For Rahel, who had spent most of her childhood in one library or another, learning to read a new language was a thrilling puzzle.

She looked up at the ceiling, picturing the letters in her mind. With the i in place of the e, it would be pronounced . . .

"Zippy," she said experimentally, and received an instant translation from her implant. "Does that mean you're fast?"

Lhyn beamed, pride and warm approval washing outward.

"I'm organized." Zeppy indicated the door in the bulkhead behind him. "Are you ready to see the heart of the *Phoenix*?"

"I toured engineering two days ago. They said that was the heart of the ship."

"They would," he scoffed. "Engineering could produce all the power in the galaxy and it wouldn't do any good without operations. We keep it flowing."

"Maybe they're the heart, while you're the arteries and vessels," Lhyn said diplomatically.

He narrowed his eyes, then gave a short nod that did not shift a single hair on his head. "I'll accept that. Shall we?" He tapped the small pad to the right of the door, which immediately slid open as the hidden scanner recognized his face. Rahel stepped toward it.

Lhyn didn't move. "I'll see you at the other end of the tour," she said.

"You're not coming?"

"Not fond of enclosed spaces, remember? That's about as enclosed as it gets." Lhyn looked past her into the opening, then shook her head and turned away. "Call me when you're done."

"Damn shame, that is," Zeppy said as they watched her walk down the corridor. "I don't believe in capital punishment, but there are times when I'd make an exception. Seeders, I'd do it personally." Satisfaction rippled through the air. "The captain almost did. Wish I'd been there to see it."

"What did she do?"

"Got ten minutes alone with the asshead who hurt Dr. Rivers and taught him what hurting really means. Broke his knee and smashed his jaw into a thousand pieces."

Rahel tried and failed to imagine the perfect officer of her admittedly short acquaintance beating up a prisoner. "That doesn't seem like something she'd do. Not unless it was self-defense."

"Oh, it was." The satisfaction thickened. "She did him the favor of taking off his restraints, and he attacked her. Damn stupid fool didn't realize he played right into her hands. Gave her the perfect excuse and by the Seeders, she took it. I heard she put him down in three moves."

"How do you know this?" Rahel was still skeptical.

His gray eyebrows rose. "This is Fleet. Gossip goes through here faster than a quantum com. Somebody in Tlahana Station security saw the footage, and away it went. There isn't a person on this ship who didn't cheer when they heard it." He turned abruptly and stepped through the door. "Come along, then."

Rahel followed him into a narrow passage that stretched straight back from the opening. Though the light level was normal, it seemed darker due to the close walls and the profusion of conduits, pipes, ducts, and grouped cables that snaked along them, as well as overhead and occasionally underfoot. The latter were covered by low, three-sided ramps that allowed Zeppy and Rahel to walk up and over the obstruction, protecting them from tripping but increasing the danger of cracking their skulls against overhead pipes.

Zeppy rattled off an impressive litany of labels as he walked and pointed in various directions. "That carries power to half this deck. That one? Power to the other half. Feeder duct to the carbon scrubbers. Fresh air outflow. Sewage, you never want to need access to that one. Reclaimed water. Intraship com . . ."

Rahel listened with half an ear, distracted by the sudden realization that other than Zeppy, the intrusive broadcast of emotions had stopped pounding against her.

Cautiously, she lowered her blocks.

They were still there, all the emotions of the Gaians within her range on the other sides of these walls. But her awareness of them was muted. It was as if this space were the emotional equivalent of an acoustic dead zone, where feelings were emitted and then canceled out.

She took a deep breath and thought it might have been the first one she'd enjoyed since boarding this ship. The freedom was exhilarating. Her headache, a constant and growing companion since the first day of her punishment, receded just enough for her to realize how she had unconsciously adapted to the pain.

Zeppy stepped onto a ramp and ducked as his tall hair brushed the underside of a pipe.

"Is that why you have your hair like that?" Rahel asked. "A sort of warning system?"

He let out a guffaw. "It wasn't my intention, but it surely does do the job." Turning around, he added, "I have a tech who'll do anything to avoid taking jobs in the chases. He's bald. Every time he goes in, he comes back out with a new knot on his head. You'd think that after all the years of working here he'd know where the pipes are, but—" He slapped a hand against the pipe. "Nope. Bangs his head every damn time. So yeah, we think good hair is an evolutionary adaptation for working in operations."

The pipe under his hand carried reclaimed water; Rahel could hear it sloshing through in rhythmic pulses. All around her were similar sounds of a living ship: power humming through cables and conduits, occasional creaks and crackles, the whoosh of precise mixtures of gases through ducts. Here, too, she could smell the more mechanical scents she had expected upon first boarding the *Phoenix*. The clean, woodsy scent of the ship's corridors and living spaces had startled her until Captain Serrado proudly explained how the profusion of plants throughout those same spaces acted as a filtration system, carefully chosen to neutralize inorganic scents and freshen the air. They also served as carbon dioxide scrubbers, and many were used as a source of fresh food.

But this space—this was what she had imagined a starship to be. Close, crowded, pungent, and brimming with the sounds of life. The engineering section had been full of the sounds of machinery, but she liked this more.

She *loved* the emotional peace.

"Lhyn was right," she said, gazing around. "This is more like an artery than a heart. It's . . . impressive. And cozy."

Approval wafted off his skin. "Didn't expect you to see it that way. Most people don't like the chases."

"I grew up in the alleys of the Whitesun docks." At his confusion, she added, "Places respectable people were afraid to go. But I was never afraid of them. They were my home. The alleys were where I learned to be who I am."

He nodded. "Some of my techs could tell a similar story. Just between you and me, the ones who learned their craft the hard way? They're the best workers of all. And they don't complain when I send them into the chases."

"Chases. What does that mean?" She tapped behind her ear, where the lingual implant resided. "I know that's what you call these spaces, but it doesn't make sense."

"It's from back before the spacefaring days. A chase was the lane between fields on a farm. Or an access road between adjoining properties." He held out his arms. "Now it's the access space between adjoining sections of a deck. The lanes between living quarters, offices, labs, storage—this is where the *Phoenix* lives and breathes." With a snort, he dropped his arms. "Not in *engineering*. Didn't you notice on your tour how big their heads were?"

She laughed, charmed by such unexpected approachability in a high-ranking officer. The chief of engineering hadn't been nearly this affable. "I'm new here. I'm trying hard not to offend anyone."

"So you'll discreetly say nothing, I know. It's all right." His eyebrows rose again. "Although you said a lot when you took down Pearson and his goons."

Her amusement turned into a groan as she thought of the punishment awaiting her after lunch. "If I had it to do over again, I'd have let them take me down."

He looked her over. "I don't think you could. I know your type. I know Pearson's type, too. He needed to have some respect pounded into his head, and those kinds of lessons . . ." He clicked his tongue against his teeth. "Let's just say that officers can't always teach the lessons that should be taught. We'll occasionally look the other way when someone else does it for us."

She remembered Captain Serrado's clipped speech and irritation while reading off the list of injuries. But there had been something else, too, something Rahel hadn't been able to name because it felt so out of place. Now, sensing the same thing from Zeppy, she had a name for it: satisfaction.

"You're glad I put seven security officers in the medbay?"

He stared at her, then slapped his hand against the overhead pipe. "I can neither confirm nor deny that. Come along, let me take you to the brace shaft. If you like this, you'll love that."

She followed him down the narrow chase, marveling at this space that felt so much like a secret discovery. She couldn't spread her arms without touching the walls, and though she understood how some people would find it constricting and frightening, she felt right at home.

Up ahead, the chase ended at a metal door that was distinctive for having only one panel, versus the two that made up most doors on the ship. It made sense given the narrow dimensions of the space.

Zeppy tapped the pad and grumbled when nothing happened. "Thought I told Swanson to fix these. She must have missed this one. They had a short in the power supply." He lifted the small orange panel to expose a keypad beneath, then quickly tapped out a code.

Rahel watched, feeling vaguely guilty but unable to stop herself from memorizing what was obviously an access code. She knew from prior studies that every door on the *Phoenix* had a face recognition scanner. When a crew member was programmed for that door, or that department, tapping the lock pad initiated a facial scan so efficient that the pause between the tap and the door opening was undetectable.

No one had gotten around to explaining what happened if the scanner didn't work. Now she had the answer—and Zeppy's access code as well.

The door slid open and Zeppy stood aside, his emotions bright with anticipatory pleasure. "After you."

She turned sideways to edge past him and gasped at the sight.

A circular shaft dropped beneath her feet for thirteen decks and extended over her head for sixteen more. Affixed to the curved wall behind her was a ladder that ran the entire length of the shaft, passing through holes in the landings that punctuated each deck.

Like the chase, the brace shaft was lined with pipes, conduits and cables. But it was at least five times wider than the chase had been, and that, plus its vertical nature, gave it a spacious feel.

"Why is it here?" she asked as Zeppy joined her on the landing.

"Keeps the ship from flying apart under a stress load. Brace shafts are a structural necessity when you're building a ship with thirty decks. We run critical equipment through here, too. Double use of the same space." He stepped onto the ladder and wrapped his hands around the side rails. With a sudden burst of merriment, he said, "See you on nineteen."

He made a quick hop, braced the sides of his boots against the outsides of the rails, and slid down the ladder without touching a single rung. Two decks below, he slowed and gracefully stepped onto the landing. "You coming?" he called up.

She stared down at him with a grin she could not control. "How do you stop?"

"It's mostly in the feet and elbows. Shift so that more of your boot soles are rubbing on the rails; they act as brakes. Wait," he added, and tapped a control on the wall.

Over the background hums and whooshes, Rahel heard a sliding sound as a plate slipped forward and locked itself against the ladder at his feet, neatly closing the hole in the landing that the ladder passed through.

"Well, that takes away the thrill," she grumbled.

She hadn't meant for him to hear, but he chuckled. "Captain Serrado would have my head if I let anything happen to you. Besides, this is a safety regulation."

Which he hadn't observed himself, she noted, but refrained from saying it aloud as she climbed onto the ladder. Holding on tight, she braced her feet on the outside rails—and went nowhere.

"Too strong for your own good," Zeppy said with a laugh. "I heard that about Alseans. Loosen your grip."

She had already figured that out and was sliding down before he finished speaking. At first it was slow, until she found the right amount of pressure with her forearms and feet. Then she zipped down with a whoop of pure happiness, though the freedom of speed didn't last nearly long enough before she had to brake. She was determined to stop before hitting the safety plate, and her dismount wasn't as graceful as his. But that was a matter of time and practice, both of which she intended to find as soon as possible.

"That was *fun!"* she said, breathless with glee. "Can we do it again?"

He smiled at her. "I heard security was after you, once you got through training. Now I see why. Want to go for three?"

"Decks? Yes!"

"All right, let me go first. You'll need to start slowing after the second deck."

"Understood."

"Less than two weeks and you're already picking up Fleet speak," he said approvingly. "You'll fit right in. As long as you don't make a habit of talking about what senior officers feel."

"Or anyone else?" she asked, acknowledging the gentle admonition. "I don't mean to make people uncomfortable. It's just—you broadcast everything. I don't know which things you care about and which things you don't."

He scratched his chin. "I suppose that's a little harder to learn than ship's schematics. Might be the best policy to not say what you sense until you know it's all right."

She remembered Shigeo's assumption that she was here to serve Captain Serrado in exactly that way: saying what she could sense. Perhaps the best policy was simply to keep quiet until an officer asked for her input. But if she didn't tell them what she could sense, how would they know what to ask?

"You're thinking too hard," Zeppy said. "Maybe that wasn't my place to say. Maybe you'll be good for us. A big dose of brutal honesty, like backwashing the water pipes."

Laughing at his own joke, he tapped the control pad behind the ladder. The safety plate at their feet slid open, while three decks below, another plate closed. He swung onto the ladder with a jaunty ease, braced himself, and slid down. As before, he came to a perfect stop above the landing, then stepped off as lightly as if he had just walked down a flight of stairs.

Rahel's whoop of joy was louder this time as she enjoyed the extra deck of flight. She gripped too hard and too soon, nearly biting her tongue with the abruptness of her braking, then laughed as she dropped the rest of the way.

"Have you ever done all thirty decks?" she asked.

"Nobody's done thirty decks, and you're not going to be the first." He opened the door into the chase. "Next stop is the switching block."

She followed him, a wide smile still on her face. That had sounded like a challenge.

5

TRUST

Dr. Wells cornered Rahel as soon as she arrived for her punishment shift. "Look, I know I'm not your favorite person right now, but I'm still your doctor. I don't ask how you're feeling to annoy you. I ask it because I need to know."

"I'm fine, just like I was yesterday and the day before that." Rahel withstood the appraising stare, relieved that her time with Zeppy had reduced her headache enough to render it easily masked.

"All right. If you start to feel—"

"I'll tell my doctor." Rahel turned away. "If you'll excuse me, I have beds to strip."

This shift was the worst one yet, the unrelenting pressure of heightened Gaian emotions battering down her blocks a full two hours before she could flee. The moment it ended, Rahel raced out of the medbay lobby and went looking for the nearest chase access. She found it across the corridor from a particularly beautiful display of Filessian orchids and tiled artwork, something she would normally appreciate but now saw only as a directional marker. Her head pounded as she waited, pretending to admire the mosaic while crew members passed behind her. At an opportune break in the traffic, she lifted the access panel, tapped in Zeppy's code, and entered the chase.

For five steps, she strode as quickly as she could, desperate to escape into this haven with its soothing noises and close walls. Then the tight band around her forehead eased, bringing a relief so profound that her breath hitched. She stopped and leaned against the wall, gulping air as if she had been underwater.

Once her body had adapted to the lack of pain and she could breathe normally again, she set off down the chase. It soon intersected with another chase running in a perpendicular direction. She paused, picturing the ship's map she had been studying, and turned right. Her guess proved correct when she came to yet another chase, this one a short branch ending at a familiar-looking door. Zeppy's code worked its magic, and the door slid open to reveal the soaring space of a brace shaft.

Her morning plan of practicing on the ladders no longer had any appeal. Exhausted, she sat on the landing with her back to the wall and let the emotional quiet soothe her ragged edges. It was ironic that she would find peace in a place so full of noise, but there was a soothing feel to these hums and gurgles. They were the sounds of a ship that lived.

She had loved the breathing of Wildwind Bay as it surged up and down against the pilings of Dock One. The *Phoenix* was a very different creature, but it breathed as well. It had merely taken her this long to learn where she could hear it.

For ninety minutes, Rahel stitched herself back together in her newfound sanctuary. She might have slept there overnight had she not promised to give Lhyn a lesson in Alsean outcaste culture that evening. Walking back into the emotional noise of the corridors felt like leaving a cozy home to enter a raging, destructive winter storm.

The next afternoon, memories of that peaceful retreat were all that kept Rahel going through the worst headache she had ever experienced. By the middle of the shift, she could not turn her head at a normal speed without setting off agonizing flares that threatened to shut down her consciousness altogether.

The physical limitation made it difficult to complete her latest assignment of cleaning a surgical bay, but she eventually managed and walked out with her tools in one hand and the bag of medical waste in the other. Focused on the effort of maintaining her fragmented blocks, she was surprised by the sudden appearance of four Fleet Medical staff, two pushing a gurney while the others hurried alongside, snapping out numbers and orders to each other. She hadn't heard them coming and threw herself to the side, but not in time. The leading edge of the gurney clipped her hip, sending her spinning. Fireworks exploded in her brain, tools flew in all directions, and the bag of waste hit the floor and burst open.

"Sorry!" one of the doctors called. A nurse kicked the bag aside to make room, and they thundered past without another glance. Their heightened emotions trailed after like the wake of a fast-moving boat, slapping up against Rahel's exposed and raw senses, but it was the fear that threatened to capsize her.

She had glimpsed the older man lying on the gurney, his eyes open unnaturally wide and staring sightlessly at the ceiling. His terror was primal, the bone-deep panic of a dying creature that clung to life despite knowing it was over. Rahel had never felt anything like it.

Her chest tightened, forcing her to lean against the wall and gulp air. There was a pressure in her throat, straining for release, but she could not allow it. She could not allow anything. She was a hair's width from total collapse, and this was not the place for it.

The debris strewn across the floor was terrible evidence of her weakness. Distracted by her pain, she had forgotten to seal the bag. The nurse had been extremely clear on the importance of isolating medical waste, and she had just spread it all over a highly trafficked area.

With shaking hands and a roiling stomach, she slowly crouched and began to collect the disgusting waste she had already cleaned up once.

"What happened?"

Dr. Wells stood at the edge of the mess—the last person who should have seen this. A blazing lecture was surely on its way.

Rahel ignored the question. Speaking was not an option at the moment. Cleaning the mess was her single focus.

"Rahel?"

She dropped a wad of bloody cloth into the bag, so intent that she didn't notice Dr. Wells move until two hands were on her shoulders. They pushed her back on her heels even as she tried to reach for another wad of red-stained cloth.

"Stop it . . . stop . . . Rahel, stop!"

The loud command in High Alsean startled her into stillness.

"Are you going to tell me you're fine now?"

She kept her gaze on the floor, where the lack of visual detail aided her tenuous control.

A vehement stream of words burst from Dr. Wells, spoken in a guttural tongue that Rahel's language chip could not translate. The grip on her shoulders shifted to beneath her arms and began to lift.

"Come on. Get up, I can't lift you by myself. Rahel!"

The shreds of shielding she had pulled together were not enough to hold back alarm from such a close source. But that couldn't be right. Nothing unsettled Dr. Wells.

Her focus broken, Rahel raised her head. "What's wrong?"

Dr. Wells let out a choked sound. "Me, that's what. I didn't realize—" She cut herself off, then spoke more calmly, still in High Alsean. "Tell me what happened. Are you in pain?"

Though she wanted to deny it, there didn't seem much point when even shaking her head would probably make her pass out. She brought a hand toward her forehead, but her wrist was caught before she made contact.

"Don't. Your hands aren't clean. It's your head? You have a headache?"

A headache? That was the understatement of the day. Her head didn't ache. It stabbed with agony, as if her skull was two sizes too small to contain her brain.

"Yes," she whispered.

Dr. Wells gently pressed a finger behind her ear. "Here? Near your lingual implant?"

"No."

"Good," she muttered under her breath. "At least I can rule that out. Rahel, I need you to stand up and come with me. Can you do that?"

"No, the mess—"

"I'll call someone to take care of it. That's not your job now. You're done."

"I'm not done, I have one more day—"

"You are *done.* First Guard Sayana, I'm ordering you to come with me."

An order made sense. It was something she could follow, a beacon in the grayness of her surroundings. Without a word, Rahel stood up. When Dr. Wells moved, she walked right behind.

She stood passively while her hands were cleaned in a decontamination booth, then allowed herself to be settled on the omniphasic diagnostic bed. Multiple scanners slid along their tracks above, below, and to either side of her, the noise level making her cringe. It seemed that all of her senses were raw, not just the empathic ones. Her previous scans in this bed had impressed her with their near-silence.

The scanners reached her feet and came back up for their second pass. She closed her eyes and clenched her jaw, waiting for them to finish. At last, the noise stopped and the bed tray slid out, depositing her into the mercifully dim diagnostic room.

Dr. Wells stood nearby, scowling at a display. "I don't know how you were standing upright. Your head must feel like a slow-motion implosion. Right behind the eyes? And the left side of your forehead?"

Wanting off the bed, Rahel made the mistake of trying to sit up and speak at the same time. Her "yes" turned into an embarrassing groan. There was a flurry of movement and an arm around her shoulders, bringing with it a surge of emotion that she desperately wished she could block.

The next thing she knew, she was in a treatment room with no memory of how she had gotten there. The door closed, shutting out the noise of the medbay.

If only shutting out the emotions were that simple. Rahel closed her eyes and dug the heels of her hands into her forehead, a trick she had learned would alleviate some of the pain.

"I know this didn't just happen. Why in all the purple planets did you not tell me it was this bad? I checked in with you every day!" Dr. Wells bustled around the room, opening cupboards and drawers.

"Never show weakness," Rahel mumbled. *To an enemy*, was the rest of the phrase, but she would not say that aloud.

The cool tip of an injector touched her throat, followed by a tiny sting as it hissed.

"I wish I could use something stronger, but this is safe with your Alsean chemistry. You should start feeling better in about ten minutes."

A clatter indicated the injector being tossed onto a tray. She resisted the touch that tried to pull one of her hands away.

"I need to put on a diagnostic band," Dr. Wells said. "It will only take a second."

Rahel let go long enough for the wide bracelet to be snapped around her wrist.

"Thank you." After a moment of silence, Dr. Wells sighed. "Rahel, I'm sorry. I should have seen this. Shippers, you're good at hiding your symptoms, but still—I should have seen it. Dammit," she finished in a whisper.

Rahel turned onto her side, away from the emotions that were being broadcast so loudly.

"Would you like me to take out your braid? It might help reduce the tension."

Anything that could help was worth a try. Rahel gave a minute nod.

Dr. Wells was so careful that Rahel didn't feel her pull the band off the end of her braid. But she certainly felt the gentle motion of fingers unwinding the twists and combing through her hair.

In an eruption of memory, she was lying with her head on Sharro's lap, looking out onto the sparkling blue waters of Wildwind Bay as Sharro caressed her hair and face and talked about whatever came to mind.

The pain abruptly diminished. Her diagnostic band beeped.

"What—?" Dr. Wells stopped her motions and picked up Rahel's wrist.

The memory shattered and the pain roared back, worse now for that brief moment of respite. Rahel pulled her wrist away and curled into a tighter ball. "What you were doing," she croaked. "It helped."

"This?" The touch returned.

Within seconds, Rahel's body relaxed enough for her to uncurl. She wanted to say *Yes, that,* but the reduction in pain was too overwhelming.

"Fascinating," Dr. Wells murmured, her spiky emotions softening into curiosity. "Can you let me see your diagnostic band?"

Rahel slid her arm upward, onto the pillow.

"Look at that. This isn't from the analgesic; it hasn't had time to take effect. It's a direct result of this stimulation."

"It's home." Rahel cleared the rasp out of her throat and found she could speak in a normal tone. "Sharro's done this for me since I was sixteen."

"Sharro. Your mother's bondmate?"

"And my friend. Mentor. Mother, in a way, but not really. It's hard to explain."

After a pause, Dr. Wells said, "I would like it very much if you felt able to explain it to me." She brushed Rahel's hair away from the side of her face, fingers ghosting over her temple. "Is this all right?"

"Mm. Anywhere on my head, neck, face . . ." Rahel rolled onto her back, now able to manage the pain.

Dr. Wells was sitting on an elevated stool next to the bed, looking down at her with an expression Rahel had not seen before. The emotions she was broadcasting—those weren't for her. Or at least, not all of them.

"You had someone," Rahel said without thinking. "A daughter?"

Dr. Wells froze, a wave of shock billowing off her skin, and Rahel held her breath. She had done it again, stepping where she shouldn't, but she didn't want to say anything else for fear of making it worse.

"A son," Dr. Wells said at last. She tucked a wisp of hair behind Rahel's ear and let the touch trail down her jaw. "A beautiful son who was going to change the world, but he never had the chance. He died of dannerite fever when he was two."

"I'm very sorry." Rahel had never heard of the disease, but she understood the grief.

"So am I. He's why I'm here." Dr. Wells lightly scratched Rahel's scalp as her emotions sharpened into a decision. "I had another life before joining Fleet. I was twenty-one, happily married, raising my son, and working in crop genetics. Our planet had only been terraformed a generation earlier. We were still in the phase of developing crops that could withstand the environment, the diseases, the fungal infestations . . ." She trailed off. "I loved my work. I loved my life."

Rahel was barely cognizant of the pain, too fascinated by this glimpse into the formidable doctor.

"Then the fever hit. Almost forty percent of our planetary population went down with it. The fatality rate was . . . inconceivable. I didn't think any disease could be that virulent. My grandmother taught me herbalism—that was the start of my interest in medicine—but she was one of the first to get sick. I tried everything she ever taught me." Her gaze was distant, focused on events long past. "The best I could do was make it less painful for her. Then Grandpa got sick. Then my husband's parents, most of our cousins and aunts and uncles and friends—half the town was sick, and the other half nearly killed themselves trying to take care of them."

She ran a fingertip up each of Rahel's forehead ridges in turn, then brushed back her hair. "When Josue showed symptoms, I prayed to the

Seeders. All night long, I tried to keep him cool while promising that if they would only save him, they could take me instead."

Dr. Wells never swore to the Gaians' Seeder gods, Rahel realized. She swore in the name of the Shippers instead—advanced aliens thought to have shipped early Gaians all over the galaxy.

This was the story of when she had lost her faith.

"At some point, I fell asleep. When I woke up the next morning . . ." She shook her head, clamping down on the grief with a proficiency that could only come from long practice. "My memories of the next few days aren't clear. But I remember my husband running in, saying that a Fleet Medical ship was in orbit. There were shuttles landing everywhere. There was one right in the middle of our town. A very kind doctor came into our house, examined me, and gave me an injection. He said I was lucky; the disease hadn't gotten far."

"You had it, too?"

She nodded. "And I realized that if the Seeders did exist, they were cruel beyond understanding. They were going to take us both. Fleet Medical got in their way."

She traced Rahel's cheekbone ridge. "The fatality rate for the infected was ninety-one percent until Fleet Medical arrived. Grandpa survived, and a handful of my cousins and friends. My husband lost his parents, I lost Gramma . . . everyone was devastated. But none of that compared to losing my son." Her fingers drifted upward, into the hair at Rahel's temple. "There's a famous poem on my planet, about how love isn't love if it fails. That poet was a fool. Love fails for all kinds of reasons. It fails when both of you lose too much, and you don't have enough left to help each other. He grieved by drawing into himself and forgetting he still had a wife. I grieved by getting angry."

"That doesn't surprise me," Rahel said.

Dr. Wells let out a short laugh. "It wouldn't surprise anyone, would it? I was angry at the Seeders, the fever, my planet, everyone whose children survived—and I had to do *something*. I could never be that helpless again. So I left. I dissolved the marriage contract, caught a shuttle to the core worlds, and tested into a medical program. Gramma's lessons gave me a head start. My specialty is still genetics, but these days I focus on Gaians. And one Alsean," she added with a tiny smile. "I joined Fleet the day I graduated."

She rubbed Rahel's scalp with one hand and checked her diagnostic band with the other. "You should be feeling better."

"I am. Thank you." Rahel thought she should tell Dr. Wells she could stop now, but it felt much too good and she did not want to give it up.

"No one here knows I had a son. Josue was my life before Fleet. He's . . ." Dr. Wells lifted her free hand, then dropped it on her thigh. "Separate. I'll ask you to keep my confidence."

"I swear on my honor. But why did you tell me?"

"You already knew."

"Not the—"

"And I need you to trust me. So I'm trusting you first."

Rahel frowned. "I don't understand."

"Never show weakness?" Dr. Wells reminded her. "Your health is my responsibility. I failed because you didn't trust me enough to tell the truth when I asked how you were feeling. And I didn't want to risk what little trust you had by forcing you into tests you said weren't necessary."

Rahel lowered her gaze. She had never considered how her deception might affect Dr. Wells.

"I'm sorry I yelled at you the day you were bullied. You've probably heard about my temper."

"I didn't have to hear," Rahel mumbled. "I experienced it."

Dr. Wells sighed. "The reason I came to find you was because I had a late lunch with Lhyn. She gave me quite a lesson on warrior honor and respect. Not to mention the prestige your rank holds on Alsea, and how it must have felt for you to be lectured in front of everyone in the lobby."

She nudged Rahel's head up until their eyes met. "Would it make you feel better to know that when I learned what really happened, I made just as much noise in Captain Serrado's office as I did here?"

That Dr. Wells had been angry *for* her had not entered her wildest imaginings. "She must have enjoyed that."

"She's used to it by now." Dr. Wells gave her a tentative smile. "It might also help to know that she sent those bullies to serve their sentence in the waste reclamation department."

"Is that any worse than what I've been doing?"

"Oh, much worse. Staff are rotated through that duty. No one is assigned there longer than a week at a time, or we'd have troopers jumping ship every time we docked at a space station. She put them on the night shift, too. That's when the flush-throughs and maintenance happen. The really dirty jobs."

Rahel pictured those unpleasant blindworms dealing with concentrated amounts of effluent and found that it did indeed make her feel better. "I didn't realize she was that angry with them."

"We both were. Now, I'm going to ask you a question, and I want you to tell me the truth. Are you feeling emotional pressure right now?"

She could lie no longer. Not with the story of a child's death still lodged in her heart; not when Dr. Wells was blaming herself for missing what Rahel had taken every precaution to hide.

"It's harder here than anywhere else on the ship. But it's not as bad now. It helps when you . . ." She trailed off, touching the doctor's sleeve.

Dr. Wells took the hint. As she brushed Rahel's hair away from her forehead, she said, "How long have you felt the pressure? When did it start bothering you?"

Rahel closed her eyes. "Dr. Wells, I'm sorry."

"How long, Rahel?"

This was it. She would be sent back to Alsea a failure. The alternative restitution for her crime was two cycles of labor in Salomen's fields, a lenient punishment she would welcome if it didn't mean losing both her own dreams and what Salomen had worked so hard to give her.

"Since the first day," she confessed. "It wasn't bad until I had to work here. I thought I could manage it, but it kept getting worse and worse."

It was a great credit to the doctor that her touch never faltered, despite the surge of anger that filled the room. "The first day. Then almost every test I've run on you, every baseline I've established, is garbage data. I know *nothing* about the effect of emotional exposure on you except what I'm seeing right now."

"I'm sorry," Rahel repeated. She forced herself to open her eyes, to face the doom approaching at the speed of light.

Dr. Wells was watching her with narrowed eyes and a tight mouth, frustration written in every line of her face.

"We need to work on limiting your exposure," she said at last. "And getting you regular doses of the physical contact you need to reduce the nerve signaling."

Startled by the incomprehensible response, Rahel stuttered, "I—I don't know what that means."

"You were caught in a signaling loop. Your nerves were sending pain signals to your brain, which responded by sending out alarm signals, which caused your nerves to send more pain signals." Dr. Wells tapped her fingers on Rahel's scalp. "This interrupts the loop. So now I know what causes it, and I know how to stop it. All I need to learn is how to prevent it."

Rahel stared up at her, stunned speechless.

"What's wrong?"

"I, um, didn't expect that."

"You didn't expect medical care?" Dr. Wells scowled. "That had better be a joke."

"No, I mean—that's not—I didn't—" Rahel's breath was suddenly insufficient, and she had to tilt her head back to draw in a shuddering gulp of air.

"No you don't. Rahel, look at me. Breathe with me. Deep, slow breath in, come on."

Rahel shook her head, then stopped as the stabbing pain reminded her that was not a good idea. "I'm not hyperventilating."

"Please tell me what's happening, then. Because everything I thought I knew about you is wrong."

Everything Rahel thought she knew was wrong, too. "Are you going to throw me off the ship?"

"What? Why would you think that?"

Dr. Wells's shock was all the answer she needed. "I thought if you and Captain Serrado found out I was too weak, you'd find a high empath with better blocks. Or a low empath who doesn't need them."

A thundercloud formed on Dr. Wells's face, the commensurate anger rising in her emotions. Rahel waited nervously for the explosion.

"You—" Dr. Wells began, then fell silent, fuming. When she spoke again, her words were clipped. "You are not a tool we're sending back if it doesn't work as expected. You're the first of your kind, a medical and sociological treasure. Did you really think I didn't anticipate issues? I knew you'd be under emotional pressure. That's why I tested you, asked you every day—" She stopped again, her jaw clenched so tightly that Rahel feared for her teeth. Then she rubbed her own forehead, let out a long exhale, and spoke in a calmer tone.

"We're having a cultural misunderstanding. You're used to working alone and depending on yourself. That's not how it works here. You're part of a team now. You have people whose jobs are to look after your professional growth and your physical well-being. We're here to *support* you, not to test you and throw you out if you don't pass!"

Her anger still curled up like steam off hot shannel, but it was not aimed at Rahel. This was protective, and Rahel had a sudden vision of the kind of mother Dr. Wells would have been. When that was taken from her, she had channeled her ferocious instinct into healing others.

The lecture that had blistered Rahel's skin looked different in this light. It hadn't been meant to humiliate. It was the reaction of a healer faced with seven patients she had viewed as needlessly injured.

"What a disaster," Dr. Wells muttered. "I never imagined—but I should have."

"No." Rahel struggled up onto her elbows. "No, you shouldn't have. This is not your fault—"

"Lie down." Dr. Wells planted a hand in the center of her chest and pushed her down. "Stop being a damned warrior for one second. Do you think I've never seen a patient who hid her symptoms? Or her pain? You're not the first patient to try to fool me, not by any stretch. You're just the first who succeeded this well." Her anger eased slightly, lightened by a wry amusement that Rahel could not fathom. "And believe me, that's going in my article when I write it. You've ruined it for every Alsean coming after you."

Rahel's baffled frown seemed to increase her amusement.

"Let me tell you what's going to happen now." Dr. Wells ran gentle fingers through Rahel's hair, her touch at odds with the fierceness of her emotions. "You're going to repeat every test you've ever taken here. Every single one. And this time, you're going to give me *honest* answers. Because this time, you know two things. One, you don't have to lie to protect your position. And two, if you do lie, you'll be endangering every Alsean who serves in Fleet after this. Because we'll be treating them with corrupt data that you gave us by lying. I think you're too honorable to commit a crime like that."

A crime?

Rahel chewed on that thought until Dr. Wells finally spoke again.

"The analgesic should have kicked in by now. How do you feel?"

As if she'd taken a hard blow to the head from a stave, but that was just her mental state. "It still hurts, but much less. Dr. Wells, I don't need to retake all the tests. It wasn't a problem until I started working here. I swear."

"Did you feel any emotional pressure at all? Did you feel tense, anxious, tired? Have any trouble sleeping?"

"Shek," Rahel grumbled. "Yes."

"You're retaking every. Single. One." She smiled at Rahel's heartfelt groan. "Glad you understand. Now, I have an idea for how to reduce your emotional exposure, but I'll need to run some tests. Let's get you to your quarters first."

"My quarters?"

"Well, I'm certainly not going to keep you here. You said it's harder here than anywhere else."

Rahel stared, speechless again.

"For the love of flight, it's called medical care. It's what I do." Dr. Wells slid an arm beneath Rahel's shoulders and helped her sit upright. Leaning back enough to meet her eyes, she added, "Telling me how you feel is not showing weakness. It's helping me help you, and every Alsean who comes after you. All right?"

As Rahel slid off the bed, that supporting arm never leaving her shoulders, she thought of a tiny child who had not lived long enough to truly know his mother. He was only a spark of memory now, guarded and kept separate from everyone else on the crew—but Dr. Wells had shared him with her, despite her deception.

She's really a kind person, Lhyn had said, and why in Fahla's name had Rahel not believed her? Lhyn never lied, and her insight into others was unerring.

Rahel reached up to touch Dr. Wells's hand where it wrapped around her shoulder. "Thank you for telling me about your son. I'll keep him safe."

Dr. Wells did not answer. But her arm tightened, and even though the emotions were uncomfortably strong, Rahel refused to show it.

6

TEAM

Rahel did not have to finish the final day of her sentence. Captain Serrado apologized, saying that punishments were never supposed to cause physical distress, and then handed her a special duty assignment. While with Lhyn, she was to pay attention to the emotional reactions of people around them and determine possible threats.

Lhyn had provided the testimony that convicted both the man who had tortured her and the politician who hired him. She had done further damage by granting numerous interviews after the trial, speaking candidly and with devastating precision of her experience. As a result, she had almost single-handedly destroyed the political ambitions of the Defenders of the Protectorate and swung public opinion regarding the dangers of Alsean empaths.

"There's nothing like torture and attempted murder to make the other side look good," Serrado said wryly. "When Alsea gave Lhyn citizenship in recognition of her sacrifice, it swung the scales even more. But the DOP isn't dead. The true believers just crawled under rocks. I want to know if there are any on my ship." She paused. "Any that are a threat to Lhyn, that is. And only if you can do this without compromising your health."

"What are my orders if I find a threat?"

"Report directly to me. Unless it's active and imminent, in which case, neutralize it by any means necessary."

Rahel wasn't familiar with the Gaian version of what Lhyn called "speaking between words," but judging by the furiously sharp emotions saturating the office, Captain Serrado wouldn't mind a firm takedown if it came to that.

When the captain dismissed her, she found another officer waiting for her on the bridge.

"I've come to take you to your new quarters," Dr. Wells announced.

They were in base space, moving at what Captain Serrado said was a sedate pace toward the Setis Prime relay station. The dual bridge displays, which took up the entire floor and the hemispherical ceiling, were filled with the glowing red and orange mists of base space and the lumbering cruise ship whose sick passengers were clogging up the medbay. Dr. Wells appeared to be floating amid the ghostly streamers, the bow of the cruise ship just behind her left ear.

Rahel bit back a smile at the image of her as a Seeder god, smacking down an irritating ship that buzzed too near. "I didn't know I had new quarters," she said.

"You do now." Dr. Wells turned away.

Rahel fell into step beside her, marveling again at the disconnect between the solid floor beneath her feet and the vacuum of space her eyes insisted she was walking through. She loved coming here.

"Did you know that almost everyone gets nauseous the first time they see these bridge displays active?" Dr. Wells asked. "Especially when the ship is moving. Even more so in base space. It takes most bridge crew at least a week to get accustomed to the sensory dissonance. Some never do. They can't work here."

Rahel felt sorry for those unknown crew members. "I think it's spectacular."

"You thought exiting base space was fun, too. Ninety-eight percent of Gaians need foramine to get through an exit transition without vomiting, but not you."

They walked past the crew at the work stations lining the circular walls and entered the lift. After the limitless sight lines of the displays, the lift felt like a tiny box.

"What are you trying to say?" Rahel asked.

"Deck six, section two. I'm trying to remind you that while you consider your empathic sensitivity a weakness, you're remarkably resilient in ways that most crew members would pay for. Captain Serrado would probably give a year's wages for the ability to skip her foramine doses."

"You said foramine reduces reaction time. No warrior would do that willingly."

"I never said she took it willingly." Dr. Wells kept her gaze fixed on the doors, a small smile visible at the corner of her mouth. Rahel would bet a bottle of Whitesun Rise that Captain Serrado had been flattened by the intractable doctor at least once.

The lift came to a stop, its slightly blue lighting returning to normal. It was one of the tiny miracles that everyone on the ship took for granted, but Rahel was still amazed that she could drop five decks, shift to a rapid horizontal movement, then come to a complete halt, all without feeling a thing.

They emerged into a hushed, plush corridor and turned left.

"Um. These are the VIP quarters," Rahel said.

"I'm aware."

"My new quarters are here?"

In lieu of a verbal answer, Dr. Wells stopped in front of the last door and gestured at the pad beside it. "Go ahead, you're programmed in."

The scanner pad responded instantly to Rahel's touch. The door slid open and recessed lighting came to life, revealing luxurious quarters at least three times larger than her current ones.

Directly across from the entry was an L-shaped couch set in a corner, its short end punctuated with an elegant triangular table whose diagonal edge flowed to the doorway of what must be the sleeping quarters. Rahel trotted over and peeked in, confirming her guess and exhaling in amazement at the size of the bed. VIP quarters were made for guests who either came in triplets or entertained all night.

The bed's pedestal had the usual drawers, but that much width gave her more storage space than she could possibly fill. That wasn't counting the closet or the additional drawers built into the bulkhead beside it.

She turned in place and looked into the living area, spacious enough for stave practice. At its far end was a small kitchen, and making a visual break between the two was a dining table set beneath the wall display. A desk sat on the other side of the room, arranged so that a person working there could look up and see the display.

In her current quarters, the wall display made an excellent substitute for a window, showing astonishingly realistic scenes from a menu that she was still working through. She had thought it an ingenious solution for the lack of actual windows and hadn't given much consideration to its size.

This display made hers look like a kerchief. Its bottom edge was at hip level, the top was flush with the ceiling, and it took up the entire length of the bulkhead from the entry to the kitchen.

"Phoenix, set display to Alsea One," Dr. Wells said.

Startled by the request, Rahel glanced at her but was distracted by the enormous display coming to life with the last view she had expected to see on this ship.

It was as if she were standing on the east bank of the Fahlinor River, looking across its wide expanse to the verdant lawns and colorful landscaping of Blacksun's State Park. Behind that was dense forest dotted with the domed tops of the six great caste houses, the grand, glassed dome of Blacksun Temple, and the imposing height of the State House. The Fahlinor's soothing burble filled the room, accompanied by a light breeze rustling through leaves and instantly recognizable birdsong. It brought a rush of familiarity and an equal dose of homesickness.

"I never saw this in the menu." She stopped and cleared the hoarseness from her voice, hoping Dr. Wells hadn't noticed.

"It's not in the menu. It's a private program. Lhyn recorded it while she and Captain Serrado were on Alsea. Captain Serrado gave me permission to download it to your system."

Reeling from that casual bomb, Rahel managed, "The captain gave me her personal program?"

"Actually, I think Lhyn did." Dr. Wells put her hands on her hips, surveying the quarters with visible satisfaction. "Nice place, don't you think? These are the same size as the senior officer quarters. Although we were able to decorate ours any way we wanted. You can change things around, but I think you're stuck with the furniture." She motioned toward the bulkhead opposite the entry, which featured tile art and several alcoves filled with an assortment of flowering and foliage plants. "Normally, the botanists take care of those. Now that you're living here, you'll either have to care for them yourself or else give the botany section entry rights."

"But I don't understand. Why am I living here?"

"Remember I said I had an idea for reducing your emotional exposure?

This is it. Our tests yesterday established the range where you're most affected. I put in a medical transfer and told the chief of personnel that the quarters next to you and across the corridor are the last ones to be assigned. Unless the *Phoenix* is packed to the brim, you won't have any neighbors." She pointed toward the bedroom. "Your bathroom shares a bulkhead with a chase, and on the other side of that is storage." Sweeping her hand across the length of the rear bulkhead, she added, "Nothing but storage there, too. All of the VIP quarters are backed by storage. This should be an emotional dead zone, where you can retreat and recover from your daily exposure."

Rahel didn't know what to say. "I—Fahla's farts and fantasies," she blurted, reverting to High Alsean in her surprise. "I never thought—"

"Fahla's farts and fantasies?" Dr. Wells repeated, then roared with laughter. "Has Lhyn heard that?"

"Um, yes, I think so. Possibly?"

"Possibly? You need to find out for sure, because if she hasn't, she should."

The interruption had given Rahel time to find her words. "Dr. Wells, thank you. I didn't expect anything like this. This is . . ." She looked around, a smile growing as she realized what she couldn't sense. "Fantastic. There's no one here. I don't feel anyone but you."

"Good. I'm just sorry it took me so long to realize that you needed more consideration than we were giving you." Dr. Wells gave her an arch look. "Of course, if you hadn't lied to me since the day you walked on board . . ."

"I didn't want to be—"

"Weak, I know. Perhaps you could accept that you're *different*, and that's not the same thing as being weak."

She could hardly grasp the magnitude of what Dr. Wells had done for her. And none of it would have been possible without Captain Serrado's support. VIP quarters and no one near her? They were treating her like someone special, someone they truly wanted to accommodate.

Like a valued member of the crew.

She closed her eyes and took a deep breath, preparing for the storm she was about to unleash. But if she didn't do it now, it would surely cause more harm later on. Hadn't she just learned that lesson?

"I need to tell you something," she said.

"Hm. Why do I get the feeling I'm not going to like this?"

"Because you're not." Rahel moved over to the couch and sat near the corner.

"What is it?" Dr. Wells asked, taking the seat at right angles to her. "Something else you've been hiding?"

"No. Well, yes, but not in a medical sense." There were no words to make this easy. "I used Commander Zeppy's access code to get into a chase."

The disadvantage of being able to sense only one person, she realized, was that she *really* sensed that person. Though Dr. Wells was physically still, a symphony of emotions washed outward until her expression set into something hard.

"Why would—? You weren't even done serving your first sentence! Are you so eager for another one?"

"You haven't misjudged me!" Rahel could not bear the unspoken doubt, so strong that it hammered against her. "I swear you haven't, if you'll just let me explain."

"Please do." Dr. Wells crossed her arms and leaned back with a sharp, expectant stare.

"When Commander Zeppy took me into a chase, I felt better than I had since the first day. I could still feel the emotions, but they weren't . . ." She rapped her knuckles against her head. "They didn't *beat* on me. Suddenly I had a choice whether to acknowledge them or not, instead of spending every waking moment trying to keep them out. It was such a relief."

Dr. Wells said nothing, but she uncrossed her arms and was watching with a concern that erased the sharpness.

"Then he took me into a brace shaft. Fahla, it was beautiful. And I had fun. I enjoyed myself for the first time—" She stopped. "I'm sorry. I knew it was wrong, but after my next punishment shift, I couldn't go another minute without that relief. Commander Zeppy had to use his code when a scanner didn't work. I memorized it and used it to get into the nearest chase to the medbay. The brace shaft was easy to find and it—it was a little bit like home. Like sanctuary. I would have slept there if I could. Yesterday in the medbay, the pressure was so much worse and the thought of getting back to that brace shaft was the only thing—but I didn't make it." She was embarrassed by her babbling, but the need to redeem herself was so strong that she couldn't think properly.

"My sainted Shippers." Dr. Wells leaned forward, planting her elbows on her knees and resting her face in her hands. "What am I going to do with you?"

"I'm sorry. I didn't know that you would—" Realizing that was better left unsaid, she closed her mouth and looked miserably around the luxurious quarters. It was Fahla's own joke that she would lose them before moving in.

"You didn't know I'd take care of you?" Dr. Wells raised her head. "No, you wouldn't have. Between my temper and your self-reliance, we've gotten ourselves into the deep end of the sewage, haven't we?"

Startled by the *we*, Rahel could only look at her.

"Did you know that security tracks all access logs? When you used his code, Commander Zeppy was recorded in two places at once. An event like that gets flagged by the system. Then someone starts looking at the security cam footage. I'm guessing the only reason you haven't been questioned is that whoever is in charge of reports hasn't seen that one yet. There's still time for us to head it off." Her eyebrows rose. "That's shocked you. Good. Maybe it will start to sink into that thick skull of yours that *you are on a team.* And team members look out for each other." She frowned in thought. "I wonder if Alsean skull density really is greater. Need to measure that." With a quick head shake, she refocused on Rahel. "There's only one way to fix this, and we need to move on it now. Phoenix, location of Commander Przepyszny?"

Rahel was impressed by what sounded like perfect pronunciation. Then she realized what was coming next.

"Come on," Dr. Wells said, leading the way to the door. "You have another apology to make."

The lift ride to operations wasn't nearly long enough, and Rahel felt fifteen cycles old as she stood in front of Commander Zeppy's untidy desk and apologized for using his access code. Then she listened in amazement when Dr. Wells smoothly cut in, explaining that Rahel had engaged in self-medication due to a failure in treatment and a case of poor communication that she hoped was being resolved this very moment.

"I don't want my name and section being splashed all over the report Captain Serrado would have to send back to Gov Dome," she added.

"You know Protectorate Security is watching this pilot program just as closely as Command Dome. I'd like to keep your name out of it, too."

He eyed her knowingly. "For being so careless as to let an alien empath see my code?"

Rahel stood still, afraid to move a muscle as the two section chiefs faced off over her.

"Commander, this isn't a power play and I'm not threatening you. Ask Rahel about my intentions if you want. I know damn well I'm partly responsible for this. I also know there are people back in Gov Dome itching for a reason to shut this program down. Let's not give it to them."

"Well now," he said in a drawl, "you've hit me in my soft spot. The last thing I want is to give those pad pushers what *they* want. I'll call security and tell them we had a fritzing scanner corrupting its access logs." He pinned Rahel with a stern look. "Did it ever occur to you to simply ask me for access?"

On second thought, she felt ten cycles old. "No, Commander. I'm sorry."

He let out a soft grunt. "Didn't think I was that intimidating. Not sure if I should be happy about that or not."

"It's not—" She hesitated. "You weren't intimidating. You were professional and an obvious expert. I never thought I *could* ask. I mean, with any reasonable expectation that you'd say yes."

"I'm the one she thought was intimidating," Dr. Wells said.

To Rahel's surprise, Zeppy burst out laughing. "Everyone on this ship thinks that, Doctor. I have to say, it's a treat to have you here, trying to keep your ass out of the same fire mine would be in. Let's call this a lesson learned for all three of us, hm?" His eyes twinkled as he turned to Rahel. "The way you love sneaking around, you'll fit right in with security. But you'll need to learn a bit more about how the systems work. And how *we* work. Is there something you'd like to ask me?"

At first Rahel didn't understand. Then she stood straight and said, "Commander Zeppy, I want to thank you for showing me the chases and the brace shafts. I didn't know such places existed, or how beautiful they could be. Is it possible for me to have access to them? Without needing an escort?"

He pursed his lips, looking as if he were carefully considering the request, but his amusement bubbled and fizzed. "Nicely spoken. You're the first person to ask me that and you'll probably be the last. Not many people see them that way." After a theatrical pause, he said, "I can give you access on two conditions. One, you don't touch *anything* in there except the doors."

"I promise." She couldn't believe it was this easy.

"And two, you don't slide more than three decks on the ladder." His gray eyebrows climbed upward. "Don't think I didn't see the look on your face. You might be an empath, but that doesn't mean we can't read you too."

With effort, she held his gaze. "I understand. I swear I won't go more than three."

He nodded. "Just in case your word isn't worth what I'm told it is, there are sensors and security cams all over this ship, and that includes the chases and brace shafts. If you break your promise, I'll revoke your access so fast you'll still be dizzy two days later."

That stung. "Commander, I've only broken my word once in my life, and it was one of the biggest mistakes I ever made. I take my honor seriously."

"I can see that. All right, then." His fingers danced over the deskpad, sending shapes and digits scattering across his transparent display. A few more taps resulted in a green glow before he blanked the display. "There's your access. Thank you for asking me."

Rahel was so startled that she didn't respond until Dr. Wells elbowed her. "You're welcome," she said quickly. "Thank you for being so kind."

Zeppy chuckled. "Can't say I expected anything like this when I woke up this morning, but it's been an entertaining day. Captain Serrado has no idea of the headache we just saved her."

"And ourselves," Dr. Wells said. "I'd like to thank you as well, Commander. I appreciate your understanding."

"I'm not so old that I don't remember what it was like to be her age and brand new in a posting. Looks like you aren't, either."

"The day we get to that point is the day we should retire." Dr. Wells shared a smile with him before adding, "I want to take Rahel back into a chase and run some tests on what she senses. Your expertise would be helpful, if you have time to come with us? Something in there is muting the power of emotional broadcasts. I'd like to find out what."

"Well now, you've piqued my interest. I can't resist a mystery." Zeppy palmed a small electronic device off his desk and slipped it into his tool belt as he rose. "Let's go."

One day ago, Rahel could not have imagined that she would be standing in a chase with Dr. Wells and Commander Zeppy, reporting the strength of her emotional pressure on a scale of one to ten at varying points in the space. The two of them buzzed with interest and excitement, trading theories and ideas while she watched with an oddly detached bemusement. Despite the evidence before her, she still wasn't certain any of this was real.

After taking more measurements than could possibly be necessary, Dr. Wells thanked Zeppy and took Rahel back to her old quarters. "I have a little free time before lunch," she said, looking around at the sparse decor. "Would you like some help packing up?"

The detachment abruptly dissolved as Rahel stared at her. A single sentence had affirmed that she hadn't lost her new quarters, wasn't in trouble, and was still part of this team that had suddenly become the most important thing in her new life. Overwhelmed by relief, she turned away to hide what were surely reddened eyes.

Dr. Wells's quiet voice came from close behind. "I reread your medical file last night. Some of the details make more sense now. Such as the way physical touch is tied to your mental health, and why you've flouted your culture's taboo against warmrons for your entire adult life."

"It's a senseless taboo," Rahel muttered.

"I'm not qualified to offer a sociological assessment. But from a medical point of view, I'd say it's more than senseless. It's harmful." Dr. Wells paused. "I'm also seeing the irony in the fact that Fleet has a similar taboo."

"It does?"

"I'm constrained in how I can employ physical touch as well. Both as a section chief and as a doctor. I could hug a child in my care, but we don't get too many of those on a warship. So if you need a warmron, I'd be glad to offer one."

Sincerity shimmered on the surface of her emotions, just above the caution and wariness. There was a reason she had made the offer to Rahel's back.

Rahel turned. "You called it a warmron."

"I've come around to Lhyn's point of view. It's a nicer word than hug."

"I probably would have said no to a hug. But a warmron . . ." She opened her arms and found herself wrapped in the first warmron she had enjoyed since leaving Alsea.

Dr. Wells was a little stiff at first, but soon relaxed. "You're good at this."

"Lots of experience." Rahel could hardly get the words out. She had not known how much she needed this until now.

"More than me, that's for sure. At least, recent experience." Dr. Wells slid a hand up her back. "If Josue had lived, he would have been a little younger than you. And probably just as stubborn, given that he had my genes."

Rahel coughed out a rusty chuckle.

"This is not me wanting a substitute," Dr. Wells added.

Her worry was strong enough to unwind the blockage in Rahel's throat. "I know. I can feel it." She tightened her arms, then let go and stepped back. "Thank you. For everything. I'm sorry I've been such a trial, but I'm learning."

"Seems I am, too." When Dr. Wells smiled, it transformed her face. "Shall we pack you up?"

"It won't take long. I only brought a few things with me."

"Such as those?" Dr. Wells gestured at the two wooden daggers hanging over the small couch, their inlaid patterns gleaming in the lights. "They're beautiful. I wanted to ask you about them yesterday, but it wasn't a good time."

Yesterday she had been barely coherent and still stunned that Dr. Wells would help her. "They're very special to me. It's a long story."

"I'd like to hear it. Besides, as long as you're telling me a story, you're not getting into trouble. I could use the rest."

The joking words were accompanied by a lightness of emotion that Rahel could barely believe. So much had changed in a single day. "Dr. Wells?" she said tentatively. "I'm glad you're on my team."

As the startled pleasure warmed her senses, she reflected that once in a great while, she managed to say the right thing.

7

TRANSITION

Two days after moving into her new quarters, Rahel found herself in the briefing room off the bridge with Dr. Wells and a case full of portable medical equipment. They had reached the Setis Prime relay station and were preparing for the exit transition into normal space.

"I don't understand why I have to retake this test," Rahel protested. "It has nothing to do with emotional pressure. I didn't lie about anything I was feeling the first time."

"Not being empathic, I have no idea when you were lying and when you weren't." Dr. Wells was far too amused as she slid a silver metal circlet onto Rahel's head. "And your memory might not be perfect. Now, if you hadn't lied, you wouldn't be retaking this test, because I'd have confidence in *all* of my data. Since I'm now questioning every bit and byte of it, I have to redo it. And since you're feeling guilty about misleading me and putting me through this extra work, you're going to help without whining."

Rahel clamped her jaw shut against the retort. Warriors did not whine. Ever.

Dr. Wells tapped the back of the circlet. With a hum that Rahel could feel more than hear, the circlet's tabs tightened against her skull.

"This is not a whine," Rahel said. "But that feels like a hairy watcher walking around on my head."

"I accept that as a non-whine." Dr. Wells turned away to fiddle with something in her case, but Rahel didn't need to see her face to know that she was barely holding in the laughter.

"I'm glad you're finding this so enjoyable," she grumbled, and had to smile as the doctor's shoulders shook.

"I'm not—" Dr. Wells gave up and laughed aloud. "Fine, I am." She waited as a display sprouted from her case, then tapped a few controls and turned around. "It's just a joy to see you being you, instead of trying so hard to be the perfect stoic soldier. Your psychological history led me to expect a very different person than the one I saw in my medbay every day. I'm glad we're done with that."

"Dr. Wells." The captain's quiet voice penetrated every corner of the room as it came over the com. *"Every section is checked in but crew services. You've got about three minutes. Are you and First Guard Sayana ready?"*

"We're ready."

"And you've taken your foramine?"

"Of course. Unlike some of the crew, I don't wait until the last possible minute to take mine."

Rahel was startled by the blatant disrespect. Everyone knew Captain Serrado never took her foramine until right before transition.

"Just making sure you didn't forget while focusing on your test," Serrado said mildly. *"Some of the crew can be single-minded. See you on the other side."*

"Single-minded, hmph," Dr. Wells muttered as she checked the lock-down straps that would keep her equipment in place. "She has no idea."

"Are you whining when you're the one who started that?" Rahel asked.

Dr. Wells looked up with wide eyes and prickling indignation, which dissolved as soon as it had appeared. "All right, you earned that point." She gave a strap one final tug and sat in the chair next to Rahel. "I just can't stop myself with her. She makes it too easy."

"You two sound like a bonded couple."

"I suppose we do. She's the best captain I've ever served with, you know. I'd never give that kind of grief to a captain I didn't like. Now, my last captain . . . he was competent but a bit of an asshead. Had an ego that wouldn't fit in the same room as mine." She paused. "Right, that wasn't quite what I meant to say."

"I probably had a glitch in my lingual implant," Rahel said. "It didn't really translate."

"Oh, well done."

"All sections report ready. We'll be entering normal space as soon as the Plush Life *has gone through."* Captain Serrado's voice was still calm, but Rahel's heart rate increased as the blue lights that had been flashing on the upper walls of the room shifted to a much faster blink rate.

She focused on the display that took up the entire wall at one end of the room. Protectorate display technology was remarkable; she would never have thought this was anything other than a window onto the glowing mists of base space. Ahead and to the left, the cruise ship was stopped next to the relay station, a silver cylinder that dwarfed the ten-deck ship beside it. The station was narrowed at the bottom—or what Rahel perceived as the bottom—while its other end was ringed by two layers of instruments and antennae. These stations with their massive quantum beacons provided the only means of navigation through base space, where normal physics did not apply. They were also the means by which quantum coms were able to communicate without noticeable latency over distances Rahel still couldn't wrap her mind around. Yesterday she had enjoyed a session with Lanaril, her counselor back on Alsea, followed by a call to Salomen. Both calls had been indistinguishable from using a vidcom back home, yet Alsea was over a hundred light years away.

Along a straight line directly ahead of the cruise ship, the base space matter began to shift. Rahel knew from her studies that the line was caused by a pikamet beam, a type of radiation that enabled transitions into and out of base space.

At first, the matter moved slowly, but it soon picked up speed until it was roiling and whirling, rushing outward from the pikamet beam in all directions. The beam itself was now visible as a line of darkness, empty of all matter. It expanded until it was greater in diameter than the ship itself, and then—

"Shekking Mother on a burning boat!" she blurted as the *Plush Life* contorted itself into a grotesque parody of a ship, normal at the stern while the bow was stretched and pulled into a pinpoint. The point vanished into the nothingness of the pikamet beam and sucked the rest of the ship behind it, the entire thing elongating and flattening into something no living being could possibly survive.

With a blinding flash of light, the ship vanished. Another light show occurred not one second later when the base space matter reversed direction, crashing back into the void left behind and exploding in an expanding sphere of red and orange. As the shockwave blasted over them, the *Phoenix* shivered, creaking and groaning softly under the stress.

Then all was still.

"Fire without flames," Rahel whispered in awe. On her first exit transition, the *Phoenix* had been alone. She hadn't seen what it looked like from the outside.

"I've done this too many times," Dr. Wells said. "Forgotten how miraculous it is. You're making me see it in a new light."

"It *is* miraculous. I'd go through another punishment week in the medbay to see that again."

"Not on my watch, you won't."

Rahel blinked at her sudden ferocity and was about to respond when Captain Serrado's voice came over the com.

"The Plush Life *is through. Brace for transition."*

Rahel held on to the arms of her chair and watched as the base space mists directly ahead of them began the same dance, first gradually shifting and then rushing away from the beam that stabbed into them. The blackness grew into a yawning emptiness that took up the entire display—and then the display cracked.

Rahel twitched, startled by the unexpected effect.

Wrinkles propagated through the display and onto the bulkheads. With an eerie lack of sound, the display crumpled and was sucked down a tiny hole. The bulkheads, ceiling, and floor followed, stretching and vanishing into the emptiness that rushed toward Rahel with an otherworldly speed.

Dr. Wells, sitting next to and slightly ahead of her, twisted into a blur of black, green, and silver fabric that streamed into the hole. As the colors of her uniform vanished, all Rahel could see was the light brown of her hair, stretching across the whole galaxy and then disappearing altogether.

Rahel's feet were sucked in and her legs crumpled, the distortion rushing up her body until she ceased to exist.

This was the moment that she wished all Alseans could experience.

She had no eyes, yet saw everything. She had no ears, yet heard the universe murmuring to itself in a language that she could almost understand. There was no space and no time, only an infinity between spaces that was surely the home of Fahla herself, who held Rahel's hand as she was stretched and disassembled, then spat back into existence with an abruptness that left her laughing.

Dr. Wells was swallowing hard, fighting a nausea that made the air heavy around her. At the end of the room, the newly whole display showed the darkness of normal space punctuated by a million stars, with the *Plush Life* shining just ahead.

"Whoo!" Rahel thrust her fists overhead. "That was fantastic! What a ride!"

"Well, I guess that wasn't a fluke." Dr. Wells stumbled briefly as she went to check her equipment. "You really aren't affected."

"Are you joking? Of course I'm affected. It's like three days' worth of stims in one dose. It's shekking amazing! I feel like I could fight ten warriors with one hand behind my back."

Dr. Wells was scrolling through an incomprehensible readout, textual characters and numbers moving past at a rate Rahel couldn't begin to translate. "Amazing is a good word for it," she said, still reading. "If I'm right, this isn't just you. I think it's your species. We'll need to test more Alseans, but I have a feeling you're all immune to transition effects."

"That's a surprise." Captain Serrado stood in the open doorway. "Are you sure, Doctor?"

"Obviously not. I have a sample size of one. But from what I'm seeing here? It's not Rahel's personal chemistry. It's her Alsean brain."

Captain Serrado walked inside, allowing the door to shut behind her. "I suggest we keep that quiet for now. No need to spread that around when you don't have the data to support it."

"Well, of course—" Dr. Wells stopped. "Why do I have the feeling you're not concerned about evidentiary backup?"

"I have you for that. What I'm concerned about is certain people in Protectorate Security getting ideas they shouldn't have yet. If ever."

The understanding that passed between the two officers was so profound that Rahel felt it go right through her chest. There was deep history there.

"I'm happy to serve in any capacity I can," she offered. "That's why I'm here."

"And we value that." Though her voice was calm, Serrado's dark blue eyes reflected the strength of her emotions. "We just need to be sure that capacity stays reasonable."

She was slightly shorter than Dr. Wells and had the same slender build, but where Dr. Wells moved with a careless grace, Captain Serrado had a warrior's tense readiness. She kept her shoulder-length black hair clipped back, and her uniform always looked as if it had come straight from the laundry services, flawlessly pressed and without so much as a speck of lint to mar its perfection.

"Protectorate Security is always looking for an advantage," Serrado continued. "Any advantage. If Alseans are immune to exit transitions, then imagine what a warship could do with strategically placed Alseans at the helm and a few weapons controls."

"While the Gaians on the other ship are coping with transition nausea and slower response time from the foramine," Dr. Wells said. "Sometimes your mind scares me, Captain. That wouldn't have been my first thought. Or my second or third."

"I don't understand. Why is that a concern?" Rahel asked. "There's only one of me."

"There won't always be. In the meantime, I'd prefer that Dr. Wells determine the rate and type of experimentation you're subjected to."

"You can't possibly—he doesn't have that power here." Dr. Wells moved to Rahel's side, hands on her hips. "I'm the final say on anything to do with her health."

"You are as long as I'm captain and you're my chief surgeon. Let's not give him a reason for any personnel changes."

"I don't think I like this *him* you're talking about," Rahel said. "Should I know who this is?"

"No," they said simultaneously, then looked at each other. Dr. Wells nodded slightly, giving precedence.

"Not unless or until it becomes necessary," Captain Serrado said. "Dr. Wells, if you're done with your test, I believe we have a patient transfer."

"I'm done, and we do." She slipped the circlet off Rahel's head and replaced it in a slim silver box. "See you in the shuttle bay at fifteen forty-five?"

"We'll be there. Rahel, ready for your shuttle bay tour?"

Rahel was too surprised to hide it. "You're my guide?"

"Lhyn thinks shuttle operations are boring, so she's taking the afternoon off. And every now and then, they have to let me off the bridge so I don't go space happy."

A small snort came from the direction of Dr. Wells, who was lowering the medical display back into its portable case.

"Something you want to add, Doctor?"

"No, not at all. Just clearing my throat."

Serrado looked back at Rahel, who raised her hands.

"I think this comes under the category of things I can sense that I shouldn't say aloud."

"She's learning!" Dr. Wells closed the case and settled its strap over her shoulder. "Lead or get out of the way, please. I have patients to attend to."

8

A BAY WITH A VIEW

Rahel had passed through the shuttle bay upon first boarding the *Phoenix*, but remembered few details from that first overwhelming day. Now she walked beside Captain Serrado and marveled at both its vastness and the number of crew members bustling through it.

The bay was six decks high and housed eight shuttles ranging in size from large to gigantic. Six of them glowed with the silvery semi-organic hullskin that characterized all Gaian ships, but two others shone black beneath the lights. They were designed to handle the nanoscrubbers in Alsea's atmosphere, which attacked any ship with hullskin due to the foreign radiation it produced. No other ship in the Protectorate Fleet had Alsea-capable shuttles.

Each shuttle had its own support crew, Serrado explained. Space travel was rough on hardware, and failures could be catastrophic. No shuttle would fly until the crew chief signed off on its readiness.

"Then the crew chiefs are the ones in charge?" Rahel asked.

Serrado's lips twitched. "Don't tell the pilots."

She conducted her tour with the enthusiasm of a child in a sweet shop, a startling contrast to what Rahel had previously seen of her. Lhyn's earlier words about public and private personas suddenly gained new meaning, and she wondered how many people on the ship had seen their captain like this.

"If we're ever separated from the *Phoenix*, this is the one to be on," Serrado said, spreading her arms as they stood inside the largest shuttle. "It's considered the captain's because of the size and luxury, but I'll tell you a secret." She lowered her arms and spoke in a confidential tone. "I hate it. I want a shuttle I can enjoy flying. This is like flying a train."

Rahel chuckled before she could stop herself, then looked up to see the captain smiling at her.

"It really is. We have a phrase in Common that you might not have heard yet. 'Turns on a tack.' Know it?"

"Um. No. But I can imagine what it means. Something that can turn on one wing?" Rahel put one arm down and the other up, then rotated around her downward-pointing hand.

"Yes, exactly!" Captain Serrado laughed, a full, joyous sound that lifted Rahel's heart. "Turns on one wing, I like that. Might be better than ours. More visual." She repeated the phrase in High Alsean and added, "I'll have to ask Lhyn if she knows that one. She'll love the alliteration. Anyway, this beast does the opposite of turning on one wing. It needs half a planetary orbit to come around."

She walked Rahel through the shuttle, pointing out some of the differences between it and the one they had flown in from Alsea, then led her across the busy bay to the far end. The exit tunnel loomed far over their heads, three decks high and wide enough to easily accommodate the largest shuttle.

"I remember flashing lights when we arrived," Rahel said.

"Guidance lights." Serrado tapped the lock pad beside a small door, which slid open to reveal a stairwell. "You'll see them when the shuttle leaves with our last patients." She jogged up five flights of stairs and opened another door into a small room crowded with lit panels, a dizzying array of switches, and two crew members in operations uniforms. They were seated by a large window overlooking the exit tunnel, but at the sight of Serrado they leaped up with matching shivers of nervousness.

"Captain!" The short male reached out to stop his chair's spin. "We didn't know there was an inspection."

"There isn't. Just a tour. Unless you feel an inspection is needed?"

Beside him, the taller woman shook her head vigorously. "No, Captain. Not necessary at all. Everything is in perfect working order and we're ready for launch and retrieval."

Rahel frowned. "Captain—"

Captain Serrado raised a hand without looking at her. "Good, because I'd rather leave the inspections to Commander Zeppy."

They relaxed immediately, smiling at her use of the commander's nickname.

"I'm taking First Guard Sayana to the end," Serrado continued as she turned away. "Don't be alarmed when the bay door opens."

With a nod to the too-relieved crew members, Rahel followed her through another door into a narrow passageway lined with windows.

"This runs all the way to the bay door." Captain Serrado stopped by one of the windows. "Were they lying? About being ready for operations?"

"No. But they were very nervous. They really didn't want you to look around."

Serrado took the clip out of her hair and pocketed it, then ran both hands through the freed strands as she gazed onto the empty exit tunnel. "All right," she said quietly, leaning a hip against the windowsill and crossing her arms over her chest. "Rahel, you can't contradict crew members in front of them. Not unless they're actively lying about something you believe to be a danger to the ship or its crew."

"You don't want to know?"

"You think I didn't know they were trying to avoid me nosing around? It could be anything. They could be hiding a bottle of alcohol, or had inappropriate reading material on their screens. Maybe we caught them in the middle of a kasmet game. Any of those would be actionable, but they're not things I want to deal with. I leave that to my officers. As long as they're ready for operations, I'm not going to breathe down their necks about playing a game in the quiet half-hour before they need to start flipping switches."

"Because you're the captain. You're prioritizing."

With a wry smile, Serrado said, "I used to be the kind of captain who *did* breathe down everyone's necks about the little things. I bled Fleet colors and expected everyone else to do the same. Then I did a tour of duty at Protectorate Security in Gov Dome. That opened my eyes to the kind of commanding officer I didn't want to be."

"Protectorate Security," Rahel remembered. "Is that where you met him? The one you're worried about?"

"Be careful that you're not too smart for your own good."

"I'm sorry, I'm trying to learn when—"

"I know," Serrado interrupted. "I'm not angry. But then, you know that."

A spike of discomfort pricked against Rahel's senses. For the first time, she realized that Captain Serrado was one of those who didn't feel at ease with an empath.

"I wasn't actively reading you," she said, swallowing the sudden sting of loneliness. "But I'll block you now."

"Wait." Captain Serrado stared out at the tunnel, her discomfort growing. "Dr. Wells tells me you need to reduce the amount of time you're holding up your blocks."

"She thinks the effort affects my production of some brain chemical with a name I can't remember. But you're the captain, I'm sure she didn't mean—" She stopped at the odd sound that erupted from Serrado's throat.

"I'm sure she did. I'm supposed to be setting an example for the crew. If I can't learn to be around an empath . . ." She turned her head and met Rahel's gaze. "Tell me what you're sensing now."

"Um. You're not comfortable. Neither am I," Rahel added, and was encouraged by the streak of amused understanding that lightened the captain's emotions. "You're worried, but that's not at the surface. It's deeper, like it's something you live with."

"I think you'd find that in any captain worth her bars. What else?"

Rahel shrugged. "There isn't much else. You wanted to stop me in the control room, but that ended as soon as we left. You're concerned, I think for me. Before that, you were enjoying this tour. It felt good. I'm sorry it's gone."

"You enjoy sensing positive emotions?"

"Of course! Don't you? I mean . . . if you make someone laugh, don't you enjoy that? Or when you know Lhyn is happy?"

Slowly, Captain Serrado nodded. "I hadn't connected that sort of sensing with what you do."

"Being sonsales doesn't mean you're blind. It means you don't have this particular sense." Rahel tapped her head. "But you still see."

"And yet the definition of sonsales is someone blind to emotions."

"Yes, but we made that definition before we knew there was other intelligent life in the universe. A sonsales is an *Alsean* who is blinded in this sense." She tapped her head again. "You never had it to begin with. How can you be blind in a sense you never had?"

Captain Serrado smiled. "Are you sensing my enjoyment right now? That was an excellent argument."

"It's hard to miss."

"Good. Then I'm ready to get back to enjoying our tour. But one bit of business first." She pointed over her shoulder to the door behind her. "If you'd told me what you sensed in there, those two would have told everyone they know that the Alsean empath is spying for the captain. Neither of us would come out of that in a good position. Do you understand?"

"I think so."

"That doesn't mean I never want to know. You're a resource; I'd be remiss to shut you down. Use your judgment. If you think I need to know something, tell me in private. If you sense an imminent danger, don't wait for privacy."

"Understood."

Captain Serrado examined her, then gave a single nod and pushed off the sill. "Come on, we still have the best part."

Despite her shorter height, she moved rapidly enough that Rahel had to extend her stride to keep up. They walked the length of the exit tunnel and stopped at the final window overlooking a closed bay door. Beneath it was a panel similar to those in the control room.

"There aren't many places on the ship where we can see out." Serrado flipped one switch, then another, and the panel came to colorful life. "I know Lhyn took you to Deck Zero. It's her favorite place on the *Phoenix*."

"It's spectacular." The entire top deck was a landscaped park, topped by hullskin that could be rolled back to reveal transparent material. It was the closest thing Rahel could imagine to actually flying among the stars.

"It is. It's also never empty. But there are little spots like this all over the ship, where we can glimpse the same thing without sharing it with half the crew." Serrado tapped a code into the panel.

A deep thunk resonated through Rahel's feet, followed by the sound of air rushing past the window. A vertical seam appeared in the center of the bay door, growing wider as the two halves slid back, their bulk vanishing into pockets on either side of the tunnel.

"Goddess above," Rahel breathed.

"Beautiful, isn't it?"

Rahel touched her fingertips to the window. On the other side were a million stars blazing in the darkness, so densely packed that she couldn't imagine trying to draw constellations among them. Farther away were the elegant columns of a nebula, fingers reaching out to grasp something just beyond sight. Brilliant glows scattered amongst the fingers gave away the nebula's secret: it was a star nursery, studded with protostars, their birth cries igniting the gas around them in a triumphant announcement that could be seen across the galaxy.

"Beautiful doesn't begin to describe it."

"I have the same problem." Captain Serrado put a palm against the window, a satisfied smile on her face as she gazed out. "Tell me, what do you feel right now?"

"Awed. Exhilarated." Rahel paused. "Peaceful."

"What are you sensing from me?"

Rahel met her eyes. "All the same things."

The smile grew. "You're right. I do enjoy sensing positive emotions."

9

TESTS

"Captain, there aren't enough thanks in the galaxy for what you and your crew did for me." The man's wrinkled face creased into a toothy grin as he held out a hand. "Never expected a warship to come to my rescue."

"I'm glad we were here when you needed us." Captain Serrado accepted his hand, her eyes growing comically wide when he used the grip to pull her in and plant a loud kiss on each cheek.

Rahel pressed her lips together to hold in the laugh. Never in their short acquaintance had she felt the captain so startled. But it seemed that just as on Alsea, elders here had a certain leeway when it came to social expectations.

The man's bondmate stood beside him at the foot of the shuttle ramp, equally wrinkled but with snow-white hair where his was a steely gray. "If I may, Captain?" She put gentle hands on the captain's shoulders and drew her in for a similar but quieter set of kisses. "It's our way, to thank someone for a special gift or service. I can think of nothing more special than saving my husband's life."

"Yep!" The man patted his stomach. "Came in for a belly bug, almost went out with an aneurysm. We met the boss doc on the *Plush Life*. He looks very fine in his dress whites, but I'd surely be dead if he'd been the one operating on me." He turned to Dr. Wells. "Now, *your* boss doc! She knows her fingers from her toes."

"I like to think so." Dr. Wells's smile was genuine; she liked this blustery man. "Of course, I'm not the one who operated on you. But I do know how to put together a top-notch team."

"Seems everyone on this ship is top-notch. You even have the first Alsean."

Rahel found herself the center of attention and the object of expectation on all sides. No one had told her she would have to say anything!

"I'm, um, not on Dr. Wells's medical team. But I agree with you, she has an excellent staff."

"First Guard Sayana is being modest," Dr. Wells said. "She just completed a rotation in medical. In fact, I believe she was present when you were taken to surgery."

Rahel froze, then looked at the man more closely.

Great Mother, she would never have recognized him. She'd had only the briefest glimpse before being overwhelmed by his terror. She had never asked Dr. Wells about him, certain of his death and not wanting confirmation.

And here he was, grinning at her.

"Oh," she said. "Yes, I was. It was . . . a true learning experience."

Unseen by the others, Dr. Wells winked at her.

She got through the rest of the leave-taking without sounding too idiotic, thank Fahla. While their guests were taken aboard, she accompanied Captain Serrado and Dr. Wells to the shuttle operations office.

"You could have told me," she said as they stood at the transparent wall overlooking the bay.

"You could have asked," was the unsympathetic reply.

"I didn't want to know he was dead."

Captain Serrado chuckled. "She has such faith in your team, Doctor. There go the guidance lights, see them?"

The small shuttle was lifting off, and sure enough, there were flashing lights inside the exit tunnel, just as Rahel had remembered.

"I felt him," she said, watching the shuttle rise until it was level with the tunnel entrance. "One of my warriors died in my arms during the Battle of Alsea, and that wasn't half as bad as what I felt from him. I never imagined he could live."

The shuttle flew past its parked brethren and into the tunnel, its rear navigation lights the last thing to pass from view.

"Rahel."

She turned to face Dr. Wells, who was suddenly serious.

"I knew that sensing him was difficult for you, but I didn't realize it was that bad. I wanted you to understand that you *were* part of my team, if only for those few days. Everyone who works on my staff has some part in what we do. It wasn't just the surgeon who saved him. It was the nurses, the support staff, the fact that his surgical bay was prepped and ready. It was the clean linens and sterilized equipment. I may be the chief, but I can't do any of it alone." She glanced up at the exit tunnel, its guidance lights still flashing. "And I wanted you to have an emotional contact with him that might balance out what you felt before. If I overstepped, I apologize."

Her first thought was to say it was fine, to assuage the edge of regret she sensed. But behind the words lay a sharp appraisal, and Captain Serrado had an expectant air, as if something important was happening here.

And a well-meaning lie would still be a lie.

"I wish you had told me before, so it wasn't such a shock," she said. "But I appreciate that you thought about balancing that emotional contact. It did help. A lot."

Dr. Wells nodded, the faint tension in her emotions relaxing. "Thank you for being honest."

Rahel relaxed as well, understanding that she had passed another test. Dr. Wells had insisted that she was not being tested, but she knew better now. She was a trainee again, starting over in a completely new world, and tests were part of training. Her initial mistake had been in thinking Lhyn was her only instructor, the only one for whom she did not have to be perfect. She had never expected the senior officers of this ship to have the time or inclination to help train a new officer so fundamentally uninformed and unprepared. But Dr. Wells had forcefully proven otherwise, Captain Serrado had taught a quiet lesson not half an hour ago, and even Commander Zeppy gave her a second chance instead of being justifiably angry about her use of his access code.

"I know this might be difficult to believe," she said, "but I prefer honesty. I spent most of my career with Prime Warrior Shantu working as...well, what you would call a spy." She glanced at Captain Serrado and saw the recognition there. "Honesty wasn't often an option. And the last time I worked on a real team was the Battle of Alsea. This is new for me, but it feels right."

"Do you remember what I said to you the first time we met?" Dr. Wells asked.

"Besides the hour-long medical lecture on my lingual implant surgery?"

Dr. Wells chuckled. "Yes, besides that. I said they chose you well. I stand by my assessment."

"Now there's a vote of confidence," Captain Serrado said, turning toward the doors. "It took me much longer to manage that from her. Congratulations, First Guard."

Rahel followed as they wound past the crew at their work stations, wondering if she could get the story behind that statement out of Lhyn.

"This has been one of those days when nothing happens the way I expect," Captain Serrado added.

"Is that a good thing?" Dr. Wells asked.

"Oh, definitely."

The doors opened at their approach, as no access code was needed to exit the office, and they walked into the empty corridor together.

Empty, that is, but for the stocky young man who turned from his study of the mosaic on the opposite wall. "Captain!"

"And that, unfortunately, is something I always expect," Serrado finished in a low voice. "Yes?"

"Commander Zeppy sent me," he said, starting across the corridor. With him came a malevolent excitement, dark red and sticky, and a suffocating wave of lethal intent.

Rahel shifted to a ready stance and pulled her stave grip from its holster as he took another step, smiling at them and giving every external appearance of a friendly crew member. The dissonance between what she saw and what she felt made her skin crawl.

He reached into the pouch hanging from his utility belt. "The commander wanted me to show you—"

The end of her stave smashed into his sternum, sending him flying. He collided with the wall and slumped to the floor, his hands fluttering uselessly at his chest as he gasped for air.

She'd had no room to swing, not with the captain and Dr. Wells bracketing her. But she had long ago learned the best move for taking out an opponent in a close space: by extending her stave straight into their body. It required the right positioning and a rock-solid hold on the grip, but when done correctly, it was devastating.

"Rahel!" Dr. Wells shouted, leaping forward. Rahel caught her with one arm around her waist, holding tight as she struggled. "Dammit, let me go! What the Hades are you doing?"

"Stand down, Doctor!" Captain Serrado barked.

Relieved at Serrado's instant understanding, Rahel kept her grip on the doctor while pointing with the hand still holding her stave. "In his tool bag."

Serrado crossed the corridor and knelt next to the man, keeping a wary eye on him as she checked the bag. Her hand came out holding a phaser, its green activation light glowing. It was charged and ready to fire.

Dr. Wells stopped all movement. "Oh, stars," she breathed.

Serrado deactivated the phaser and slipped it into the back of her waistband, then unfastened the man's belt and used it to flip him over. Ignoring the shriek he let out upon landing chest down, she stripped the belt and began checking it for weapons.

Dr. Wells flinched at the pain-filled scream, but made no attempt to aid him. "Phoenix, medical team to my location," she murmured. "Gurney required. Prisoner transport."

Rahel released her, assured that she would not rush over and put herself in danger. Her own internal com was silent, but she could imagine the com traffic currently blowing through the ears of the medical staff.

Captain Serrado had called in a security team at the same time and was now patting down the attacker's pockets. Satisfied that he was no longer a threat, she scooped up the belt and crossed to Rahel.

"Who was the target, you or me?" she demanded.

Rahel had been watching his eyes as he approached. When he looked at the captain, she had sensed excitement and anticipation. But when he looked at her . . .

"Me," she said.

Serrado's expression shut down. Her terror made the air difficult to breathe, yet she appeared to be a warrior in complete control as she dropped the belt by the doors, strode over to the incapacitated man, and yanked him onto his back.

This time, he only managed a gurgle.

"Who sent you?" she snarled.

He rolled his eyes up at her, then closed them as another agonized squeak escaped.

"Answer me, damn you! Was it the Defenders of the Protectorate?"

"I don't think he's capable of speech," Dr. Wells said.

"Then nod or shake your head. Did the DOP send you, yes or no?" Serrado's fury was mounting as he continued to ignore her, until it nearly equaled her fear.

"If he's getting too annoying, I can stop that noise." Rahel refused to acknowledge Dr. Wells's shocked glare.

"Don't tempt me. Phoenix, locate Lhyn Rivers. Respond to Rahel Sayana and me."

The ship's calm voice sounded inside Rahel's head. *"Dr. Lhyn Rivers is on Deck Zero, aft side of Bridge Hill."*

Captain Serrado stood up as a squad of security officers came around the corner at a dead run. While they swarmed the man, she pulled the phaser from her waistband, reactivated it, and held it out to Rahel. "It's not much different from a molecular disruptor. Trigger's here, don't touch it unless you're ready to shoot. Can you use it?"

Rahel retracted her stave and snapped it back into its holster. Accepting the phaser, she said, "As a last resort, yes. I'll always prefer my stave."

"Good. Get Lhyn and take her to my quarters. Don't leave her side, don't let anyone in, don't trust anyone but me. *Run.*"

Her fear gave wings to Rahel's feet. She pushed through the security officers and raced to the nearest lift. Its doors opened just as she reached it, disgorging four crew members in the green and silver of Fleet Medical. Impatiently, she waited for them to push out the gurney, then leaped inside and called out, "Deck Zero, aft entrance!"

The lights shifted blue and she drummed her fingers against her thigh, hating even these few seconds of forced inactivity. After what felt like an hour, the lights returned to normal and the doors slid open, revealing gardens whose beauty made no impression on her now.

She shot out as if propelled from a rail gun and raced down the curved paths, cursing the fact that not a single one of them led directly to the hill in the center of the park. It was built over the domed ceiling of the bridge, a duality of purpose that she had admired on her first tour through here. She had also admired the careful landscaping design, which obscured all sight lines and made the park seem larger and more private than it was.

She wasn't appreciating any of that at the moment. When the path began to veer away from Bridge Hill, she cut across the landscaping, leaping over flower borders and crashing through shrubbery until she landed on another path at the base of the hill's terraced plantings.

Lhyn was sitting on a bench halfway up, her legs crossed at the knees and her focus on the pad she held in one hand. Six people were in her immediate vicinity, all too far for Rahel to sense.

Six potential assassins.

"Lhyn!" she called.

Lhyn's head came up. A smile ghosted across her face before she saw the phaser in Rahel's hand. She scrambled to her feet, shoving the pad in her sleeve pocket.

By the time Rahel was in sensory range, Lhyn was already frightened —but not for herself.

"Is she all right?" were her first words when Rahel drew near enough.

"She's fine." Rahel stopped beside her and did another sweep of the six crew members. They were startled, wildly curious, and blessedly free of the malevolence she had felt from the attacker.

"Then what—"

"I'll explain later. Right now, I need to get you to your quarters. Come with me."

"Explain what? Just tell me!"

"Not now. My orders are to get you to your quarters immediately. We'll talk there." She set off at a fast trot, tugging Lhyn with her, and was relieved at the lack of resistance.

The journey across the park was fraught with potential danger. *Don't trust anyone but me*, Captain Serrado had said. For the captain of a warship to give that order . . .

Everyone was a threat until Rahel could sense them. That was no easy thing with Lhyn so close, pouring out even stronger emotions than normal.

When they finally reached the lift, three troopers were walking into it. Rahel set a foot in the entrance, preventing the doors from closing. "Get out."

"What?" asked a baffled trooper.

"Captain's priority. We need this lift now."

They looked behind her. "I don't see the captain," the largest of them said. "Haven't heard anything over the com, either."

"Get out now!" Rahel snarled. When they still hesitated, she reached in, grabbed the talkative one by his shirt, and hauled him out. He stumbled over his feet and nearly fell.

The other two blanched and hastened out. One muttered imprecations under his breath, but Rahel was already pushing Lhyn ahead of her. "Captain's quarters."

When the doors closed, she slumped against the wall and let out a breath.

"Now will you tell me what's happening?"

"In your quarters."

"Fucking stars, would you—"

"No. Lhyn, please. I can't focus on talking and sensing at the same time."

"Oh." Lhyn clasped her hands together and stood looking at her uncertainly. Then she turned to face the doors.

They passed the next few seconds in silence, and when the doors opened again, Rahel put a warning hand on Lhyn's arm before stepping into the corridor. Only when she was sure that the four people walking through it posed no danger did she beckon Lhyn out.

One of the captain's privileges was living right across from a lift entrance, leaving three strides between Lhyn and safety. Rahel faced outward, phaser gripped low and ready, while Lhyn tapped the lock pad. As soon as the door slid open, she turned and stepped past her into the room, scanning it visually and sensing with all her might.

Clear so far.

She pulled Lhyn in and held up a hand, silently telling her to stay put. Then she sidled up to the only doorway in the quarters and focused.

No emotions hit her senses, and when she stepped inside, she breathed a sigh of relief. The bedroom wasn't large enough for anyone to be outside her range. She checked the closet to be sure, then looked into the bathroom. Only then did she deactivate the phaser. Not having a holster for it, she loosened her belt and tucked in the phaser as she walked back to the living area. "It's safe."

"Good. *Now* will you tell me?"

She held up one finger. "Sayana to Captain Serrado. Lhyn is safe and we're in your quarters."

"Understood, thank you. Stay there until you hear from me. Tell Lhyn that I don't have any answers yet, but she'll know as soon as I do." The call ended before Rahel could acknowledge the order.

"I don't know much," she said. "Someone tried to kill me outside shuttle operations, and then Captain Serrado sent me to protect you. She doesn't know what's happening either, but she'll tell you as soon as she does."

Lhyn frowned. "Someone tried to kill *you?* Then why—" Her eyes widened as dread slithered over Rahel's senses. "Oh, stars, not the DOP. Not here."

"Captain Serrado asked if that was who sent him. He wouldn't answer."

"Defenders of the Protectorate." Lhyn spat the words as if they tasted foul. "I loathe that name. Defenders of torture and murder is more like it. They're the ones most likely to want to kill you. And if you're a target, so am I."

"You don't know that."

"No, but it's a safe assumption. The trial just ended two months ago. I've given seventeen interviews since then. They want to shut me up." She dropped her head back. "Okay. Okay. I can do this. It's not difficult. I'm trapped on a ship with one or more DOP operatives and Ekatya is scared enough to send you after me, but that's . . . that's . . ."

Her breathing accelerated, the primal fear so powerful that Rahel shivered with it.

"Lhyn, you're safe." She reached for Lhyn's hands and willed confidence into her terrified friend. "You're safe, you're in your quarters, and I won't let anyone touch you. Do you understand? They'll have to get past me first. And I'm yanked right now."

Lhyn's breathing arrested. "You're—what? Yanked?" The rising terror receded a hair. "What does that mean?"

So that was how one stopped a scholar from having a panic attack: distract her with a puzzle.

"I'll tell you what it means after you breathe with me." Rahel kept her grip on Lhyn's hands and lifted them as she inhaled, then brought them down on the exhale.

Lhyn's breaths were still too short, but after a few repetitions, she aligned her breathing with Rahel's. The fear died back to a manageable level, and a small smile quirked her lips. "Did you do that on purpose? Put a little linguistic snack under my nose?"

"No, but I learned something from it." Rahel relaxed; she wouldn't have to call Dr. Wells after all.

"So did I. Thank you."

"Always."

Lhyn squeezed her hands and let go. "So?"

"It's Whitesun slang. I'm yanked means I'm angry. I yanked you off means I made you angry." She shook her head. "It doesn't sound the same in Common."

"I'm yanked," Lhyn said in High Alsean. "You're yanked, Ekatya's yanked . . . who yanked you off? You're right, it doesn't sound the same at all. I can hear the etymological roots in High Alsean."

Rahel had to smile. "There was never any question as to which caste you would join, was there?"

"Not for a second. I'm scholar to the bone." Lhyn took a deep breath, her hand over her chest. "Shippers, I thought I was done with those. Who tried to kill you?"

"I don't know him. He was in an operations uniform."

"Perfect disguise," she muttered. "How close did he get?"

"Physically? Close enough for me to break his sternum when I sensed his intent. He never got his weapon out."

"Ouch. Suddenly I'm very happy to have you here with me." Lhyn relaxed further, the fear receding to a point where Rahel could feel her consciously pushing it into the background. "Would you like something to drink while we wait? Ekatya has a shannel dispenser."

"She does?"

"A gift from Andira." Lhyn was crossing the room toward the kitchen. "She probably got tired of hearing Ekatya complain about how much she missed it on patrols."

Rahel followed, taking in the details of the room and wondering if she would ever get used to Lhyn referring to Lancer Tal by her first name. "The Savior of Blacksun is a shannel addict?"

"You have no idea."

"Can you make a rajalta?"

Lhyn reached up to pull two cups out of a wooden rack. "No, more's the pity. Next time you go to Whitesun, bring back a crate of those toasted seeds. Ekatya will be your friend for life." She paused as she set the cups next to the dispenser. "It says a lot that she sent you after me and not anyone from her own staff."

Rahel had hoped she wouldn't think of that. "Captain Serrado knows how to use her resources."

"Yes, but she also doesn't know who to trust." Lhyn activated the dispenser, and the familiar whooshing sound filled the kitchen. "I think you're going to be busy over the next few days."

10

TARGET PRACTICE

Ekatya was not good at having nothing to do.

Her security chief was handling the investigation, Dr. Wells had taken the would-be assassin into surgery, and Rahel was guarding Lhyn, leaving Ekatya with no plausible means of involvement. She had managed a short diversion on the bridge, overseeing the shuttle retrieval and putting the *Phoenix* back on course for their next rendezvous. They would be meeting the cargo ship *Tutnuken*, which was carrying defender mines for the Alsean base space exit point.

But now they were underway, everything was running smoothly, and Commander Lokomorra had thrown her off the bridge. Respectfully, of course—her executive officer was always respectful, even while couching it in informal language. He reminded her that she had left him in charge, observed that he was fully capable of overseeing operations when the ship was doing nothing more than transiting, and gently suggested that her tension might be contagious to the rest of the bridge crew.

She could argue none of these and returned to her quarters, where the door opened to reveal Lhyn seated at the dining table, the chair opposite her tipped onto its back, and Rahel standing in front of Lhyn, phaser out and ready.

"Oh," Ekatya said weakly. "I should have told you I was coming."

"And deny me the chance to see how fast she moves? My stars," Lhyn said, watching Rahel deactivate the phaser and set it on the table. "I didn't even have time to be nervous."

"I did," Rahel muttered.

"I'm sorry, I really wasn't thinking." Ekatya crossed the room and righted the chair. "Hope I didn't take too many years off your life."

"Only a few." Rahel thumped a fist against her chest. "Captain."

"Settle," Ekatya said in High Alsean, and enjoyed the startled expression. Her First Guard had not expected her to know that command.

Good. It was nice to be able to surprise an empath. At least, intentionally.

"You're in my quarters," she added. "This is the one place on my ship where I don't want to be the captain."

"Yes, Cap—um." Rahel looked panicked.

"You could call her Ekatya," Lhyn said with a wicked smile.

"No, I don't think I can."

Ekatya wasn't ready for that, either. "Captain is fine. Just leave the military expectations outside the door."

"With respect, Captain, I'm here with military expectations."

"True, but only regarding Lhyn. Not me."

"It's like watching a pair of tribal representatives negotiate. Would you two sit down?" Lhyn gave them three seconds to get comfortable before demanding, "What do you know?"

"Not enough." Ekatya took out her hair clip and set it on the table next to the phaser, then ran her fingers through her hair. It was a nervous habit that helped her think, one she had never noticed until Lhyn pointed it out.

There were disadvantages to being partnered with an anthropologist.

"Is he DOP?"

"That comes under the 'not enough' category. He came aboard with that last batch of troopers at Station Erebderis. He has a perfect record with Fleet and no known associations with the DOP. His Fleet record says his name is Warrant Officer Erik Helkenn, but Commander Cox doesn't believe it. I'm inclined to agree with him, disturbing as that is."

"Why is that disturbing?" Rahel asked.

Ekatya looked at her in surprise, then nodded. "Right, you spent most of your career using an alias. It's disturbing because that sort of deception shouldn't be possible in Fleet. How powerful is this man that he managed such a high-level set of falsified records?"

"He didn't feel powerful," Rahel said thoughtfully. "He was too excited. Maybe he was like me. I couldn't create my second set of records, but I worked for someone who could."

"That's the truly disturbing part. Anyone who could do that would be as powerful in our system as Prime Warrior Shantu was in yours."

"Well, what has he said?" Lhyn wanted to know. "Didn't Commander Cox question him?"

"He tried. Dr. Wells wouldn't allow it. Something about him barely being able to breathe, let alone talk." Ekatya caught Rahel's eye. "That was some move. I didn't even see you draw your stave."

"It was an easy shot." Her tone was dismissive. "It's hard to miss the sternum."

"You were specifically aiming there?"

"Of course. I hit where I aim."

On anyone else, that might have been a boast. After seeing Rahel in action, Ekatya suspected it was a mere statement of fact.

"Then why not his arm?" she asked.

"That would have knocked out one arm but left him in play. I didn't know what he had on his belt. There could have been another weapon."

"You're taught to target the center body mass, then." Not seeing the expected comprehension, Ekatya drew an illustrative circle around her own torso. "We're taught to aim here. It's the largest target guaranteed to have stopping power. And easier to hit than the head."

"That's not a big target, that's at least six small targets. Sternum, heart shot, ribs above the lungs—"

"You really *were* aiming for his sternum?"

"She just said she was." Lhyn reached out with a look of distaste and pushed the phaser to the far side of the table.

"Yes, but I thought . . . how small a target can you hit that way?"

"I used to practice with cinteks."

"You practiced hitting small coins." Ekatya could not stop her grin. "This I have to see."

"I don't have any cinteks here—"

"Don't worry." Ekatya was out of her chair and halfway to the bedroom. "I have something about the same size."

She returned with the soft pouch holding her kasmet game pieces, a gift from her grandfather and one of the few things she had carried away from the wreck of the *Caphenon*. The little squares clattered softly as she pulled one out and set it upright on the table's edge. "Can you hit that?"

"Of course."

"Forget the tribal representatives," Lhyn said. "I should have said eight-year-olds."

"Just because you don't value strike accuracy doesn't mean it's childish." Rahel rose from her chair.

"I didn't mean it like—wait, you're going to do it?" Lhyn shoved back her chair and popped up as if it were on fire. "I'm getting on the other side of the room."

"Good idea," Rahel said, looking past the game piece to the wall. "It'll ricochet." She pulled her stave and activated it.

Ekatya, who had been opening her mouth to say *Go ahead*, saw nothing but a blur. She didn't see Rahel aim or take even a second to judge distance. It was an instantaneous movement, a sound of sliding metal, and a *pop, ping* as the game piece vanished from the table and bounced off the wall.

Rahel lunged to the side, hand outstretched. Retracting her stave, she opened her hand and revealed the wooden square.

"Stars and Shippers! That is . . ." Ekatya could find no words.

"Not a real challenge."

"Not a challenge? You didn't even brush the table!"

"Sure, but it was a stationary target. Opponents don't usually stand still and let me aim." Rahel gave the piece back to Ekatya. "Mouse—um, my old friend, he used to make me turn around before he put the cintek on our table. So I wouldn't know where it was."

Ekatya looked at the piece in her hand, then at Rahel. "Turn around."

As Rahel turned her back to the table, Lhyn plucked the piece from Ekatya's palm. "Let me."

"I thought this was childish?"

"This is a fascinating example of a training technique not used in Fleet culture. It's research."

"Whatever you say, Dr. Rivers." Ekatya was secretly delighted to see her showing no fear after what must have been a terrifying afternoon.

Lhyn fetched a glass from the kitchen, turned it upside down, and placed it near the rounded corner of the table.

"Are you sure—" Ekatya stopped at Lhyn's look. "Fine, but I'm not cleaning that up if she misses."

"I don't miss," Rahel said.

Lhyn balanced the game piece atop the upturned glass and moved to Ekatya's side. "Go," she said.

Rahel turned, smiled as she dropped to a crouch, and knocked the piece into the kitchen. With a series of *pings*, it hit the far bulkhead, bounced off a cupboard, and fell to the floor.

The glass did not even vibrate.

"Wow." Lhyn's face could hardly contain her grin. "That was *amazing*." She fairly skipped into the kitchen to retrieve the game piece.

"Phenomenal accuracy." Ekatya watched Rahel retract and holster her stave. "Salomen didn't tell me about that."

"Given how I met her, I never wanted her to think about that."

Lhyn came back and dropped the piece into Ekatya's hand. "Everyone in this room has made mistakes, Rahel. Big ones. It's what we do afterward that makes the difference, don't you think?"

Ekatya missed Rahel's answer when the soft click in her head heralded an incoming call. *"Captain, this is Dr. Wells. I've finished the surgery."*

"I'll be right there."

11

ACTIONS AND REACTIONS

"It was a longer operation than I expected." Dr. Wells was seated at her desk, which, as usual, was cluttered with odd bits of paraphernalia. "The last time I saw a sternum like that was on a skydiver whose descent boots failed. He won't be on his feet any time soon." She counted off on her fingers. "Cardiac contusion, pulmonary contusion, hemothorax—he's lucky to be alive. The only reason he *is* alive is because he went into surgery so quickly. If Rahel makes a habit of using that move, she probably has a string of dead bodies behind her."

Ekatya rested her elbows on the padded arms of the guest chair and steepled her fingers, presenting a picture of relaxation while she studied the tension in Wells's body language. "We know Alseans have denser bones to go with their denser musculature. I'd guess Rahel learned that as a neutralizing strike and doesn't realize how much damage it causes in Gaians."

"I don't know what this does to Alseans. But I'll find out in a few hours. I left a message for Healer Wellernal in Blacksun. It's still early morning there."

"It's late afternoon here," Ekatya said mildly. "Why not ask Rahel? You'd get your answers faster."

"Rahel is not a doctor."

Ekatya bit back the obvious response and tried a different tack. "This is a warrior so traumatized by what she saw in the Battle of Alsea that it took a government intervention to save her. She's still in counseling via quantum com. I think it's safe to say she doesn't make a habit of killing people."

"But we don't know that, do we? Her employer is dead, her records were falsified, and all we know of her history is what she told her counselor."

"Who is a high empath," Ekatya reminded her. "Lanaril would have known if Rahel lied."

"A person can hide truths without lying."

"I think professional counselors are equipped to detect that, too. Especially high empath ones." Ekatya dropped her hands in her lap. "What is this really about? You can't be this upset that she responded to a lethal threat with appropriate force."

"You call that appropriate force? She took on seven bullies at once and managed relatively mild injuries on all of them. This was one man and she nearly killed him. Why?"

"Because I told her to."

It wasn't often she had the opportunity to stun her chief surgeon into silence.

"We had a talk about appropriate responses to what she can sense. I told her to take action immediately if she senses an imminent danger. Not that I expected that order to come around so quickly." Though Ekatya was certain Rahel would have responded the same way regardless of permission. That was pure training and instinct.

"Action," Dr. Wells scoffed. "There's a word with plenty of room for interpretation."

"If Rahel hadn't sensed that threat, she'd be dead. Not even her reflexes could have stopped a close-range phaser shot. I asked about her choice of targets, and I'm satisfied that she made the best tactical decision. Let's set that aside and get to the real issue. Why are you suddenly afraid of her?"

"I'm not—" She subsided at Ekatya's look of disbelief. With a sigh, she picked up a delicate paintbrush from her desk and began twirling it between her fingers. "She held me back."

When nothing else was forthcoming, Ekatya said, "I understand why that would distress you. Your instinct is to give aid. But the danger—"

"No. She held me back and it was like being clamped in a vise. I couldn't—she's unbelievably strong." Dr. Wells huffed an unamused laugh. "I don't often fall into the chasm between knowledge and understanding. I know Alsean musculature is denser than ours. I know she's stronger. But she held me with *one arm* and I couldn't get out. She caused so much damage with a single strike that I spent two hours repairing it." Her gaze was fixed on the paintbrush, now held between both hands as she bent it into an arc. "A strike I couldn't even see, and I was standing right there."

Ekatya crossed her hands in her lap. "So, you've just discovered your personal project isn't a cuddly pet."

"Oh, don't you—I never thought she was a pet!"

"But cuddly?"

For a moment, Dr. Wells looked close to eruption. Then the steam seemed to dissipate.

"There's a certain endearing quality about her," she admitted. "She wants so badly to do it right. Earn our approval. At the same time, she's tough and obstinate and smart as a box of foxes. I guess I'm rethinking what that intelligence and toughness might mean."

"They mean we have an extremely capable warrior serving with us."

"Too capable," Wells muttered.

Insulted by the implication, Ekatya swallowed her retort and reminded herself that she was talking to a surgeon. "Her need for approval was exploited in the past. Yes, she's made mistakes. But they were based in loyalty. Now she's given that loyalty to us."

"To you," Wells corrected. "Not to Fleet."

"To Salomen Opah, if we're splitting hairs, and I think she'd do anything in her power to uphold that oath. Which includes serving me and Fleet. She's working hard to learn what that means, to pick up both the written and unwritten rules. She needs help with that. I hope she won't lose yours."

The sharp *snap* of the paintbrush startled them both.

"Dammit. That was one of my favorites." Wells threw the pieces onto her desk. "Did you hear her? She offered to 'stop that noise.' She would have, if you'd given the go-ahead."

"The operative word here is offered."

"The problem is the offer!"

"She's *learning*, Doctor. She spent years working undercover for the Prime Warrior. Spying isn't clean work. But she kept this clean. She took decisive action to neutralize a lethal threat, and that is all she did." Ekatya held up a hand. "We need to take this down a notch. I understand that you're dismayed by the reality of what she is. I'm not, but maybe I have the advantage of being a killer myself."

Shocking Dr. Wells twice in one afternoon; this was a record.

"Did you forget that I killed at least three Halaamans a year ago?" she asked. "Probably more; I don't know. I'm sure about those three because I watched them die in my scope. But if we're talking sheer numbers, then we'd have to include a Voloth invasion group and Hades, that's in the thousands. Rahel could spend the rest of her life doing nothing but killing and she still wouldn't catch up with me. I don't scare you because you know what I do. You know what to expect."

"I didn't expect that." Dr. Wells picked up one of the paintbrush halves, apparently incapable of not doing something with her hands. "I know what you're saying. But . . ."

"But?" Ekatya prompted when she didn't finish.

"I deal in broken bodies, Captain. I've seen more than my share. I just haven't—"

When she stopped again, Ekatya thought she saw the problem. "You haven't seen it happen. You've only seen the aftermath."

"She was so calm about it! Caught me in half a second, held me without even trying, and offered to shut him up if you wanted. I can't reconcile that with the woman who needs hugs, who was sweet enough to —hm. Never mind."

Though wildly curious about that unfinished thought, Ekatya let it go. "That calm is the result of years and years of training. I *want* that in an officer. I want it in you."

"I'm not—"

"For instance, I'd be terrified to cut a person open and rearrange their internal organs," Ekatya interrupted. "But I know you're calm when you do it."

Dr. Wells snapped her mouth shut. "Should have seen that coming. Fine, point taken. She was doing her job."

"She was. She neutralized him and saved her own life without taking his. If she'd wanted to, she could have put her stave through his eye socket. One quick second to turn his brain to jelly."

"What a charming visual, thanks for that. And that would be a lucky shot."

"No, it wouldn't. Ten minutes ago, I watched her use the same move to knock a kasmet piece off a glass without touching the glass. Trust me, if she wanted him dead, he'd be dead."

Wells dropped the broken paintbrush, leaned her elbows on her desk, and rubbed her face. "I'm overreacting, aren't I?"

"Seeing violence is different than seeing the effects of it," Ekatya said gently. "You were shocked. It's understandable."

"I didn't think I was capable of shock anymore." She propped up her head with two fingers against her temple. "I guess we're all learning things today."

"I certainly did. Rahel needs hugs?"

"I told you that. She needs physical contact to mitigate the effects of emotional pressure."

"Yes, but I didn't realize 'physical contact' was doctor-speak for hug. Do you have a sign-up sheet somewhere? I bet half the crew would put their names on it."

"As if I'd expose her to that. I won't let her medical needs become a point of vulnerability. Especially not now, when she's still learning how to negotiate the social interactions."

"You're very protective."

"I'm—" She caught on and glared, making it impossible for Ekatya to hold back her amusement any longer. "That was a nasty trick."

"Psychology is part of the job description, remember?"

"Is smugness part of it, too?" At the sound of the door chime, she sat upright, once again all business. "Thank you. I'll consider your words of wisdom, and I use that term loosely."

"Would it kill you to admit I'm right?"

"No, but it would probably reduce my life-span." She tapped the deskpad to admit her guest.

The bulky frame of Commander Cox stood in the doorway. "Captain," he said in a surprised tone. "I was on my way to see you next."

"You have news?"

"I'd have more if I could speak to the assailant." Shifting his gaze to

Dr. Wells, Cox added, "Someone forgot to inform me that he was out of surgery."

"Out of surgery, yes. Conscious and able to talk, no. I said I'd inform you when you could speak to him."

"It would have been a professional courtesy to keep me updated on his condition regardless."

"I informed the captain and have been speaking with her since then. Or do I not have a full grasp of the chain of command?"

"Commander, please come in," Ekatya said, hoping to defuse this bomb before it went off.

The chief surgeon and chief of security had gotten along like oil and water since the day they met, probably because they were too much alike. Both were brusquely outspoken, cared little for the egos that got bruised along the way, and were undisputed rulers of their domains. Every time they were in a room together, Ekatya could see the hackles rising as they subtly tried to establish dominance.

Cox crossed the room with a heavy tread. He was slightly bow-legged and had a square look about him: wide nose, strong jaw, blocky shoulders, and a torso the same width as his hips and thighs. It made him look overweight, but he was solid muscle.

He dropped into the chair next to Ekatya and rubbed his hands on his thighs. "Commander Kenji is still in Helkenn's quarters with a couple of data analysts, taking apart his com system. My officers are wrapping up the room search. So far we've found no communications out of the ordinary and nothing in his possessions." He pulled the top two tabs on his jacket. "Except for his orders."

"You just said there was nothing unusual in his communications," Dr. Wells observed.

"This wasn't in his com system. The odd bit is that it wasn't hidden all that well. I think we were supposed to find it." Cox reached into his inside pocket and produced a transparent evidence bag. Inside was a piece of paper folded into a packet and sealed with putty.

"Shipper shit!" Ekatya snatched it from his hand and exchanged a look of horror with Dr. Wells before examining the design impressed into the seal.

Cox looked between them with a furrowed brow. "You've seen this before."

"To my eternal regret. This is from Sholokhov."

"Sholokhov? The director of Protectorate Security? That doesn't make sense."

Ekatya pinched the bridge of her nose. "You weren't here for our first mission. You missed some of the finer details."

"I read everything in the logs."

"Everything I included, yes. I didn't include this." She held up the packet. "Sholokhov uses a low-tech encryption system and hand-written orders for his most secretive ops. When I worked for him, I saw him sign and hand off hundreds of these. The seal is from one of his signet rings, and he uses different ring faces for different orders."

"Ingenious," Cox said.

"You'll never go wrong counting on Sholokhov's intelligence. Did you read it?"

"Imaged it." Cox activated his pad and passed it over. "You won't like it."

"I already know that."

She read the orders and clenched her hand so tightly that it was a wonder the pad didn't shatter. Her breath quickened as she sat motionless, paralyzed by fury and the lack of any professionally appropriate outlet for it.

"What does it say?" Dr. Wells's voice was uncharacteristically small.

Not trusting herself, Ekatya gestured at Cox.

"It's a kill order for First Guard Sayana. Captain Serrado was to witness the hit."

Wells stared, her jaw slack. "What—why—he's the one who signed off on the pilot program! She wouldn't be here if he hadn't approved it!"

"I don't get it either." For once, Cox dropped his challenging attitude toward Wells. "I especially don't understand why the captain was supposed to see it. That guaranteed Helkenn's detainment. Unless he had the galaxy's most ingenious escape plan, he was on a one-way trip to the brig."

"Second-guessing Sholokhov is a fool's game." Ekatya had found her voice. "You never have as much information as he does. But in this case, I think I can come up with a reasonable theory."

"Are you going to share it?" Cox asked when she paused.

Slowly, she shook her head. "Not yet. I think this might be at least partly personal, and I want to give him a chance to prove me wrong before I say anything."

"It's *personal* that he put a kill order on the first Alsean warrior to serve in Fleet?" Cox bristled. "Why, because you were the one to propose the program?"

"I didn't propose it. That came from the Alsean government."

"But you did support it," Dr. Wells said. "You were named in it. They didn't ask to put an Alsean on any other ships, or with any other captain. Would he—" Her voice cracked and sank to just above a whisper. "Would he really kill Rahel for a grudge?"

"No. He'd kill her because she's a game piece." Ekatya handed the pad back to Cox and stood up. "Now if you'll excuse me, I need to make a call."

12

KASMET GAME PIECE

It never seemed to matter what time of day or night it was in Gov Dome; Sholokhov was always in his office. Ekatya thought she should probably be flattered that her call went through rather than being screened by his assistant, but being the focus of Sholokhov's attention was rarely a good thing. He was brilliant, dangerous, and second only to the President and the Assembly Leader in authority. She no longer reported directly to him, but that only meant he didn't write her orders. Displeasing him could considerably accelerate her retirement.

It had been a year since she last saw him. He looked exactly the same, with his hooked nose, bushy eyebrows, and unsettling blue eyes contrasting with his black skin.

"A pleasure as always, Captain. To what do I owe it?"

"Remember what I said last year about professional courtesy? I take it back. Let's not bother."

"Ah, I knew you'd see it my way. So much more efficient, wouldn't you say? Do tell me a story, then. I'm most anxious to hear it."

"Your kill order failed. Sayana passed your little test."

He showed no reaction. "He's dead?"

That gave her pause. "You wanted her to kill him? I'm afraid I'll have to disappoint you. She's a better warrior than that. She neutralized him in half a second."

"Impressive." He nodded. "Most impressive. And not what I expected."

"You expected a barbarian," she said flatly.

"Did she use a sword?"

"Oh, for the—no. She used a stave."

"A stave! Even better!" His smile would have frightened a berserker boar. "What an intriguing combination of primitive and advanced these Alseans are. A whole new evolutionary branch with mental powers we can only dream of, held back by a culture two steps above hunting and gathering."

She took a breath to tamp down her rage before speaking in a careful tone. "What was the purpose of this?"

"It was important to know her capabilities. It's all very well to read reports from biased and questionable sources, but I prefer facts."

The jab at Lhyn's research was infuriating, but she would not give him the satisfaction of seeing it. "And what *facts* do you think you've acquired? All you know is that she neutralized an assassin."

"I know that she is, in fact, capable of sensing lethal intent. And that's a mid empath; imagine what their high empaths must be capable of! I know she acted immediately on what she sensed, because if she hadn't, she'd be dead. I know that despite sensing murderous intent, she chose to neutralize her enemy instead of killing him. How did she do that, by the way?"

She did not want to give his man even one more data point than he had already gathered, but making an enemy of Sholokhov was not just a career-ender. It could be a life-ender as well.

"She hit him in the sternum."

He made a rolling gesture. "Don't make me dig for it, Captain. I've been waiting to hear how this game played out."

Three different responses went through her mind, all equally inadvisable. "He followed your orders to the letter. He waited until we were together and ambushed us outside shuttle operations, pretending to be a crew member with something to show me. That 'something' turned out to be a phaser."

Sholokhov rested his chin in his hand, listening with apparent fascination.

"She had her stave out before I even saw it and incapacitated him in one strike, then told me to look in his belt pouch. I found the phaser charged and ready to fire."

"Did she know which of you was the target?"

"Yes. She did."

"Amazing," he murmured. "They really are what your Dr. Rivers says they are."

She couldn't help herself. "Did you ever consider that Dr. Rivers is a scientist who concerns herself with academic integrity? That her conclusions are the most accurate she can draw?"

"I considered it. In fact, I'm certain she's one of those people who worries incessantly about getting every speck of truth put in place. I'm also certain she has an emotional attachment to Alsea which may cloud her judgment. There's no need to hiss at me, Captain. I think the best of your favorite doctor. It's no reflection on her that I needed to verify her conclusions. If we're going to be bringing Alsean empaths into Fleet operations, we need to know what they're capable of."

"And you could think of no better way to do this than to order an assassination attempt on my ship?"

"We're in new territory here," he said with a careless shrug. "That woman is the first of her kind. If she was what your Dr. Rivers claimed, then she was never in danger. If she wasn't . . . better to know that sooner than later."

She was at risk of grinding her teeth flat. "What am I supposed to do with your assassin now?"

"Prosecute, of course. What did you think?"

"Do you value all of your employees that highly? No, never mind, I already know the answer to that."

"He's not an employee. He's a low-level thug who got himself into a bad situation. I offered a way out. It's not my problem that he thought immunity for past crimes meant immunity for new ones, too."

That "low-level thug" had joined her crew with a shining record scrubbed clean by Sholokhov. The idea that she had so little control over the quality of her staff made Ekatya's hair stand on end.

"In other words, you promised him immunity if he'd do one simple job for you, and now you're throwing him out of the airlock."

He leaned back, affecting a pose of casual ease. "Ah, there she is. The righteous Captain Serrado, upholding justice for all. Believe me, the sentence he'll get for attempted murder is far less than he would have gotten otherwise."

Lovely. She probably had a serial killer in her medbay.

Holding up the packet, she said, "You realize that this is evidence for the prosecution. How were you planning to keep your name out of it?"

"I didn't send that. It's a clever forgery, but sadly, the forger put the wrong seal on it. It doesn't match the seals I used on the date that packet was written. I'll confirm that and so will my assistant."

"Perjury's not a concern for either of you, then?"

This smile was slightly less terrifying. "Still upright and uptight, I see. You're so concerned with the minutiae that you lose sight of the big picture. It makes you a great captain, but you'd fail my job in half a day."

"I'd never want your job." When he chuckled, seemingly pleased by the statement, she pushed her advantage. "It seems to me that after causing so much trouble on my ship, you owe me a small favor."

Though his chuckle stopped, he was still smiling. "And what is it you think I owe you?"

"Reassurance. I have a data analyst team in Helkenn's quarters right now, searching for links to the DOP. If they find any, will those links be real? Is there any real danger to Dr. Rivers?"

He gazed at her for several uncomfortable seconds before shaking his head. "They'll find real links, yes. Which you will use to prosecute, and which will make certain members of the DOP even more nervous than they are now. A situation I intend to maximize. But no, there are no other DOP sympathizers on your ship . . . that I know of." He leaned forward again, resting his forearms on his desk. "I recommend you never let Dr. Rivers set foot on Tashar, though. Not even Command Dome would be safe for her."

"I had no intention of it."

"Good. I'd like a full report on this incident by tomorrow morning. If there's nothing else, I'm going to dinner." He waited a moment. "No? Then good night, Captain."

His image vanished and was replaced by the priority blue emblem.

She dropped her head back and let out a long exhale. "Stars and Shippers, I hate that man," she mumbled.

It *was* personal, despite his grandiose statement about the big picture. He hadn't needed her eyewitness account; he could have picked up the details from Commander Cox's report. But he had wanted her there as a reminder that even on her own ship, he called the shots.

That his juvenile need to prove his supremacy had terrified Lhyn . . . Her fingers itched to wrap around his throat. He had saved Lhyn not too long ago, and at the time she thought she would be forever grateful to him.

Forever wasn't as long as it used to be.

With a few taps to her deskpad, she pulled up the recording she had made of the call. Though she had no delusions about ever prosecuting Sholokhov, a little insurance couldn't hurt.

It came as no surprise that the recording had failed.

13

BEAKERS

The murder attempt marked a shift in attitudes toward Rahel. Lhyn said it would have happened eventually, but Sholokhov's "test" accelerated the process. Where before she was the alien empath, now she was an innocent crew member who had been attacked on their ship by a DOP radical.

She didn't understand it until Lhyn explained, "This isn't just a job for most of them. The *Phoenix* is their home. You were attacked in their home. They're angry about that."

"How does that lead to this?" Rahel gestured at the crowded corridor they were walking through, lined on both sides with shops and services for the crew. "They're *smiling* at me." Even those who remained uneasy were making an effort to appear friendly.

"How would you feel if you had a guest staying with you, someone you didn't particularly like or feel comfortable with, and then an outsider attacked her in your living room?"

Rahel stopped walking.

Lhyn took two more steps, realized she had lost her companion, and backtracked. "Did a blinding light go off in your brain?"

"Dazzling. Now I feel stupid for not seeing it."

"Don't do that." Lhyn moved closer, exuding an intensity that Rahel could not look away from. "Everyone has their own kind of smarts. Mine is in understanding patterns. Language, behavior . . . they're both sets of patterns. Don't underestimate what you have here." She tapped Rahel's temple. "The way you learn and adapt to what you're learning—it's phenomenal. You're setting a high standard for the Alseans coming after you."

"I'm going to miss you when this patrol is over." Already she could hardly bear to think about it.

"Because I say nice things to you?"

"Because you're not just my guide. You're my friend."

Lhyn's eyes softened. "You're mine, too." She pulled Rahel into a warmron, her affection cresting like a wave hitting the sea wall. It was an almost physical force, and Rahel pitied Captain Serrado for not being able to sense it. If Lhyn's friendship felt like this, what must her love be like?

"I might be coming along on more patrols," Lhyn said as they separated. "This hasn't been nearly as bad as I expected. Lanaril was right. She said I needed to see for myself that I'd healed enough to be comfortable here."

Rahel now knew enough about Lhyn's torture to understand why she wouldn't go into the chases. She had been held in a windowless room to destroy her sense of time, leaving her with a desperate need to *see*. It explained why Deck Zero, with its open spaces and transparent ceiling, was her favorite place on the ship.

"I haven't sensed that kind of discomfort in you," Rahel said. "Except for . . ." She waved a hand, not wanting to finish.

"My panic attack? That hardly counted. If you'd ever seen any of my big ones, you'd know that was nothing. Besides, you didn't let it go anywhere. I told Ekatya about the linguistic snack, by the way. She's sorry she didn't think of it first."

Later that day, Captain Serrado called Rahel into her office and thanked her for that very thing. "You did more than protect her," she said. "You made her feel safe. I won't forget that." Then she swore Rahel to secrecy about the true circumstances of the attack.

It felt eerily familiar. How many secrets had she kept for Shantu? Now here she was, in this new life that was supposed to be about truth and honesty and working as a team, and she was ordered to lie to her shipmates.

She might have been more upset if not for the fact that Serrado was incandescent about the whole affair. It was difficult to stay angry while being swamped with such fury on her behalf. She found herself wanting to calm the captain, telling her that it was all right, she hadn't been hurt and she was glad Lhyn wasn't a target. That was a tremendous understatement, in truth. She would never forget feeling Lhyn's panic and the valiant way she fought it back. As a veteran of night terrors herself, Rahel could only honor Lhyn's courage and vow to protect her from situations where she would need to employ it.

But if she ever met Director Sholokhov in person, he had better hope there was a solid wall of weapons-grade glass between them.

The days passed in a blur as Lhyn continued their tours and lessons. In the late afternoons, she would wave from the entrance of a chase as Rahel took a break from empathic noise. With Zeppy's approval and Dr. Wells's encouragement, Rahel was on her way to mapping out the full network. There was a second ship hiding within these passages, a ship few were aware of. Rahel made it her home and set about learning every corner of it.

She used the matter printer in her quarters to print up several soft mats and stored them behind the ladders in the brace shafts. Each shaft had its own sweet spot, a place where the noise cancelled itself out to create a bubble of relative quiet. These became her tiny, private centering rooms. She would roll out the mat, lie down with her hands on her pelvic ridges, and quickly drop into the mental space that repaired her frayed edges.

When she emerged—often on the other side of the ship from where she had entered—Lhyn would be waiting with an offer of "cultural immersion," her term for relaxing in one of the three bars on the *Phoenix*. Among other things, Rahel was learning the astonishing variety of non-alcoholic drinks available on a Fleet warship. Her favorite so far was the Synobian Sparkler, which sent stinging spikes of fizz up her nose and made her smile with every sip.

It was during one of these cultural immersions that Warrant Officer Roris brought her weapons team to their table.

"This is the warrior I watched beat down Pearson and six of his toadies," Roris said proudly. "I'm just sorry I didn't see her crush that DOP slime. Sayana, meet the best shots on the *Phoenix*."

"She's not boasting," Lhyn said. "They keep winning the drills. Ekatya says that one of these days, she's going to have to pull them off the roster during a drill so the other teams have a chance."

The four troopers glowed with pride while striving to appear casual. Roris began the introductions, getting as far as the second name before Rahel's brain clicked.

"Great Mother, you're *that* Roris!" she blurted. "You were all in the Battle of Alsea! You stopped the first invasion!"

If their pride was bright before, it positively glittered when she told them how famous they were on Alsea. Roris called over the bartender and ordered a congratulatory round, and Rahel spent a glorious afternoon listening to stories told by the people who had lived them—people she had never dreamed of meeting, much less drinking with.

Three rounds later, Lhyn left for her quarters and Rahel followed her new friends to their weapons room for an introduction to the destructive capabilities of the *Phoenix.*

"Lhyn hasn't shown me this yet," she said, gazing in awe at the massive launch tubes.

Roris chuckled. "If you're waiting for Dr. Rivers to show you our firepower, you'll be waiting until retirement."

"Beakers don't like to think about the 'war' part of warship," Trooper Torado said. He was a big man, with hair the color of sand and a sunny emotional presence that put Rahel at ease.

"Beakers?" she asked, making a pouring motion.

That amused them. "Yeah, language chips aren't so good at slang, are they?" Trooper Ennserhofen said. "It's Fleet speak for academics."

"They like to stay up in their labs and offices and forget we're down here." Trooper Blunt was half the size of Torado, with colorless eyes and white hair in a tail. "Didn't Dr. Rivers program your language chip? She probably left that out on purpose."

"Not to limit you," Roris said, heading off Rahel's defensive ire. "It's just that she hates the word. Captain Serrado mentioned it once."

They invited her to their favorite training room and insisted that she demonstrate Alsean hand-to-hand techniques. She sparred with each of them in turn, grinning at the sheer physical joy of it, and quickly learned that small, quiet Blunt was the one to watch out for on the mat. Torado was big but slow, and not at all embarrassed by his friends' jibes when

Rahel pinned him. Looking up at her from his prone position on the mat, he said, "Yeah, but I have the best view in the room."

"Fill your eyes," she retorted. "It's as far as you'll get."

He laughed with everyone else, and she soaked up the camaraderie like a desert flower in the rain. Warriors were warriors, it seemed, even when separated by genetics and culture.

At the end of her demonstration, she was pronounced "good enough" and nearly flattened by their congratulatory back slaps. She went back to her quarters walking half a body length off the ground.

Within a few days, Roris and her team had introduced Rahel to what felt like half the crew. Roris held a unique social position, moving easily through both the lower ranks and the commissioned officers. She was accomplished, respected, and liked, even by Captain Serrado. Her approval was a ticket to general acceptance among the crew.

It was ironic, Rahel thought, that the mistake that had sent her to a week of awful punishments would turn out to be the means of integrating into her new life.

Most evenings, Dr. Wells came by for what she called treatment and Rahel called the highlight of her day. If all medicine felt this good, no one would ever want to leave the medbay.

She had answers now. Living in a shouting, clanging cacophony of empathic noise was causing her body to produce high levels of stress hormones. Physical touch suppressed the stress, allowing her hormone levels to normalize.

She tried massage first, with a prescription from Dr. Wells that gave her a medical priority. But massage from a Gaian was nothing like massage from an Alsean. The skin contact was too much, especially given the therapist's distaste and borderline fear of touching her. Rahel left that session in worse condition than she had entered it.

A second therapist did not mind her alien body but was still nervous about her empathy. Though she appreciated his effort to work past his discomfort, it was impossible to relax while anxiety was literally rubbed into her skin.

When she reported the second failure, Dr. Wells looked like a thundercloud.

"They can't help how they feel," Rahel said, hoping to shield those therapists from the wrath of Fahla. Ever since the murder attempt, Dr. Wells had been even more protective.

"I can't help how I feel either," Dr. Wells snapped. "They have no business serving in Fleet if they can't handle something different. Pampered little . . ."

The last word was in her native language. Rahel didn't know what it meant, but she could make a good guess. "Yelling at them won't help me," she pointed out.

"No, but it would make *me* feel better." Dr. Wells tilted her head back and blew out a breath. "Fine. If you want something done right, do it yourself. I'll come by this evening after my shift."

"Um. I don't think it will be therapeutic if I'm the last chore you have to get done today," Rahel said carefully. "I need someone who enjoys what they do."

Dr. Wells looked stricken as her anger evaporated. "No, I didn't—dammit. Rahel, you're not a chore. I'm just disappointed in the quality of care I've been able to get for you."

That was ludicrous. "You had to pick me up off the floor. I couldn't have won a fight with a fairy fly, and you solved that in minutes. I haven't had any real problems since I started being honest with you. You don't think that's quality care?"

"It's not enough," Dr. Wells insisted. "It's all preventative. I still don't have anything in place to reverse the buildup. I don't have a *treatment*."

"Yes, you do! You gave it to me that day! What you don't have is a regular provider for it." Why didn't Fleet have comfort givers? It would solve so many problems.

"Which is why I'm coming by your quarters." Dr. Wells held up a hand. "I promise not to be angry when I get there."

Rahel couldn't help herself. "You have a medication for that? You should take it more often."

"Very funny." But it worked; her emotions softened. "What I did when you were in your signaling loop—that was an old instinct. One I haven't used in a long time."

"Since Josue."

She gave a sharp nod. "I wouldn't consider it a chore to use those skills again."

It was healer language and justification for something Sharro could have said in five words: *It would give me pleasure.* But Dr. Wells couldn't say that. The lines these Gaians drew between what was acceptable and what wasn't defied understanding. If Dr. Wells could benefit from the same treatment she was offering, where was the harm?

They did not use the positioning she was accustomed to with Sharro, which would have entailed lying down with her head in Dr. Wells's lap. Rahel couldn't imagine it, and Dr. Wells did not invite it. After trying several arrangements, they settled for having Dr. Wells sit on the couch while Rahel sat on the floor between her feet, facing away. It gave them the mental distance they needed to keep this from becoming uncomfortably intimate.

Yet it was impossible to feel Dr. Wells's fingers combing through her hair, or sliding gently along the sides of her face, and not relax into something that wasn't quite a doctor-patient relationship. Over time, they talked about everything from medicine to cultural differences to food to life in Fleet. Not even Lhyn's lessons could cover the breadth of useful knowledge that a career Fleet officer could.

"I was hoping we could make the equivalent of an empathic white noise transmitter," Dr. Wells said one evening. "Something that would reproduce what the chases do for you. But Zeppy told me today it can't be done. The equipment wouldn't be portable. The best we could do is install a system in your quarters, but you don't need that here."

"Thank Fahla. I thought you were going to say I'm being kicked down to my old quarters."

"That would be cruel, wouldn't it?"

Rahel glanced over her shoulder.

"Oh, don't give me that look. I may be tough, but I'm not cruel. The problem is that you're always going to need this. Not every day, but certainly on a regular basis. You might think about eventually finding someone else to help. I hear you've made quite an impression on Roris and her team."

"In other words, you can't be my only provider."

Dr. Wells ran her hands down the sides of Rahel's neck and rested them on her shoulders, the gesture that meant she was done for the evening. "As much as I enjoy this, you shouldn't limit yourself to one person."

Rahel smiled, wondering how long it would take her to realize what she had just said.

"My schedule isn't always stable," Dr. Wells continued, oblivious to her admission. "There will be times when I can't be here, and I can't accept the idea of you going into decline because I'm tied up in an emergency. But you need to be careful about who you accept. I've seen the crew members following you with their tongues hanging out. That's not a qualifying factor."

"Don't worry. Tongue touches don't normalize my stress hormones."

Making Dr. Wells laugh had become one of Rahel's favorite things. It always felt like an accomplishment.

"You're starting to sound like a doctor," Dr. Wells said approvingly. "Very academic."

Academic. The word caught Rahel's attention.

The next morning, she asked Lhyn if their daily tour could end with a treatment.

Lhyn was more than amenable; she was enthusiastic. "I used to do this with my youngest sister when we were kids," she said, settling on the couch and patting her thighs. "Put your head here."

What was impossible with Dr. Wells was easy with Lhyn. Rahel went down with what she thought must be a visible cloud of bliss over her head. The position was so familiar that her body sagged under its own weight.

"Why did you stop?" she asked as Lhyn began combing her hair back. "With your sister, I mean."

"We grew up. Went different ways. I'm the only person in my family to set foot off-planet. They don't even vacation anywhere else."

Rahel could not fathom having easy access to galactic exploration and choosing not to use it. "It's good you're living on Alsea," she said. "We appreciate you more."

Lhyn chuckled. "Now that is the truth and a half."

By the end of their time, Rahel was so relaxed that she had almost fallen asleep twice. Even better, she had no qualms about offering to return the favor.

"I thought you'd never ask." Lhyn flipped her long body around and stretched out with a happy sigh. "Good thing you have the fancy quarters with the me-sized couch."

Rahel looked down at her smooth face with its lack of ridges and marveled that an alien was in her lap. As she ran her fingertips across Lhyn's forehead and down the side of her face, a chuckle escaped.

Lhyn's brilliant green eyes opened. "What?"

"I've never felt an alien before." She traced Lhyn's cheekbone, fascinated by the presence of a vestigial ridge beneath the soft skin. "You're like a child. Your ridges are here, but they never came to the surface."

"You are so fortunate that I know what you mean. Otherwise I might take offense at being told I'm undeveloped."

Rahel grinned, undeterred. "You're like a child in your emotional broadcasts, too. Hoi, that could be the answer! Maybe Gaians are a branch of undeveloped Alseans."

"There's a research proposal that would never get off the ground. 'Hello, I'm here to ask for funding to prove that Gaians are evolutionarily nonprogressive relative to Alseans.' I'd be thrown out the door."

"Take me with you. I guarantee that nobody will throw you out of any doors."

Lhyn closed her eyes, her expression showing nothing but her emotions suffused with a warm sense of safety. "Thank you. Now stop talking about my retarded development and pet me."

Laughing, Rahel complied with orders.

14

PROPOSITION

Lhyn was the ideal partner for Rahel's medical needs, but she was not a member of the crew. Even though she promised to come on more patrols, Rahel needed another candidate, one who would always be on board.

The answer came the next day, when she and Lhyn were taking a cultural immersion break in the Blue Rocket, their favorite bar.

"Mind if I interrupt?" Commander Lokomorra stood at their table with a bright orange drink in his hand.

"Not at all, have a seat," Lhyn said. "What is that?"

"Neutron star. Guaranteed to blow off your outer layers and strip you down to the core." He pulled out a chair and settled in, directing a smile at Rahel that brought out deep dimples on both sides of his mouth. "First Guard Sayana, well met."

From the moment of their introduction, Lokomorra had used the Alsean greeting. She liked him based on that alone, and her estimation had only grown since then.

Commander Lokomorra was the ship's executive officer, second only to the captain, but he wore his authority with ease. Where Rahel found Captain Serrado intimidating, Lokomorra was friendly and approachable, emanating a calm emotional presence that was at odds with his fierce physical appearance. He was tall and well-muscled, with close-cropped black hair interrupted by what she had initially thought were two shaven bands running from his temples to the back of his head. In fact, those bands were made up of permanently destroyed hair follicles, a body alteration common to the megacity where he had grown up. Another common alteration was the set of tattooed black lines rimming his dark brown eyes.

But his most eye-popping feature was the thick, forked beard capped off with two beads at the end of each fork. Alseans did not have body hair. Male Gaians seemed to have an astonishing profusion of it, unless they removed it every day—a chore Rahel couldn't imagine having to perform.

Lokomorra smoothed one hand over his beard, pulling the two halves together until the beads clicked against each other. "Can't stop staring at this, can you?"

"No," Rahel said honestly. "If you go with Captain Serrado on her next leave to Alsea, every person you pass will be staring at that."

"But they'll stare politely," Lhyn interjected. "I speak from experience."

"They stare at your beard, too?"

Lhyn shot him a look of exasperation and turned to Rahel. "This is why Fleet officers should stay away from humor of any kind. They're not good at it."

"I'll bet you don't say that to the captain." Lokomorra slumped bonelessly in his seat.

"Ekatya is the exception to every rule."

"I'm sorry to hear that." He leaned toward Rahel and spoke in a loud whisper. "There's a rule about how a captain's bridge performance can predict her performance . . . off the bridge, so to speak."

"Sometimes I can't believe she brought you on," Lhyn said. "You are her polar opposite in so many ways. And no, not that way," she added before he could speak.

"Ah, you've heard the stories." He looked pleased. "That rule applies to the executive officer, too."

Rahel stared at him. "You're not telling the truth."

"Oh?" Lhyn's attention sharpened. "Did you make up the whole rule or just the part about how it applies to you?"

"The whole rule. Do you know, I'm normally considered an excellent liar. It's useful in dealing with personnel or diplomacy." He sipped his electric orange drink. "Well. They're the same thing, really."

"Can you have sex with anyone on the ship, Commander?" Rahel asked.

Lokomorra coughed with his mouth shut, his cheeks blowing out to an alarming degree as he tried to keep his drink contained. Across the table, Lhyn hurriedly set down her glass and laughed.

"What?" Lokomorra managed.

"I said, can you—"

"No, no, I heard you. I was—why would you ask that?"

"Lhyn said Captain Serrado was lucky to find her, because Fleet regulations say a supervisor can't have sex with anyone who reports to them or works in their section, and captains oversee all sections, so they can't have sex with anyone on the ship. I just realized that as the executive officer, you oversee all sections, too."

"See?" Lhyn said. "This is what I mean by how fast you learn. I can't believe you remembered that. And then you took it to the next logical step."

"Why do I feel like I'm in a classroom?" Lokomorra thumped his fist against his chest and cleared his throat. "You're right. I can't have sex with a *Phoenix* crew member. The section chiefs have options in ten out of the eleven sections, but the executive officer and captain are special cases. That's why 'captain cuts loose on the space station' is such a popular theme in erotica." He frowned. "They never make it about execs, though."

"You never get any physical contact. Except on leave."

"That's correct."

"I think we might be able to help each other." Rahel felt Lhyn startle, but when her friend said nothing, she forged ahead. "Would you like to come to my quarters after your shift tomorrow? We can pet each other."

Lhyn snorted, covered her mouth, then leaned back and laughed uproariously. Lokomorra appeared to be paralyzed, his eyes so wide that the whites showed all the way around the irises.

"I'm sorry?" he said.

"Does that mean no?"

"No, it means—what the Hades does that mean?"

Rahel had lost track of the conversation. Was he asking what she meant, or what he meant?

"Oh my fucking stars, that was priceless," Lhyn gasped. "I wish I had a recording of it." She laughed again and wiped her eyes. "Rahel, when I said pet me, I was using the first definition of the term. There's also a slang definition. It means sexual contact."

"Oh. Why didn't you say so?"

"I didn't think it would come up in casual conversation!"

"Let me see if I understand." Lokomorra's shock had receded from the blaring horn it had been a few seconds ago. "You want non-sexual physical contact and you think I want it, too."

"I don't know if you want it. That's why I asked."

He turned to Lhyn, who was laughing again.

"Sorry. Sorry," she wheezed. "I can explain, just give me a second." She held up one hand, sipped her drink, and cleared her throat. "Rahel, since you're asking the commander, can I assume you're lifting the confidentiality clause on your medical needs where he's concerned?"

Rahel nodded.

"Right. Commander, Rahel is under constant pressure from the empathic noise generated by all of the unshielded minds on this ship. It has harmful effects if it builds up too much, but Dr. Wells discovered that the pressure can be reduced through physical touch. Simple things, like touching here, and here." She demonstrated on her face and neck. "Or brushing fingers through her hair. Dr. Wells has been doing the treatments, but she advised Rahel to find alternative, ah, helpers for the times that she's not available."

"So I asked Lhyn, and she's perfect." Rahel enjoyed Lhyn's satisfaction before facing Lokomorra. "But she won't always be on board, so I need a backup. I know you're sexually attracted to me—"

"Ouch," Lhyn murmured.

". . . but I also know you're very disciplined and you don't allow that attraction to influence your behavior. I respect that kind of discipline. From what I've seen, you're an admirable warrior and I'd trust you to help me without trying to take advantage. Of course, if you *did* try, I'd crush you."

"Ouch is right," Lokomorra told Lhyn.

"And I thought that since you can't get your sexual needs fulfilled on the *Phoenix*, maybe me touching you will at least help." Rahel took a deep breath and leaned back in her chair.

"That's what you meant by helping each other," he said.

She nodded.

He picked up his glass, drank half of it, set it down, and began to chuckle. That set Lhyn off, which made Lokomorra laugh harder, and Rahel sat baffled while they howled. She really didn't see what was so amusing.

"This is just crazy enough that it might work," Lokomorra said at last. "Besides, how could I resist an invitation like that? I'll want to eat first, which I assume I won't be doing with you since this isn't a date. Shall I come by your quarters at twenty hundred hours?"

Relieved that this confusing conversation had ended so well, Rahel said, "Yes, that will be fine."

"Can I set up a recorder?" Lhyn asked.

15

PETTING

Lokomorra was exactly on time, wearing loose-fitting trousers and a short-sleeved shirt with an open neck. He poked his head in the door and looked around. "Did she?" he asked.

Two words into the conversation and already Rahel was confused. "Um. I don't understand."

"Did she set up a recorder?"

"Oh!" She chuckled, relieved that it was this simple. "No. I don't think she was truly joking, though. If I'd said yes, she would have done it."

"Don't I know it." He came the rest of the way inside, smiling broadly despite the awkward tint to his emotions. "Glad to see you got one of the sweet suites. You should have had a senior officer cabin to begin with, but there are only as many of those as there are senior officers."

"I didn't mind my first quarters, except for the fact that I couldn't get away from empathic broadcasts. But now that I'm used to these, it would be hard to go back."

"Yeah, it's always easy to adjust up."

She tilted her head. "You're speaking from experience."

"That really does take some getting used to. It's a long story. The short version is that I grew up in a place that valued law and order a lot less than Fleet. I ran around with some pretty tough people and lived in some pretty tough places. What I have now . . ." He grinned, showing his dimples. "If I could go back in time and talk to my younger self, he'd never believe me."

"I know exactly what you mean."

"I guess you do. Even more than me. At least I knew Fleet existed." He glanced at the wall display. "Ah, I recognize this. The captain had it on in her quarters when I needed a signature from her some time back. The State Park?"

She nodded, her gaze on the quiet beauty of the Fahlinor River and the glorious Alsean architecture beyond it. "I hated Blacksun when I first saw it. It wasn't my home. There was no Wildwind Bay, the docks were tiny, it was landlocked . . . but this part of it, this part I could love. Now I watch it and it hurts. But in a good way. It's hard to explain."

"You're homesick," he said gently. "It hurts to see any part of home and know you can't be there. But it feels good at the same time. Like it's filling a void."

"You understand."

"Most anyone on the crew would."

But she hadn't asked just anyone on the crew to her quarters. She relaxed, certain that she had made the right choice. "I think you should go first, so I can show you the kind of touching I mean."

"Thank the heavenly stars, I was hoping you'd say that. I didn't want to do it wrong and embarrass myself."

She led him across the room and sat near the corner of the couch. "Take off your shoes, lay down, and put your head here." She patted her thigh.

"Got it." He toed off his shoes.

"What—" Rahel choked back a laugh. "What are those?"

With a wide grin, he said, "These are my conversation starters. I have a little brother, and we used to fight all the time. But I wasn't allowed to hit him, no matter how obnoxious he was, so I'd tell him to kiss my feet, which is *very* obscene where I come from." He lifted a foot, encased in a bright yellow sock with a pattern of pursed red lips in various sizes. "Two years ago, he gave me a set of these for my birthday. I have them in six colors."

"But doesn't that mean he's kissing your feet? Figuratively?"

"He grew up to be about twice as big as me. He can joke about kissing my feet."

She looked up at him and wondered how massive his brother must be. "Do you wear those on duty?"

"Now, see, this is the part where I'd normally wink and say in an exaggerated tone, 'Of *course* not,' and you'd assume I actually meant I did. But I can't do that with you because you'd know I'm lying."

She puzzled over that. "Why would you pretend?"

"Ah . . . flirting?"

"Oh. I don't flirt."

"Yeah, I noticed that when you said you knew I was sexually attracted to you. That's pretty much the anti-flirt." He sat beside her. "I don't know how to do this smoothly."

"Haven't you ever put your head in someone's lap?"

"Not since I was twelve or so."

"Really?" She couldn't imagine. "Is it forbidden in your home culture?"

"No, but it's not something tough men do. I thought I was a tough man. Eventually I learned that wasn't the kind of man I wanted to be, but most of the women I've been with . . . well. They weren't empathic."

"They saw the tough man," Rahel said, and he nodded. "You do look ferocious, with that beard and your body alterations."

"But I like the way I look. When I was that twelve-year-old kid, I dreamed of having a beard like this." He stroked it, clacking the beads together. "Why should I have to change how I look to get people to see past the outside?"

Rahel thought of Mouse, with his tiny body and missing central forehead ridge. "You shouldn't."

"Alseans must have a lot of advantages."

"We can still misjudge each other. Or pretend to be what we're not. But in most cases, pretending doesn't last past skin contact." She touched his leg. "Swing those up, scoot down, and put your head here." Too late, she remembered that she had meant to print a small pillow for this. But Lokomorra was getting into position and she couldn't get up now.

His head was heavier than Sharro's, heavier than Lhyn's, and how could she touch his jaw through all that thick hair? The sheer foreignness hit her like a stave to the chest.

"Katsuro," he said, breaking her out of her momentary panic.

"What?"

"My name. If I'm going to have my head in your lap, you can't call me Commander Lokomorra."

His matter-of-fact statement helped her to a calmer space. "Rahel. Not First Guard Sayana."

"Well met, Rahel."

"Well met, Katsuro. Are you ready?"

"I'm ready. Pet me."

That made her laugh, and suddenly it was all right. She slid her fingers down his temple and skated along the cheekbone, then up the bridge of his nose and into his short hair.

"That feels good," he murmured.

"I know."

His eyes were shut before the end of the second minute, and a deep contentment purred out. By the time she had lightly scratched all around his scalp and moved to his throat, he lifted his chin without a hint of awkwardness.

"There's a truth to physical touch," she said, sliding her fingers past the collar of his shirt. "It transcends words and even emotions. It's wired directly into the body, I think. The body knows." Her fingers danced back up his neck, skipped over the coarse hair of his beard, and returned to his surprisingly soft cheeks. "The first time someone touched me this way, I was a scared girl who had no idea how much I needed it. But my body knew."

"I hope whoever touched you that way was honorable," he said quietly.

"She was and she is. I was selling my body before that. A very different kind of touch."

His eyes remained closed and he said nothing, but sympathetic anger rose from his skin. She rested her hand on the center of his chest, palm flat, trying to communicate her own lack of pain. "It was a long time ago. I have no regrets. That path led me to Sharro—that's her name—and it led my mother to her as well. Now they're bonded and having a child together. Fahla might not be able to save us from hurting, but I think sometimes she finds ways to make it lead to a worthwhile place."

"I like that philosophy. I believe in the Seeders, but I don't expect them to take care of me. I think it's up to us to make something good out of the bad things that happen." His lips curved into a wry smile. "I see what you mean about the truth of this kind of touch. I don't usually discuss philosophy until the fifth date. And I don't usually get to the fifth date."

"I don't see how you get to a second date if you're only dating on space stations."

"That's a sad fact." He rolled his head to one side as her fingers combed through his hair, subtly inviting her to focus there. "You're right, my body knows. I haven't been this relaxed in years. Not even after . . . well. One of those dates."

"Sexual satiation isn't the same thing as relaxing in trust."

He chuckled. "Says the anti-flirt."

"It's the truth. Is flirting all about lying, then?"

"Huh," he said after a moment. "I had a response ready, and then I thought about it, and damn. It kind of is, sometimes. But other times it's about having fun with someone who understands the game."

"I'll ask Lhyn," she decided.

"Er, she might not be an expert on the matter. But I want to be there for that conversation."

They stopped talking then, but it wasn't uncomfortable. She explored his alien features and marveled at the similarities and differences, while he sank deeper and deeper into a state of relaxation.

She sensed the moment that he fell asleep. His broadcast shut off as if a valve had been turned, leaving a faint trickle of diffuse and unreadable emotions. It lasted perhaps one minute before his entire body jerked and the broadcast resumed. His eyes flew open, a look of such surprise in them that she stifled a laugh.

"Sorry," he muttered, pushing up to a sitting position. "I don't know how that happened."

"Why are you apologizing?"

He scratched his fingers through his hair and shook his head vigorously. "It's bad form to fall asleep on your partner. Even though you aren't my partner. That kind of partner. Oh, Hades, never mind, my brain's not working."

"I think you need to readjust your expectations. We're not having sex."

"Noticed that," he said, rubbing his eyes.

"On Alsea, when a warrior like you relaxes enough to fall asleep with someone else—when the purpose isn't sleep—that's a compliment. I'm happy you did. It means you trusted me." She wondered if he would trust her if he knew of her past crimes, then pushed the thought away. This was her new start. She had earned it. The adjudicator's signature confirmed it.

Then why did it feel like she was lying to him?

"I think I have a much better idea of the kind of touching you mean now." Katsuro was smiling at her. "Switch?"

"Switch," she agreed.

His thigh, when she rested her head on it, was considerably broader than she was used to. His hands were also bigger, but he inhabited his body with the ease of a trained warrior and kept his touch light. Too light, in fact, and with her encouragement he grew more confident.

At first she kept her eyes open, fascinated by the new view of that phenomenally alien beard. But as his caresses gained the smoothness of practice, she let her eyes fall shut and began to drift, letting out a happy hum of pleasure.

Katsuro's enjoyment was shattered by a spike of alarm, accompanied by dark dread and the red heat of embarrassment. Startled by the sudden shift, Rahel sat up and turned.

She froze at the sight of his trousers. Just below the crotch, the loose fabric was pushed up by some object underneath. Even as she stared in horror, it *moved.*

She was across the room in half a second. "Shekking Mother on a burning boat!" she shouted in High Alsean, then remembered to speak in Common. "What is *that?* Are you all right?"

He fell back with a groan and covered his face. "Fuck a rock, I haven't been this embarrassed since I got a stiff one in math class."

The alarm had vanished, pushed out by a new and larger wave of mortification. She edged closer, assured that at least there was no danger. "What happened? What *is* that?"

"I'm never going to have children. I'm only going to be able to have this conversation once in my life, and this is it." Slowly, he raised his head. "It's my penis, and I can't believe I said that."

She frowned. "Your—no, that can't be right. I saw images. Dr. Wells told me about it. It hangs down, like every male mammal on Alsea."

Groaning again, he planted his elbows on his knees and dropped his face into his hands. "I'm going to have a talk with Dr. Wells."

"Talk to me first. Do you have—is it a disability?"

"No, it's not a disability!" He looked her in the eye for the first time. "It's working perfectly well, thank you. Just not when I want it to. Sucking Seeders, I was trying everything. And then you made that sound, and . . ." He waved a hand. "It reacted."

"You mean that's normal?"

"Normal for a fifteen-year-old," he mumbled.

"But—it reacted? By itself? Isn't it part of you?"

"Trust me, sometimes I don't think it is. Yes, it reacted. I tried to stop it, but sometimes it can't be helped. It's just biology. I got an erection even though I didn't want one. Can we talk about something else now? Philosophy would be marvelous. Or religion. Tell me more about your Fahla."

She sat on the other leg of the couch, keeping the corner between them. "I still don't understand. Alsean mammals have penises, and they don't change direction."

"Oh, for fuck's sake."

"And you weren't very aroused. I know how erections work; we studied that in biology before I left school. It requires sexual arousal to increase the blood flow to the erectile tissue."

"That might be the most unsexy set of sentences I've ever heard. Next time I want to kill an erection before it starts, I'll remember that. Right after I remember you leaping across the room." He took a deep breath and let it out slowly. "All right, let's get it over with. Yes, erections are caused by increased blood flow, and yes, the penises of male Gaians can, er, change direction when they expand. It makes it easier to enter a female."

"Oh!" she exclaimed in sudden understanding. "Because yours don't aim forward like other male mammals."

"Correct." His embarrassment was beginning to retreat. "And there are different kinds of sexual arousal. There's the part that happens in the brain, which I guess is what you sense, and the part that happens down here." He waved a hand in the general direction of his crotch—which, Rahel was fascinated to note, was now lacking any sign of the erection. "The part that happens down there isn't under our control. We can get erections in our sleep."

"Really? That seems counterproductive. Also uncomfortable. What happens when you roll over, is it like landing on a small tree branch?"

He stared at her in disbelief and a tinge of horror, then threw his head back and laughed. She couldn't help smiling at the sight, despite having no idea what was so funny. At least he wasn't mortified any longer.

"If I had a stiff one like a tree branch, I'd either be bragging in the Blue Rocket or looking for help in medbay, I'm not sure which. It's not *that* hard."

"Oh. You said you tried to stop it. How did you do that?"

"Unsuccessfully."

This time, she caught the humor and snorted a laugh. He laughed with her, and the last vestiges of discomfort fled the room.

"I think about things that are as far from arousing as possible," he said. "Cleaning out the waste reclamation tanks, for instance."

"Ew."

"See? That should have worked. It didn't. Then I tried thinking about what happens if an entire cargo of stolen defender mines goes on the black market."

"I understood the first one. This one . . ."

"All the senior staff are worried about it since the *Tutnuken* missed the rendezvous."

She had heard about the cargo ship, of course. After arriving at the rendezvous and finding empty space, the *Phoenix* was now backtracking the *Tutnuken*'s likely route from its last stop. But no one had mentioned mines.

"I thought we were just trying to find a lost ship. It was carrying a load of weapons?"

He nodded. "Captain Serrado doesn't want to say anything until we have more facts. It may have had mechanical issues."

"You don't believe that."

"Are you guessing, or do you know?"

"You feel doubtful. Not assured."

"I'm definitely doubtful. If it had mechanical issues, why didn't the crew send a message? A ship would have to take a lot of damage before the quantum coms stopped working. It doesn't make sense. What makes sense is that someone knew that ship was carrying mines and hit it for the black-market value."

"What happens if they go on the market?"

"Nothing good," he said grimly.

She studied him. "You feel like *that* about it and it still didn't stop your erection?"

"You see now?"

"Amazing. I'm going to ask Dr. Wells why she didn't tell me about this."

"You are not!" He looked at her more closely and narrowed his eyes. "You were kidding."

She offered an innocent smile. "Lhyn says learning to tease is a critical part of fitting into the culture. Am I fitting in?"

"Far too well," he grumbled.

16

TUTNUKEN

"Still no response, Captain. I've even tried the laser com and radio. They're not answering."

Ekatya studied the blocky cargo ship off their starboard side, coasting on nothing but inertia with its dead, dark engines. She had ordered a matching speed while staying far enough away to be cautious, then magnified the view so the ship took up half of the bridge display.

Overhead, under her feet, and on the port side was nothing but stars. Normally, she felt at home when surrounded by open space, but it was making her itchy now. There was nothing here to explain why the *Tutnuken* had cut its engines. They were nowhere near a space station, planet, moon, or even an asteroid. This location was four days away from the ship's last stop. Nor had it deviated from its planned route—the *Phoenix* had practically run over it while backtracking the flightpath on file.

The ship showed no signs of piracy. There were no scorch marks or holes in the hull, no open airlocks, not even scraped hullskin from the grapplers of a boarding pod. The massive midship cargo door was tightly closed. If the *Tutnuken* had been hit for its mines, the pirates had boarded without a struggle and tidied up when they left.

Right below her, on the second level of the central bridge dais,

Commander Lokomorra swiveled his chair around to face her. "There's only one way to find out what's going on over there."

"External investigation first," she said. "I'm not authorizing a boarding party until we've looked in the windows."

As chief of security, Commander Cox led the investigative team, closing the gap between the two ships in a shuttle escorted by three fighters. For the next hour, the bridge buzzed with activity while the team nosed all around the silent ship and sent back baffling results.

The engines were completely cold. A close examination of the hull confirmed its integrity. Thermal scans showed wildly divergent temperatures, with some areas retaining normal heat while others were barely warmer than the space they were flying through.

"So, partial environmental failure and they sealed off those areas." Ekatya was studying the thermal scans on the display, superimposed over the real-time visual of the ship.

"Could have been automated," Lokomorra said.

"If their automated systems were working, we'd have a distress beacon. Or at the very least, an IDT."

That the ship was traveling without even an identity transmitter was the strangest thing of all. IDTs were self-contained and usually the last thing to fail in the event of catastrophe. The only reasons to not have one were either total destruction of that part of the ship, or deliberate disabling for stealth movements.

A cargo ship contracted to Fleet for a simple delivery had no reason for stealth movements, unless . . .

She looked down at Lokomorra. "Do you think they were double dipping?"

He pursed his lips, then gave a slow nod. "Might explain a few things. If they've got something in that cargo hold they're not supposed to be carrying, they wouldn't be motivated to put out a distress call."

"I was hoping you'd tell me I was being cynical." That was just what she needed, a corrupt contractor mixing defender mines with contraband.

"You can be cynical and still be right."

Commander Cox appeared on the part of the display currently showing the shuttle's quantum com. "The drone is in place," he said. "Look at this."

After conducting every other scan, the team had launched a drone to literally look in the ship's windows. Unlike a warship, the *Tutnuken* had no need for an impervious battle hull. Its bridge had several large windows, and their drone was hovering outside one of them.

Ekatya stared at the video feed. "There's *no one* up there?"

Cox shook his head. "Looks like they set the autopilot and left."

"That violates about twelve laws," Lokomorra said.

"And a bunch of Fleet regulations. All right, Commander, I think we've seen enough. Call back your drone and come back to the barn."

"Boarding party?" Lokomorra said when Cox signed off.

"Boarding party," Ekatya agreed.

It was Rahel's first time in a section chief meeting. Though she held no Fleet rank nor even any supervisory responsibility, she was considered a senior officer by virtue of her Alsean Defense Force rank, not to mention her status as the only Alsean in Fleet. Until now, however, her training had taken priority over the issues discussed in most section chief meetings.

Captain Serrado had said this one would be different. She had not exaggerated.

Rahel sat two seats away from her, between Commander Lokomorra and Dr. Wells. The other ten section chiefs were arrayed around the large oval table, with Zeppy and Shigeo directly across from her. Every eye was on the display taking up the far wall.

The last time Rahel had been in this briefing room, the display was a window onto the red mists of base space. Now it was divided into eight video feeds. Given the partial failure of the ship's environmental systems, each member of the boarding party wore a full envirosuit complete with helmet cam and sensors, which streamed their data to this room. A holographic representation of the *Tutnuken* hung suspended above the table, with eight red dots showing the location of each *Phoenix* crew member as they fanned out into the cargo bay.

At the moment, the video feed labeled Korelonn was enlarged for easier viewing. Lieutenant Korelonn was second in command of security and leading the boarding party, which consisted of six more security officers and one data systems analyst. His helmet cam was panning across endless racks of gray crates stacked to the ceiling of the cavernous bay. All bore two symbols: one of Fleet and another that looked like a stylized explosion.

"Looks like they're all here," he said.

The crates loomed larger as he walked toward one rack. His gloved hands reached out to snap open a series of locks on a crate, then swung down the front panel. Inside, nestled in cushioning material, was a black disk that looked to be half the size of the table Rahel was sitting at.

"How does that work?" she whispered to Lokomorra. It seemed a vanishingly small target for a ship to blunder into.

"They're attracted to pikamet radiation," he whispered back, watching Korelonn check the mine. "They'll be activated by any ship coming out of base space. If the ship doesn't send the right code, the mines will swarm it."

Korelonn closed that crate and spot-checked three others. The other seven feeds showed similar activity.

"Thirty-two checked, thirty-two intact," Korelonn said.

"I think it's safe to say they weren't hit by pirates." Next to Zeppy, Commander Cox folded his arms across his chest. They both had dark skin, but the resemblance ended there. Cox was shorter and much wider, with hair that laid flat rather than standing straight up. Where Zeppy's eyes were round and amused, Cox's were narrow and penetrating—a fairly good indicator of their personalities, Lhyn had said.

"They were hit by something," Captain Serrado said. "We just boarded them by force and haven't heard so much as a peep. Lieutenant, I don't want your team setting foot outside that bay until you've checked every meter of it. Let's not have any surprises."

"Understood, Captain."

"And keep your eyes peeled for contraband."

Rahel thought that was a particularly gruesome Common phrase. Who peeled eyeballs?

As the team searched among the racks, Commander Cox caught Rahel's attention. "We need to get you trained in an envirosuit. We could use your talents over there. Be nice to know if anyone is waiting outside that bay."

Beside her, Dr. Wells kept her gaze on the display, but her emotional signature flashed red with annoyance and a darker shade of fear.

Rahel carefully did not look at her. "I look forward to that part of my training. But your thermal scanners have a longer range than I do."

"Yeah, but our scanners don't have an intent readout. I can think of a hundred times when that would have come in handy." He pointed at the display. "In situations like this, it could be the difference between life and death."

Dr. Wells turned her head to shoot a glare across the table. "Perhaps we should worry more about getting First Guard Sayana properly trained and less about using her as a tool."

Rahel opened her mouth to say that missions like this were what she *wanted* to do, but Captain Serrado beat her to it.

"First Guard Sayana has a great deal to offer several sections. You can all fight over her later, when she's finished her training and knows what she wants."

"I'm not fighting over her." Shigeo offered his irreverent grin. "Though who knows, maybe plants grow faster if she projects happy feelings on them."

"I could try." Rahel smiled back, hoping to convey her appreciation for his diplomacy. "I haven't learned to project, but I did listen when a classmate was learning. Plants might be a good first target."

"I think I found something," said a female voice.

The video marked Kitt, a lieutenant from data systems, was showing a rack of crates that looked like all the others—except for the holes in the front panels.

"Hold your position, Lieutenant." Captain Serrado had her forearms on the table and was leaning forward, intently studying the video feed. "What in all the purple planets did that? It looks like they were melted through from the inside."

Korelonn jogged over to join Kitt. "Thermal readings show nothing in there." His hand appeared in the video, holding a knife.

Rahel raised her eyebrows, instantly approving. Despite what Captain Serrado said, the only sections she was interested in joining were weapons or security. From what she was seeing now, security was far out in front. The weapons teams didn't get to board mystery ships with knives in their belts.

Korelonn tapped his knife blade on one of the melted bits dripping from the edge of a hole. "It's hard. Whatever melted this did it a while ago." His hand vanished, then reappeared sans knife. Carefully, he snapped open each lock. "Kitt, get behind me."

Both video feeds shifted as they moved to the side of the crate. Kitt's visual frame was now largely filled by Korelonn, and her heart rate was climbing. His remained steady, a testament to his training.

He dropped the front panel and waited.

Nothing happened.

"Stay there," he said quietly, and stepped in front of the crate. "Huh. Okay, I don't know what this is. It looks like a pile of black rocks."

"Lieutenant Korelonn." Kade Jalta, chief of the science section, pushed her blonde hair behind one ear as she focused on the display. "Your light has an ultraviolet setting, right?"

"It does, yes."

"Will you shine it on those rocks, please?"

His hand reappeared, now holding a slender black cylinder. When he clicked it on, both he and Kitt let out an awed "Whoa."

The nondescript black rocks were now brilliantly glowing crystals, covered in a vibrant web of violet and orange lines. Rahel had never seen anything so beautiful. Her crafter mother would love it.

"Don't touch them." Commander Jalta turned to face Captain Serrado. "Well, now we know what the crew was hiding. That's unrefined teracite. And judging by the dense lattice, it's weapons grade."

Serrado's tight jaw was the only sign of her anger. "Lovely."

"What's teracite?" Shigeo asked.

"It's the part of a Delfin torpedo that makes the boom," Jalta answered. "Dangerous even in the unrefined state. And not very common."

"Teracite is why the Delfins are our largest yield," Serrado added. "It's also why we carry so few of them. Every time we launch a Delfin, we're firing the equivalent of a small shuttle in terms of cost."

Shigeo looked down the table to the chief of weapons. "Guess that explains why your budget is so much bigger than mine."

"When you need teracite for your orchids, we'll talk about budgets," Serrado said. "Commander Jalta, is there anything about the properties of teracite that explains those melted holes?"

"Not a thing. I have no idea what made that. But I sure don't like it."

"Me either." Korelonn's voice came from the display. "I like this even less." He shone his ultraviolet light on the floor below the crate, revealing a faintly glowing line that faded out as it progressed. "Something melted those holes and walked away." His light traced over the floor in front of the other crates and found multiple glowing lines. "A bunch of somethings."

"Oh." Jalta looked shocked. "I *really* don't know what would do that."

"They've got stowaways," said Captain Serrado. "Something that came in with the teracite. Check the rest of the cargo bay, see if anything's moving."

"We've already done a thermal sweep," Korelonn said.

"If the stowaways are cold-blooded, the thermal sweep won't find them," Jalta pointed out.

"Visual check," Serrado said. "Your first priority is the safety of your team. Second priority, download their navigation logs. Third priority is finding out what happened to the crew."

"Understood." Korelonn snapped off his light. "All right, everyone, you heard the captain. Let's go for a walk."

Ekatya watched the red dots on the holographic model of the *Tutnuken* hovering above the table. Lieutenant Kitt was on the bridge, working to break into the computer and download the captain's and navigation logs. One security officer watched over her. The rest of the team had split into two groups of three to search for the ship's crew.

"This section still has environmental controls," Korelonn reported. His team's three dots had crossed into the engine room. "But not gravity."

"That's strange." Zeppy caught Ekatya's eye. "That means it wasn't a power loss to the section. It was something that specifically targeted the gravity plating."

"Lieutenant," a security officer said. "I've got blood."

"Blood as in, someone scraped their hand on equipment? Or blood as in—oh." Korelonn's video feed now showed the same thing his teammate's did: perfectly round globules floating through the air.

"That's a lot of blood," Dr. Wells said. "Those aren't droplets, they're blobs. You need consistent flow to get something that size. You're looking for someone with a punctured artery or major vein."

"So, dead?" Korelonn asked.

"Unless they got immediate help from someone who knows how to seal a bleeder."

"You could have just said 'yes,' Doctor," Ekatya murmured.

Dr. Wells glanced over. "Do you want accuracy or not?"

"I think what the doc meant was 'probably.'" Commander Cox looked far too pleased.

"The *chief surgeon* meant what she said," Dr. Wells said curtly. "That ship has a medic on the crew manifest. If whoever lost that much blood got to the medic in time, you're not looking for a corpse. But you do need to be looking in their medbay."

"Not necessary, Doctor." Korelonn had rounded a bank of carbon dioxide scrubbers reaching from the deck to the ceiling. Floating behind them was a man in brown coveralls. At least, Ekatya thought it was a man based on the body shape. Given the condition of the head and neck, it was hard to tell.

Cox leaned forward. "That doesn't look like any weapon I'm familiar with."

"I don't think it was a weapon." Korelonn held up his light, this time set to the laser pointer. The bright green point settled on an area of the ravaged neck that showed—

"Are those *teeth* marks?" Cox blurted.

"Lieutenant, please focus in on that," Dr. Wells said.

The helmet cam zoomed in, filling the display with a gruesomely close look at melted and torn flesh. The wound was so deep that the severed ends of veins and arteries were visible, as well as a gleam that Ekatya thought might be the trachea.

"A little *too* close," Shigeo muttered. He looked slightly green.

Ekatya checked to see how their newest officer was handling this. Rahel was intent on the display, her face showing nothing but curiosity.

"That does look like teeth marks around the edges," Wells concluded. "But from small teeth."

"From whatever crawled out of those crates?" Korelonn asked.

"Your guess is as good as mine. The melted tissues—that's consistent with a highly potent acid. What I find interesting is the lack of blood in the wound. In zero gravity, the blood would adhere to itself and the surrounding tissues. What's floating was jettisoned under pressure. Once that pressure ran out—" She pressed her lips together in thought. "The most obvious reason would be that it was removed."

Kade Jalta appeared nearly as green as Shigeo. "You're saying something with small, sharp teeth tore open his neck and drank the blood?"

"Can we see his face, please?" Wells frowned and pushed her head forward, as if trying to get a closer view. "What the Hades *is* that? It looks like some kind of glue." She sat back, shaking her head. "If that's impermeable to air movement, he would have been unconscious in a few minutes and dead in a few more, even without the blood loss."

The dead man's face was hidden beneath splatters of a pearlescent whitish substance. One spread across his eyes; another covered most of his lower face. His mouth was wide open but still sealed, as if he had tried desperately to breathe through the slime.

Ekatya took a deep breath in unconscious reaction, imagining what it would have been like to have both nostrils and mouth sealed off. Her skin crawled at the thought.

"Captain, I'd like to autopsy this man," Dr. Wells said.

"Absolutely not," Cox snapped. "The risk is—"

"Mine to decide." Ekatya shot him a hard look.

He snapped his mouth shut with a flash of irritation, then took a visible breath as Ekatya stared him down. "My apologies, Captain. It's my opinion that the risk is far too great to bring anything aboard from that ship. Especially when we have no idea what did that. It could be inside him, for all we know."

"Which is my *point*," Wells said in an exasperated tone. "We won't know anything until I can autopsy the victim. If there's anything inside him, level ten isolation procedures will keep it there. Just like it does for highly contagious diseases."

Next to her, Rahel frowned across the table at Cox, clearly unimpressed with his assumption of authority. Ekatya was too, but she had already slapped him down and besides, she agreed with him.

"I understand your position, Dr. Wells, but at this point in time, there's no pressing reason to take the risk. Lieutenant Korelonn, tie off that body so it doesn't drift and mark the location. We might want to come back for it. See if you can locate any of the other crew members. But the moment Lieutenant Kitt is done with her download, I want you all back here. Let's get answers from those logs before we go poking into any more dark corners."

"Yes, Captain." Korelonn's camera pulled back and his gloved hands were immediately busy in the frame, hooking a length of cable through the dead man's belt.

Cox leaned back in his chair with a triumphant expression but had the sense to keep his mouth shut.

"Captain," Wells began.

"I hope you're not going to ask me to reconsider."

"No. I understand you're putting the safety of this crew first." She pointed at the display. "But whatever did that is nothing we've seen before. If I can't autopsy the body here, I'd like to do it over there. They have a medbay, and an envirosuit is the equivalent of level ten isolation anyway."

"Not if something with sharp teeth tears open your suit," Cox said. "Or melts it with acid."

Rahel did not move, but her eyes spoke volumes. Ekatya had a feeling that if she approved Wells's request, she'd have to approve intensive envirosuit training for Rahel as well.

"I'll take your request under advisement. Let's see if the logs tell us anything first. Lieutenant Kitt?"

"I'm through the main security wall and into the navigation logs," Kitt said without waiting for the question. "The captain's logs will take a little longer."

"Thank you. Sorry to add more to your list, but we'd like the medical logs as well."

"No problem, those are under the same level of security as the nav logs."

Kitt was as good as her word, reporting both the nav and medical logs downloaded five minutes later. While she worked on the captain's logs, Korelonn's group went to the medbay and found a second victim on a bed, also with the asphyxiating goo sealing her eyes, nose, and mouth. But her throat was intact.

"Bizarre." Kade Jalta had gotten over her initial horror and was showing the curiosity that Ekatya expected from her chief of science. "This makes me think we're looking at a predator that uses asphyxiation to neutralize prey. Which would make the throat wound a means of consuming it. So why not consume this one? Did it get interrupted? Was it storing the food until later?"

"Could have been an opportunistic kill," Lokomorra suggested.

"Um . . ." Rahel cleared her throat nervously. "What if it's not about prey? What if that's a defensive measure?"

Everyone looked at the image on display. The woman's mouth was open as wide as the man's had been, a vivid sign of her panicked final moments.

"Defensive measures that kill?" Jalta said thoughtfully. "It's not the norm, but it does happen. You think we're looking at a prey species, rather than a predator?"

Rahel glanced at Ekatya, who nodded. "You're a senior officer, First Guard. That gives you a voice here."

"Thank you. I, um, I don't know what kinds of things are out here, but in Wildwind Bay we have a fish species that can squirt mucus from glands on its body. It clogs up the predator's gills, and the fish gets away while the predator is trying to get rid of the mucus. Fishing crews hate it because if they catch it by accident, it contaminates their nets and turns their decks into a slippery mess. This just . . ." She waved at the display. "Reminds me of it."

"That might tie in with the holes we saw in the crates," Dr. Wells said. "This species could produce different compounds for different purposes. Acid, to dissolve certain objects, and mucus, to plug others."

"This is total speculation," Cox began.

"Captain Serrado?" Lieutenant Kitt's voice interrupted. "I have all the logs."

"Excellent. Lieutenant Korelonn, get your team together and come home. Maximum decon protocols."

"Acknowledged."

No other crew members had been found, though there had not been sufficient time to check every room of the ship. Nor was there any sign of the creatures that had killed at least two crew and probably more. Ekatya had more questions than answers, a state of affairs she hated.

She didn't breathe easily until the shuttle had cleared the cargo ship and was safely on its way back to the *Phoenix.*

17

LOGS

Ekatya's hope for quick answers was dashed when Lieutenant Kitt informed her that she had loaded the captain's logs on her workstation and run right into a second, harder layer of encryption.

"He was keeping some big secrets," she reported. "It'll take me a few hours to break this."

Nor were the medical logs much help. "There's nothing here," Dr. Wells said after reading through them. "Their medic held a Class Three certification. Good enough for bumps and broken bones, not for dealing with unknown life forms. He doesn't list anything on that patient in the medbay that we couldn't see from looking at her, but I can tell you she was the first victim. He never saw the one in the engine room. The last entry is four days ago, at sixteen twenty-one."

"What did it say?" Ekatya asked.

"He responded to injuries incurred in a fight between two crew members. Tempers were frayed, he said. That's it. My guess is, he was one of the next to die."

Even the navigation logs were a washout. Not because they hadn't recorded the *Tutnuken*'s whereabouts, but because someone had corrupted a significant chunk of data. The data systems techs were painstakingly reconstructing it, but it would take days.

Though Ekatya's shift had ended, she was not about to go off duty while a ghost ship hung off her starboard side and the only answers were locked in encrypted logs. She did leave the bridge long enough for dinner in her quarters, but what was supposed to be a quick break somehow turned into a full hour, which she blamed on an unrepentant Lhyn.

"A rested brain makes better decisions," Lhyn said in her best academic's voice.

That, Ekatya thought later, was probably the jinx that got her in trouble.

She kissed Lhyn at the door, crossed the empty corridor to the lift, turned in place, and promptly lost her breath.

Lhyn was leaning against the door jamb of their quarters, casually sliding her finger down the front seal of her Alsean shirt. It smoothly split apart, showing nothing but skin beneath.

"Oh, that is cruel," Ekatya said. "You could have done that during dinner."

"Then you wouldn't have finished. Nutrition is important." Lhyn ran a fingertip between the shadowed curves of her breasts, then slid her hand out of sight beneath the open shirt. "Enjoy your overtime."

"Evil, evil woman." Ekatya shook her head at Lhyn's wicked grin and added, "Bridge."

Her last view as the doors shut was of Lhyn making a kissing motion.

For once in her life, she wished the magnetic lift would move slower. She was going to need more than a few seconds to get that vision out of her head and snap back into work mode.

The light took on its usual blue cast, indicating movement—and then vanished, along with the lift's propulsion and inertial dampeners. Taken by surprise, Ekatya slammed into the side wall and hit the deck in an ungraceful heap, unable to break her fall properly given the total darkness.

Red emergency lighting came on a second later.

"Nice timing," she groaned, rolling onto her back. "Serrado to Przepyszny!"

"Yes, Captain." Zeppy sounded annoyingly calm in her ear.

"Can you explain to me why the lift just failed in my brand-new ship?" She pushed herself into a sitting position and grimaced at the twinge in her shoulder.

"It . . . what? Hold on, let me check."

She rolled out her shoulder, found it sore but functional, and scooted back to rest against the wall. If this thing started up again without inertial dampeners, she was not about to be caught standing.

"The power is out in that whole section. What the—Captain, I don't know how this happened."

"Well, find out," she said shortly. "And fix it."

"Of course, but, er . . . it's going to take time to diagnose the problem. I'm sorry, Captain, but you should probably get comfortable."

"Lovely." She heaved a sigh and began calling her staff for updates on the *Tutnuken*'s logs. That didn't take more than five minutes. She sat in the dim, silent lift for another two minutes, then called Lhyn.

That conversation kept her occupied for twenty-five minutes, but Ekatya had never been good at not having control. Sitting helpless in a stuck lift was the very definition of it.

"I'm getting out of here," she said, pushing herself upright.

"They're fixing it," Lhyn said patiently. *"Trust your crew."*

"I do trust my crew. And I'm getting out of here. There's no reason why I should sit here and wait."

"Besides the fact that lift shafts aren't designed for anything but lifts?"

"They're designed for emergency access."

"Right. For emergencies."

"This counts."

"Ekatya!" Lhyn let out a short laugh. *"Now if I were in there, it* would *be an emergency. You don't need to be literally climbing the walls."*

Suddenly cheerful now that she had a goal, Ekatya opened the emergency kit panel and pulled out a small headlamp. "I love your laugh. Have I ever told you that?"

"This is a transparent attempt to distract me from arguing with you. And yes, you've told me. But it's nice to hear."

"It *is* nice to hear. Your laugh, I mean. You do it so much more now."

"Ekatya . . ."

"It's true. You stopped for too long. When you laughed again—I mean really laughed, not that quiet little chuckle—that was when I knew you'd be all right."

There was a loaded silence while she pulled the lever and watched ladder rungs slide out from the front wall. A lift car had magnetic interfaces on the bottom and all four sides, leaving only the roof as a means of exit.

"Why are you saying this to me when I can't hold you?" Lhyn asked.

"Because it's one of those things I couldn't say." She settled the headlamp in place. "When I didn't want to say anything that might hurt you or remind you. Then I stopped having to worry about it so much, and I guess I forgot that I never told you." A tap activated the light.

"You are the most exasperating woman."

Ekatya could easily envision the smile that went with that. A soft one, with too-shiny eyes and love sitting right at her fingertips.

"Alsea has been so good for you." She climbed up to the ceiling and pressed the release for the hatch. "I wish we could have gone there right after."

"Me too. But I had to get the physical healing done first."

The hatch slid back, and she climbed one more rung to poke her head through. Her light stabbed into the inky blackness of the lift shaft stretching out on either side. She had known from the angle of her impact into the wall that the car had stopped in a horizontal section. Thank the Shippers for small favors; at least she wouldn't be climbing up a vertical shaft.

"You know what else has been good for you?" She hauled her upper body through the hatch and turned to sit on its edge.

"What?"

"Teaching Rahel."

"Noticed that, did you?"

"It's hard not to. You come home lit up. You're full of stories every night." There wasn't much space between her head and the roof of the shaft. Uncomfortable with the closeness, she pulled up her legs and spun in a half-turn. Now her legs dangled over the edge of the car.

"Like the one about asking Lokomorra to pet her?"

Her laugh sounded strange in this deadened space. "I'm still waiting for the right time to poke him with that one. And still not over my disappointment that you couldn't set up a recorder."

"Me either! One of these days, she's going to tell me what happened."

With one foot on the top rung, she flipped around and began the climb down. "Don't hold your breath. You've probably run into the brick wall of Alsean warrior honor."

"She's almost as exasperating as you are. But a joy to teach. You really lucked out with her. You realize that, right?"

In more ways than one, Ekatya thought. Rahel did indeed hold an impressive amount of potential, but right now her greatest service was in the way she had been a catalyst for Lhyn's newfound confidence. Ekatya wasn't sure whether it was the act of teaching, or the fact that Rahel hadn't known her before the torture and didn't treat her any differently because of it, but that relationship was exactly what Lhyn needed now.

"I do realize it." She stepped off the last rung and began walking toward the nearest shaft access. "I lucked out with her instructor, too. I'm hoping I can convince that instructor to reprise her role in the future. Rahel's only the first, you know. There'll be others."

"You might have to offer that instructor better pay," Lhyn said. *"I heard there was something in the contract about taking it out in trade, but there hasn't been enough trade."*

Ekatya let out a startled bark of laughter. "Is that why you were killing me at the door?"

She didn't hear Lhyn's response, too focused on the worst sound imaginable at the moment: that of power returning to the lift shaft.

Fucking Hades, she hadn't told Zeppy she was climbing out. He didn't know she was in here.

"Serrado to Przepyszny," she shouted, automatically cutting off her call with Lhyn. "Power it down! I'm in the shaft!"

She ran, frantically cataloguing any possible metal in her clothing or pockets and thanking the Shippers that buttons had gone out of style in Fleet uniforms.

Oh, no, her pad. She ripped open the sleeve pocket and fumbled it out just as the magnetic field came up to full strength. The pad was yanked from her fingers with enough force to sting and flew straight to the wall, sticking with a clang that reverberated in her ears.

Had that still been in her sleeve, she would have been pulled off balance and probably fallen—which would have been very, very bad, she thought as the lift car's external lights came on. She reached a maintenance alcove, barely deep enough to hold a body, and threw herself into it with one second to spare.

The car roared past, ruffling her hair with the speed of its passage. She leaned back to check for any other cars, then jumped out and set a new speed record to the nearest access door. With her heart hammering in her ears, she tumbled into the blessed safety of a chase and slammed the door behind her as the lift shaft went dark again.

Leaning against the door, she caught her breath and mumbled, "Better decisions my ass." Resting her brain during dinner had done her no good at all. Lhyn was going to tear a strip out of her hide, and she had no excuses.

"Captain! Are you all right?" Zeppy sounded frightened.

Ekatya inhaled deeply and schooled her voice to sound normal. "Well, I'm still three-dimensional. No thanks to whoever failed to notify me that the repairs were complete."

"Murray didn't tell me, he must have—Captain, I'm sorry. I'll bust him down to sewage maintenance. He should have known better, I don't know why —" He paused and spoke with slightly more calm. *"Thank the Seeders you weren't hurt."*

It wasn't entirely Murray's fault, and Ekatya gave Zeppy points for not mentioning her own failure. While it was true that protocol required warning her before resuming lift operations, it was also true that she had been shockingly careless.

"Thank the ship designers for those maintenance alcoves," she said. "Though I think they could be a little deeper."

He made a choked sound. *"They're not made for anyone overweight, that's a fact. You're sure you're all right?"*

She closed her eyes, remembering the wind that had blown past her with the high-speed passage of the lift. "I'm fine. But there's a pad in that shaft that I'm not about to go back for."

18

PREY

Murray threw his tools back in the kit, grumbling to himself. Commander Zeppy had read him the riot act, and fine, he should have called in the fix, but why wasn't anyone pointing out that the captain shouldn't have been in the damned shaft? If she'd stayed in the lift like any normal person, she wouldn't have been in the slightest danger. It wasn't his fault she decided to wander off like a drunken cadet.

"But no," he mocked. "It's hurry up and get it fixed, Murray, top priority, the captain's in there, get it done." He had found and fixed the problem in record time, and what had that earned him? The shit shift.

He slammed the lid on the kit, furious at being punished for such a small mistake. Grabbing the handle, he stood up—and slammed his bald head into an overhead pipe.

"Aah! Shit! Shit shit shit! Every damned time!" He dropped the kit and bent over, pressing the heel of his hand against his scalp. A vicious kick sent the kit onto its side, which made him feel better for half a second until the lid popped open, strewing tools all over the floor of the chase. He hadn't latched it properly.

"Well, that's perfect." He examined his hand and rolled his eyes at the blood. That would be another scab for everyone to tease him over. Zeppy knew he hated working in the chases but sent him anyway because he was the best person to get the captain out of a stuck lift. Now he had a banged head, another mess to clean up, and an assignment doing sewage maintenance.

Zeppy had been so angry that he hadn't let Murray get a word in edgewise about the strange cause of that power outage. In fifteen years of working Fleet ships, Murray had never seen anything like this. It looked like an animal had chewed through the main power conduit. But Fleet ships didn't have stray animals running around, and even if something *had* chewed through the conduit, the resulting electrocution would have cooked it. He had no idea what could cause that kind of damage.

Once the pain in his head had died down to an aching throb, he knelt and began gathering up the scattered tools. A pair of grips had slid beneath the ramp covering a conduit in the floor, because that was just his luck. He went to his hands and knees with a grunt and reached for the handles poking past the edge of the ramp.

Something moved in his peripheral vision.

"What the—?"

A part of the wall detached itself and changed to the color of burnt wood. He froze, still with his hand extended, and stared at the alien creature not one meter away.

It looked gelatinous and might have fit into his toolbox if not for the proliferation of tentacles ringing the base of a bulbous, featureless body. Greenish flashes of light sparkled under its glistening skin as it slid along the wall toward him. A tube extended from the upper part of the body and waved back and forth, as if it were *sniffing* him.

"Fuck me sideways!" He threw himself backward. "Murray to—"

A whitish blob shot out and slapped onto his face, gluing his nose and mouth shut. Frantically he scrabbled at it, but it had already hardened into cement. Stretchy cement, he discovered during an involuntary gasp for air. He could open his mouth, but nothing came through.

A second blob splattered across his eyes. He squeezed them shut on impact, an instinctive act that might have saved his sight had this glue not hardened just as quickly. Blind and panicked, he flailed about, alternating between fruitless efforts to dislodge the suffocating cement and wild attempts to keep the alien away.

He was running out of oxygen when the heavy weight landed on his head, bypassing his windmilling arms and sending him over backward.

The creature rode him down and scraped needle-sharp teeth into his scalp, right where he'd banged his head into the pipe.

With a muffled scream he grabbed at it, but his fingers could find no purchase on its gelatinous body. It was stuck to his head like a giant suction cup. Still he tried, driven by pure instinct, until his muscles gave out and his arms dropped to the floor.

The last thing he felt was another weight jumping onto his chest.

19

ANSWERS

Ekatya was making her way out of the chase when Lhyn called, worried about the abrupt end to their conversation. So soon after her own scare, she hadn't been able to lie or even come up with a softened explanation.

The silence after her short description of events was ominous. She stood still, one hand on an overhead pipe as she waited for her comeuppance. Even expecting it, she was startled by the level of fury that blistered her ears.

Until Lhyn's voice abruptly changed and she choked on her words.

"You can't take chances like that! Do you know what happens to a tyree with a broken bond? Do you even think about what you'll leave me with? If you're going to kill yourself, do it for a good reason, not because you're fucking bored!"

The shuddering breaths were worse than any anger. Ekatya would rather face six admirals and Director Sholokhov at a court-martial than hear Lhyn cry because of her.

"I'm sorry," she said helplessly. "It was stupid and—" And she had been distracted while talking to Lhyn, which she was not about to say now. "I didn't think."

"No kidding." Lhyn's voice was steady once more, though considerably quieter. *"So many times I've worried about you on dangerous missions. It*

never occurred to me to worry when you're not even doing anything. If you die on your own damned ship because you're being a grainbird, I'll never forgive you."

"That's fair. I'd never forgive myself, either. Lhyn, I really am sorry."

"I know. It's a good thing I'm the one training Rahel and not you. I'll do a better job."

The laugh burst out before she could stop it, likely fueled by her near miss. To her great relief, Lhyn chuckled as well, and she knew the storm was over. All in all, she had gotten off lighter than she deserved.

Two hours later, she sat in her office, still haunted by the memory of that call. She had never given much thought to the risks of her job, beyond training and planning and taking all precautions to minimize them. In her line of work, she *couldn't* worry about the risks. That led to hesitation, and hesitation led to failure.

But it wasn't just her own life she risked now. Lhyn was tied to her through the first-ever Gaian tyree bond. There was a physical and mental cost to breaking it. And she had nearly done it because she couldn't bear not being in control.

With a groan, she rested her elbows on the desk and rubbed her face. "You *are* a grainbird," she muttered.

Her desk display lit up with an intraship call from Lieutenant Kitt. She sat back and tapped it on. "Tell me you have good news."

"Well, I have news. I can't say it's good."

"Two section chief meetings in one day," Rahel said as she sat next to Commander Lokomorra in the briefing room. "Is this normal?"

"Nope. But it's not abnormal, either."

"That's helpful."

Dr. Wells pulled out the chair on her other side. "It happens in crisis situations, when information is unfolding as we go."

Commander Zeppy flopped into the chair across from her, blowing out a long breath as he landed. He looked weary, and his emotional signature was far removed from the usual confidence that Rahel sensed from him. When Captain Serrado entered the room, he watched her with a spike of worry and guilt.

Oddly, the captain was exuding a similar level of guilt. She met Zeppy's eyes with a small smile, communicating something that relieved him but not her.

Rahel would have given a great deal to understand what that was all about.

Eight other section chiefs filed in and took their places around the table, followed by the last one escorting someone new. Commander Kenji, chief of data systems, was a striking man with golden eyes and bronze skin. His long black hair was tied in an uncountable number of tiny braids, and he was as peaceful emotionally as he looked on the surface.

At his side was a younger woman Rahel had never seen before. She moved with a jerky, contained energy, and her hair was a thick mass of tight curls that added to the sense of constant motion.

"Commander Kenji, will you please introduce the lieutenant?" Captain Serrado said as they sat down together.

"Certainly. This is Lieutenant Kitt, my star data jacker. You heard her voice on the mission team."

Kitt sketched a nervous wave. She had seemed calmer on a ghost ship with unknown life forms than she was in this room.

"Hello, Lieutenant," Dr. Wells said in a friendly tone. "Good to see you when you don't need my services."

"Hi, Doc." Kitt's anxiety eased. "So they *do* let you out of the medbay."

"Only for meals and meetings."

Toward the end of the table, Shigeo chuckled. "That's what you get for choosing medicine. You should try botanics; we get to wander all over the ship."

"Yes, but you deal with fertilizer."

Kitt's smile was quick but genuine, and her emotional signature relaxed further.

Having recently been the new person in this room, Rahel was fascinated to see the section chiefs offering the same courtesies to Kitt that they had to her. She had thought they were treating her differently because she was Alsean, but now realized they simply wanted to put any new person at ease. It made sense when she thought about it: nervous people were not as reliable when giving information.

"Kitt is exceptionally good at cracking encryption," Commander Kenji said. "She's also good at scanning large numbers of files and pulling out relevant data. Rather than have me read through everything she's found and then relay it to you, I thought it would be easier to have her report to us directly."

Commander Cox leaned forward. "You've cracked the captain's logs?"

"I have. I know where they got that teracite." Kitt slipped a data wand into the port at her seat and tapped the deskpad. At the center of the table, a holographic star system popped into existence. Three gas giants orbited a yellow star, each surrounded by a dizzying array of moons. The outermost planet sported a magnificent set of rings, but it was the second planet that drew everyone's attention when a bright green box appeared around its largest moon.

"Oh, don't tell me." Commander Jalta slapped her hand on the table and scowled at the image. "The Enkara Preserve? Those flaming shits!"

"What's the Enkara Preserve?" Zeppy asked.

"A moon teeming with lifeforms we haven't yet catalogued. It's protected under the Non-Interference Act. No sentient life, but buckets of non-sentient marine species—one of the most diverse and rich worlds we've ever found. It's off limits to anyone without a research permit. And getting a permit is only slightly easier than getting the Seeders to answer a prayer."

"I take it that means the penalty for an unauthorized landing is high," Shigeo commented.

"Prison term, huge civil fine, and lifetime revocation of travel permits," Cox said. "Now I understand why they corrupted their nav logs."

"And didn't call for help when they were in trouble," Lokomorra added.

"But they didn't just land." Jalta's fair skin was tinged with pink. "They *mined.* They tore up the substrate for teracite. Who knows how much damage they caused?"

"Then they brought some of that life back with them," Captain Serrado said. "Organisms that killed them and destroyed their ship functions within forty-eight hours. Lieutenant?"

Kitt sat up straighter. "They didn't figure out what was going on until it was too late. It started with little things. Doors losing power, so they had to open them manually. Lights going out, sections losing gravity. Then it hit their engines, and while half the crew was busy with that, the other half died when the atmospherics failed in their sleeping quarters and the alarm didn't trip." She looked over at Dr. Wells. "Including their medic. It was the night of his last log entry. Nobody went into the medbay after that."

Wells nodded.

"That's why we didn't find many bodies," Kitt continued. "They don't have a morgue, and with power going out all over, they didn't want to use the freezer. So they stuck them in an airlock and cut the power to it."

"Sensible," Dr. Wells said.

"Sensible?" Down at the end of the table, the chief of engineering was appalled. "Sensible would be having the most basic failsafes built in so people don't die in their sleep! How do they lose oxygen flow to an entire section and not notice?"

"It's not a military ship," Kitt answered. "The captain was the owner, and I don't think he spent much time drilling them on disaster response. I also don't think he spent much money on safety controls and redundant systems."

The chief grumbled his disgust. "How did these people ever get a Fleet contract?"

"Lowest bidder," Serrado said, her gaze on Kitt.

"They'd already lost five crew and things were going wrong all over. That was when they finally checked the cargo bay and figured out they had what they called an infestation."

"Assheads," Jalta snapped.

"Their words, not mine."

"I understand that. Sorry, keep going."

Kitt's curls bounced as she nodded. "The captain still thought they could handle it, which is why he didn't call for help."

"Plus his profit from the teracite sale doubled. He was dividing it by six instead of eleven." Lokomorra raised his eyebrows as every head turned to him. "Don't tell me I'm the only one thinking like a black marketeer."

"You're the only one who does it naturally," Rahel murmured.

He glanced over, briefly showing both dimples. On her other side, Dr. Wells leaned in and whispered, "You're going to explain that to me later."

"I think Commander Lokomorra might be right," Kitt said. "He didn't say as much in his logs, but I got the feeling the captain wasn't too sorry about losing low-level grunts. Especially when two of them were hired just for the teracite mining. Anyway, what they didn't realize until the end was that all of these problems weren't from their accidental passengers randomly messing up systems. They were looking for food."

"I thought that was obvious from the man with his throat torn out," Cox said.

"Yeah, but I don't think he was a target. They're not looking for meat, they're looking for silicates and minerals. They use some sort of acid excretion to dissolve bulkheads and then chew up anything that tastes good. Including power conduits and lots of parts a ship needs to keep its crew alive. They killed that ship by nibbling it to death. The rest of the crew died because of environmental failures."

Zeppy made a strangled sound.

"There are small amounts of minerals in blood," Dr. Wells said. "Iron and calcium. Copper, zinc, magnesium . . . It's not much, but if that's their food source, Gaians could very well be targeted."

"Looked like more was floating in the air than they could possibly have sucked down," Lokomorra said.

Dr. Wells let her hands drift upward. "Whatever they are, they're not used to zero gravity."

"Didn't you say marine life?" Shigeo asked. "How are they surviving out of water?"

"That cargo crew wasn't mining underwater. I doubt they had the knowledge or the gear. They certainly didn't have the time. This must be an intertidal species." Jalta saw more than one confused look and added, "Species that live within the tidal zone."

Rahel still sensed quite a bit of confusion. Had none of these officers ever lived near an ocean?

"Okay, remedial lesson." Jalta picked up her pad and gave it a tap. The hologram of the solar system winked out and was replaced a few taps later with a mostly oceanic planet being orbited by a single, large moon. Directly beneath the moon, the planet's ocean bulged up toward it.

"That's what causes a high tide," she said. "The gravitational pull of the nearest celestial body. Of course, this isn't to scale."

Kenji chuckled. "Good thing. If it were, the people on that planet would have daily tsunamis the size of mountains."

"Trust a beaker to crunch the numbers." She shot him a smile and then pointed at the matching water bulge on the opposite side of the planet. "At any given time, there are usually two high tides. One directly beneath the moon, because it's pulling the water up, and one on the other side, because it's pulling the planet away from the surface of the water. And those bulges drain water away from the rest of the planet, so these sides get low tides." She indicated the sides at right angles to the moon. "Of course, planets with multiple moons have a more complex system, but this is the simple version. Intertidal species live in the zone that's affected by tides—they're underwater at high tide, and in shallow tide pools or above water at low tide."

"But they still need water at some point, right?" Cox asked. "Then whatever is over there is going to dry out and die before long."

Jalta shook her head. "The Enkara Preserve is different. It's not a planet being affected by its moon. It's a moon being affected by its planet. Those tides really are like tsunamis, and it takes seventeen days to go from high tide to low tide. Another seventeen days to get back to the next high tide. If this species isn't dependent on tide pools—if it's actually dry at low tide—then it's adapted to surviving for thirty-four days without water."

Cox looked disgruntled. "So we can't just wait them out."

"Well, we don't know when they were picked up. It might have been at the end of the tide cycle. They might be dried out and dead right now."

Rahel wasn't listening any longer. She was watching Zeppy, whose worry had been spiraling upward for several minutes.

"Commander Cox," Zeppy said slowly, "your team went through maximum decontamination protocols, right?"

"Of course. The shuttle was sterilized in the exit tunnel, and every member of the mission team went through decon."

"What are you thinking?" Captain Serrado asked.

"I'm thinking that since you were stuck in the lift, I've had six other repair orders for odd little power outages. I thought it was just a weird day. But if those creatures target cables and conduits looking for minerals . . ."

The stress level in the room spiked.

"I don't like where you're going with this," Serrado said. "Did Murray indicate anything strange about the power outage that took out my lift?"

"Uh . . . no, but I didn't exactly ask him." He glanced up at the ceiling and said, "Przepyszny to Murray."

No one made a sound as they waited for his tense expression to ease.

"Przepyszny to Murray, what's your location?"

He swallowed and shook his head at the captain.

"Phoenix," Captain Serrado said calmly, "locate Technician First Class Murray. Respond to my location."

"Technician First Class Murray is on deck four, chase twelve-F, junction seven."

Zeppy sucked in an audible breath. "That's where he got your lift running again. He shouldn't—his shift ended ninety minutes ago."

Serrado's expression was grim. "Phoenix, display the security cam at Murray's location in the bridge briefing room."

The wall display activated, showing the tight confines of a chase—and a uniformed body lying on the deck. Rahel thought the head was facing the cam, but it didn't look like a head.

Commander Cox stood instantly. "I'll take a team."

At Rahel's side, Dr. Wells was already speaking quietly into her com, ordering her staff to prepare for an autopsy and have a gurney ready outside the chase entrance.

"Is there any way that could have been caused by something mechanical?" Serrado asked. "An accident?"

Zeppy looked back at the display and blanched. "I don't think so." His eyes closed as he fought a wave of fear so strong that Rahel felt the hair rise on the back of her neck. "Commander Cox, you need me. You don't know where that is, and your team shouldn't be checking pads for directions while you're navigating the chases and maybe running into fish things that kill people."

Rahel stood up. "Let me take them." When Zeppy stared at her in silent conflict, she turned to the captain. "I know where it is. And no disrespect meant, but if anything is still there, I'm better qualified to help."

Captain Serrado studied her, then gave a single nod. "Commander Cox, take First Guard Sayana with you. Assign her a phaser. If you find anything, capture is preferable. Killing is the last resort."

"Understood." Cox met Rahel's eyes and tipped his head toward the door. "Let's go, First Guard."

20

CHASE

The last time Rahel had been a subordinate on a team of warriors, she was nineteen cycles old and finishing her training. It was not a role she fit into easily, a fact made clear when Commander Cox stopped her at the junction of two chases.

"Are we getting close?" he asked quietly.

She nodded. "At the end of this one, it's a right turn and then straight ahead."

"Good. Take the six."

In Fleet speak, that meant the rear position. She would be following Cox and two others.

"Commander—"

"We needed you to get us here. We don't need you to get yourself in trouble."

"I am a trained warrior," she began, the blood already hot in her face, but he interrupted.

"You're trained on Alsea, not here. Not yet. If I let anything happen to you, Serrado will have my head on a platter and Wells will have my ass in a sling. Take the six."

If he *let* anything happen to her! As if she weren't perfectly capable of taking care of herself.

He stared her down, jaw set and clearly done talking.

Scowling, she stood aside and let them pass, then swung in behind them. It was ridiculous. She had led them all the way here, clearing all the chases to this point, and now she was being treated like some breakable package they had to take care of.

She was so deep in her fuming that she didn't register the emotions at first. Someone was in this chase with them. Unlike the security officers, who were variously anxious, cautious, and determined, this person was lost and homesick.

They reached the end and turned right. It was a straight path from here to the end of the chase, with no place to hide.

Cox stepped up on a ramp protecting a conduit, then down the other side, his two officers following closely behind. Rahel paused atop the ramp and looked over their heads, now able to see all the way to the door that marked the end of the chase and the entrance to a brace shaft.

It was empty but for the body on the floor. Yet the emotions were still there.

Had that unreal image on the security cam been some sort of error? Was Murray still alive? But then Cox would be broadcasting relief, not this insulted anger.

Cox moved slowly forward, weapon out and ready. "That looks a lot nastier than it did on the cam. Whatever did this is something I'm not risking lives for. If you see it, shoot it."

Rahel watched in confusion from her slightly elevated perch, then turned in place. No one had magically appeared in the chase behind her. They were alone.

Perhaps the emotion-dampening effects of the chase were weak here. On either side were machine rooms and storage spaces, good places for a person to hide away. Maybe someone was leaning against the wall and their emotions were transmitting through at full strength?

She dismissed the thought, irrelevant now, and focused on the immediate danger. Cox was past the body and checking the remaining length of the chase, a brittle determination hardening his emotional signature. His baton was in its holster; he had no intention of using it to disable.

The other officers spread out, looking in all directions with their weapons charged. Rahel stepped off the ramp and followed, stave grip in hand. She scanned the ceiling, walls, and floors for anything out of place and wondered if she should remind Cox that Captain Serrado wanted this creature captured.

Waves of horror and fear poured over her as the other two officers reached the body. It was far too much to tolerate, and she raised her blocks as she took one last look around. Then she turned to face the cause of that emotional torrent.

Murray's eyes, nose, and mouth were covered by the same whitish substance she had seen on the *Tutnuken*'s victims. But that wasn't the worst part.

It looked as if most of his skull had melted. It wasn't broken or bashed in; it was simply gone.

As was his brain.

She closed her eyes and reopened them, but the image hadn't changed. It was so entirely out of her experience that she felt nothing at all.

"It's long gone." Cox had returned to the body. "Anyone see anything?"

They all shook their heads.

He holstered his weapon and put his hands on his hips, staring down at the corpse. "Cox to Dr. Wells. Yeah. He's got the same crap stuck to his face as that engineer on the *Tutnuken*. Looks like you'll get to do your alien goo autopsy after all."

21

INFESTATION

Ekatya reached the door of the security office at the same time as Commander Cox and Rahel. Cox's squarish face had acquired a look of dogged determination, while Rahel was expressionless.

"The body's on its way to Wells," Cox said as he led them through the door. "My officers will be sticking close to the doc in case there are any surprises."

"I'm sure she's loving that," Ekatya said.

"She will if anything pops out of that body."

"It's a good precaution," she agreed. "First Guard, will you give us a moment?" She watched Rahel move to the far side of the room and turned to her chief of security. "Why not leave Rahel with her? They have a special relationship. She'd be far less likely to irritate."

"I'm not *trying* to irritate Wells. That's just a happy side effect." He caught her glare and sighed. "Sorry. A little humor to ease the last half hour."

"I understand the need. But save it for a different audience." She waited for that to sink in before redirecting. "If it's not about irritating Dr. Wells, why not Rahel?"

"I want her in my section," he said simply. "She took out seven of my people without getting a scratch on her. She stopped an assassin before he cleared his weapon. She's good, but she doesn't know anything about how we work."

"And she won't learn that by guarding a body in the medbay."

He nodded.

"You might have some competition with the weapons section." She couldn't help the smile, despite their situation. "Just what every captain wants, a section chief fight over a new officer."

"I won't have competition with weapons if she decides she wants us." He gestured toward the door. "It's a shit situation out there. But it also gives me a chance to show her what we do."

"All right. Let's go see what we can see."

She called Rahel back and followed Cox across the outer office, through a door, past the control room with its wraparound wall displays, and through another door to his office. Half the vertical space of one wall was taken up by a currently inactive display; in front of it was a comfortable reclining chair with control panels in its wide arms.

Cox dragged over two chairs from his desk and set them next to the larger one. "Take mine, Captain."

"Thank you." She sat down and let herself ease back into the reclined backrest. "How do you ever get out of this thing? Or stay awake in it, for that matter?"

He chuckled. "Practice. Phoenix, queue up security cam footage from deck four, chase twelve-F, junction thirty-one. Time index today, nineteen thirty-seven."

The central portion of the display blinked awake, showing the view from a cam that Ekatya knew was positioned over the brace shaft door. Murray was a short distance away, frozen in the act of packing up his tools.

"This is right after Zeppy called him," Cox said. "So we knew he was alive at this point. Phoenix, play log."

Murray threw a tool into his kit, his body language exuding anger. He was saying something, but the cam's microphones could not pick up his voice over the background noise in the chase.

He finished putting away his tools and stood, only to crack his head into an overhead pipe. Immediately he dropped his tool kit and folded over, facing away from the cam with his hand pressed to his scalp. Ekatya winced in sympathy, then shook her head when he kicked the kit and spilled his tools all over the chase floor.

"I know who that is," Rahel said unexpectedly.

Cox stopped the playback. "You already knew who it was."

"No, I mean—" She looked embarrassed. "Commander Zeppy told me about him. A bald tech who banged his head every time he went into the chases. Because he doesn't have any hair to act as a warning system when he gets too close."

Ekatya pictured Zeppy, with his hair standing straight up for at least five centimeters. "Well, if anyone has a warning system, it's Commander Przepyszny."

"Isn't that the truth," Cox said. "Phoenix, resume."

Murray looked at his hand and wiped it on his trousers before gathering up his tools. He got down on his hands and knees, reached toward a conduit ramp, and froze.

"What is he—oh, Shippers," Cox breathed. "What *is* that?"

Ekatya would have sworn nothing had been there before. Now there was definitely a creature in the chase, clinging to the wall less than a meter from Murray.

"Phoenix, pause. Excuse me, Captain." Cox activated a panel in the armrest of her chair and slid his finger down its length. On the display, a green crosshair moved from the top to the side, settling on the creature. With a few taps, he zoomed in on it.

Given the size of the melted holes in the teracite crates, Ekatya had expected something much smaller. This looked like it weighed ten kilograms. It gleamed wetly, soft-bodied and flecked with green lights under its almost black skin, and it had seven, no, eight—ten legs? Where were the eyes?

"Serrado to Jalta," she said. "Report to Commander Cox's office immediately."

"On my way."

Cox flicked his finger across the panel and sent the still image to another part of the wall display. Then he pulled back the zoom and resumed playback.

Legs rippling in a smooth, eerie dance, the creature slipped along the wall toward Murray. It stopped and extruded part of its upper body into a thin tube, which swayed sinuously back and forth.

Murray threw himself backward. The moment he moved, a jet of whitish fluid flew from the creature's body toward his face. As he desperately clawed at his nose and mouth, a second jet covered his eyes.

His terror was so palpable that Ekatya could almost taste it. She wanted to turn away, to stop the playback of what they all knew would be a horrifying death. But Murray was her crew member. He had died while performing his duty. She owed it to him to bear witness.

He waved his arms wildly, defending against an unseen predator one moment and raking his fingernails down his face the next. The creature timed its leap perfectly, sailing over his arms to land on his head. The force of impact knocked Murray flat on his back.

His head was toward the cam, giving them a perfect view of the creature attached to him. It didn't budge as he slammed to the floor, and Ekatya remembered Jalta talking about tsunami-sized high tides. Anything that could cling to rocks when that kind of water was moving past would be unbothered by this collision.

By now Murray must have been nearing unconsciousness, yet he fought on, trying with all his remaining strength to pull the creature off his head. His fingers slipped and scrabbled, growing weaker every second, until his arms dropped to his sides and his body seemed to deflate.

"There's another one!"

Ekatya had seen it at the same time as Rahel: a second creature dropping from the ceiling to land on Murray's chest. It sat still, apparently watching the first one, which didn't seem to be doing anything.

Except . . .

"Fucking Hades," she whispered. Beside her, Cox made a small noise of horror.

With that characteristic rippling movement, the creature had flowed off Murray's head to the floor. His scalp had disappeared, and the exposed skull looked soft and misshapen.

The second creature flowed up over his face and fastened itself over the warped bone.

"Cooperative hunters?" Rahel said.

A light knock preceded the entrance of Commander Jalta, who stopped inside the door. "Holy crap."

Rahel rose from her chair and offered it. Jalta sat in a daze, her eyes never leaving the scene.

The two creatures traded places twice more, moving backward and forward with equal ease, before breaking through the skull and exposing the brain beneath. One settled in to feed for several minutes, removing what looked like a third of the brain—and the skull walls with it—before moving off and letting the second take over. It appeared to eat its fill, leaving only a small amount for the first to finish. When it was done, the remains of Murray's skull looked like an empty cup.

They left the body behind and rippled up the wall to a bundled set of cables running the length of the chase. Clinging to the top of the bundle, they moved away and were quickly out of view.

Cox pulled up the next cam in the chase, found the right time index, and set it to play.

The creatures came into view and paused where a duct crossed the top of the chase. They flowed up to the junction of duct and wall and again took turns sitting over a specific point.

A small hole appeared in the duct, its edges melted just like the crates had been on the *Tutnuken*. Ekatya would have sworn that hole was too small for them, but they elongated themselves, squeezed inside, and vanished.

"I think that's a feeder duct to the carbon scrubbers," Rahel said.

Cox stopped the playback. "They could be anywhere. If they're melting holes—there's no way to guess where they'll come out."

Ekatya looked past him to Jalta, whose face had not recovered its normal skin tone. "Commander Jalta, are you all right?"

"Huh." She rubbed her face with both hands and shook them out. "Sorry, this is a little difficult to take in. Watching predation on other animals is one thing. Watching it on one of us . . ."

"I understand. Do you recognize the species?"

The question seemed to jar her back to business. "I think I've seen it before, actually. In an article on the Enkara Preserve. Give me a second." She pulled the pad from her sleeve pocket and began searching. "Commander Cox, could you send me that still image? I can do a comparison search on the Enkara database."

"Certainly." He reached over to the panel on the reclining chair, and Ekatya pushed herself out. "Captain, it's—"

"You need the controls. I need to move anyway."

As he slid into place, she stepped over to Rahel and spoke quietly. "How are you doing?"

"I'm fine."

Ekatya touched her arm and drew her to the opposite side of the room. "If I could detect a lie through a palm touch, would you still tell me you're fine?"

Rahel's shoulders rose with a large inhale, and she let out the air slowly. "I wanted to explore. I didn't quite have this in mind, but it's, um." She looked vaguely ashamed. "What happened to him is horrifying. But I don't feel horrified. This is something from another *world*, Captain. Not even you know what it is. I want to know more about it."

"I can see Lhyn's influence on you."

A smile brightened her face. "I liked learning new things long before I met Lhyn. I practically lived in the library growing up."

"Oh, yes, the Head Librarian. Lhyn mentioned that you introduced her in Whitesun. I've been informed that she's going back there at the end of this patrol. I hope your librarian has the patience for a cargo transport's worth of questions."

"She had the patience for me," Rahel said. "I think she can handle Lhyn."

"Got it." Kade Jalta looked up from her pad. "It's *Resilere miin*."

"Could you repeat that in Common?" Cox asked.

"There isn't a Common name for it. But the scientific name means, er . . ." She checked the pad. "Resilient miner. They lay eggs above the high tide line and—oh, you're not going to like this. The parents protect the eggs until they hatch."

"Why won't we like that?" Ekatya asked as she and Rahel returned to the front of the room.

"Because the eggs take three tidal cycles to develop. Meaning the parents survive more than a hundred days out of water."

Cox groaned. "You're right. I don't like that at all."

"Better to know what we're dealing with," Ekatya said. "What else?"

"There isn't much more. They've never been seen by the underwater probes. We wouldn't know about them at all if one pair of researchers hadn't come across a nesting group and set up cams."

"They nest in groups?" Rahel asked.

Cox sagged in his chair. "There are more than two. I'll bet my new custom boots on it."

"Possibly." Jalta spoke absently, reading her pad. "At this point, we might know more than the authors. They observed the *Resilere* digging nests in a rocky substrate and theorized that they were using an acidic compound to dissolve the minerals. And that they might be getting nutritional benefit from those minerals, which could explain how they survived three tide cycles with no other food. Once they hunkered down with their eggs, they didn't come out to forage. The cams didn't record them again until they emerged with their hatchlings at high tide and guided them into the water." She flipped past a few images. "They were imaged in two different color patterns. One matched their nesting rocks, and the other was what we saw here." She gestured at the enlarged image on the display. "The authors thought *Resilere* might be camouflage artists. But no one has seen them on any other substrates, so it was just a theory."

"Not anymore," Ekatya said.

Jalta looked up, her brows furrowed. "What?"

Cox was already resetting the time index of the first log. He found the moment when the *Resilere* had first appeared, then backtracked several seconds and paused. "Anybody see it?"

Ekatya stared until her eyes were crossing but couldn't find it.

"There," Rahel said.

"Where?" Jalta rose and took a step closer. "Shippers, I *still* can't see it."

Rahel walked up to the display and held her finger above the surface. "Here. This is the main body, and here are the legs." She traced an outline.

"Arms," Jalta said. "They're thought to serve more of the function of arms. But I'm still not—oh! Look at *that*."

From one blink to the next, Ekatya's vision adjusted. "Great galaxies. That's incredible camouflage."

"Not just color." Jalta's voice was awed. "Texture, too. It's imitating the cables!"

The *Resilere* was crouched next to a junction where several cables entered horizontally and exited vertically. Its skin was rippled outward in such a way as to look exactly like a set of cables, right down to the spacing in between them. Both the color and texture matching were perfect.

"We could have walked right past them and never known," Cox said.

"Like the mission team did on the *Tutnuken*." Ekatya could picture it. "They were probably in the cargo bay the whole time."

"Then why didn't they attack?" Cox asked.

"Lack of opportunity? Already full? The bigger question is, how did they get here? I want a look at the shuttle bay logs from when the mission team landed." As Cox turned to his controls, Ekatya thought aloud. "That shuttle was closed up while the team was out. The *Resilere* couldn't have gotten inside without melting a hole in the hull."

"Which my team would have noticed," Cox said, fingers flying over the armrest panel.

Jalta snorted. "Sure, from the sudden cold breeze when they were flying back."

"No, I mean before that. Korelonn did a visual inspection before they left. He didn't see anything amiss. Here we are." He looked up as the scene on the wall display shifted to show the open space of their shuttle bay.

The shuttle was descending to its parking space. As they watched, it powered down and disgorged the team members, who exited the frame while techs flocked in.

"Fast forward," Ekatya said. "The crew chief didn't report anything strange, so I doubt the *Resilere* did anything until after the post-flight checks and maintenance were done. We don't need to watch an hour of that."

Cox scrubbed the footage forward until the shuttle stood alone. "Phoenix, resume playback at the point where anything changes in the frame."

Movement drew Ekatya's eye. A line of *Resilere* was emerging from beneath the shuttle and collecting around a point on the deck two meters away.

"How many *are* there?" Jalta's voice was hushed.

"Too many," Cox growled.

Ekatya counted at least nine but kept losing track as they shifted around.

At a command from Cox, the playback froze. Glowing red outlines were rapidly drawn around each body, and a number appeared up in the top right corner.

"Twelve, crap," Jalta said. "And they're not all sticking together or we'd have seen ten more in that chase."

The playback resumed. Ekatya watched, mesmerized, as the *Resilere* took turns melting a hole in the deck plating. She still could not detect any distinguishing features on their bulbous bodies, but given the way they moved in all directions without reorienting themselves, perhaps there *wasn't* a front or back side.

The final shreds of deck plating dripped away, leaving behind a dark hole. The *Resilere* dropped through, one by one, and the shuttle stood alone once more.

"They really are cooperative," Rahel said. "Not just in hunting. This is pack behavior."

"Lovely. Intelligent, cooperative brain-eaters on my ship." Ekatya shook her head. "Did they just hitch a ride on the bottom of the shuttle? How is that even possible? They're adapted to a marine existence but they're impervious to vacuum? And why weren't they fried in the exit tunnel during decon?" She turned to Cox. "Did the decontamination procedure fail?"

He shook his head. "Already checked that. Both the equipment records and the visual logs. Every centimeter of that shuttle was properly sterilized. Somehow they survived it."

"Enkara gets bombarded with radiation from its planet," Jalta said thoughtfully. "It doesn't penetrate very far underwater, but organisms on the surface would get fried if they weren't adapted for the exposure. The *Resilere* are on the surface for over one hundred days, practically bathing in radiation. The radiation in our decontamination beams probably wasn't a challenge."

Rahel cleared her throat. "I have an idea about the vacuum."

"Let's hear it," Ekatya said.

"I was thinking about the fish markets in Whitesun. There are a lot of species sold live even though they're not in water any longer." She pointed at the image of the *Resilere* still on the display. "If they're surviving for so long out of water, they must have some way of sealing themselves off so they don't dry out. If they can do that for water, maybe they can do it for air."

"Very likely. In fact, it's probably the same biomechanics sealing off both water and air." Jalta looked at the display with an awed expression.

"*Resilere* is the perfect name for them. They're adapted for one thing: resilience."

"I'd love to share your enthusiasm," Ekatya said. "But I have to call Command Dome. We've been invaded by a species that can survive vacuum and decontamination procedures. They can melt bulkheads and skulls. Until we neutralize this situation, we're under quarantine."

22

DEFENSE

"Give me some good news," Ekatya said as she entered Dr. Wells's office.

Wells started so abruptly that her chair moved. "Whatever happened to knocking?"

"You called me here. I assumed you were expecting me."

"I wasn't expecting you to just blow in."

Ekatya stood in front of her desk, too keyed up to sit. "I've got a dead man in your morgue and a pack of alien life forms rampaging around my ship, melting holes in it. Social niceties are not high on the list right now. Give me some good news."

"I guess I'm lucky I can do that, then." Wells pushed back her chair and walked to the lab bench set on the far wall. "Here. Put these on."

Ekatya tugged on the thin gloves.

Having donned her own in half the time, Dr. Wells reached into a shallow dish and picked up a thin sheet of something white and fibrous, about half the size of her palm. "Take this and see if you can tear it."

"Is this the—"

"Yes. Murray died of asphyxiation because of this. Given what the *Resilere* did to his skull, asphyxiation was a blessing."

It took five seconds of effort to know she would never tear this material. She shuddered at the thought of having it plastered across her face and held it out. "Is the fact that he suffered less than he might have the good news?"

Dr. Wells ignored her outstretched hand. "No. Well, it probably should be, but that's not what I wanted to show you." She held up a small spray bottle full of clear fluid. "This is the closest approximation I can make to the seawater of Enkara. I looked up the chemical composition and programmed my matter printer." Two quick squirts soaked the patch Ekatya still held in her palm. "Now try."

The fibrous patch had already absorbed the water and increased in volume. Ekatya poked at it. When she lifted her finger, some of the fibers came with it, leaving a gooey string stretched between finger and palm. Rubbing her finger and thumb together merely spread the goo.

She picked up the patch between forefingers and thumbs of both hands and tried to tear it, an act that didn't so much divide it as spread it into a thinner patch covering a larger surface area. With a little more effort, she managed to break the fibers and end up with two separate sections.

Dr. Wells wore a triumphant smile as she held up the spray bottle. "We have a tool of self-defense. I've already programmed this into the general matter printer menu. If you tell everyone to print one out and carry it at all times, we can prevent any more deaths by asphyxiation."

Ekatya stared at the bottle, then the mess on her gloved hands. "Maybe I'm getting too old for double shifts. I don't understand what just happened."

"That's because you've been talking to Cox. He sees enemies everywhere he looks. Captain, think about what we saw on that cargo ship. Only one person wounded, one more dead from this, and all the rest dead from environmental failure. And we know these creatures can get nutrients from minerals."

She still wasn't getting it.

Wells pointed at the goo. "Under normal circumstances, the *Resilere* would be utilizing this underwater. The fibers bind with seawater and swell up. Their purpose is to block, not seal. Remember what Rahel said, about the fish that clogs up the gills of predators? I think that's what this is. It's their *defense*. They go after the sense organs—blind the predator, make it choke, make it stop. It's not meant to kill."

"All right," Ekatya said slowly. "But they did kill three people."

"I don't know what happened to the two on the *Tutnuken*. But I watched the footage of Murray. He wasn't attacked until he made a sudden movement. And did you see where the *Resilere* landed? Right where he split his scalp on the overhead pipe. Where he was bleeding."

"Blood." She looked up in sudden realization. "The minerals in blood."

"It was an opportunistic feeding." Dr. Wells picked up a small, flat-bladed tool and began scraping the goo off Ekatya's gloves. "Our scalps have a unique vascularization. The blood vessels attach to a fibrous connective tissue, so they're not vasospastic."

"Which means what, in non-doctor speak?"

"They don't constrict when they're severed." She flicked the goo back into the shallow dish and returned to her scraping. "That's why scalp wounds bleed so heavily. My guess is, the *Resilere* went after the blood on Murray's head, severed more vessels in the process, got inundated with the blood flow, and kept going. Then it hit the skull plating and found a dense source of calcium, phosphorus, fluoride, magnesium—a cornucopia of valuable minerals. And under that, the brain is packed with nutrients." Another flick of the tool, and she set it down and snapped off her gloves. "You can take yours off now."

Ekatya pulled hers off more carefully and pushed them into the discard bin. "You're saying it started out wanting to lick his head and then found out how tasty we are."

"I'm saying we're completely unknown to them. Maybe they prey on bone matter and brains of Enkara species, or maybe they really are mineral specialists and those teeth are for breaking apart softened rock. Either way, they haven't evolved to prey on us. But they've been yanked out of their environment and they're starving."

She had no intention of laughing, but it erupted before she even knew it was coming. "I thought you and Cox weren't getting along because you're so similar. You couldn't be more different. He's strategizing to eradicate an infestation and you're ready to collect them as pets."

Dr. Wells bristled. "That's simplistic and offensive. And really surprising, coming from you."

Hades, she needed to get a handle on herself. "I'm sorry, I didn't mean—it's been a very long day."

"I've put in the same double shift you have and autopsied one of our crew on top of it. I'm not insulting you." Wells was not giving any ground.

"Right." Ekatya put her back to the lab bench and leaned against it, staring out the windows that overlooked the medbay lobby. "As of ten minutes ago, this ship is under quarantine. Not exactly the mark I wanted on my record after losing my first warship." She turned her head to meet a slightly more sympathetic gaze. "I didn't mean to insult you. I spoke too freely because I consider you a friend."

"Well, shit." Dr. Wells sighed. "Now you've neutralized my mad, and I was enjoying it."

They watched each other silently, expressions easing at the same time, until Wells's twitching lips gave Ekatya permission to laugh again. Wells chuckled with her, and having company in this inappropriate levity made Ekatya feel better than she had since the *Tutnuken* missed its rendezvous.

"We're friends?" Wells asked.

"I hope so."

"Does that mean I can look forward to more nasty insults? I only ask so I can be prepared. Similar to Cox, *really*."

Ekatya snickered. "Sorry. But you have to admit that you share a certain . . . direct style of communication."

"I speak clearly because I'm a scientist. He does it because he has no tact or consideration. Or vocabulary, now that I think about it."

Holding up her hands, Ekatya said, "I'm not going anywhere near that."

"You brought it up!"

"I know. I'm still not going anywhere near it."

Dr. Wells leaned a hip against the lab bench and folded her arms. "Has your day been long just because of the *Resilere*, or is something else going on?"

She hesitated. "As a friend?"

"As a friend."

It was a leap. But she needed someone, and who better than the woman who had never been afraid to take her on?

She pulled out her hair clip, pocketed it, and scrubbed her hands through her hair. "I was an idiot today, and Lhyn called me on it. I scared her so badly that she cried. Only for a few seconds, and then she was fine, but my heart—" She shook her head. "I'm responsible for over twelve hundred people, and most of the time it's a weight I can handle. But sometimes I wonder what the Hades I'm doing and who thought it would be a good idea to leave me in charge."

"If you didn't wonder that now and again, you'd be the kind of captain I refuse to serve under." Those sharp green eyes held none of the surprise or judgment she had feared. "You're not a machine. You get to be imperfect."

"The problem is that when I'm imperfect, people can die." Ekatya looked away, focusing on the potted trees lining the far side of the medbay lobby. "Or I hurt someone who should never be hurt."

"Nobody gets through life without being hurt. Sometimes the ones who get hurt the most are the ones who least deserve it."

Something in her tone brought Ekatya's head around. "We're not talking about Lhyn anymore, are we?"

For several silent seconds, Wells stared out at the same trees that had previously held Ekatya's attention. "I'll tell you the story," she said at last. "Later, after we're through this. But I think . . . I'd like you to know."

"I have the feeling that will be a great honor."

A wicked gleam entered her eyes. "Not that great. I already told Rahel."

And just like that, the weight lifted. "That was revenge for the Cox comment, wasn't it?"

"If we're going to be friends, you should know I give as good as I get."

"As if I didn't know that before? Wait, isn't there supposed to be an advantage to being friends? Where does that come in?"

Wells shrugged. "I don't know. You'll have to tell me when you figure it out."

Dr. Wells was not going to be an easy friend, Ekatya thought. But then, nothing worthwhile ever was.

23

ON EDGE

Rahel was in the Blue Rocket with Roris and the weapons team when Captain Serrado made her all-call announcement. The bustling bar went silent as she calmly explained that Dr. Wells had discovered how to defend against the *Resilere* and their cement-like excretion. She ordered crew members to travel in pairs for safety and to carry a spray bottle of Enkara seawater at all times, effective immediately. Then she explained their theory regarding the non-predatory nature of the *Resilere*, at least with Gaians, and cautioned everyone to avoid any sudden movements should they run into one.

"I have every faith that we will resolve this situation quickly," she concluded. "In the meantime, look after each other. We'll get through this as a team."

The bar remained silent for a few seconds before resuming its prior noise level, but there was no laughter now. Rahel winced under the onslaught of heightened emotions and threw her blocks into place.

Blunt was looking at her with sympathy in her colorless eyes. "Can't imagine how that must feel."

"I can block it. Well, most of it. This many people in this small a space . . ." She lifted her hand and drew a circle with her forefinger, indicating the room. "I'd need to be a high empath to block all that."

"You're in for a rough few days," Roris said. "It's only going to get worse from here. This may be a warship, but most of these people are beakers and support staff. The most dangerous thing they've ever faced was their senior year practical exam. They'll be scared."

"Especially if we keep having mechanical issues," Torado added. "I heard someone else got stuck in a lift. If operations can't stay ahead of that, they'll end up closing them down."

The others groaned. "That'll suck air," Blunt said. "Just what I wanted to do, climb down thirteen decks to our weapons room."

"You don't have to climb down thirteen decks." Rahel grinned. "You can slide down them. But you do have to climb thirteen decks back up."

"Thanks, you're a ray of starshine."

Roris's assessment was prescient. There were power outages all over the ship the next day, including four that affected the lifts. One section on deck eight lost gravity for three hours. Deck nineteen had a flood when the *Resilere* melted a hole in a water reclamation pipe. The operations and engineering staff were running ragged while security chased ghosts without getting so much as a glimpse, and the crew's stress level spiked to a point Rahel had not thought possible. The relentless pressure on her blocks swiftly blossomed into a familiar pain behind her eyes. Nor could she retreat to the chases, which were now off limits to anyone but repair crews and security staff.

Lhyn was entirely unaffected by the general fear and saw no reason to interrupt their training.

"I don't mean to sound like an arrogant warrior," Rahel said, "but I'd expect a scholar to be a little more nervous."

Lhyn shrugged. "I guess there's something to be said for being tortured. My threshold for things to get worried about is a lot higher than it used to be."

Rahel snapped her mouth shut and resolved never to say anything that stupid again.

The day after that, the *Resilere* chewed through so much critical infrastructure that Captain Serrado was forced to shut down lift operations on seven decks and ask all non-essential crew to stay in their quarters or approved gathering places. It would limit the areas of concern for both security and the repair crews.

If Rahel thought that might slow down the gossip machine, she was mistaken. When she and Lhyn went to the Blue Rocket for a training break, they heard about every flood, power outage, and melted hole sighting on the ship. They also heard about the failure of all attempts to live trap the *Resilere*. Dr. Wells had created blocks of minerals she thought would be attractive to them, and Commanders Cox and Jalta had come up with acid-proof containers to lock them in. But the *Resilere* were either uninterested in the food blocks or too smart to be caught.

Near the end of the day shift, two operations staff surprised a *Resilere* while fetching replacement conduit for a repair. It ran away, but not before hitting one of the women in the face with its defense excretion. The Enkara seawater saved her from suffocation, but the majority of the crew did not focus on that part of the story. They focused on the fact that there had been another attack.

The ship-wide stress level hit new heights, and Rahel spiraled into a pain that was nearly as bad as her punishment week. She was on the third day since her last treatment and now realized her error in recruiting Katsuro Lokomorra: a crisis that prevented Dr. Wells from treating her would likely involve him, too.

She should have asked Lhyn for help earlier. Now Katsuro was covering the bridge, Lhyn was having dinner with the captain, Dr. Wells was busy in the medbay, and Rahel was paying the price for her stubborn warrior pride.

She was resting on her couch with the lights dimmed when her entry chime rang. With a groan, she sat up and waited for the spikes of pain to subside, then slowly stood.

The chime rang again before she was halfway across the room, making her head throb.

"I'm coming," she mumbled. "Stop pressing the shekking chime." Calling up her reserves of strength, she stood straighter and opened the door.

"I thought so," Dr. Wells said. "You look like you've been dragged through Tartarus backward."

"I feel like it. What are you doing here?"

"Seeing to a patient."

It was exactly what she needed, had in fact been dreaming about while lying on the couch with explosions going off in her head. But it was demoralizing, having Dr. Wells take time out of a crisis to come here. She was supposed to be a warrior, not a shekking patient. The whole ship was on high alert and she was disabled.

Without a word, she turned around, retraced her steps, and collapsed on the couch. She didn't have the strength to keep her eyes open; sitting upright on the floor was out of the question.

"You *are* in bad shape."

The fact that it was true didn't make hearing it any easier. "Let's get this done so you can go back."

"Well, you're making me feel wanted." Dr. Wells's voice came from above her.

She pressed the heels of her hands against her forehead and said nothing.

After a long moment, she heard the rustle of fabric and felt the air move as Dr. Wells knelt next to the couch. "Can you move your hands?"

"No," Rahel said shortly. Having Dr. Wells this close, exuding so much emotion, was pushing her to the edge. She had no patience left for this dance around what should be appropriate for their relationship. "Would you please sit on the couch?"

"I would, but you're on it—"

"At my head."

Though surprised and a little dismayed, Dr. Wells did as asked. Rahel barely waited for her to settle before pushing up far enough to rest her head on the doctor's leg.

The surprise doubled, but the dismay vanished. Coming up from deep beneath was an old, forgotten pleasure, familiar yet made strange from lack of experience.

The touch of fingers along her scalp felt like the first drops of rain after a drought. Rahel had not realized how tense she was until her entire body went limp, every cell understanding that relief was at hand.

"Sainted Shippers," murmured Dr. Wells. "That was quite a reaction."

Rahel tilted her head, able to move it freely for the first time in hours. She wasn't yet capable of speech, too focused on the blessed relief pouring into her from these hands.

Perhaps five minutes passed before she could bring herself out of her daze. The combination of this position and the knowing touch of Dr. Wells's fingertips had taken her straight from near-agony to a kind of stupefaction.

Dr. Wells deserved better.

"I didn't mean to make you feel unwanted," she said. "I wanted this so much I was fantasizing about it."

A low chuckle sounded over her head. "I remember the days when people used to fantasize about me. It never looked like this, though."

The smile felt foreign on her face. "Then their imaginations were limited. Why are you so sure people don't fantasize about you now?"

"I'm a little past the usual age bracket."

"If that's true, this entire crew is blind and stupid."

She had not thought Dr. Wells capable of shyness.

"Thank you, Rahel. That's one of the nicest things anyone has said to me in some time. Is this the position you prefer?"

"It's how I've always done it with Sharro."

"Why didn't you ask for it in the first place?"

She opened her eyes and soaked in this new view of Dr. Wells, so similar to Sharro in some ways and her polar opposite in all the others.

"Would you have been comfortable with it?" she asked.

Dr. Wells traced a fingertip along each of her forehead ridges. "No. Would I have done it anyway, knowing it was what you needed? Yes."

"Then I would have been uncomfortable knowing you were uncomfortable. Like the massage therapists."

"Hm. There is that." Gentle fingers moved along her jaw and down her throat.

"You Gaians have such strange boundaries," Rahel mused. "You don't just keep the truth from others, you keep it from yourselves. You'll do something that makes you uncomfortable because you think it's your duty, but you have to find excuses to do something that gives you pleasure because you can't accept why it does."

"What does that mean?"

She was tired of pretending that she didn't know. "You're trying so hard to make sure I'm not a substitute for Josue that you can't admit you do have some maternal feelings."

The thigh under her head tensed. "I don't have—"

"I'm an empath. You can lie to yourself, but you can't lie to me."

Anger hit like a falling wall of bricks. "How dare you," Dr. Wells said in a too-quiet voice. "I told you about my son in *trust*, and now you're throwing it in my face? Get up."

Shocked, Rahel pushed herself upright. She wasn't even fully vertical before Dr. Wells launched off the couch, fury sparking off her skin.

"If I try to continue this treatment now, I won't be any better than your first massage therapist."

"Dr. Wells—"

The upraised hand stopped her. "Phoenix, call Lhyn Rivers."

It was the protocol for a personal call, one that could be left unanswered if the recipient didn't want to talk.

"Lhyn, I'm sorry to interrupt your dinner, but I need your help. No, no, it's not an emergency. Rahel needs a treatment, but I'm not in a position to offer it right now and Commander Lokomorra is on duty. Good, thank you. I'll send a security team to escort you *after* you've finished dinner, all right? No, she'll be fine until then. Thanks again." She looked up. "She'll be here in half an hour."

"Dr. Wells, I didn't mean—"

"I'm not sure what you're looking for," Dr. Wells said sharply. "But I'm quite sure I'm not it."

"I already have two mothers, I'm not looking for another one! Would you please listen—"

"And next time," Dr. Wells said as if she hadn't spoken, "don't let your damned pride keep you from asking for help when you need it. Lhyn could have helped this morning, when you were already together. You wouldn't have made yourself incapable of serving this crew, Lhyn wouldn't need to make a special trip with a security escort, and I wouldn't have taken two security officers off their rounds to bring me here. Think about that."

She was out the door a second later, leaving Rahel speechless on the couch.

~

"Wow." Lhyn's eyes were full of the concern that was billowing through the room. "What happened between this morning and now?"

"I was a grainbird." Rahel stood aside to let her in.

"For not asking me earlier? True, but there's no harm done." Lhyn frowned. "At least, not to me. You look like the south end of a north-bound fanten, though."

The Alsean phrase made her chuckle, but that threatened to turn into something else. She clenched her jaw against it and shook her head. "I'm sorry. I should have asked. I didn't think it would get this bad, and I didn't want to bring my medical needs into our training."

Lhyn pulled her into a warmron. "You need to stop thinking of it as a weakness."

Such uncomplicated affection was balm to an aching wound, and when Lhyn tugged her to the couch, she followed and went down without a word of protest.

"Fahla, that feels good," she groaned as Lhyn's fingers combed through her hair.

"You know who else has discovered she likes this? Ekatya. I was telling her about it earlier, and she didn't understand how something so simple could be this powerful for you. So I demonstrated. Don't tell the Voloth, but I now know how to completely disarm the great Captain Serrado."

"I don't think she'd have the same reaction with a Voloth."

"I do have some special powers with her."

"You have them with me, too."

Lhyn's pleasure was shot through with sparkling pride. "Maybe I have a special touch with warriors."

Rahel caught her hand and held it against her shoulder. "Thank you."

"Of course. You think I'd leave you in pain when it's so easy to fix?"

"No. Thank you for everything." She pressed the hand to her cheek and let go.

"Oh. Well, you don't need to thank me for that." Lhyn cupped her cheek for a long moment before resuming her caresses. "What's really wrong?"

Rahel would never understand Gaians. She had told Dr. Wells the truth and driven her away. Now she wasn't saying anything, yet somehow Lhyn still knew.

"I don't think I'm going to succeed at this," she said.

"Lying on my lap? I think you're succeeding just fine."

She smiled despite herself. "You'll have to practice more if you want anyone to believe you're obtuse."

"I'll work on it. What aren't you succeeding at?"

She closed her eyes as Lhyn's touch drifted across her forehead. "Being on this ship. Learning how to be part of the crew. You need someone who understands emotions instead of stepping all over them."

"Who do you think you stepped on?"

"Dr. Wells. She's so furious I don't think she'll ever speak to me again."

Of all the possible reactions, she didn't expect Lhyn to laugh.

"You think you're failing because you pissed off the woman whose temper is legendary? If that's your metric, *everyone's* failing. Ekatya pissed her off two days ago."

"But they're still talking, aren't they? She thinks I betrayed her trust. She's not the kind of person who comes back after that."

"Did you? Betray her trust?"

"No! I just...told her a truth I should have kept to myself."

"Can you tell me what happened?"

She shook her head. "That really would betray her trust."

Lhyn's fingertips pushed beneath her shirt collar, then traced up the length of her throat. "I wish I could help, but honestly, I used to get myself in trouble all the time for telling too much truth. It's one of the reasons I love living on Alsea." Gently rubbing a cheekbone ridge, she added, "The best advice I can give is to wait. Give her time to come down from her mountain and think more clearly. She knows you wouldn't hurt her on purpose."

"Does that matter? Whether the hurt is accidental or on purpose, it's still there."

"Does it matter when someone hurts you by accident during a sparring match?"

Rahel wasn't at all sure that was the same thing, but Lhyn was right. She couldn't do anything but wait.

24

COMMUNICATION

There were several more outages during the night, one temporary loss of environmental controls, another flood, and zero *Resilere* sightings. Captain Serrado had called a section chief meeting first thing in the morning to brainstorm for new ideas on how to capture them.

Rahel's quarters were not in an area hit by a general outage, but the lift in her corridor didn't respond. She reported the failure to the main operations desk and walked to the nearest chase entrance. Surely the injunction against using chases and brace shafts didn't apply to a senior officer who had been called to a meeting?

A niggling voice told her that it probably did, but she was too happy to be back in the chases to pay it much attention. She took a deep breath and smiled at the thought that the scent of machine oil was now associated with peace and relaxation.

Despite keeping a careful eye out, she saw nothing unusual in the chases. The door to the brace shaft was a little sticky, and she made a mental note to report it—later, when she couldn't be told to leave.

Standing in the shaft felt like coming home. She stood on the landing, eyes closed, and reveled in the welcoming hum and gurgle of machinery. The *Phoenix* might have a few unwanted parasites, but she was healthy and breathing normally.

Her eyes popped open at the sudden wave of loss. Someone else was here.

She braced herself against the railing, leaned out, and looked upward. There was no movement on the ladder or any of the five landings above her. Below, the shaft descended for another twenty-four decks and appeared to be empty.

But the loss was still there, and now she could feel that it was coming from lower down.

She swung onto the ladder, started to slide, and stopped herself.

Sudden movements were guaranteed to startle any *Resilere* that might be hiding in here. She had her Enkara seawater, but the idea of having to use it held no appeal.

She pulled her feet back onto a rung and slowly climbed down to the next landing. No one was there, but the emotions were stronger.

The second landing was unoccupied as well.

On the third, also empty, the emotions were so powerful that whoever was broadcasting this had to be *right here*. It was as if they were invisible.

Her mind caught on the thought.

No, it couldn't be.

Could it?

Clinging to the ladder just above the landing, she began a visual sweep of the brace shaft walls, looking for anything even a hair out of place.

"Shekking Mother," she whispered when it came into focus.

A *Resilere* was attached to the wall two meters above the landing, partially covering the control pad that toggled the ladder access plates. It even sported the vertical lines that made up the edges of the pad.

And it was the source of the emotions.

"You are *sentient*," she murmured. "And a long way from home."

She couldn't help feeling sympathetic. Here she was, an invited member of the crew with one person dedicated to helping her fit in, yet she had still spent most of last night desperately missing home and the ease of living with people she understood. This creature had been torn from its home and thrust into a foreign environment entirely against its will. No wonder it—

She stood on the weather-worn boards of Dock One, the heavy, salty air of Wildwind Bay ruffling her hair. The western horizon was sharp as the edge of a blade, cutting a line between sea and sky, while the east was pink with sunrise and full of lowering clouds laden with rain. Behind her, the bells of Whitesun Temple rang out the time, a sound she had always loved—

The vision faded. She stared in shock at the *Resilere*, now looking nothing like a control pad. It was rounded, more elevated on its ten tapered arms, with greenish lights playing beneath the surface of its dark, translucent skin. The lights sparkled and flashed in a rapid pattern she couldn't follow, then slowed before ceasing altogether.

Had it shown her that vision of home?

If so, it could read her thoughts.

I won't hurt you, she thought as clearly as she could.

There was no response.

Belatedly, she realized she had thought in High Alsean. Did the language matter? But she couldn't think in Common; she could only speak it with the aid of her lingual implant.

A moment later she laughed at herself. Of course the language mattered, and unless this creature was a *Resilere* version of Lhyn, it wouldn't understand High Alsean *or* Common. It would understand its own language. Yet she had been drawn here by its emotions—and the vision had come after her surge of sympathy.

She had never learned to project emotions. That was a skill reserved solely for high empaths. But she had been in the room when Salomen Opah was tutored. She had heard the instructions and knew the basics.

For the first time in her life, she tried to push emotions out of her body.

Protection, safety, no harm . . . safe, safe, protect . . .

The vision took her by surprise. One moment she was in the brace shaft, the next she was—

In a detention cell, wrapped in her mother's arms and caught in such a storm of weeping that she could not hold herself up. The relief was overwhelming; she felt safer and more protected than she could ever remember. Her mother was here. Finally, her mother was here, and she would never let go—

She blinked, astonished at the strength of the memory. She had been just shy of her seventeenth birth anniversary when her mother came to get her out of detention, and she hadn't remembered it that clearly in a long time.

Lights flashed across the *Resilere*'s skin, then faded again.

"Great Goddess above," Rahel said. "You're *talking* to me."

25

BREAKTHROUGH

Ekatya drummed her fingers on the armrest, growing more irritated by the second. Commander Lokomorra and eleven section chiefs sat around the briefing room table, many still in low conversation while others glanced expectantly at the door.

Rahel was five minutes late, and if there was one thing Ekatya did not tolerate in her officers, it was tardiness. She was about to make the call when her internal com activated.

"Sayana to Captain Serrado."

"First Guard," Ekatya said in an even tone. Every head at the table turned to look at her. "You're late. What's holding you up?"

"Um. A conversation." Her voice was hushed.

"A conversation? We're waiting for you in the briefing room and you're chatting in the corridors?" She could hardly believe her ears; this didn't sound like Rahel at all.

"Not in the corridors. In a brace shaft."

"In a—"

"I'm talking to a Resilere."

Ekatya's brain froze. She glanced at Dr. Wells, whose eyebrows rose in question.

"Where exactly are you?" she asked.

"Brace shaft J, deck nine."

"Phoenix, display the security cams for brace shaft J, deck nine, in the bridge briefing room. Direct my com there as well."

A chorus of gasps and murmurs greeted the two views of Rahel crouched by the railing of a brace shaft landing. The cams were over the doors on opposite sides of the landing, each viewing her from the side.

On the wall near the ladder was a *Resilere.* It was not camouflaged, and much too close to Rahel for comfort.

"I'll get a team together." Cox pushed his chair back.

"That would be a mistake," Rahel said softly. "Captain, please don't let anyone come in here. It's not attacking me because it knows I won't hurt it. If anyone else comes in broadcasting aggressive emotions, I'll get a face full of goo or it will run away. Or both."

"Stand down, Commander Cox."

"Captain—"

"We've been hunting these for three days with no luck. This is our best chance to learn about them. First Guard, explain what you meant by talking to it."

"I will, but first—can you patch this call and the cam footage to Lhyn? I need a linguist."

"Phoenix," Ekatya said, "include Lhyn Rivers on this call and send the briefing room display feed to my quarters. Lhyn, this is a public call. Our display should be changing in a moment."

"Okay. What's going—fucking stars! What is she doing?"

Rahel smiled. "Good morning, Lhyn. I met a friend."

There was a heavy pause. *"You're completely insane."*

"If you could feel what I'm feeling, you'd wish you were here. The *Resilere* are sentient and empathic."

That set off a cascade of quiet but vehement voices, Kade Jalta's rising above the rest.

"How in flaming Tartarus is that possible? Does she know what she's saying?"

"I do know what I'm saying." Rahel shifted slightly, causing a collective intake of air as everyone waited to see if the *Resilere* would attack.

It didn't move, but a series of greenish lights flashed across its rounded body.

"Did everyone see that?" Rahel asked.

"Bioluminescence," Jalta said. "The researchers saw it when the *Resilere* were guiding their hatchlings to the water."

"I think it asked if I'm all right."

"Are you kidding us with this?" Cox grumbled.

"Why do you think that?" Lhyn wanted to know.

"I was getting a cramp in my foot. The *Resilere* could sense my discomfort. I just had a memory of my childhood friend asking me if I was all right."

Jalta leaned forward. "You think it communicates with you telepathically?"

"I think it communicates with the bioluminescence, but I can't understand that. I *can* understand its emotions. That's how I found it—I sensed it feeling lost."

"Can you sense other animals?"

"I've never heard of anyone sensing animals."

"I have," Ekatya said. "But it was the two highest empaths on Alsea. If Rahel is sensing this *Resilere*, that's a good argument for sentience. How do you know it's empathic?"

Rahel looked pained. "I was, um . . . I was feeling lost, too. When I sympathized with it, I had a vivid memory of a place back home that means a lot to me. Then I tried to project a sense of protection, to tell it I wouldn't cause harm, and I had another vivid memory of my mother protecting me. It's using images. Memories. My memories."

"It can't do that if it can't see your memories," Jalta pointed out. "Which would indicate telepathy."

"Not necessarily," Lhyn said. *"Rahel's memories may be her interpretation of its communication. Their languages are too different. If one speaks in sounds and the other speaks in light, they don't have a common frame of reference. Except for emotion."*

"Then Rahel's memories are a form of translation?" Ekatya asked.

"It's a strong possibility. Or the Resilere *may simply be reflecting her own emotions back to her."* Her voice shivered with excitement. *"Which is often the first step in communicating across a language barrier—repeating what you hear. Rahel, have you heard it make any sounds?"*

"No, but I'm in a brace shaft. There's a lot of background noise."

"It makes sense that the *Resilere* would use light," Jalta said. "It's visible for a good distance both above and underwater. Sound doesn't carry nearly as well in air. But it carries a *long* way underwater. The number of marine species that communicate through sound is . . . well, when you get up into the more intelligent species, it's practically all of them. I'd be surprised if the *Resilere* didn't use sound as well."

Commander Kenji spoke up. "You need a frequency analyzer. Something that can detect and quantify the various sound frequencies in the area, so you can separate mechanical noises from the *Resilere*. I have the equipment, but First Guard Sayana wouldn't know how to use it."

"I would. We also need to be recording the bioluminescence from closer and above, not just the security cam views. And we need detailed notes on the exact nature of the emotions Rahel is sending and sensing, and the memories she's experiencing as a result." Lhyn's inhale was audible on the com. *"I need to be there."*

Ekatya forced herself not to react, to stare straight ahead at that display as if her heart hadn't fallen out of her chest.

"Lhyn, no," Rahel protested. "It's a brace shaft!"

She was worried about claustrophobia? Lhyn could have her skull melted if anything went wrong!

"I'm aware of that. But if you think I'm going to let Kane Muir ruin my chance at a historic event in linguistics, you don't know me at all."

Ekatya closed her eyes. Lhyn rarely referred to her torturer by name. That she did now was a good indicator of how strongly she felt and how unlikely it was that she would let anything stop her.

"This is a bad idea," Cox said. "First Guard Sayana's empathy might be the only reason she's safe in there. Dr. Rivers won't have that protection."

"She'd have mine," Rahel said thoughtfully. "I think I could tell the *Resilere* that she's a friend."

You think? Ekatya wanted to shout.

"We're still not sure what motivates them," Cox said. "We don't know why they ripped the throat out of that crew member on the *Tutnuken*."

"I have a theory on that." Dr. Wells spoke for the first time. "We've had two attacks on the *Phoenix*—"

"So far," Cox muttered.

". . . both of which were instigated by sudden movements, and only one of which was fatal." She shot him a quelling look. "That one involved a bleeding wound on the victim that the *Resilere* went after.

Doesn't it make sense that the victim on the *Tutnuken* also had a wound?"

"Pretty hard to get a bleeding wound on the throat," Cox said. "It's not something you tend to smack into things."

"But he was trying to make repairs in zero gravity. Lieutenant Kitt told us that the captain didn't put much effort into emergency drills. What happens to a crew member who's panicked about the state of his ship and the deaths of his colleagues, *and* working in a difficult environment he's not trained for?"

"He'd be banging all over that room," Commander Zeppy said. "Bouncing off corners and edges and losing tools."

Wells pointed at him approvingly. "Yes! I think he injured himself, and that's what the *Resilere* went after. As long as Dr. Rivers and First Guard Sayana are *extremely* careful about staying free of bleeding injuries —and I mean not even scraping their knuckles on the ladder—they should be fine."

Ekatya glared at Dr. Wells, whose only reaction was a slight flinch around the eyes.

"I'm just waiting for all of you to realize that my safety isn't the concern here." Lhyn's voice was perfectly calm. *"The concern is that this ship is under quarantine. It'll stay that way until we can get the Resilere off it. How long do we have before they cause a problem with the fusion core that we can't fix? Or wipe out both the main and redundant environmental systems in a section? We have a chance to communicate with them. It could be as easy as asking them to let us take them home."*

"We do know exactly where they came from," Kenji said. "My analysts pieced together enough of the nav logs to get the coordinates where their shuttle landed on Enkara."

"I'm going in. All I need is the equipment."

And my permission, Ekatya thought, but that seemed to be a foregone conclusion.

"You should take some of the mineral blocks, too." Dr. Wells was avoiding eye contact with Ekatya. "The better fed that *Resilere* is, the less likely it is to do something unexpected."

"They didn't eat them before," Rahel said.

"We were using them as bait before. They might feel differently if it's a risk-free offer."

"I agree with Dr. Rivers's risk assessment," Commander Lokomorra said. "She's also the most qualified person we have for this. We shouldn't waste too much time discussing it."

Ekatya was happy to discuss it for the rest of the day. The longer they waited, the better chance she had of that *Resilere* simply walking away.

And then she'd never hear the end of it from Lhyn.

She looked at the display, where Rahel sat in apparently peaceful companionship with the unmoving *Resilere*.

"First Guard," she said. "I'm putting the safety of Dr. Rivers in your hands."

"Understood," Rahel said quietly.

"Dr. Wells, I want you ready at that brace shaft door in case anything goes wrong. Commander Przepyszny, I'll be accompanying you and Dr. Rivers as far as we can go. Commander Kenji, get her equipment ready as soon as possible."

"Security should establish a presence above and below them," Cox said.

"No." Rahel's soft voice was surprisingly vehement. "They're empathic, and I don't know what their range is. Security officers will be broadcasting wariness at best, aggression and fear at worst. This *Resilere* needs to feel safe. It's staying with me of its own free will. It can leave just as easily, and I can't stop it."

"Set up security at the chase entrances on decks eight and ten," Ekatya ordered. "If necessary, you can run in from there."

"Captain, that's not close enough to be effective."

"It will have to be." She looked at Zeppy and Kenji, both of whom had pushed back their chairs in preparation for a quick exit. "We'll meet at the chase access nearest brace shaft J on deck eight. Dismissed."

26

COURAGE

Commander Cox accompanied Ekatya to her quarters to pick up Lhyn.

"I notice Sayana flouted the order to travel in pairs," he said as they stood in the lift. "Not to mention the one about staying out of chases and brace shafts."

Ekatya nodded. "One of the hardest things she's having to adjust to is the idea of working on a team. She spent her career relying on herself."

"It's going to get her in trouble if she doesn't adapt."

"I have faith in her. She's already made great strides. We can't expect her to be a perfect Fleet officer in one patrol." She glanced over. "Still want her in your section?"

"Are you kidding? My entire section spent three days chasing ghosts and she's in there *talking* to one. I want a dozen like her. But I'll need a migraine prescription while she and I hammer out a working relationship."

Ekatya couldn't help laughing. "Sounds like you're prepared."

Lhyn was waiting for them, wearing comfortable clothing and carrying a backpack. "Do you have the mineral blocks?" she said by way of greeting.

Ekatya held out a small sack. "Compliments of Dr. Wells. Is there room in there for Kenji's gear?"

Lhyn stowed the sack. "I've got room for everything. Let's go."

"Dr. Rivers?"

She looked at Cox as if she hadn't noticed him before now. "Yes?"

"I don't like heights. It would probably take two shuttles and some unbreakable cables to drag me to the edge of a cliff. You're very brave."

He had surprised a smile out of her. "Thank you, Commander. I might be asking you to repeat that about five minutes from now."

"I'll repeat it as many times as you need," he said, raising himself twenty points in Ekatya's estimation.

On deck eight, Kenji was standing next to Zeppy outside the chase entrance, a pack in his hands. "Oh, you've already got one," he said. "I should have known."

Cox went over to his three security officers while Lhyn stashed a pile of gear in her pack and exclaimed over its quality.

"I *knew* the military was getting all the good stuff!" she said.

Kenji offered a crooked grin. "There have to be some compensations for not having a cushy academic chair."

"Cushy, ha." She shouldered the pack. "I'm about to face my worst fear, and it's not even the brain-sucking alien."

"If Commander Cox says you're brave, you can publish it. His record is impeccable." Ekatya leaned over and spoke directly into Lhyn's ear. "I still think you're the most courageous person I've ever known."

Lhyn jerked back and stared at her. "Everyone, please look somewhere else," she said, and pulled Ekatya into a passionate kiss.

It was six kinds of inappropriate. Ekatya didn't care. She gave as good as she got, trying to convey a book's worth of words and feelings into one gesture.

Lhyn abruptly pushed her away and turned to Zeppy before Ekatya had quite recovered. "I'm ready," she announced.

Zeppy opened the chase door and stepped in. Lhyn looked into the dark, narrow entrance, took a deep breath, and walked in after him. Ekatya brought up the rear.

They progressed in silence until the first ramp over a pipe. "Watch your step," Zeppy said. "And your head."

"Got it, thanks." Lhyn ducked as she stepped onto the ramp. "Why are the chases so narrow?"

"Space limitations. Thank your lucky stars you're on a Pulsar-class ship. On some of the smaller ships, you can't even walk upright in the chases. You have to crawl on your hands and knees."

Lhyn shuddered. "Nightmare. I'm amazed Fleet can attract anyone into operations if that's the sales pitch. 'Join operations! Learn to repair broken power junctions on your hands and knees!' Doesn't have much romantic appeal."

"Well, when you put it that way, it doesn't. Fortunately, my sales pitch was different. It was more like 'Join Fleet, go into operations, earn a high rank and good pay fiddling around with the things you love.' I could have stayed home and worked in my mother's machine repair shop."

"Why didn't you?"

"I wanted to see the galaxy. She thought I was insane. But here I am, a commander and section chief. I think I made the right choice."

"I think you did, too," Ekatya said.

"She has to say that," Lhyn confided.

"I know," Zeppy said in the same low tone. "She's pretty good about saying the right things."

"*She* can hear you." Ekatya smiled to hear Lhyn snicker. So far, so good.

Or at least she thought so until they reached a T-junction and Lhyn stopped right in the middle of it.

"Shippers." She dropped her head back and closed her eyes. "It goes on forever."

"It goes on for another thirty meters," Zeppy said. "Then it's a left turn and ten more meters and you're at the brace shaft door."

"Do you need a hug?" Ekatya asked quietly.

"No! Don't touch me." She licked her lips, shook her head, and opened her eyes. "Sorry. I need all the space I can get."

"I think you'll feel better in the brace shaft," Zeppy said.

She let out a harsh laugh. "Right, in the center of the ship. At the farthest possible point from any exit or window. I'll feel much better there." She hitched the pack higher on her shoulders and pointed with her chin. "Lead the way."

Ekatya hated being this helpless. There was nothing she could do except follow along behind and hope Lhyn's strength held out.

When they reached the brace shaft door, she was careful to stand an arm's length away from Lhyn while she called Rahel. "We're in position. Can I send Lhyn in?"

"Yes. Hopefully I've told it I'm expecting friendly company."

She could wish for something better than "hopefully," but it was all they had.

"Captain. If it goes after her, it will have to kill me first. I promise you that."

That helped more than she would have expected. "A promise from an Alsean warrior," she said. "I know the worth of that. Thank you, First Guard. She's coming in."

"What did she say?" Lhyn asked.

"Go slow and trust her."

Her eyes narrowed. "That's not a promise."

"She said she'll take care of you."

"Uh-huh. Still not a promise, but I don't have time to wiggle it out of you. Commander?"

Zeppy opened the door and stepped as far to the side as he could in the tight confines. "Good luck."

"Thanks." Lhyn went through the door without another word or look at Ekatya. It slid shut behind her, leaving them in the humming solitude of the chase.

27

BRACE SHAFT J

Rahel was aware of Lhyn well before the brace shaft door opened one deck above. The chases might be an emotional dead zone, but they didn't block the broadcasts of people inside them. Heavy dread rumbled into the shaft space, shot through with bolts of terror. The *Resilere* flattened itself and went back into camouflage mode, wary and watchful.

She could not let Lhyn come down yet, but how to say that without making her even more afraid?

"Rahel?"

"Right below you. Lhyn, stop a moment and breathe." She envisioned giving Lhyn a warmron, hoping that would help her project the right emotions. *Affection, protection . . . friend, no threat.*

"You make it sound so easy. There's not enough air in here for that."

"Yes, there is. Lean out on the rail and look up. See the ceiling?"

"Yes," Lhyn said after a pause.

"Now look down."

"Whoa. That's a long way."

"Longer than most of the corridors you walk through. This is just a big, airy corridor standing on end."

The terror lessened, hovered, then suddenly shrank into discomfort.

"Commander Cox would *really* hate this view," Lhyn said.

Rahel didn't understand the comment, but it didn't matter when the *Resilere* was puffing itself out again, its wariness decreasing.

"Come on down," she said.

Lhyn's soft-soled boots appeared on the ladder. Her long legs seemed to take up half the space between decks before her body cleared the ladder opening. She stopped four rungs from the landing and scanned the wall, looking for the *Resilere.*

"Oh," she whispered. "You're trying to be invisible again. My stars, look at you."

Lhyn was a true scholar, Rahel thought. Her remaining fear diminished the moment she laid eyes on the *Resilere*, and it was responding, its skin losing the colors that matched it to the wall and control pad.

"Is it okay with me?"

"It's happier now that you're feeling more at ease. Just keep your movements smooth and slow."

"Smooth and slow, like good foreplay."

Rahel clamped her jaw shut, but a snicker escaped. "We're not recording this yet, are we?"

"Are you kidding? This has all been recorded from the moment you called Ekatya." She descended to the landing, slowly freed herself from her pack, and removed a portable cam from it. Then she went back up a few rungs to attach the cam to the wall above and to the side of the *Resilere.*

It ruffled its skin into a bumpy texture.

"Still all right," Rahel said to her now-frozen friend. "It's curious about what you're doing."

Relief wafted down as Lhyn activated the cam. "Then we have something in common." She joined Rahel by the railing and pulled a boxy piece of equipment from her pack. "Frequency analyzer," she said, powering it on. The main display showed a confusing series of waves and spikes, while numbers appeared on several smaller screens below.

She laid a pad next to the analyzer and activated the virtual display, then set it to show the feeds from the two security cams plus the one she had placed. A second pad went next to the first, its virtual display transparent until she said, "Dr. Lhyn Rivers, *Resilere miin* first contact. We're aboard the SPF *Phoenix,* brace shaft J, deck nine. Date today."

Her words appeared on the virtual screen, along with the day's date in Common reckoning.

"Good," Lhyn murmured, and pulled a small sack from her pack. Settling on her knees next to Rahel, she said, "Commander Kenji, are you getting the feeds?"

Rahel watched the question spell itself out as Kenji spoke in her ear.

"Three visual, one audio, plus the output from the analyzer and your dictation. We're running."

"We have the video as well." That was Captain Serrado. *"It looks nice and calm in there."*

The *Resilere* had let its skin go smooth again. Now a wave of lights flashed across it, and Rahel was—

Looking up at her mother, who was bent over a block of metal and inspecting it for flaws. "It's going to be a sculpture of a mother and child," she said. She was so tall and strong, and Rahel wanted to grow up to look just like her—

She blinked. "That definitely was not reflecting my own emotions back. I think it wants to know if you're my mother."

Her words appeared on the dictation pad, but Lhyn's eyes were glued to the analyzer. "Incredible. That's not an emotion, it's a complex question." She looked back at the *Resilere*, a cloud of joyous awe rising from her. "It shows that they view family relationships as important, and this one is actively seeking to understand our relationship. And yes, they do use sound. A low frequency we're not capable of hearing."

"I saw it too," Kenji said. *"I'm isolating it now and pulling it to a separate record."*

"Thank you, Commander. If you can take care of the audio records, I'll be glad to not have to worry about it."

"Consider it done."

"How can it be communicating questions through emotions?" Rahel asked.

"I have no idea. This is truly alien. What was the memory you experienced?"

Rahel described it, trying not to be embarrassed by the knowledge that Serrado and half the section chiefs were listening in on this.

"I think you have the right interpretation," Lhyn said. "It's significant that you saw that memory from the point of view of yourself as a small child. Can you tell it we're friends?"

"I can try." She recalled the memory of Lhyn giving her a warmron in the middle of a crowded corridor. That she had done it in such a public place, so counter to Alsean taboo, had given the gesture an even deeper meaning that she now pushed out, hoping it would somehow translate. *Not of the body but of the heart. Not family. Friend.*

She had barely finished the projection when the *Resilere* flashed excitedly and Rahel was—

Watching a brown-haired, brown-eyed boy sit up on the empty bricked street of the Whitesun bayfront and flash her a bloody smile. "We should go before musclehead there wakes up," he said, then stood and brushed himself off. As they walked through the nighttime sounds of the docks, he offered, "My name is Mouse."

The hum of the brace shaft returned, grounding her in the here and now, and she could not see the *Resilere* clearly for the tears in her eyes.

"What happened?" Lhyn asked gently.

"It, um." She rubbed her eyes dry. "It understands the concept of friends."

"I'm sorry, Rahel. But I have to ask what that memory was."

She cleared her throat. "The first time I met my best childhood friend. The person who taught me what friendship truly was. I was fifteen, he was seventeen, and I'd just saved him from a beating by two bullies twice his size."

Lhyn picked up her hand and squeezed it, keeping her sympathy unspoken and off the record. "So, one of the most momentous meetings in your life."

She squeezed back and smiled. "One of them."

Lhyn ducked her head, an embarrassed pleasure coming through their skin contact. "It used Mouse before, didn't it? Or your mind did, when the *Resilere* asked if you were all right."

"Yes, but this was much more powerful. It was like living the moment all over again. We were right next to the docks, and I could *hear* the ships pulling at their moorings."

"Emphasis," Lhyn mused. "Or perhaps the first was your mind's interpretation of a question, while this was an actual projection by the *Resilere*. If they can project the way Alseans can, that might affect the strength of the memory."

That made sense. It also made Rahel dread what other memories this exercise might conjure up. There were things she didn't particularly want to share with half the senior officers of this ship.

As if she had heard the thought, Lhyn produced a mineral block from the small sack beside her. "Shall we try something a little less emotionally loaded? Let's see if we can communicate the concept of food. Which has the added benefit of giving it a reason to stay with us. I'd like it to associate us with good things, not just an absence of bad things."

Rahel accepted the palm-sized gray cube and considered how best to do this. "I don't think it's a good idea to hold it out."

"Get it as near as you can." Lhyn pointed to the floor directly beneath the *Resilere*.

Rahel pushed herself to her hands and knees, crept forward, and stretched out her arm to place the cube.

The *Resilere* ruffled up its skin, two arms slipping partway down the wall before retracting.

"Curiosity?" Lhyn asked.

Rahel nodded as she sat back. "And no fear."

"I think they use body language as well as the other forms. Rumpled skin seems to be a bit like us raising our eyebrows."

They waited, but the *Resilere* showed no further sign of interest.

"I guess that would have been too easy." Lhyn extracted two wrapped bars from her pack and offered one to Rahel. "Sweet bars. Maybe eating will make it easier to convey the picture. What emotion would that be? Satiation?"

"Or a kind of assuaging, if we were really hungry." Rahel unwrapped her bar and took a bite. "Yum. It'll help that you brought my favorite flavor."

"They didn't give me my degree for being stupid, you know." Lhyn waggled her eyebrows and bit into her bar with a smirk.

"That's probably the penultimate word I'd associate with you." Rahel would never say out loud what she was sensing: that Lhyn had lost the last vestiges of her discomfort, too caught up in the thrill of discovery.

"Right, then I have to ask. What's the last word?"

"Short."

Lhyn covered her mouth. "You almost got crumbs blown in your face."

"I'm glad your parents raised you properly. All right, let me focus."

She held the next bite in her mouth, concentrating on the contrast between the sweet and tart flavors. Then she tried to project the enjoyment, the satisfaction, the sense of fulfilling a need.

"Bioluminescence," Lhyn said, but Rahel didn't hear her next words. She was—

Walking into a tavern in her filthy uniform, exhausted and wanting nothing more than a plate of fanten. Two plates, if she could get them. She hadn't eaten since before dawn and would devour her own boots if she didn't get food soon.

"Sorry, warrior," the owner said. "There's none for you."

She shook her head. "That was strange."

"What?"

"Another memory, but it never happened," she said, staring at the *Resilere*. "I mean, it didn't happen that way. It was the day of the Battle of Alsea. I fought the Voloth all morning and spent all afternoon sifting through the wreckage of Brasalara—um, my birth town. It was past evenmeal by the time I got to an inn, and I was starving. The owner gave me a free room and as much food as I could shovel down my throat. But that wasn't what I just saw." She met Lhyn's eyes. "In this vision, he said there was no food for me."

"No food for you?"

She nodded.

"Implying that there *was* food, but you couldn't have it."

They both looked at the *Resilere*, then at the gray block sitting on the floor beneath it.

"Is it because we used them in traps?" Rahel wondered.

"Maybe it thinks the block is out of reach. It hasn't moved off that control pad since you got here, has it?"

"No." She considered the distance, then sighed. "I have to try."

"Be careful."

"I notice you're not trying to talk me out of it."

"Would it do any good?"

"No." She checked to make sure her Enkara seawater was easily accessible, then rose up on her knees.

"Wait." Lhyn pulled yet another pad out of her sleeve pocket. "I'll hate to lose this, because I've customized it. But better that than your hand. Put the block on this and offer it."

"Good idea." Rahel accepted the pad and crawled slowly forward on her hands and knees.

The *Resilere* rumpled its skin, then got even bumpier as she approached closer than she had before.

No threat, she told it. *Helping.*

Keeping her movements slow and easy to follow, she held the pad level, set the block on it, and raised it up.

A small tube formed near the bottom of the *Resilere*'s body, the same thing she had seen on the footage of the fatal attack but in a different location. It swayed back and forth, then retracted.

Two arms rippled down and wrapped around her forearm before she could blink.

"Fuck, Rahel!"

"Don't." It hadn't hurt her yet. "Don't move, don't be afraid."

The arms elongated, sliding in coils around her forearm and the bare skin at her wrist. Given the way the *Resilere*'s skin shone, she had expected it to feel wet. But it was cool and dry, soft with an undertone of grit. Like sand under a sheet, she thought.

It tightened its hold and pulled, demonstrating an effortless strength. Rahel rested her other hand on her stave grip, not yet resisting and hoping she wouldn't have to.

A third arm looped down and felt around the edges of the pad. Then it touched the mineral block.

She was released so abruptly that she almost landed on her backside. The pad fell to the floor and the arms whipped back up, one of them forming a tight loop around the block. It curled inward to disappear under the *Resilere*'s body, and Rahel was—

Sitting at a table in the tavern, embarrassed by her filthy hands and the fact that she was so exhausted she hadn't even thought to clean them. But the food smelled so good and she was so starved—she was not about to wait.

The first bite exploded with flavor and she thought she might actually drool.

Rahel sat back on her heels and wiped the corner of her mouth, shocked to find she *had* drooled.

"Get away from there, please." Lhyn's tone was carefully controlled. "Soon?"

She reached for the pad.

"Leave it—Shippers," Lhyn said as Rahel picked it up. "Stubborn warrior!"

She crawled back and held it out. "You said it was customized."

"I also said it wasn't worth your hand!" Lhyn snatched the pad, anger and residual fear vying for dominance. Then she froze, her earlier emotions swept away by wonder. "Oh, my stars. *Look* at it!"

The *Resilere* was alight with bioluminescence, not just green this time, but also blue.

"Is it projecting?"

"Not right now," Rahel said. "But earlier—it was another memory. The same one as before, except the right ending this time. And one more thing. I was embarrassed in the memory because I was so dirty, but I couldn't take the time to wash my hands. The food was too important."

"This is *fascinating*," Lhyn breathed. "Embarrassment—that's an advanced emotion. You can't be embarrassed unless you have a defined set of behaviors that you consider acceptable."

"It was starving." Rahel was certain of that. "But it still wouldn't come down to the floor."

"Might be tactical." Captain Serrado spoke for the first time since they had begun. *"It might feel too vulnerable on the floor."*

"But it didn't have to come all the way to the floor to pick up the cube," Rahel said. "It could have come halfway down and been able to reach it."

"Maybe it's not a matter of wanting to move." That was Dr. Wells's voice. *"Maybe it's a matter of* whether *it can move."*

"What are you thinking, Doctor?" Serrado asked.

"We know they can survive out of water, but we don't know how long it's been for them. They might be at the end of their endurance. I'd like to try something. Zeppy, can you arrange for a tank of Enkara seawater? Something you can bring through the chases to my location?"

"I can do that," Zeppy answered. *"Give me five or ten."*

"As chief of security, I should point out that if they're at the end of their endurance, we have an easy solution to our problem." Cox cleared his throat. *"That said, it would be a damned shame if we let them die."*

"I'm shocked," Dr. Wells said. *"I didn't think you'd care."*

"I don't care for homicidal rampaging aliens. But based on what we've all seen? This is something for the record books."

"Don't make me reassess my opinion of you. It's too much work."

She sounded sarcastic and slightly amused, a combination unique to her. It made Rahel smile despite the sting of knowing she was only privy to this glimpse through their shared duty. She glanced at the door to her right. Dr. Wells stood behind it, barely a body length away, yet unseen and unreachable.

It was a perfect metaphor, Rahel decided.

She shifted into a cross-legged position, tired of being on her knees and confident that she wouldn't have to spring into action for at least a few minutes. Bracing her elbows on her legs, she rested her chin on her fists and watched the *Resilere* sparkle.

"Let's go over your projections while we wait." Lhyn matched her position, dictation pad in hand. "You told it I was your friend, not your mother. How did you do that?"

"Speaking of embarrassing," Rahel mumbled.

"Sorry." But she didn't look sorry. She looked like a child in a sweet shop, and Rahel couldn't help being affected by her enthusiasm.

"I thought about the first time you gave me a warmron," she said. "And how it meant so much because you did it in a public place."

They worked their way through the details of that and the subsequent projections, as well as checking Lhyn's notes regarding the memories. By the time they were all caught up, the *Resilere* had stopped sparkling.

"Should we offer another one?" Lhyn asked.

"Zeppy's almost here with the tank," Dr. Wells said. *"If that influences your decision."*

"Tank first," Rahel said. "If that's the issue, it's more important."

A minute later, Dr. Wells came back on the com. *"We have the tank right outside. Rahel, can you warn it somehow? Tell it something unthreatening is coming in?"*

"I'll try."

With careful movements, she unfolded her legs and stood upright. She didn't know how much her mental imagery mattered, but on the chance that it did, she pictured herself playing in Wildwind Bay, off Dock One where all the children learned to swim. She remembered diving in the water, the happiness of splashing about, the buoyancy, the *wet.*

The *Resilere* sent no answering memory. It merely exuded loss, the way it had when she first found it.

"I don't think that did what I intended," she said. "But it might accomplish the same thing."

She walked to the door, projecting *safe* and *protection* and thinking of Lhyn and warmrons. Then she tapped the lock pad.

Zeppy stood behind a transparent tank of water on a low, wheeled cart. It was narrow enough to fit in the chase, came up to her mid-thigh, and held enough water for three or four *Resilere*.

"That must have been fun to push through." She refused to look at Dr. Wells, who was right behind him with the tank's lid.

"Just another day on the job," he said with a quick grin.

She backed up, keeping one eye on the *Resilere* and another on the progress of the tank, until it was fully on the landing. Zeppy was wildly curious about the *Resilere* but only glanced at it once while stepping back to the door.

"Good luck," he said.

The door slid shut.

"Now what?" Lhyn looked from the tank to the *Resilere*, which was ruffled with curiosity. "Splash it?"

"Not a bad idea." Rahel moved so that the tank was between her and the *Resilere*. Then she pulled up one sleeve, put her hand in the cold water, and splashed noisily.

The *Resilere* puffed itself up, four arms rippling out on the wall, but remained in place.

"Hm. Let's try a little wave splash." She cupped her hand and threw the water.

It jerked as the drops hit, shrinking its arms. Then they elongated again and two more joined them, all writhing along the wall. It looked frightening, but Rahel felt no threat. "It's wondering," she said. "Tempted, but reluctant to move."

She splashed it again.

With a suddenness that surprised a squeak from Lhyn, the *Resilere* dropped to the floor and flowed toward the tank. Its arms reached up, examining the smooth sides and the cart's wheels.

Rahel swooshed a small wave of water over the edge, thoroughly drenching the *Resilere*. It drew back slightly, then shimmied up the side of the tank and plopped into the water.

She staggered backward into the railing, stunned by the rush of emotion swamping her brain. She was—

Standing by the windows in Lanaril's study, looking at Salomen with joy in her heart and tears in her eyes. In a handful of words, Salomen had removed the threat of prison and offered her greatest dreams instead, with no thought of repayment. She was friend, savior, Bondlancer, and the vessel of Fahla all rolled into one, and Rahel had no words to express her gratitude.

"If you knew how much I want to give you a warmron right now," she said.

She came back to herself with Lhyn holding her arm and looking worried.

"You nearly went over the railing. What the Hades happened?"

"Oh, Fahla. I can't describe that. Joy, desperate relief, elation, gratitude..." She offered a tremulous smile. "We did the right thing."

The *Resilere*, which had been exploring the confines of its tank, now sank to the bottom and spread out. Its arms reached into every corner and its body pulsed, swelling and shrinking with a regularity that made Rahel think of a heartbeat. Blue and green bioluminescence danced over its skin.

"What was the memory?" Lhyn asked.

Why did they all have to be so damned personal?

"It was the day Salomen told me I wasn't—being punished." She had almost said *going to prison* but stopped herself in time. "And that she had arranged for me to come here, to be Alsea's first space explorer. I went from thinking my life was going straight down the toilet hole to thinking no one on Alsea could be as lucky as me. I didn't know how to tell her how much that meant to me."

She would not speak of Salomen's acceptance of the warmron on this public record. It was one thing to flout the taboo herself; she had never feared the social consequences. Revealing that Alsea's Bondlancer had also broken that taboo had a whole different level of consequences. But she didn't think it was a coincidence that the memory had included her offer.

"My stars, look at it. I can't speak its light language, but even I can see it's happy."

"Well done," Captain Serrado said. *"If this is a negotiation, we've surely proved we're here in good faith."*

A surge of determination and hope hit Rahel's senses at the same time that the *Resilere* exploded up and out of the water. It rippled down the side of the tank and back to the wall, its movements noticeably smoother than before.

"It's leaving?" Lhyn was wide-eyed.

"I don't think so." Rahel watched it flow up the wall. "I think it—shekking Mother!"

The *Resilere* had gone straight up to the joint between the wall and the landing above and was now tugging at a *second* one that neither of them had noticed. It had blended in perfectly with the shadows and the joint.

And it wasn't moving.

The first *Resilere* tugged harder, and with a crackling, ripping sound, they both fell to the floor.

"Ouch," Lhyn whispered.

The second *Resilere* seemed to be in a solid state, frozen in the shape of the crease it had tucked itself into. There was a right angle to its body, and the first was having a difficult time moving it.

She knelt on the foaming boards of Dock One, a breath away from drowning as a storm-lashed wave rose and crashed over her. With all her strength she clung to the boards, refusing to die, and the water drained away.

A fish was left behind, flopping desperately on the hard wood.

Rahel was moving before the last wisps of memory faded. In three steps she reached the struggling *Resilere*.

"Rahel—"

"It asked for help." She scooped up the frozen *Resilere*, which was surprisingly heavy and bore no resemblance in texture to the first. This wasn't sand under a sheet, it was sand packed into a shape and left to dry.

The first *Resilere* kept pace with her as she turned for the tank, then raced ahead and rippled up its side. It waited atop the edge, half its arms in the water and half out, until Rahel reached the tank and plunged her precious burden beneath the surface. The water soaked her uniform jacket all the way to the shoulders.

The first *Resilere* dove to the bottom of the tank and began gently tapping its arms on the second. Rahel let go and withdrew, dripping water.

"There goes my professional objectivity," Lhyn said. "I'm about ready to cry. Do you think it'll be all right?"

"I know the first one hasn't given up hope." Rahel stripped off her jacket and laid it over the railing. "And I know why it refused to move."

"Shippers, you're right. Of course! That's what it was doing all along, protecting its . . . friend? Mate?"

She shrugged. "I hope we find out."

"I do, too," Captain Serrado said.

"I think that holds for all of us. Even Commander Cox."

"Thank you, Dr. Wells," Cox said. *"Though I firmly deny any moisture in my eyes."*

"How did you know it asked for help?"

Rahel didn't look away from the two *Resilere* as she described the memory of the fish on Dock One.

"You saved the fish," Lhyn said when she was done. "Let's take that as a good omen."

"Lhyn, can you pull your cam and set it up near the tank?" Captain Serrado asked.

"Sure thing." Lhyn trotted over to retrieve her cam from the wall. She radiated urgency as she reattached it to the cart, moving swiftly to keep from losing any visual record of what was happening in the tank.

As it turned out, she could have taken her time. For ten long minutes Rahel saw no change in the frozen *Resilere*, nor did she sense a second emotional presence. The first never ceased its stroking and never lost hope. Then, for no reason that she could discern, it erupted into a flashing pattern of bioluminescence. The greenish lights chased each other around its body and then turned blue. Those lights followed the same pattern, but when it was completed, the next pattern was not green again but a new color: red.

One of the frozen arms of the second *Resilere* twitched at its very tip.

"We're seeing signs of recovery," Lhyn said for the benefit of the record. "A small amount of movement at the tip of one arm, but that's more than we saw before. And the first *Resilere* is putting on one Hades of a light show. It's just added red to the repertoire."

Within a minute, all ten arm tips of the frozen *Resilere* were twitching. Gradually it continued to soften, the arms flexing along more of their length, until the sharp corner on its body abruptly fluffed into a more natural, rounded shape.

"I still can't sense it," Rahel said. "The body is recovering, but the emotional presence isn't there yet."

"Like coming out of a coma," Dr. Wells said. *"The mind often lags*

behind the body, especially after significant physical trauma. I'd guess losing so much water that you solidify would count."

Rahel had to remind herself that Dr. Wells wasn't talking to her. She was simply putting her thoughts on the record.

Every five minutes, Lhyn made another verbal notation on the status of both *Resilere.* Shortly after the fifth update, Rahel felt a new emotional presence nibbling at the edges of her senses.

"It's regaining consciousness," she said.

The first *Resilere* sped up its light show to a dizzying pace.

Two minutes later, the second *Resilere* lifted itself up and began touching the first. Rahel smiled as she soaked in its amazement and joyful surprise.

"It didn't think it would live," she said. "It's startled to find itself still alive. Startled and happy."

The first wrapped itself entirely around the second, and Rahel—

Was wrapped in a warmron with Salomen, an unbelievable gift on top of all the others. "Thank you," she said into Salomen's shoulder. "For being my friend, for giving me my dreams . . . for being you."

She blinked away the moisture in her eyes, then crouched down and pressed her palm against the side of the tank.

Without hesitation, the first *Resilere* released one arm from its partner and matched the gesture, its skin flat against the clear tank material and sparkling with blue lights.

"You're welcome," Rahel said.

28

TRANSLATION

Feeding the *Resilere* was much easier when they were in the tank. Rahel simply dropped two mineral cubes in the water and sat down to watch them eat—which really meant watching them sparkle with bioluminescent patterns while consumption went on invisibly beneath their bodies.

The most startling thing about getting them in water was the sudden appearance of eyes, which emerged on hand-high stalks from a central point atop their bodies. The flexible stalks twisted this way and that, offering what looked like perfect vision in all directions. The eyes had a violet reflective sheen and two vertical pupils. Rahel thought they were rather cute, though she chose not to put that on the record. Commander Jalta theorized that the *Resilere* protected their eyes inside their bodies while exposed to air but could still see, just with a more limited field of view. *"It makes sense when you think about the radiation exposure above water,"* she added. *"And they probably don't have the same need for wide visual range on dry land. There aren't many land species on Enkara. That means less predation."*

"Good reason to lay eggs above water, too," Rahel said.

They no longer had any way to tell the two *Resilere* apart physically, but one consistently swiveled an eye stalk to follow Rahel's movements while keeping the other on its partner. The confirmation that this was their original acquaintance occurred when they dropped in two more mineral cubes. The *Resilere* watching her ignored the cubes. The other snatched one up.

"Two cubes from starvation to satiation," Lhyn observed. "You cook up an excellent meal, Dr. Wells."

"Believe me, I'm adding that to my Fleet record."

Shortly after the tank was occupied, Lhyn had requested a hydrophone and a waterproof speaker, which Rahel had carefully placed on opposite ends of the tank. While the *Resilere* were busy eating, Lhyn was busy correlating sound and bioluminescence patterns with words and concepts, both from current activities and the interactions she had recorded earlier.

"I think they speak a richer language with light than with sound," she concluded. "It would take a long time and a team of empaths to figure it out. But we've already got a few valuable words. If I'm right, we can say *mother, friend, food,* and *help me*—though it might be *help us.* And *mother* might actually be *parent.* We can also say *not for me*, but there was an element of exhaustion and hopelessness attached to that, so I can't tease it out without more data." She pulled up a separate screen. "We've got a lot more in terms of conceptual translations. They understand and can convey wariness, curiosity, embarrassment, surprise, loss, and gratitude. Then there are the combinations. When you splashed Rez—"

"Rez?"

"I'm not going to keep calling it 'the first *Resilere.*' Don't worry, when I write up the article I'll use proper terminology."

Rahel hid a smile. "I wasn't worried. Rez is . . . nice."

Lhyn gave her a narrow-eyed look. "Nice. Right." She glanced at the feeding *Resilere*, her expression softening, then went back to her notes. "So, you splashed Rez, and we got a combination of temptation and reluctance. When it went in the water, we had a whole bucket of concepts: joy, relief, elation, gratitude, and you said later there was a sense of salvation. And we had another bucket when you helped with Rez-Two." She looked up, clearly waiting for the comment.

Rahel held up her hands. "I'm not saying anything. Rez-Two is a good, strong name. I might name my own child that."

Lhyn chuckled. "Alsean culture will never be the same. Anyway, we have hope, determination, desperation . . . and the same things when

Rez left the tank to get its partner. I can't tease them apart yet. When Rez-Two recovered, we had amazement and surprise, and I'd guess there's a concept of life and death in there, but that's too far out of reach right now. And my stars, what Rez was saying when it was stroking Rez-Two! I see so many recognizable patterns, plus a whole lot more I can't make heads or tails of. It was talking nonstop, along with that light show."

"The way I'd talk to a loved one I was trying to bring out of a coma?"

"Possibly? We can't make assumptions based on our own frame of reference. There may have been a real physiological connection going on there. It might be that the sounds and lights and empathic projections all tie together to create something else. Something bigger, that we have no way of understanding because our brains don't work that way."

Rahel thought she understood. "You mean like empathic healing."

"Among other possibilities, yes."

They watched the tank, where Rez-Two had picked up the remaining mineral cube and was tucking it under its body.

"Make that three cubes from starvation to satiation," Rahel said. "I guess Rez was just very, very hungry. Rez-Two was beyond that."

"They certainly don't function like us," Dr. Wells said. *"After starving like that, a Gaian would have to reintroduce food carefully. Too much would shock the system."*

"That's true of mammals in general," Jalta interjected. *"But not exothermic species. Dr. Rivers, I've located the video footage of the* Resilere *on Enkara guiding their hatchlings to water. Would that be useful to you?"*

"Yes, it would!"

"It's on your pad. Video only, no sound."

Lhyn flipped through a few screens and pulled up the footage. They waited until Rez-Two finished eating and had rejected a fourth cube, at which point both aliens were producing the same sound pattern. Rahel's corresponding memory was a flash of lying on the couch, her head in Sharro's lap. It carried little emotional weight, unlike many of their earlier interactions.

"Comfort," she told Lhyn, and described the memory.

"Good, we can add that to the word list. And it's an excellent starting point for making inquiries. I'm going to replay the sound pattern for curiosity." Lhyn tapped her pad.

Both *Resilere* ruffled up their skins, focusing all four eye stalks on Rahel.

"That has resulted in the body language I previously associated with curiosity," Lhyn said for the record. "Both *Resilere* are paying attention. Let's see if we can answer our earlier question. I'm going to play the word for friend."

Rahel waited. A moment later both *Resilere* lit up with green bioluminescence, and she was taken through a flurry of memories: giving Mouse a double palm touch on her sixteenth birth anniversary, laughing with Salomen by the waterfall, watching her mother and Sharro at their bonding ceremony in Whitesun Temple.

"Huh. That was . . . confusing."

"What did you see?"

"Nothing consistent."

Lhyn listened to the descriptions with intense interest. "Not consistent for us," she said. "We draw a distinction between friend and partner. They might not. But they've definitively agreed that they're very important to each other." She turned the virtual display on her pad and held it against the wall of the tank. "I'm going to play the word for curiosity, then mother or parent, and then show them the video."

As expected, the two *Resilere* rumpled up attentively. But when the video began to play, their skins went smooth and flat before erupting into a dizzying display of red bioluminescence. It looked different than the pattern Rez had played for Rez-Two, Rahel thought. More discordant, as if—

She was standing in front of three burning pyres, on a field filled with two hundred and eight more. The air was wavy with heat and loud with the crackling of flames.

"I stayed," her mother said, staring at the pyres of her other two children. "I helped them, and I kept building that future . . . and look at it now. Gone." The tears rolled down her face, and when Sharro pulled her into a warmron, she let out a sob that broke Rahel's heart.

"Oh, Fahla," she croaked. She could still smell the burning wood. "They're parents. They've lost their children."

Lhyn stopped the playback immediately, her horror matching Rahel's. She dropped the pad and rubbed her face, then lifted her head with a haunted expression. "How do we say we're sorry?"

"I can try." Rahel projected her regret and sympathy, and received a faint answering memory of apologizing to Mouse after a fight. It was as if the *Resilere* were too emotionally taxed to respond with any strength. But they were calming, and their light patterns were slowing. "I think they understand."

"They probably already knew we felt terrible." Lhyn glanced over at the frequency analyzer and shook her head. "There's the pattern for loss. Do you think the other ten that we saw in the shuttle bay footage were their children?"

"If that's the case, they were adult children," Dr. Wells said. *"At least, judging by size."*

"I doubt it." Commander Jalta sounded thoughtful. *"I think they might have solved a mystery I've been wondering about. Has anyone else questioned why they didn't leave the teracite while it was being mined? They must have felt it happening."*

Rahel and Lhyn stared at each other in dawning realization.

"You think there are eggs in that teracite," Commander Cox said. *"Then why would they abandon them now?"*

"Maybe they already hatched, and the young died of desiccation," Dr. Wells said.

Rahel heard her mother's words again, describing the devastation of her losses in terms of both family and future.

"They had no future," she said slowly.

"What do you mean?" Lhyn asked.

"Even if the eggs haven't hatched, they had no future. The *Resilere* are intelligent. They're communicating with us over an impossible language barrier. And they're empathic. They would have known there was no life left on that ship. Not until our mission team arrived."

"Are you saying they took a chance attaching to our shuttle in the hopes of saving their own future?" Captain Serrado's doubt was evident in her voice.

"Is that any less believable than what we've already seen?"

"It doesn't seem unreasonable, Captain." Zeppy spoke up. *"Based on the damage we saw, and the captain's logs, the* Resilere *were all over that ship. We thought they were looking for food, but what if they were really looking for water? It could be as simple as hoping they'd find water somewhere else."*

"He's right." Jalta sounded excited. *"I don't know of any species where the*

parents will voluntarily die with their children. It's a genetic imperative to survive, to try for another generation."

"We've had four floods on different decks from punctured water reclamation pipes. I thought it was random damage, but they're looking for water here, too."

"But fresh water doesn't help," Jalta said. *"They need Enkara seawater. Fresh water would be like putting us in a room full of carbon dioxide and expecting us to breathe."*

There was a long silence on the com before Captain Serrado spoke.

"Well, if there are unhatched eggs in that teracite, then we might have a way to bring our Resilere *out of hiding."*

29

LOGISTICS

Ekatya didn't often have a section chief meeting in the middle of a corridor, but she didn't want to get too far from Lhyn and Rahel. Nor did she want to pull Dr. Wells out of range of an immediate response. Instead, she picked up Cox outside her chase and took him down one deck to meet Wells, Jalta, and Zeppy at their chase entrance.

"I can't recommend this, Captain." Cox held up his hands when Dr. Wells shot him a poisonous look. "I understand the desire, I really do, but we've had a hard enough time with twelve of these. What if those eggs are viable and they hatch? We could have a few hundred little *Resilere* running around who don't know we're not food."

"They don't feed on us by choice," Jalta said patiently. "Sayana proved that. The *Resilere* had a good grip on her and let her go. It wanted the mineral block."

"But it's not just us at risk, is it? It's also the ship."

"Have to say I'm cringing at the idea of a hundred small versions of these chewing through power cables. And babies tend to be voracious." Zeppy pursed his lips. "But we could minimize the risk by putting the teracite in acid-proof containers. If the eggs do hatch, the babies wouldn't get out."

Wells crossed her arms over her chest and looked thunderous. "You'd trap them without food or water?"

"No, of course not—"

"I don't want the *Resilere* to die," Cox interrupted. "It's obvious they're very advanced. But we have to consider the safety of our people as well. If we save the adults, we've saved the next generation and minimized the danger to this ship."

"Isn't it a matter of preferred environments?" Jalta asked. "If we provide food and a seawater tank for the hatchlings, why would they go anywhere else?"

"That does make sense," Ekatya said.

"It's still a risk—"

Cox got no further before Wells turned on him.

"These are *parents*," she said furiously. "Parents whose emotional response to losing their children is so strong that Rahel couldn't control her voice. Stop thinking like a self-important asshead and start thinking like someone with a damned heart."

"Dr. Wells," Ekatya tried, but Wells mowed right over her.

"That cargo crew destroyed an entire population. This is the equivalent of us finding out that the Voloth landed on a settled planet, shot up a village, and flew off with prisoners, including children. We have an *obligation* to save them, but you think saving babies is too great a risk!"

Cox turned red. "You are drawing insulting and *irrational*—"

"That's enough!" Ekatya shouted.

They went silent.

"Commander Cox, I agree with you about the risks." She held up a hand, stopping Wells before she could speak. "That said, I believe they can be minimized. Zeppy, print up the appropriate containers, something we can slide those packing crates into. Then we need a place where we can set up an environment for the eggs and their parents."

Zeppy snapped his fingers. "Water is the key, right? And space. We could use hydroponics. That's the best place on the ship for handling water flow, and there's plenty of room. We could move the plants and reprogram the rain cycle for one zone so it rains Enkara seawater."

"That's a great idea," Jalta said enthusiastically. "It might even attract the adult *Resilere* without us trying to round them up. If they've been looking for their seawater, why not provide it?"

"Call Shigeo and tell him what we need," Ekatya told Zeppy. "He can get started moving plants while you print up the transport containers and get them to the shuttle bay. Then take a team down and set up the environment. Make it so we can seal it off remotely if we end up with hatchlings trying to climb out. Commander Cox, get us that teracite and take it to hydroponics. We'll move these two *Resilere* there and start calling for the others. I trust Lhyn and Rahel to figure out a message."

"What if I get to the *Tutnuken* and find a pile of dead hatchlings?" Cox asked.

"Then leave the teracite and come back. I don't think we'd have anything to gain by showing the *Resilere* their dead hatchlings."

"You need me," Jalta said. "I can determine the viability of the eggs. No point in bringing them if the embryos didn't survive."

Ekatya nodded. "Agreed. Any other comments or questions?"

They stood silent.

"Good, dismissed. Dr. Wells, a moment?"

As the others moved off, she stepped inside the chase and waited for the door to close behind Wells. "What the Hades was that? It's one thing to have an opinion, but that was a personal attack."

"He's running risk assessment calculations on parents and children! That is—"

"His job," Ekatya interrupted. "If he weren't thinking in terms of minimizing risk, I'd be looking for a new chief of security. I *expect* him to stay above the emotional level, just like I expect you to operate from a position of compassion. Your duties put you at opposition sometimes, but that's no reason to insult him."

Dr. Wells started to respond, then closed her mouth and slumped against the door. "Don't tell me I have to apologize to him. I really don't think I can."

Ekatya studied her. "Are you all right?"

Wells dropped her head back. "I don't know. This situation . . ." She lightly thunked her head against the door, then raised it and met Ekatya's concerned gaze. "Can I just say that I've had some old issues unburied over the last few weeks?"

"Does it affect your decision-making capacity?"

"Other than wanting to take Cox's head off? No." She paused. "It has to do with that story I said I'd tell you."

"I take it now isn't a good time for it."

She shook her head.

"All right. But when this is over, I'm coming to your quarters and we're going to share a bottle of iceflame. You can get roaring drunk and tell me your story."

Wells offered a weak smile. "I'll bring an injector of kastrophenol."

"Make it enough for two doses. After the week I've had, I'm ready to drown in that bottle with you."

"It's a deal." She gave a sharp nod, then sidled past and set off down the narrow chase.

Ekatya watched her with a frown. "Right," she said under her breath. "Now for Cox."

30

POOL PARTY

Captain Serrado put everything in motion.

Rahel sat with Lhyn and two *Resilere* in their throbbing, humming brace shaft and imagined the scurrying. Commanders Cox and Jalta were winging through space to board the cargo ship and look for viable eggs, Commander Shigeo and his botanists were rearranging part of the hydroponics bay to create a small slice of Enkara, and Commander Zeppy was working with his staff to put together the infrastructure.

She glanced at the tank with its healthy *Resilere* and added a few more names to her mental list. Dr. Wells created the mineral blocks, had this tank brought here, and was the first to look past the horrifying footage of Murray's death and postulate that the *Resilere* were not rapacious predators. Lhyn had already learned enough of their language to help deduce the possible existence of eggs on that cargo ship, and it was her work with Rahel that had helped save these two.

Of course, none of it would have happened had Captain Serrado not trusted Rahel's instincts and given the full support of this ship's resources.

So often, Dr. Wells had tried to tell her that she was part of a team. Rahel had accepted it intellectually, but she hadn't truly understood until now. She might be the primary liaison for the *Resilere*, but she couldn't have done any of this on her own.

She was startled from her musings by a memory of Mouse and a sense of anticipation from the *Resilere.*

"They're excited about something," Lhyn said. "Bioluminescence is way up and I'm getting the *friend* sound pattern. And something similar to the *help me*. Maybe just *help*?"

The words were barely out of her mouth when Rez launched itself out of the tank, flowed over to the wall directly behind the ladder, and headed down. As it vanished from sight, Rahel caught a brief visual of the fish flopping on Dock One.

"I'm going after Rez," she said. "It's asked for help again."

It was possibly the most surreal moment of her life, climbing down a brace shaft ladder while a ten-armed alien led the way. Within four rungs she realized Rez was moving much too quickly, so she pressed her boots against the outsides of the ladder rails and slid.

They passed the landings on decks ten, eleven, twelve, and thirteen before she picked up the emotional signatures.

"There are other *Resilere* nearby," she said. "At least two, possibly more."

Midway between decks fifteen and sixteen, Rez abruptly changed direction and rippled horizontally along the wall, passing beyond the landing to the open shaft beyond. It stopped next to one of the conduits that ran the length of the brace shaft—and the melted hole right beside it.

Rahel descended to the landing and leaned over the railing while reporting her location and the hole, as well as her increased sense of what she now thought were three additional *Resilere.*

"We can be sure that their empathic range is better than mine," she added. "Rez felt them from at least six decks away. I didn't pick up on them until we were two decks away. Hold, there's one coming out now."

Rez was already touching the arms that were reaching through the hole. It continued to touch, flashing a pattern of lights that included all three colors, and soon the other *Resilere* pulled itself through the opening and onto the wall.

"You should be seeing this, Lhyn. They're touching each other and playing the same bioluminescent pattern."

"Don't rub it in that I'm not there. I'll see the cam footage later. But I can tell you that they're talking a Hades of a lot. Their sounds carry."

"Are Rez's eye stalks tucked in?" Dr. Wells asked.

Rahel hadn't had a chance to notice. "Yes," she said after a closer look.

"That seems to prove Jalta's theory, then. Rez is well hydrated but still protecting its eyestalks out of water."

Another set of arms appeared in the hole.

"Here comes the second one . . . and it's out. That was fast. They're all lit up with the same patterns. I think it's a greeting."

"You think, or you're sensing it?" Lhyn wanted to know.

"Both."

"Excellent," she said happily. *"I'll add it to the vocabulary list."*

"There's the third. It's moving much more slowly. Oh, this is hard to watch," Rahel said when it painfully pulled its body through. "It looks almost as bad as Rez-Two did. It's mobile, but barely."

The third one moved in hitches and starts, clearly in distress and unable to keep all ten arms on the wall at the same time. One arm would slip free and dangle, then be pulled up only for another one to slip. Slowly, it followed Rez and the other two toward the landing.

"Wait! There's a *fourth* one!"

It had popped out of the hole much more smoothly, and Rahel had the feeling it had done exactly what she would do: bring up the rear to make sure a disabled friend didn't get left behind.

The five *Resilere* came toward her, moving at the pace of their slowest member. When at last they reached a position over the landing, the disabled one let go of the wall and dropped to the deck with a thud.

Rahel tightened her grip on the railing as the memory of the fish on Dock One hit with far more intensity. There was no doubt in her mind that Rez was asking her to help, but this *Resilere* didn't know her and was most likely starved. And how was she going to carry it up seven decks' worth of ladder?

"Rez wants me to help the dried-out one," she reported. "I don't know how to do that safely."

"I have an idea. I can bring my pack down. If you can talk the Resilere *into getting inside, you can carry it up on your back."*

"I'm not liking this idea," Captain Serrado said. *"But I don't see an easy alternative that doesn't involve us somehow telling them to stay put while we bring in another tank. Zeppy's in hydroponics; it would take him at least fifteen minutes to print one up and get it there."*

"I don't have that kind of vocabulary yet."

"And I don't think they'll wait," Rahel added. "The other four are swarming around the ladder and they're upset."

Rez sent another memory of the fish.

"Rez asked for help again. Captain, I don't know how we can possibly tell them that we're willing to help, but they have to wait. I think we might lose some of the good faith we've earned. I'm prepared to take the risk."

After a short pause, Captain Serrado's voice came on again. *"Lhyn, take your pack down. I don't want you on that landing, though. Hand it through the ladder access."*

"Got it."

Not wanting the *Resilere* to get any more stressed, Rahel moved toward the injured one. Immediately the distress emanating from the others lessened.

"I'm feeling better about it now," she said. "I'm right next to the dried *Resilere* and the others are fine with it. I think Rez told them I'm a friend. But it would be good if you could move quickly, Lhyn."

"As quickly as I can."

Rahel crouched next to the grounded *Resilere*, projecting *safe* and *protect*. Unable to resist, she reached out and touched an arm with a single fingertip.

"You're in bad shape," she said softly. "But not as bad as Rez-Two, and it's fine now. We'll take care of you."

The *Resilere* did not pull back, instead feebly twitching the end of its arm.

Lhyn's boots thudded on the ladder, the slight delay between steps telling Rahel that she was skipping rungs. With her long legs, she could do it.

Rahel stayed in contact until she knew Lhyn was close. Then she carefully stood and stepped back, to the clear dismay of the others.

Helping, she told them, and they settled down.

She caught the pack as Lhyn dangled it through, then took it to the *Resilere* and opened it as far as it would go. Fortunately, the front flap came mostly free, leaving the pack wide open.

"Time to see if this works," she said. Turning her head to the side in case the *Resilere* got ideas about flinging goo, she slid her hands beneath its body.

It twitched but made no aggressive movements.

She shifted it onto the pack, then slowly moved its arms upward.

It resisted.

She stopped and projected *safe* and *protect,* then imagined herself giving Lhyn a warmron for good measure.

The memory of the fish on Dock One exploded in her mind, startling her into looking directly at the *Resilere.* This time, when she moved its arms, it did not resist.

"It just used the same fish memory that Rez did," she said as she slowly maneuvered it into position. "Incredibly strong through skin contact."

"Wow." Lhyn's voice came from right overhead; she was leaning over the railing. "So either your brain interprets *help me* in the same way every time, or Rez actually saw that memory and shared it."

She expected the worst when it was time to pull up the seal on both sides of the pack. How could she communicate that she wasn't trapping the *Resilere* but making it safe for the journey?

To her surprise, not only did it not put up a fight, it sent the memory of her lying on Sharro's couch. Then it pulled in its arms and settled into the bottom of the pack.

"I think they *like* being in cozy places," she said. "It's feeling more comfortable."

"That's very good news," Captain Serrado said.

"Shippers, yes," Lhyn agreed. "Because I sure didn't have the words to explain."

"I'll tell Zeppy to add a few hiding places to our little bit of Enkara paradise."

Rahel continued sealing the pack until it was three-quarters closed, then projected *safe* with all her might while going through the difficult contortions of getting her arms through the straps without jostling her cargo. At last she stood and moved toward the ladder.

"Get going, Lhyn," she said. "I don't know how fast the others will move."

"I'm on it."

As soon as she began climbing, one of the *Resilere* streaked behind the ladder and headed upward with her. She thought it must be Rez, judging by its proximity and ease of movement. The others came behind a little more cautiously.

Rung by rung, moving as smoothly as she could, she made her way up. Lhyn stayed two decks above, though she kept pausing to look over her shoulder and grin at the procession.

After what felt like the longest ladder climb she had ever done, Rahel reached deck nine and breathed a sigh of relief. Rez was already waiting on the tank's edge, while Rez-Two was plastered against the side nearest Rahel, both eye stalks swiveled forward. Lhyn stood against the far wall of the landing.

The other three *Resilere* came through the ladder access and burst into excited bioluminescence, swamping Rahel with their hope and eager expectation. The one in her pack began wriggling.

"Wait," she said, easing herself out of the straps. "Just a little farther."

She set the pack on the deck and unsealed it, but before she could lift the *Resilere*, it moved off in its halting, stuttering way and began climbing the wall of the tank. Halfway up, it slipped and fell.

Rahel had expected that and caught it before it could go far. "See, this is why I told you to wait."

"You sound like a mother," Lhyn commented. Her eyes were bright, and she was exuding a complicated mixture of sympathy and joy—without a trace of claustrophobia.

Rahel helped the disabled *Resilere* up, letting it do some of the work. Rez was touching it in what felt like encouragement, and Rez-Two was reaching up from below.

The *Resilere* tipped over the edge, plopped into the water, and sparkled with brilliant patterns of blue and green bioluminescence. Rahel held on to the tank, lost again in the vivid memory of Salomen saving her.

When she came back to her senses, the other *Resilere* had left the wall and were swarming across the floor. She moved back to give them room and watched all three ripple up the tank sides and dive in. The exaltation was so strong that she could almost see it, a cloud of joy rising above the water.

Lhyn stepped up next to her, smiling at the heaving mass of happy *Resilere*.

"We're going to need a bigger tank," she said.

31

SEARCH AND RESCUE

Dr. Wells had to resupply them with mineral blocks after the new *Resilere* went through the remainder of Lhyn's stock. In the meantime, Zeppy sent one of his staff over with a second tank, complete with hydrophone and cam. It arrived at the door on the opposite side of the landing as the first.

Five *Resilere* in one tank had left them little room to move, and Rez hadn't even tried to join them. But the moment the second tank was in place, Rez jumped in, launching off the edge of the first and landing with a splash big enough to spray Rahel's shirt.

"Thanks," she said. "At this rate I'm not going to have a dry piece of clothing left."

"It's for a good cause." Lhyn didn't try to hide her grin.

"Says the dry person."

One of the others struggled up from the bottom of the pile, sending bodies sliding in all directions as they rearranged. It was slower and more careful, climbing up to the edge and stretching its arms across to the second tank. Only when it had five arms securely attached to each tank did it let go and hop over the space, slipping quickly into the water. It was already touching Rez before it reached the bottom, their bodies glittering with matching patterns of bioluminescence.

"It must be Rez-Two. It didn't want to be separated." Lhyn checked her frequency analyzer. "That's the greeting pattern, along with a few other things."

They looked at the remaining four, none of whom showed any inclination to switch tanks. "Think any will move?" Rahel asked. "They could go three and three and have more space."

"I'm beginning to suspect that the original twelve were six pairs."

"Six breeding pairs, it seems," Captain Serrado interrupted. *"We just got word from Commander Jalta. The teracite is full of viable eggs. She says they blend in perfectly, even under UV light."*

"How many?" Lhyn flashed a delighted grin at Rahel, who couldn't help responding in kind.

"They're still counting. More than fifty so far, with another crate to go. They'll be back within the hour, and Zeppy and Shigeo promise to have the environment finished by then. Can you two hold tight until it's time to move these six?"

"Sure. Can you send in some appropriate beverages while we keep the expectant parents company?"

"Let's hold off on the celebration until we're sure there's a reason for it."

"Do they suck all the fun out of Fleet officers in command training?"

"I'm not answering that," Serrado said, but Rahel could hear the smile in her voice.

"Hold tight?" she repeated.

"Wait patiently. Usually in a situation where it's hard to do."

"You have strange idioms."

"Idioms are what make a language fun. You Alseans use 'hot as a black rock on a summer day' to mean sexually aroused. What the Hades does a hot black rock have to do with joining?"

She had to laugh. "I've seen hot rocks used in massage at my old pleasure house . . ."

"Probably not the source of the idiom, but thank you for the data point." Lhyn sobered as she turned back to the tanks. "Dr. Wells?"

"Still here."

"Doesn't it surprise you that the eggs are viable? Commander Jalta said the hatching was tied to the tide cycle, but if the *Resilere* were solidifying, shouldn't that mean the eggs were past hatching time?"

"We've been theorizing about that. Maybe the Resilere *go into a kind of*

dormancy while their eggs develop, but the mining disturbed that and they ran out the clock early. If they do stay awake, we know from the research footage that they don't leave their eggs for the duration. But these Resilere *have been running all over two ships. That might have used up their internal water supply as well. It's also possible that the trip through vacuum was harder on them than we thought."*

Lhyn crossed her arms and scowled. "That cargo crew deserved what they got."

"They tempted fate and Fahla." Rahel got no further before Rez burst out of the tank again and streaked for the ladder, leaving the flopping fish memory in its wake. "I think we've got more coming in."

This time she took Lhyn's pack with her. Rez stopped at the same hole as before, lighting up in greeting as the first set of arms appeared. Two *Resilere* emerged in quick succession, followed by a third moving more slowly, then a fourth and fifth.

"I wonder if they were using this brace shaft as the equivalent of a lift," Captain Serrado said when Rahel reported the numbers. *"Since they're all returning to it."*

"I think Rez might be calling them in." Rahel watched the bioluminescence dance over their bodies.

"But I'm not getting a consistent sound pattern for that," Lhyn said. *"And it wouldn't travel that far anyway. Not in air."*

"You won't get a sound pattern if Rez is using telepathy." Rahel frowned at the wall full of *Resilere*. "Where's the last one?"

"It's not there?"

"No, and none of the others are acting like they're waiting for it."

The six *Resilere* stopped milling about and began moving—all except one, which remained by the opening. The sense of loss it exuded was all too familiar.

"They're coming your way. I'm pretty sure Rez is leading them up, but there's one left behind. If you feel safe with more *Resilere* coming in, I'll stay here and see what it does."

"I think we've proven that I'm safe with them. Besides, I have a bag full of fresh, yummy mineral blocks."

The lone *Resilere* never moved, and it seemed to take forever before Lhyn reported the arrival of the others.

"We're officially out of space again. Rez went straight for the second tank

and led two friends to it. The other two went in the first tank. I'm dropping in mineral blocks now."

Rahel pictured it in her head. "So we have four in one and six in the other?"

"Three in one. Rez stayed out. In fact . . . there it goes. It's coming down."

Rez arrived in a rush of rippling arms, going directly to the other *Resilere* and touching it before returning to a spot over the landing.

"I'm getting the call for help," Rahel said when the flopping fish appeared in her mind. "But I'm not sure—wait."

Rez moved over to the hole, then back to the railing. Then to the hole.

"Oh, no. I can't—Rez wants me to follow it again. Into the hole. How do I explain I can't do that?"

"Well, we have the not for me *sound, which might actually mean* I can't, *but I'd hate to make that mistake."*

"Too bad you can't tell Rez to carry a com," Captain Serrado said. *"Then we could track it."*

"Huh." Lhyn drew out the single syllable.

"I recognize that sound. That's your big brain whirring. What are you thinking?"

"I'm thinking we might be able to do that. Rahel, I'm coming down."

Lhyn's descent was even faster this time. She joined Rahel at the railing, pulling a speaker from one jacket pocket and her pad from another. "Right, here's what I think. We can play a greeting and a sound pattern for loss. Which could also mean lost. And Rez is extremely intelligent. So let's show it what we mean. For the record, this is Dr. Lhyn Rivers signing off."

"What?" Serrado burst out. *"Lhyn, what are you doing?"*

"Giving Rahel my com so she can give it to Rez. I can get another one from you."

"Wait," Rahel said. "You're not coming with us?"

Lhyn shook her head.

"But—you'll be alone here."

She looked up and down the brace shaft. "I'm the best person besides you to stay with the *Resilere*. They know me. They won't know anyone else. And I'm okay here. You were right, it's really a big, airy corridor standing on end." Tilting her head toward the two *Resilere*, she added,

"But Rez is probably going to drag you through a bunch of chases, and those . . . I'm dreading having to go back through one to get out of here. I can't go through more than one."

"I agree," Serrado said. *"Lhyn is the only other person I'd feel comfortable having around the* Resilere.*"*

Rahel grasped her wrist, an instinctive reach for the truth of skin contact though she didn't need it. "You're certain you'll be all right?"

"Positive."

She touched Lhyn's hand to her own heart. "I honor your courage."

"It's not—" Lhyn stopped at her sharp look. "Right," she said with a smile. "Let's play pass-the-com."

She pulled out her com and held it out while giving her pad a tap. "We're playing the greeting now. Take the com slowly. Make sure Rez can see it. Try to project happy, friendly emotions."

Rez moved back toward the landing, and though Rahel couldn't be sure where its eyes were now, she felt certain it was watching. She picked up the com with exaggerated motions, curling her hand around it as she held it up, and imagined giving Lhyn a warmron.

"Okay. Put it on the railing and back away." When Rahel complied, Lhyn gave her pad another tap. "Now we're playing the sound pattern for loss or lost." She let it run for a short time, then touched the pad. "Pick it up again."

For six repetitions, they played the sound patterns to associate holding the com with greetings and dropping it with loss. After the sixth, Rahel moved as near as she could to Rez and held out the com on her palm.

Rez edged closer, still not quite over the landing, and extended a long arm.

"Shippers, I hope Rez doesn't drop it," Lhyn muttered. "Someone will have to climb fourteen decks to get it."

The arm tip brushed Rahel's palm.

When she had offered that first mineral block, Rez had been too abrupt, too strong, with a texture of sand under a sheet as it grabbed and pulled. Now its skin was soft as a new leaf, sliding over hers so gently that it tickled. The arm tip slipped over the com and wrapped around it, holding it securely in a loop.

Lhyn tapped her pad. "Playing the greeting sound now."

Rez retracted the arm and sat on the wall for a few moments, then retreated toward the hole.

"Captain, Rez has the com and is heading—has just left the brace shaft," Rahel reported as both *Resilere* vanished through the hole.

"We're tracking. It's between decks . . . passing deck seventeen . . . it's come out on deck eighteen, chase nine-B, junction eleven."

Rahel turned toward the ladder. "I'm on my way."

32

FOLLOW THE COM

Lhyn had been right not to come, Rahel thought as she jogged through the chase. She had been led on an odd, zig-zag path that made no sense to her but was probably the result of foraging—or so Commander Jalta hypothesized. She and Cox were on their way back, carrying teracite packed with eighty-three *Resilere* eggs.

"Rez is climbing again." Captain Serrado sounded almost apologetic.

"Come on," Rahel grumbled under her breath. She spun in place and backtracked to the main chase. "Could we just pick a deck and stay with it?"

"Apparently not. On the bright side, Zeppy is delighted that you're locating all of the Resilere damage for him."

"I'm sure he is."

"Chase two-D now."

She exited into the corridor and found the nearest lift, breathlessly calling out the location as the doors closed.

"I think this might be it. Rez stopped moving at junction nine."

The doors reopened. Rahel ran down the corridor to the chase entrance, then jogged through several turns before slowing to a walk at junction eight.

At junction nine, she stopped and slowly turned in a circle. "There's no sign of—oh, wait. Here's a hole."

"I'm adding it to Zeppy's list."

She got down on her hands and knees and peered into the hole, which was next to a bundle of cables that exited through the chase wall. "He's lucky these cables weren't affected. I can't see anything. Is Rez still stationary?"

"Yes."

She pulled the light from her trouser pocket. Fleet uniform regulations required all crew to carry one of these tiny, powerful lights, and she was starting to think she needed to have a pocket sewed onto her Bondlancer's Guard uniform to accommodate it. Regular Fleet uniforms had a special one on the upper trouser leg for easy access.

Shining the light into the hole revealed the two *Resilere* working on something, though she couldn't see what. "I see them. They look busy. They're worried and determined. No," she added, pulling apart the threads of the emotions. "One is worried. The other is frantic. I think the last *Resilere* must be solidified and they're trying to pull it out."

"Can you help?"

"It's out of my reach. I can't even see it; it's behind some cables. They might be—"

The lights went out.

"Melting the cables," she finished as the red emergency lights came up. "The power just went out in this section."

"That'll make Zeppy happy. At least this should be the last little crisis they cause."

A scraping sound issued from the hole. Rahel redirected her light beam and saw one of the *Resilere* coming toward her in slow, jerky movements. Beyond it was the second, and in between them . . .

"Great Mother," she said. "They really are cooperative. They've gotten the solidified one out, but the space here is too narrow. One of them is pulling their friend toward the hole, and the other is pushing from behind."

"That is utterly fascinating." Lhyn had her new com. *"If I weren't already busy studying Alsea, I'd study the* Resilere. *An incredible linguistic challenge on top of a truly intriguing culture."* She sighed. *"I need two of me."*

"Stars and Shippers, that would probably kill me."

"Very funny, Ekatya. You should be so lucky."

"First Guard." Serrado's voice was all business again. *"I've cleared your path. There are no personnel in the corridors between the chase door and the lift, on either end."*

"Thank you, Captain." She hadn't even thought of that.

"The closest lift is affected by the power outage. You'll have to use the next one."

"Understood."

The nearest *Resilere*—Rez, she was certain—had almost reached the hole. She scooted backward, giving it room.

Arms emerged through the opening, immediately spreading out to either side. They flexed, spread further, flexed again, and spread even more. Soon Rez's body was visible. It jerked twice and popped out, several arms still extended in front.

After a few more yanks, Rahel could see the solidified *Resilere.*

"They're working hard," she said. "They've got it to the opening and are trying to get it through. Do you suppose they can sense whether it's still alive?"

"Rez knew Rez-Two was still alive," Lhyn said. *"You said one of them was frantic? I doubt it would be if its partner was dead. They're racing the clock."*

Suddenly it was far more difficult to sit still and watch the *Resilere* struggle. She wasn't sure how much of the sudden sense of urgency was hers and how much was from the *Resilere.*

Four solidified arms emerged and were gradually dragged out. Then all movement stopped.

Rez went into a frenzy of yanking, exuding a powerful mix of dismay and fear.

The frozen arms came no further.

Rez let go and fastened itself to the wall just above the hole, which Rahel could now see was entirely blocked by the solidified body.

"It's stuck," she reported. "I should have realized. They flatten themselves to get through those holes, but this one can't. Rez is trying to enlarge the hole."

"What is the other one doing?" Lhyn wanted to know.

"I don't know. I can't see anything past the body. But given how cooperatively they work, I'd bet it's enlarging the hole from the other side."

"Too bad you can't soften it up with a few liters of Enkara seawater," Serrado said.

Rahel thought of her little spray bottle and shook her head.

"Even if she had that much water, they don't have the time," Lhyn noted. *"It was ten minutes before Rez-Two showed any sign of softening."*

Drops of melted material began to spatter on the deck, a few landing on the frozen arms and sliding off. Rahel tried not to worry but couldn't help thinking they were down to the last moments of this *Resilere*'s life.

Belatedly remembering her pack, she shrugged it off and opened it up, readying it for instant action. Then she moved forward and took hold of the stiff, gritty arms, two in each hand, well away from the drip zone of that dangerous acid. Gentle pressure resulted in no movement. She stopped, gave it a few breaths, and tried again.

On the fourth try, Rez fell off the wall, pieces of molten material coming with it, and the solidified body slid forward.

"It's free!" Rahel wasted no time pulling it all the way out and laying it in the pack. She arranged the arms, closed the pack most of the way, and shouldered it as she stood. "Come with me," she said, projecting confidence, and set off at a run.

A quick glance back showed both *Resilere* rippling along the chase, Rez keeping up easily while the other fell gradually behind. She slowed her pace, not wanting to lose the last one. It hadn't had a chance to rehydrate and eat, she realized. This was probably its last reserves of energy.

She rounded a corner and broke into a sprint upon seeing the door. In her haste, she nearly slammed into it, then flipped open the cover hiding the manual hand crank. By the time the *Resilere* caught up, she had the door halfway open and was standing in the darkened, empty corridor.

If climbing down a brace shaft ladder led by a *Resilere* had been surreal, jogging down a red-lit corridor with two of them swarming behind set a new standard. It was with great relief that she saw normal lighting up ahead, a visual confirmation that this lift would work. She sped up and was waiting in the lift entrance when the *Resilere* arrived.

They hesitated, obviously confused by this box of a space with no other outlet. Rahel stepped back as far as she could while still keeping her arm in the opening. "Come *on*," she said urgently. *Safe. Protect.*

Rez came inside and tucked into a low corner. After a stressful pause, the other followed.

"Deck nine, chase eleven." She projected *safe* with all her might as the doors closed, praying to Fahla that they wouldn't feel trapped.

One did. It climbed the wall and huddled against the ceiling, out of her reach. In a heartbeat, it was camouflaged to match the lift wall.

"Well, that's better than spraying me. Captain, we're in the lift."

"I can see that, well done. Actually, I can see both of you. Rez still has the com."

The blue-tinted lights shifted back to normal and the doors opened. Rahel stepped out, nearly tripping over Rez as it darted in front of her. The frightened *Resilere* flowed down the side of the lift and shot out as if propelled. It stopped on the corridor wall, twisting its body this way and that. Confusion beat against her senses from both *Resilere.*

They didn't know where they were, she realized. Their brains could have no way to conceptualize a lift.

"This way." She stepped past the immobile *Resilere* and once again projected confidence, adding the thought of a warmron for good measure.

She would probably never know if they followed because they trusted her or because she had their dying friend on her back. Fortunately, they were only a few steps from the chase entrance.

Once she had that door open, their confusion vanished. With a flash of bioluminescence, Rez streaked ahead. Rahel ran, keeping pace with it and checking now and again to be sure the last one was still in sight. It lagged behind, struggling now, but the fear and determination clogging her senses told her that it would fight to the last moment.

They rounded a corner, then another one, and finally entered the branch that dead-ended at the brace shaft door.

"Lhyn! Open the door!"

It slid open instantly.

Rahel sprinted the final distance and burst into the relatively open space of the landing. She barely had time to notice the empty tank as she was shrugging off the pack.

"We brought in a third tank," Lhyn said rapidly, pointing at the open door on the other side. The entrance of that chase now housed one of the occupied tanks, making room for the new one on the landing. "Dr. Wells and everyone else evacuated to the corridor."

Rahel yanked open the pack, lifted the dried *Resilere*, and plunged it into the water.

"Step back," she said, urging Lhyn with her. "This one has had a hard time."

"The solidified—oh." Lhyn watched with wide eyes as the final *Resliere* limped through the door. "Oh, poor thing."

"All this time worrying about its partner and then I terrified it in the lift. But I don't think it would have made it all the way back taking the long route."

Rez flowed up the side of the tank, alight with bioluminescence. The last *Resilere* gained confidence, still moving in a stuttering motion but trusting in the final destination. It joined Rez on the tank's edge and then fell forward with a splash. Lights danced across its skin as it sank to the bottom and reached for its partner.

Rahel dropped her head back and took a deep, relieved breath. The *Resilere*'s frantic fear was gone, replaced by the same hope she had felt from Rez at the beginning.

Rez slipped into the water, taking up a position on the other side of the solid form and gently stroking it.

"Were we in time?" Lhyn asked.

"I think so. I think they know. They're not afraid any longer."

They watched in silence until Lhyn shifted away to pick up the food sack. "You should probably be the one to drop these in. Rez might need another after all that."

Rahel pulled out two mineral blocks and dropped them in, one at each end of the tank. Both were immediately accepted.

She sank into a cross-legged position and glanced across the landing. "It looks like a train of tanks pulling out of the station."

"It does," Lhyn agreed. "For our next trick, we get to convince twelve *Resilere* that we mean them no harm when we seal these for transport." She sat down beside Rahel and leaned back on her hands. "But first, let's watch a rebirth."

A rebirth, Rahel thought. She knew about those. How many times in her life had she been reborn?

"They're the phoenixes of the sea," she said. "Instead of burning to ashes, they dry into blocks. And then they rise."

"And then they rise," Lhyn repeated quietly.

33

OPPORTUNITY

Erik Helkenn—for that was the name he went by now, and he didn't think of himself by any other—had learned two things while in the medbay.

One, Dr. Wells was an excellent surgeon.

Two, Commander Cox was an excellent security chief.

The first of these played to his advantage. The second did not.

Erik had carefully maintained the guise of a wounded man, hiding his strength as it returned. In fact, it returned much faster than he expected, thanks to Wells's surgical skill. That alien freak had really done a number on him. Anywhere but here, he'd never have breathed normally again.

There was a strategic window of time between the moment he was well enough to escape, and the moment the chief surgeon released him to security. He had successfully convinced the medical staff of his weakness, but they had made an escape more difficult by putting him in a treatment room right off the main lobby and keeping his plexan wall transparent. He couldn't so much as sneeze without one of the nurses seeing. Cox had added to the problem by assigning two guards to his door.

Still, he could have managed had he made it to that window of time. At worst, he could have taken a hostage.

He knew he'd lost the chance when he heard Cox arguing with Wells right outside his door. Though the words were unintelligible, the outcome was obvious when Cox opened the door and stalked in.

"Time for a chance of scenery," he said. "You'll like it. Much quieter than the medbay. No emergencies in the middle of the night." He tossed a stack of clothing on the bed. "Get changed."

Erik picked up the plain brown uniform. The shirt had BRIG spelled out in letters half the height of his back. There would be no hiding in this.

"I'm not well enough to leave," he said. "It still hurts to breathe."

Cox's smile was not friendly. "Unfortunately for you, that's not the criteria for a transfer. The question is whether you need ongoing and *onsite* medical care. A nurse will be checking on you once a day. In your cell. With multiple guards." He crossed his arms. "Get changed."

"Can I have some privacy?"

"No."

Not even a lecture on what his privacy rights were.

Erik didn't try after that. It was too obvious that Cox wouldn't engage, wouldn't be manipulated.

The transfer involved cuffs and four security officers in addition to Cox, and the lift went directly from the medbay lobby to the security office. From there he was marched down a corridor and through a locked door to the brig, then through another locked door to his cell. There was zero opportunity for escape.

He was screwed. He had failed the assignment, and Sholokhov was not a forgiving man. The only possible salvation would be if he could complete the job.

So he waited, and he listened. Security staff were like anyone else; they loved to gossip with each other. And they didn't always pay close attention to who might overhear.

He learned that Cox was hoping the alien freak would work in his section, and that not all of his officers approved. Some had a grudge against her since she had flattened them in a fight. For a while, he thought he might be able to use that, but when three separate attempts ended with scathing looks and slammed doors, he gave up. He hated to admit it, but Fleet security staff were better trained than the goons he was used to.

He heard about the new aliens, even freakier than the Alsean, when the security staff was sent running all over the ship trying to find them. Then Captain Serrado made an all-call announcement, so it was serious.

Some poor slob got his head eaten because the aliens liked the taste of blood. Two others were attacked and one of them would have suffocated, except Dr. Wells had figured out a cure for alien face goo. And security didn't find shit.

Of course it was the Alsean who did. A freak who invaded your mind probably had something in common with brain-eating monsters. And now, he heard, she was collecting the damn things from all over the ship in preparation for taking them to hydroponics. To *save* them.

When the lights went out in his cell, he jumped to the door and peered out the window. Red emergency lighting came on, illuminating the spaces as far as he could see into the main office.

A golden opportunity.

He positioned himself, took a deep breath, and screamed.

"Help! It's in here! There's one of them *in here*! Get it out, get it out! *Help!*"

Two sets of footsteps came running down the corridor. "Stand back from the door!"

"I *am* back from the door, I'm in the fucking corner! That thing is after me! Shoot it!"

The magnetic lock disengaged with a *clunk*, and the door slid open.

He was on the guard before she was halfway in, grabbing her wrist in a pressure hold and wrenching the weapon out of it—a baton, unfortunately. He had never seen the guards carrying phasers back here.

Still, it was a weapon, and it only took one blow to put her out. The second guard tried to rush him, but Erik jabbed him in the stomach with the baton, then sent him back with an upward swing to the jaw. That cleared him out of the doorway.

He stepped over the prone officer and went through his pockets, searching for the magnetic key card. Once that was in hand, he stripped the man's uniform jacket and put it on over his shirt. It was tight in the shoulders and a bit short in the sleeves, but it hid the telltale BRIG lettering.

Swiftly he dragged the officer back into the cell and dropped him next to the woman. Then he pulled out their coms.

"Shit," he said, glaring in disgust at the man's com. "Clean your ears once in a while."

He closed the door on them and threw the coms into a far corner.

The key card handily unlocked the brig door, which—like his cell door—opened manually on slides. He thanked the Seeders that Fleet security didn't use electronic doors, palm scanners, or facial recognition in the brig. Too insecure in a power outage—what an irony. Not that he would have had an issue dragging one of the officers here to satisfy the exit requirements; they didn't have to be conscious for it. But it would have taken precious time.

A peek around the corner into the main office showed three officers standing together amid the inactive displays, distracted by a heated discussion. Another advantage: the brig was soundproofed, so security staff wouldn't be bothered by loud prisoners. Without the security feeds or any communication from the other guards, they had no idea he was loose.

They still had no idea when he walked up behind them.

Not one got a weapon out.

He checked their belts and cursed. Did no one carry a damned phaser around here? They were probably in a weapons locker, and he had no time.

Still grumbling, he pulled their coms and walked out the door into the red-lit corridor. Hardly anyone was in it, and though his wrinkled brown trousers got a few looks, the security uniform jacket stopped any questions.

He flicked his wrist, tossing the coms to one side as he walked.

The power outage meant no security cams. He couldn't be tracked as long as he stayed in the affected section. Of course, he had no intention of doing that, but it certainly served his purpose now.

Sholokhov had given him a tool to use for his assignment, a way to move around the ship without leaving a security trail. It was reserved for his escape after the job, Sholokhov had said. Under no circumstances was he to use it before the job.

Well, he was still on the job, but these were mitigating circumstances.

He walked past the first two chase entrances, dismissing them as too close to the security office. At the third, he flipped up the access panel—battery operated, because repair crews needed access to the chases at all times and especially during power outages—and tapped in the repair code.

This code, Sholokhov had said, was unique to the ship and known only to repair crews. It was a backup in case an individual code failed for any reason.

It worked. The door unlocked, and he spun the hand crank enough to slip through. On the other side, he closed it again and silently thanked Sholokhov. The man was terrifying, but he didn't make mistakes.

Neither did Erik. His time spent memorizing schematics served him well now, and he had no difficulties navigating through the chases to the brace shaft they connected to. Only the central shafts spanned all thirty decks; this one spanned twelve. He climbed down to deck twenty-one, passing into normal lighting on the way, then slipped back into a chase and made his way to the corridor.

From here it was easy enough to stroll through the corridors to the chase entrance nearest hydroponics. Once inside, he found the short side branch that dead-ended at a door opening into the hydroponics bay.

A wonderfully chaotic scene greeted him, with botanics and operations staff scurrying around as they prepared for the aliens. It was simplicity itself to melt into the background and make his way toward the other end of the cavernous space. The pair of pruning shears someone had left on a bench made a perfect weapon.

Sholokhov hadn't known what Sayana's empathic range was, but Erik had put a great deal of thought into it during his recovery. She hadn't said or done anything when he greeted the captain, only striking him when he was halfway across the corridor. There were two possible conclusions: her range was limited to half the width of a corridor, or she hadn't felt a threat until he mentally committed to the kill.

Regardless, he felt safe at this distance. Approaching her unseen would be easy in this jungle. Approaching unfelt would be more of a challenge, but if he was right about the threat, then perhaps he could create a sort of mental camouflage by thinking solely of his next step. First get from here to there. Then to there, and then to there. He planned all of his operations that way; it was second nature to him. Only at the end of his journey, with the target in reach, would he commit to the kill.

It might not work, but he had nothing to lose.

Safely apart from the busy personnel and Sayana's likely location, he scanned the area for the best hiding place and smiled. Who would think to look up in a tree?

He had barely reached a comfortable fork in the branches when

Commanders Cox and Jalta arrived with large crates bearing the Fleet symbol. His high perch gave him a perfect view of the resulting activity. Operations staff pulled the fronts off the crates and took them to sturdy platforms standing next to two large, square tanks full of water. The open crates were now above the tanks, with shallow ramps leading from them to the water.

He frowned. Rocks? They were doing all this for black rocks?

"Are we ready?" Commander Jalta called. When the answer seemed to be yes, she said, "Make it rain!"

A loud horn startled Erik so badly that he almost lost his hold on the branch. The crew members all moved away from the cleared area holding the tanks.

The horn sounded again, this time twice. With a hiss, water began spraying out of overhead pipes onto the tank area.

"Excellent!" Jalta said. "Well done, everyone. Thank you."

"Time to go," Cox added. "Everyone out!"

Erik could not believe his luck. He held his breath, watching every single Fleet crew member march out the main doors.

He was alone in hydroponics. And the alien freak was coming.

34

SALVATION

It took nearly an hour for the solidified *Resilere* to recover. Rahel felt blessed by Fahla to witness this a second time, and with three participants instead of two. The light show put on by both assisting *Resilere* was breathtaking, especially when they brought in the third color. As before, red was introduced shortly prior to the first visible twitches, and the joyous hope flooding her senses made her wish once again that others could feel what she did. Lhyn was enraptured, convinced she was witnessing an unprecedented event, yet she was still missing the best part.

When the two *Resilere* sped up their bioluminescence to the dizzying dance that indicated imminent awakening, Rahel prepared herself for the emotional onslaught. Two minutes later, the recovered *Resilere* rose up, its own skin sparkling, and was promptly wrapped in a tangle of arms.

She closed her eyes, savoring the vivid memory that burst across her mind. Salomen, offering the gift of trust on top of salvation, and her own stumbling words of gratitude . . . but this memory was twice as strong as before. The objective part of her noted that it must be due to both Rez and the final *Resilere* thanking her, while the rest of her luxuriated in the sensory flood. She could smell the cinnoralis that Lanaril had lit in her study, as well as the spicy scent of Salomen's skin. She saw the light coming through the tall windows, illuminating the park beyond, and this time she heard Salomen's voice, choked with emotion.

"I didn't ask you for anything because you gave it freely."

"How could I do anything else?" she murmured, caught up in the memory. She was certain that if she opened her eyes, Salomen would be *here*, smiling at her while Lanaril watched from close by.

"Rahel! Are you all right?"

The scents, the light, the feel of Lanaril's study faded away, and she blinked. Lhyn was watching her with guarded concern, a hand resting on her shoulder.

"You went away for a bit," she said. "I'm glad you weren't standing up."

Rahel rubbed her eyes and took a deep breath. "That was intense. They both hit me with their gratitude, and . . . whew."

"Was it the same memory as before?"

She nodded. "But twice as powerful. I was there."

Lhyn chewed her bottom lip, then offered a wry smile. "I'm so envious."

"If there was a way I could share it . . ."

"I know." She sighed. "I shouldn't be greedy. There isn't an anthropologist or linguist in the Protectorate who wouldn't sell their grandparents to be here."

"Don't forget the biologists," Commander Jalta said.

"Right, those too."

"I hate to break up the party." That was Commander Cox. *"But I'm afraid I have some bad news. Erik Helkenn has escaped custody. Ironically, it was that last power outage that gave him the opportunity."*

"We were hoping to avoid having to tell you," Captain Serrado said. *"But we haven't found him yet, which means we're having to take special precautions getting you to hydroponics."*

Cox came back on. *"There are two probable courses of action for him. The most likely is to try to escape. We've locked down the lifts, the shuttle bay, and the fighter bays. He's not getting away."*

"And the second is to come after me." Rahel met Lhyn's worried gaze.

"I'm afraid so. That's why we wanted to tell you before you came out to find the full escort waiting here. The safest place for you right now is hydroponics. It's clear and every entrance is guarded. Even if he knew your destination, which is doubtful, he won't get in. Most likely he used the computer to monitor your location. I've restricted that information, so he's blind now. But

he probably does know you were here when he was last able to check. I'd like to get you out of there."

Rahel stood up and offered Lhyn a hand, then pulled on her uniform jacket, now dry. "Then I suppose we'd better package up these *Resilere* and get them to hydroponics. Who's in charge of the third tank?"

"That would be me." Zeppy stood in the chase, behind the tank that blocked its entrance. "I need to show you how to operate the carts anyway."

"You mean you don't just push them?" she joked.

"Do you know how much seven hundred and fifty liters of water weighs? Good luck getting that up and over the ramps." He pointed at the push bars at each end of the cart. "You can control it from either bar. When you push or pull, the cart will figure out which way you want to go. Buttons are on the bottom of the bar. Left hand is go and go faster. Right hand is slow and stop. Understood?"

"Did you breathe while you said that?" Lhyn bent over to peer beneath the bar of the nearest cart. "Oh. They're green and yellow. Why didn't you say so? That makes more sense than left and right."

"But you can't even see—" Zeppy stopped. "Whatever works for you. Seeder's balls, there are more *Resilere* in this one than there is water. Shouldn't we redistribute?"

"I'm not about to try to communicate that," Lhyn said. "It's only a short trip."

Rahel dropped four mineral cubes in the tank with the newly recovered *Resilere*. Two of them were instantly snatched, while Rez ignored the remainders. "That should keep our two newest arrivals happy. We should all put the lids on at the same time."

"Agreed." Zeppy picked up his lid.

"Wait! We need to reassure them first." She crouched down and put a hand against the tank wall near Rez. As before, it matched her gesture. "Lhyn, will you watch the analyzer? I'm going to try to say *home*."

"Watching."

She stared at Rez, its eye stalks fully extended and oriented to her, and thought of Dock One at dawn, with the crisp, salty air of Wildwind Bay caressing her skin. She imagined the bells of Whitesun Temple tolling in their deep, resonant voices, and tried to project the unique flavor of joy and contentment that came from being home.

Rez played a burst of green bioluminescence, and Rahel *heard* the bells. Only for a moment, but she hoped it was enough. "Did you get it?" she asked.

"Wow," was Lhyn's answer as she tapped her pad. "It's a new word."

"It's the first word Rez ever spoke to me."

"And you managed a repeat. You're getting good at this."

"Tell me that after we've gotten them to hydroponics without terrifying them."

"I think we'll be okay," she said thoughtfully. "We have *friend*, and now we have *home*. Those are powerful concepts. Not to mention that every *Resilere* here knows you saved them."

"We saved them," Rahel corrected.

"Group effort," Zeppy put in. "Half the sections on this ship are involved now. The other half are cheering us on."

"You're the liaison," Lhyn said. "You're the one who personally put two solid *Resilere* in life-giving water. Rez trusted you enough to get in the lift, and that turned out well for it." She tapped her pad a few more times. "Right, I'm going to send both words to the tank speakers. Then we'll put on the lids, and then I'll repeat it. Ready?"

Rahel picked up her lid and took note of the soft sealant around the inside edges. "Ready."

Lhyn tapped her pad, then fetched her own lid. "Go."

They quietly slid the transparent lids over the tanks. Rahel gave hers a final push, then tried to nudge it upwards. It stayed firm.

The *Resilere* showed no sign of nervousness.

"So far, so good." Lhyn looked over at the chase, her forehead furrowed in thought. "If they're not upset, I think I'll save the replay for when we start moving."

"Then shall we?" Zeppy put his hands on the bar.

Rahel walked around to the far end of her tank, bringing up the rear of the train. "I'm ready."

Lhyn took up her own position with the middle tank. "I feel like I should make appropriate train noises."

"Rumors of your adulthood are exaggerated, aren't they?"

Looking mischievous, Lhyn said, "A lot of rumors about me are exaggerated."

"Me too, probably."

"Let's go." Zeppy began to pull.

Rahel couldn't see past Lhyn's tank, but she could feel the nervousness bordering on fear from multiple sources. Probably all six *Resilere* in Zeppy's tank. "Lhyn, play it now," she said urgently.

Lhyn tapped her pad even as she moved her tank forward.

Safe, Rahel projected. *Protect.* She thought of home, of joy and contentment, and pushed her tank.

A small motor whirred. The effort of pushing smoothed out, and the cart moved forward.

Her three *Resilere* became very tall, drawing themselves up into what looked like an alert position. But they didn't camouflage, and she sensed no anxiety. Yet.

Zeppy had to walk backward and pull the tank with him, a position Rahel did not envy. Her concern was Lhyn, whose shoulders tensed as her tank nosed into the chase. She saw the intake of breath and hunched posture, and she felt the forcible—but not completely effective—control of fear.

She also saw her own *Resilere* flattening down in reaction to it.

"Lhyn, how old were you when you left Allendohan?" she asked.

"What? Oh, um . . . seventeen."

"Really? You left your home *planet* and went tromping around the galaxy at seventeen? And I thought I was independent. Where did you go?"

"Dothanor Prime. It has twelve continents. The northernmost one is the coldest place I've ever lived. Froze my ass off."

Zeppy snickered.

"You think I'm kidding? Every time I went outside, I thought my nose hairs would break. But the university there has the best anthropology program in the Protectorate."

Her com gave a soft click, the sign of an incoming call.

"Well done, Rahel." Captain Serrado's voice was quiet. *"This is a private call. Keep her talking. Keep her mind off of it."*

"I will," she murmured.

"Thank you. Putting you back on the group link now."

The com clicked again.

"Didn't the planet have axial tilt?" she asked. "It had to get warmer sometime, didn't it?"

"Right, if you define warmer as 'only freezing your nipples off instead of your whole ass.'"

Now Zeppy laughed outright. "There must be a lot of body parts lying in those streets."

"Oh, the locals were fine with it. I think they were born with ice cubes in their mouths. It was just us foreign students suffering."

Rahel noted with considerable satisfaction that her *Resilere* were fluffing out again. Lhyn was controlling her fear more effectively.

She and Zeppy kept Lhyn engaged as they trundled along, taking turns asking questions or making observations. She wondered if Captain Serrado had contacted Zeppy as well, or if he was naturally that perceptive.

They had a brief hiccup when some of the *Resilere* in Zeppy's tank were sloshed around a little too much while going up and over a conduit ramp. Lhyn played *home* and *friend* again, and Rahel projected *safe* as well as she could. Eventually they settled down.

It was a long, slow trudge out, and she was exceedingly happy when they rounded the last turn. The distant rectangle of light signified that their escort already had the door open. "Almost there," she said. "That's the exit up ahead."

"It is? Oh, thank all the deities." Lhyn paused. "Are you sure we came out the same way we went in? I'd swear it was a shorter trip."

Rahel lowered her head and smiled.

Zeppy backed into the corridor, pulling his tank out of the way. Lhyn followed, a blast of relief billowing through the chase as she cleared the door. Rahel's *Resilere* fluffed out, their eye stalks swiveling as they absorbed Lhyn's emotion and their changing scenery. She glanced down and realized that somewhere along the way, the recovered one had eaten another mineral block.

"Welcome back," Captain Serrado said. She was standing with Commander Cox, Commander Jalta, and six security officers. The only one not wearing a sidearm was Jalta.

"You have no idea how happy I am to be out here." Lhyn walked over and threw her arms around the captain.

Serrado was startled but quickly recovered, tightening her grip and murmuring something Rahel couldn't hear.

"I am," Lhyn said, pulling away. "They helped. They kept me distracted. And I was really more worried about the *Resilere* than myself."

"Let's see if we can get them to a point where we can stop worrying about them," Jalta said.

"Sayana and I will go first." Zeppy began pushing his tank forward. "The lift could handle all three tanks, but it would be a tight fit with the three of us, too. Lhyn, you'll come in the next car."

"Understood," Lhyn and Rahel said at the same time.

Commander Cox fell into step beside Rahel. "You're learning Fleet speak."

"Better sooner than later. Commander, are you personally guarding me?"

He rumbled a soft sound of amusement. "Are you insulted?"

"Mildly. But I'll overlook it this time. I'm a little preoccupied with *Resilere*."

"You're going to test me, I can tell. But you have a lot of promise. Please tell me you're coming to my section."

"I don't know," she hedged. "Will I have to watch assheads in the brig?"

His smile dropped. "You'd be better at it than a few of my officers. They paid with a concussion and a fractured jaw, so I hope the lesson will sink in. They broke protocol going into his cell without establishing his position and compliance. The power outage was only half of his opportunity. Breaking protocol was the other half."

"Were those officers by any chance the ones I put down my first week here?"

"How did you guess?"

She shook her head. "If I join your section, I'll have to establish dominance."

"We don't work that way in Fleet—"

"Yes, you do. I've already seen it. You don't *officially* work that way, but Gaians aren't that different from Alseans when it comes to settling who's in charge."

"I'm in charge, First Guard."

"Not when you're not there."

"Seeders preserve my patience," he grumbled. "I knew I'd need migraine meds."

"I spent my first two weeks here trying desperately not to do anything wrong. That got me in more trouble than I imagined. I can't be anything but what I am, Commander. It works best if I'm true to myself."

He gave her a sideways look, one corner of his mouth tilting up. "It works best that way for everyone. I'll take your words under advisement. But we'll probably have to have a few talks about protocols and chain of command."

"Probably," she agreed, and smiled at his short bark of laughter.

When they reached the lift, she pushed her tank past Lhyn's. It made sense for her to go with Zeppy, who had no prior connection to the *Resilere*. Her presence would hopefully keep them calm, and Lhyn wouldn't feel as crowded in a car by herself. Though she suspected Captain Serrado would be accompanying her.

Cox came in with them, stepping in last and facing the doors. Rahel crouched down, looking into the tanks and projecting *safe* and *protect* for the duration of the ride. Thank Fahla these lifts were so quick; the *Resilere* barely had time to react before the doors opened onto hydroponics.

"Great Mother," she breathed. "Look at that!"

A whole section of the bay had been cleared of plants and set up with two low-sided square tanks, each of which covered a larger area than all three of hers put together.

They were the same size as the footprint of a lift, she realized.

Smaller containers in the tanks offered hiding spots, mineral blocks were scattered throughout, and the water rippled with the seawater rain falling from above. Standing on platforms were two of the packing crates she had seen on the briefing room display, back when everyone thought they were dealing with something terrifying.

In the end, the most terrifying thing had been the cargo crew.

"Don't you think I've got a flair for decoration?" White teeth flashed against dark skin as Zeppy grinned. "I could have a second career once I retire from Fleet."

"Don't count on that," Cox said. "The crates clash."

"What?"

"Wrong color. They don't go with the containers in the tanks."

Rahel snickered. She was liking Cox more and more.

Behind them, the lift doors opened and Lhyn pushed out her tank. Sure enough, the captain was with her.

"Zeppy, did you set up the frequency analyzers?" Lhyn asked breathlessly.

"I did. Speakers and hydrophones in the tanks, cams mounted for every possible angle, analyzers set to transmit to your pad and Commander Kenji's office. It's all ready, Dr. Rivers."

"Shippers, I can't *wait* to see this."

"You're seeing it from outside," Serrado said.

"Ekatya—"

"There is no predicting the behavior of twelve parents protecting their eggs or hatchlings and you know it. Everyone is watching this from outside." She met Rahel's eyes. "But I think the *Resilere* would benefit from your presence, if you feel comfortable with that."

"I do," Rahel said hurriedly. Miss this chance? Not in ten lifetimes.

Serrado nodded. "Thought you might. As Lhyn said earlier, I'd like them to associate one of us with something positive, not just the absence of negatives. If they associate you with the safety of their families, we'll have an easier time getting them home."

"Understood, Captain."

"*So* envious," Lhyn grumbled.

They pushed their tanks toward the larger ones. The *Resilere* began reacting before they got there, arms spreading across the tank walls and each other as they shifted anxiously. They saw the new environment and wanted out.

"Let's not keep them waiting," Serrado said. "Good luck, First Guard."

"Thank you, Captain."

They jogged out of the bare zone and rounded the nearest rack of plants, vanishing behind the greenery. Rahel saw only glimpses as they threaded their way through racks and past thick tree trunks, but she could see the main doors. Soon they opened, then closed again.

"We're out," Serrado said.

"Acknowledged. I'm freeing them now."

She pushed up the lid on Rez's tank. It took some effort to break the seal, but once she did, it came off in a smooth slide.

Rez exploded out and leaped into the nearest environment, then dashed into every corner as it explored. The other two followed more carefully.

She noted that the last mineral block was gone. The recovered *Resilere* must have taken it while she was talking with Cox.

There was one object remaining in the tank, however: Lhyn's com. She thought it was a good sign that Rez had concluded it was no longer needed.

When she opened the second tank, one of the *Resilere* thoroughly splashed her in its scramble out. It raced into the same environment as the others and swam to another *Resilere*, which lit up in joyous greeting as they touched each other.

Rez and Rez-Two were back together.

In the last tank, the remaining six were sliding over each other in such a constant motion that she was afraid they might hurt themselves trying to get out before she had the lid off. "Calm down," she said, for all the good it did.

They took half the tank water with them in their rush to leave. Rahel laughed as she wiped her face.

"They're all out," she reported. "And I'm drenched again."

"Don't expect me to feel sorry for you," Lhyn said. *"You're in there and I'm out here."*

"How long are you going to sulk?"

"Years."

She looked over the tanks, now full of happy *Resilere* with room to move, and realized how well-planned the environment was. The rain had been carefully arranged to cover the tanks and crates, but nothing else. It would hydrate the hatchlings when they came out, and keep the adults hydrated if they chose to sit by the crates, but otherwise, no water was wasted. The tanks themselves were plumbed with stand pipes, which kept the water at a constant level while allowing a renewing supply from the rain.

"Ingenious," she murmured.

A sudden blast of shock brought up her head. One of the *Resilere* had climbed onto a ramp and was rippling toward a crate. It went inside and burst into a brilliant pattern of all three colors, flooding Rahel's senses with euphoria.

In almost perfect synchrony, the other eleven swarmed out as well. At first, all twelve were playing the same pattern in a dizzying display, but soon there were small differences as they moved about, taking up every bit of the crates as they hung from the tops and sides. They could not stop touching their eggs, holding one in each free arm, then setting them down and picking up others.

"My stars, you should see what they're saying." Lhyn's elation could be heard in her voice. *"If you could hear in their frequency, you'd probably be deafened. What do you feel?"*

What did she feel? So much that she couldn't separate it out, much less put words to it. "Um. They are . . ." She cleared her throat. "Well, imagine you thought your children were dead, and then someone took you to a room and there they were, alive—"

"They're overwhelmed," Dr. Wells said quietly. *"Joy and relief and confusion and more joy. If they're like us in their emotional responses, it's not so easy to let go of the belief that your child is dead. It might be a while before it sinks in."*

Rahel cringed at her asinine choice of words. "Yes, overwhelming. Like having a bucket of water poured over my head and trying to feel the individual drops. I can't describe it."

One of the *Resilere* burst out of a crate, rippled into the water, and swam directly to her.

"I think this is Rez," was all she got out before Rez climbed up on the edge of the tank, not a handspan away from her, and reached out with four arms. Its eye stalks were fully extended despite being in the air, and the vertical pupils were focused on her.

She stood still as the four armtips traced over her face, her shoulders, her arms, then wrapped around her wrists and gently pulled.

"It wants—oh," she said. "It wants me to touch its body."

She let her hands come in contact, the new-leaf softness now slippery with water, and—

She was digging frantically through the wreckage of her mother's workshop, so shattered by the blast that only stones and dust remained. A gleam of metal shone through, the jagged base of what had once been a sculpture made by her mother's hand. The sight destroyed the wall she had built around her grief, leaving her open to the searing agony.

"No!" she screamed. "No! No, no, no, no . . ."

"Fahla," she gasped, tears rolling down her face. "Why are you showing me this?"

The arms coiled around her wrists, refusing to let her pull back. She took a shuddering breath, and—

"Sweet shekking Fahla in a moonbeam, it's good to hear your voice," Sharro said. "You have no idea how much we worried."

Her existence collapsed to a single, stunning possibility. Unwilling to believe, terrified to hope, she choked out a single word.

"We?"

"Hold on, let me get your mother. She's been frantic all day, and even worse since the battle ended."

She couldn't breathe. She couldn't breathe and she couldn't move, because her mother was alive, *and it was too much. The whole world was torn apart, but her mother lived.*

She came out of the memory so off balance that she would have fallen but for Rez's firm grip.

"I understand," she managed. She wiped her cheeks on first one shoulder, then the other. "Your world is torn apart, but your children live. You thought you lost them, and now they're back, but the extremes of emotion—nothing can describe it. Joy and grief, side by side."

"Rahel." Dr. Wells sounded worried. *"What is it doing to you?"*

"Showing me. Their grief at losing their eggs—no Gaian or Alsean parent could suffer any more. They were devastated. Having them back is euphoria and salvation, but . . ."

"But salvation doesn't magically erase their grief. Not yet." Dr. Wells paused, then spoke curtly. *"I'm going on record as being in agreement with Dr. Rivers. That cargo crew got what they deserved."*

Rahel hardly heard her as a new memory rose up. She was—

On the deck of Blacksun Temple in her new dress uniform, facing a regal-looking Salomen.

"I am overjoyed to stand with you now," Salomen said. "I have learned the pain of causing harm—and the great, healing gift of forgiveness."

"Shekking Mother on a burning boat," she blurted.

"What is it? What did you see?" Lhyn asked.

"My oath ceremony. When Salomen publicly acknowledged hurting me and accepted my forgiveness. I think Rez is saying they forgive us."

"And possibly apologizing for Murray," Captain Serrado said.

"Fucking stars," Lhyn muttered. *"This is so far off the charts I don't know how I'll write it up."*

Rez's arms loosened and uncoiled, a smooth slide that only gradually released her. Two arms pulled back, while the other two lightly traced her palms. Then it slipped into the water, swam to the other side, and rippled up the ramp. In moments it had vanished into the cluster of *Resilere*. She could no longer tell them apart.

She wiped her face again and looked back with a sudden realization. If she couldn't tell the *Resilere* apart, was there any reason to think they could tell Gaians apart? She was the only one who was different.

"Fate and Fahla," she whispered.

She was meant to be here.

35

SONG OF LIFE

Erik could not believe what he was seeing. Sayana had practically hugged that brain-eating alien! And now—was she wiping tears? What in all the bounteous fucks was that about?

One thing he knew for sure: she truly was a freak. Sholokhov was right to want her gone. Alseans didn't belong in the Protectorate at all, but they *especially* shouldn't be allowed in Fleet. Military might and mental invaders were a disastrous combination.

It had given him pause, though, seeing Serrado and Cox. They were obviously waiting right outside the main doors, probably watching everything on the security cams. He would have to move carefully to avoid being seen until the moment of his strike.

And then it would be over. With both the captain and Cox here, he had no illusions about his ability to get out of hydroponics. The only reason he'd gotten out of the brig was because Cox wasn't around. The man was a professional. He probably had the chase doors guarded, if he hadn't already changed the repair code.

Then again, it hadn't ever been about escaping, had it? Deep down he had known he wouldn't get off this ship. But there was a difference between prison when Sholokhov was pleased by a job well done, and prison when he was angry at a failure.

Slowly and methodically, he examined the walls and ceiling beams, marking each of the security cams that he could see. The tree was both advantage and disadvantage now, blocking the cams' view of him but also hindering his ability to find them. Still, he could see the pattern of their installation and fill in the blanks.

Now it was a matter of mapping out the route. He would need to climb down this side of the tree and dash behind that rack of plants. Then to that bushy shrub that overhung most of the path between racks, and then to that blind spot.

It helped immensely that the racks were three meters high, with upright plants on the bottom tiers and hanging plants on the top. In many places, those racks made a solid wall of foliage—and they extended for the length of the bay.

Bit by bit, he assembled his approach. When he mentally reached the point where he would have to break cover and run to Sayana, he backtracked the route. From the base of the tree, he ran it forward again, and twice more for good measure.

He shifted his weight, preparing for the first move, and glanced back for a final clear look at Sayana.

What in the name of the Seeders—?

The ramps leading into the tanks were full of small moving objects.

And Sayana appeared to be in a trance.

~

"You may be right," Commander Jalta said. *"There are birds and mammals that can distinguish Gaian faces, but only after time and association."*

"Even Gaians have trouble with it when people look different from what they're accustomed to," Lhyn added. *"Drop Ekatya on Allendohan, where we're all tall and thin and a lot of us have green eyes, and she might not be able to tell me from the rest."*

"Slight exaggeration," Serrado said dryly.

Rahel chuckled at her tone. "I understand. It's about what you're used to. Hoi—there's something happening."

The *Resilere* were rearranging themselves. Two hung from the top of each crate, dangling over the eggs, while the rest were flowing down the ramps. They entered the water but didn't fully submerge, instead remaining half out and plastered against the tank wall. Their eye stalks were extended and swiveled forward, facing the crates.

In perfect synchrony, blue bioluminescence circled their bodies. Then green. Then red. Then the blue returned, drawing a different and more complex pattern. The green and red repeated it.

Expecting a new pattern in blue, Rahel was startled to see a separation in their synchrony. The four hanging over the eggs sparkled in blue, while the eight in the water divided themselves into two groups: four with a pattern in green and four with a different pattern in red.

"This is phenomenal." Lhyn was speaking in a near-whisper, awe filling her voice. *"The sound patterns—they're identical. I mean, each group of four is doing precisely the same frequencies at precisely the same intervals, and the three patterns are interwoven and reflecting. It looks . . . musical."*

"What do you mean?"

"I think they're singing."

Never had Rahel wished so fervently that she could hear in low frequencies. She would have given almost anything to hear this the way the *Resilere* did.

Judging by the ever-increasing complexity of their bioluminescence, the song was becoming more intense, more . . . profound, she thought. They didn't move, their stillness unsettling after the constant shifting she had grown accustomed to. Even when a *Resilere* stayed in one place, at least one or two of its arms were usually coiling, extending, feeling, retracting—but not now. They were focused on their song.

So focused, she realized, that their earlier maelstrom of emotion was dying down. One by one, threads were stripped away. Confusion was already gone. Relief was gone. Grief was fading, and the joy had changed flavor. It was no longer a shocked joy of discovery. It was . . .

"Anticipation," she whispered. It had hit her senses like a stave to the chest. "They're full of joyous anticipation. They're waiting, expecting . . ."

"Expecting." Commander Jalta's voice was as awed as Lhyn's. *"Expecting their eggs to hatch. Holy crap, do you think that's possible? Eggs that don't rely on elapsed development time, or a build-up of certain chemicals. Or temperature or light levels . . ."*

"But on song," Lhyn said. *"On hearing these specific frequencies."*

"We sing our babies to sleep." Rahel could not stop her grin. "Why couldn't they sing theirs out of the egg?"

The anticipation grew, flooding her senses until she could feel it in her bones. Joy lifted her arms and increased her heart rate. It dropped her head back, opening her airway for the breath she needed now that her lungs were so much larger. Her vision darkened and her hearing dampened, until she was alone in the universe with a silent voice speaking solely to her. It caressed, comforted, encouraged. It told her that she was loved.

Vaguely she heard distant sounds, a smaller voice trying to get her attention. She had no time for such irritants. The only voice that mattered was the one she heard with her heart. It was calling her out, and she would follow it anywhere.

Her comforting, perfect universe shattered with a blinding slash of pain. Shards of reality shredded her awareness as her body crashed to a hard, unforgiving surface. She was too warm and too cold all at once.

Voices shouted at her, their words confused and unintelligible. She dug them out of her ear and threw them away, hoping that would stop the pain, but it only worsened. Her vision cleared, revealing a man standing above her and holding something that dripped red.

"Thought you'd be more of a challenge."

"What?" she whispered. She was dazed, still longing for the private universe that had been torn away. The gleeful malevolence soaking her senses could not be more shocking after what she had just experienced.

Then she remembered feeling this once before. "Helkenn."

"Not so fast with that stave now, are you? I hear these things like blood. You're losing a lot of it. Don't you think it's poetic, being killed by your pets?" With a laugh, he darted away.

She pressed her hand to her side. The blood was flowing rapidly, and her body was already weak. Whether from the emotional impact or the physical one, she had no strength to stand, let alone fight.

Rage coated her senses—protective, parental rage from multiple sources.

From her position on the deck, she couldn't see them, but she knew they were coming. And she was bleeding a hundred times worse than Murray had.

They boiled out of the tanks, two heading straight for her while the others swarmed off in a different direction. She had no time to wonder where the others had gone before a heavy weight slid onto her abdomen.

A *Resilere* was positioning itself directly over her wound.

"No." She pushed at it weakly. "I saved you!"

It settled down, unaffected by her pitiful attempts. She dropped her head back and thought of the fish flopping on Dock One.

Help me.

She'd have to thank Zeppy and Kenji later, Ekatya thought as she watched the displays. They had set up a miniature command center outside the main doors, complete with multiple displays showing the sound frequencies and cam footage. Despite having four section chiefs and Lhyn crowded around, everyone had a good view and she didn't have to pull rank to guarantee her own.

Which she most certainly would have done. Overseeing first contact with a sentient, intelligent species? She had dreamed of this since her cadet days. She could retire tomorrow and be happy.

Nor was she the only one. Lhyn was practically vibrating with excitement, Jalta was only a little calmer, and Dr. Wells had been sucked in despite her earlier efforts to maintain a professional distance. Zeppy couldn't stop grinning, and even Cox had loosened up.

It was first contact, historic research, and a birth party all in one.

"Look at that," Lhyn said as Rahel lifted her arms and let her head fall back with a beatific smile. "I'd sell my left arm to feel what she's feeling."

"I don't know about that." Zeppy glanced at her. "After those stories about Dothanor Prime, do you have any body parts left to sell?"

"They didn't all freeze off. Ask Ekatya."

"People, we're still on the record," Ekatya reminded them.

Lhyn gave a dismissive shrug. "Not really. The events are, and the data, but I stopped keeping an official voice record the moment we rolled the tanks into those chases."

"You mean my statement about the cargo crew won't go in your data packet?" Dr. Wells asked.

"Only if you want it to."

"I might. Stars above, she looks like she's going into an altered state of consciousness. At this rate we'll need the gurney after all."

"Have you seen people in those kinds of trances?" Lhyn asked curiously.

Wells nodded. "They tend to have a hard transition back to reality. They lose all sense of time and space. Proprioception goes out the window with it."

"Proprio what?" Zeppy wanted to know.

"Proprioception. The body's sense of itself." She held up a hand and turned it back and forth. "Knowing where our various body parts are in space, and which ones are moving."

Lhyn snapped her fingers. "That *did* happen to her. Several times. When the memories were especially intense, she almost fell over. She didn't hear me or even know I was there."

"I saw that. It shows how intense the sensory input is for her. I've rarely met anyone so exquisitely tuned to her body as Rahel. For her to lose that awareness, repeatedly—the *Resilere* must be extremely powerful empaths."

"And it wasn't just physical awareness," Lhyn added. "She lost empathic awareness."

"Which makes me wonder how a high empath would perceive contact with them."

Lhyn flashed a grin. "Considering the fact that we need empaths to learn their language, there's a good chance we'll find that out someday."

"Someday," Dr. Wells agreed. "Phoenix, unmute. Rahel, can you hear me?"

The video feed might have been frozen for all the indication Rahel gave.

"Rahel. This is Dr. Wells. If you can hear me, please lift your right hand."

When ten seconds passed with no movement, Ekatya shifted closer to her.

"Do we need to worry?" she asked quietly.

"Not yet. Phoenix, mute." Dr. Wells didn't take her eyes off the display. "Wish I had a bioreadout on her, but I can see her breathing. She's taking deep, regular breaths, and she's still upright. If she falls over, I'm going in."

"I'm not sure anyone should be going in now." Jalta pointed at the display showing several cam angles on the crates. "Look!"

Everyone crowded around.

"Great galaxies," Ekatya murmured. "They really are singing their hatchlings out."

A tiny *Resilere*, half the size of her closed fist, was swaying at the top of a ramp. Bioluminescence played over its little body as both of the adults hanging from its crate touched it. Their arm tips were as thick as its body, but they kept their contact so gentle that the hatchling was neither bumped nor jostled. It simply swayed, as if in keeping to a tune.

Then one of the adults gave it a pat from behind, and the hatchling began rippling toward the water.

"That might be the cutest thing I've ever seen," Lhyn said. "Look at its little arms go!"

They were a flurry of motion, propelling the hatchling toward the waiting adults. When it was close enough, a thicket of comparatively massive arms reached out as every other adult in the tank made contact. The hatchling stopped and swayed, then rippled forward again and vanished beneath the water.

"There's another one." Cox pointed at a view from the second crate.

"And a third," Zeppy added. "See it, coming out right behind?"

Ekatya glanced back at the display showing Rahel, who had not moved and still wore that blissful, unguarded smile. "I know what you mean about Rahel," she murmured to Lhyn. "I'd give a lot to feel that, too."

"Just not while being recorded, right?"

"She does have a big pair of horns." Ekatya couldn't imagine putting her vulnerabilities on public record the way Rahel had.

"Don't worry," Lhyn said, smiling at the Alsean slang. "Yours are still bigger."

"Sharper, too," Dr. Wells interjected from Ekatya's other side.

The trickle of hatchlings became a stream, then a river. Ten minutes after the first hatching, the ramps were full of little *Resilere* sparkling with bioluminescence. The adults touched every one of them, and the hatchlings always stopped and swayed when they felt a caress.

The underwater cams showed more and more hatchlings exploring their new environment. Without fail, each of them eventually found a mineral block and settled on it. Given the size differential, it looked like a person trying to eat a house.

"They have the acidic capabilities of the adults," Jalta observed. "I just saw one leave a block. It managed to round off some of the edges."

"Imagine the damage a brood of these could do to a Voloth ship," Cox said.

Dr. Wells shook her head. "Your mind is not a place I'd ever want to be."

"I'll bet the captain thought the same thing."

"No comment." Ekatya drifted over to Wells. "Any change?"

"She hasn't moved a hair. If we could bottle what she's sensing, we could finance a new ship. I'm looking forward to hearing what she has to say about it."

"That makes two of us," Lhyn said. "I wonder if it's more memories, or something entirely different?"

"If it's memories, then I'm glad she has something that makes her look like that." Dr. Wells frowned. "What—? Phoenix, unmute! Rahel! Wake up! Wake *up*, damn you, come on! Rahel! You're under attack!"

Helkenn had come out of nowhere. Before Ekatya could even move, he stabbed Rahel in the side. She collapsed immediately, her body slumping in the loose, liquid fashion of the newly dead.

Cox turned and slapped his palm against the entry pad while pulling his phaser with the other hand. He was through the doors before they were fully open, speaking to his security staff as he ran.

"Stay here," Ekatya ordered, stopping Wells in mid-motion.

"You can't expect me—"

"Yes, I can. Stay until I call." She chased Cox through the doors.

Hydroponics was normally a serene, fragrant slice of terrestrial life. Now it was an ominous maze of hiding places for a skilled assassin. She kept low, running in a crouch as she raced to catch up with Cox. He was moving rapidly but staying cautious.

A thought struck, and she patted her jacket pocket. Yes, her spray bottle of Enkara seawater was still there.

She wondered if it would be enough.

It had gone perfectly, just as he planned it. Sayana had never known he was there. Even if Serrado and Cox ran right in and killed all of the aliens, they couldn't do it before Sayana's internal organs were dissolved. Not even Dr. Wells could fix a mess like that.

He raced away, putting distance between him and the swarm of brain-suckers that were descending on her now. He had seen them starting across the tanks, already drawn by the blood. Poetic, indeed.

The route back to his tree was easier when he wasn't worried about security cams. In the unlikely event that her pet monsters took any interest in him, he planned to be out of their reach.

But mostly he wanted a good view of her death.

He rounded the end of a plant rack and saw the bushy shrub that had marked his second waypoint. Its branches slapped against him as he ducked beneath, stinging his face and making one eye water, but he ignored it and kept going. At the tree, he jumped up and caught the first branch.

A strong hand around his ankle jerked him to a stop.

Fuck. Cox had been faster than he expected.

"You're too late," he said, turning to look over his shoulder. His triumphant smile dissolved into a squeak of terror.

It wasn't Cox's hand holding him. It was a tentacle. The alien sat below, reaching a second tentacle toward his other foot while three more of the slimy monsters slithered up the tree trunk.

Frantic kicking failed to loosen the monster's grip while endangering his own. With a surge of adrenaline-fueled strength, he swung up his free foot and managed to wedge it on the branch, then strained to free himself.

One of the monsters launched off the trunk and landed on his stomach.

Another slapped onto his chest. The third impacted his head and wrapped its disgusting tentacles around his face and throat.

His foot slipped, leaving him dangling from the branch with three monsters weighing him down. He let out a despairing cry when his hands slipped free.

They clung to him even as he fell.

Searing pain roared across the top of his head. It could not have hurt more had he been set on fire.

Never in his life had he screamed as loudly as he did now. It burst from him in a long wail of agony, and he drew breath only to scream again when his torso caught fire.

It felt as if his skin and bones were melting. He thrashed and bucked, muscles convulsing as his body reacted to the unthinkable torment. His screams grew hoarser and his body was molten lava, and still he howled with every molecule of air in his lungs.

The end of his life was measured in screams, each weaker than the last, but no less agonized.

Death, when it finally came, was a mercy.

Ekatya caught up with Cox at the last plant rack before the *Resilere* environment. They peered through the profusion of hairy red leaves but saw nothing. Their position was well behind the rear corner of the nearest tank, and their view of Rahel was blocked.

But some part of Helkenn should have been visible if he were still standing, or even kneeling.

"My people are working the security feeds," Cox said. "They haven't found him yet."

"He just ran," Dr. Wells said. *"He said something to her and ran toward the starboard side. I need to get to her, she's bleeding out!"*

"He's not the only danger." Cox pointed up the row between racks, which paralleled the side of the tank. The plants would give them cover until they got past the front corner and could see Rahel's situation. Ekatya nodded and took off at a run, Cox hard on her heels.

"Six of the Resilere have left the tanks." Lhyn had reverted to a clinical tone that meant she was truly frightened. *"Four went in the same direction as Helkenn. The other two . . . one of them is on Rahel. The other is right next to her."*

Ekatya hardly heard the last sentence, her mind stuck on a horrifying image.

That image became reality when she passed the front edge of the tank. Even through the foliage obscuring her view, the sight of a *Resilere* sitting on Rahel seared itself into her retinas. A second one sat nearby, apparently waiting its turn—just as they had with Murray.

But it made no sense. They were fed; they weren't desperate.

"That's where she was stabbed," Cox hissed. He lifted his phaser and sighted in.

"No!" Ekatya shoved his weapon down and prayed that she was right. She was betting Rahel's life on it.

"Captain! They'll suck her dry!"

"Do not fire without my order!"

"Don't shoot!" Dr. Wells shouted. *"It's not attacking!"*

"Yes it is!" Cox was incredulous. "I'm looking right at it!"

"Doctor, how do you know?"

"She's still conscious. I saw her hand move. Captain, listen to me. They break down their food with acid, but if that were happening while she's conscious, she wouldn't be lying there quietly. I'm telling you, it's not attacking and I need to be there!"

Ekatya hoped her relief didn't show. "She's right. If it was secreting acid, she'd be—"

A howl of the purest agony rang through the cavernous bay, going on and on until she thought it couldn't be Gaian. At last it died away, only to ring out again at the same volume but with twice as much pain.

"She'd be sounding like that," Cox finished, his eyes wide.

"Helkenn." Ekatya stood up, looking toward the starboard side of the bay, but saw nothing. Another scream pierced the air.

"Sounds like he's getting what he deserves," Cox said grimly.

"If four of them are distracted with him, that gives us time to deal with these two." The screaming was getting worse.

"It gives *you* time. I'll check—" He held up a finger and listened, then narrowed his eyes. "We've found him. By that tree, but he's in a blind spot. I'll go and warn you when the others come your direction."

"Observation only," she ordered. "Keep your distance."

"Understood." He sprinted down the row as another scream curdled her blood.

Ekatya raced behind him, turning at the cross row and slowing to a walk when she hit the open area. She was ten meters from Rahel and had a clear view of both *Resilere*. One still sat on her abdomen; the other crouched on her opposite side. A quick glance at the tanks showed that the four *Resilere* hanging inside the crates hadn't moved, and two others remained at the base of the ramps. The river of hatchlings was still in motion, but there were fewer of them.

She wondered if they could hear the high-frequency pitch of Helkenn's screams.

When she was five meters away, the *Resilere* beside Rahel climbed over her legs and advanced toward her.

She stopped.

It stopped as well, but made itself tall and spread out its arms, red bioluminescence rippling over its skin.

"It's guarding her." Lhyn's voice was awed.

"That's just wonderful, Lhyn, now tell me how to get past it!" Dr. Wells snapped.

"Rahel." Ekatya spoke as loudly as she dared. "It's Captain Serrado. Can you hear me?"

Rahel's head turned slowly, her eyes still closed. She murmured something, but Ekatya couldn't hear it over the hiss of rain hitting water.

"Dr. Wells, did you pick that up?"

"She pulled out her com after Helkenn stabbed her." Wells sounded half frantic and half furious.

Cox spoke softly. *"I'm in visual contact with Helkenn. He's no threat."*

"Are the Resilere reacting to you?"

"No."

If they weren't reacting to Cox, with his high level of distrust, they wouldn't react to the rest of them. "Dr. Wells, get moving. Lhyn, we'll need your translation skills."

"On our way." The main doors opened before Wells finished speaking.

Ekatya crouched down to present less of a perceived danger and was heartened when the *Resilere* retracted its arms. But it didn't move back, and its red bioluminescence did not abate.

The screams were growing weaker and more hoarse. She tried not to think of what was causing them and concentrated on these *Resilere*, which were not threatening her with an agonizing death.

"We're trying to help," she said. "Can't you feel it? We need to get to her." When the *Resilere* did not react, she spoke in a louder tone. "Rahel. Tell them we're your friends."

Rahel lay unmoving on the deck.

"Dr. Wells, I think she's unconscious."

"Of course she is by now," Wells growled. *"Since you kept me waiting!"*

She and Lhyn skidded around the corner of the last plant rack and hurtled toward the tank at a dead run. Wells was operating the gurney, a large medkit sitting atop it, while Lhyn carried a pad in one hand and a speaker in the other.

Ekatya held out her arm and made a downward motion, urging them to slow down. They continued their sprint to the tank, then slowed to a fast walk before turning the front corner.

At the sight of the gurney, the *Resilere* on guard duty flashed a faster pattern of red and extended its arms to what had to be their full length. The tips twitched wildly.

Lhyn fell to her knees beside Ekatya. "I've been playing the sounds for *friend* and *help* since we came through the doors. Why aren't they responding?"

"They are," Ekatya said. "Just not the way we want."

"I don't understand!" With an impatient motion, Lhyn brushed back the hair that had escaped her braid. "Did I get the translation wrong? Oh, stars, maybe the sound patterns aren't enough. Maybe they need the empathic component, too. How are we going to do that without Rahel?"

"That might not be the problem," Commander Jalta said. *"If Rahel was right and they don't distinguish between Gaians, then we lost their trust when Helkenn stabbed her. To their eyes, she's been responsible for their salvation, while our species has done nothing but hurt them—and now her."*

That made more sense than anything else. "So they're peaceable enough to not attack us, but that doesn't mean they'll allow us to hurt her any more." Ekatya wanted to break something. All that work, all that bridge-building, and Helkenn had destroyed it in the space of one second. How could they rebuild before Rahel died?

It was only then that she realized the screams had stopped.

"Dammit!" Dr. Wells spat. "I've had enough. Lhyn, come here."

Lhyn scrambled up and moved to the gurney. Dr. Wells held a vehement whispered conversation with her, then lowered the gurney until it was barely off the deck and dropped into a crouch beside it. She looked at Lhyn, who tapped her pad and nodded.

Wells pushed the gurney forward, moving in an awkward, shuffling waddle as she stayed in her low crouch.

The guarding *Resilere* stopped flashing its red bioluminescence and retracted its arms.

"I am responsible for her," Wells said firmly. "Let me take care of her. She is mine to care for."

Ekatya's jaw dropped when the *Resilere* rippled over Rahel's legs and took up a new post on her other side. She watched Wells shuffle forward, then turned to Lhyn. "What did you do?"

"Um." Lhyn looked uncomfortable. "I promised not to say anything. She said she'll tell you when it's all over. But my stars, look at that. It's working."

Dr. Wells had reached Rahel, set the medkit on the deck, and was already clicking a diagnostic band around her wrist. The *Resilere* atop Rahel slid off, taking a position next to its companion.

"Captain, the Resilere have left Helkenn's body. They're coming back."

"Acknowledged. Dr. Wells?"

Wells shook her head, which Ekatya took to mean *I heard and I don't care*. She unfastened Rahel's jacket and rapidly sliced open her shirt, then traded the edged tool for an injector while checking the diagnostic band.

Whatever she saw there shocked her. She reared back to stare first at the wound, then the *Resilere*, before shaking off her surprise and loading the injector with three different vials. It was discharged into Rahel's throat and tossed back to the kit in a blur of movement. She snapped on gloves with equal efficiency and bent over the wound. The position put her head close to the *Resilere*, but they didn't move, and she seemed to have forgotten about them.

After the hurried, purposeful actions up to this point, the examination lasted longer than Ekatya expected. Shouldn't she be doing . . . something?

At last Dr. Wells pressed a dressing in place and sat back on her heels. "Lhyn," she called across the intervening space. "Tell them thank you. Then get over here and help me get her on the gurney."

"Don't ask," Lhyn said before Ekatya got a word out. "I don't know either." She tapped her pad several times before pocketing it and pushing the speaker into Ekatya's hands.

The four *Resilere* returned just as Lhyn was crossing to Rahel. Ekatya was braced for the worst, but they paused only to touch the other two before swarming up the sides of the tanks. Apparently, some conversation had taken place that assured them Rahel was not being threatened.

"Commander Cox, they've arrived," Ekatya said. "They went straight into the tanks."

"Good to know," he answered. *"Remind me to never get on their wrong side."*

Dr. Wells had her hands under Rahel's shoulders and was pulling up her torso.

"How bad is he?" Ekatya asked, watching as Lhyn reached for her legs. Wells wrapped her arms around Rahel's chest, and still the two remaining *Resilere* did nothing.

"It'll make for a challenging autopsy." He made a sound of disgust. *"The first challenge will be keeping the body in one piece when they move it."*

Dr. Wells counted to three, and they lifted Rahel onto the gurney. She immediately raised it and began pushing it toward Ekatya, while Lhyn closed the medkit and plucked a bloody pair of pruning shears from the deck.

"Rahel is on the gurney. We're heading to the medbay."

"Acknowledged."

The two *Resilere* climbed onto the tank walls but did not enter the water. Ekatya had the feeling they would watch until Rahel was out of their sight.

"They sealed it," Dr. Wells said when she and Lhyn reached her.

Ekatya trotted beside them as they turned the corner and moved down the side of the tank. "What does that mean?"

They rounded the second corner and picked up speed, jogging along the backs of the tanks and platforms and heading toward the lift.

"The one that was sitting on her? It coated the wound with something similar to the cement sealant. It's like—" She shook her head. "I'll know more after the surgery. But I can tell you it stopped the bleeding. Almost instantly, judging by her blood pressure and the state of her uniform. All of her vital signs are stable. Shippers, I thought I'd be replacing half her blood volume."

Lhyn rushed ahead to open the lift doors, and Dr. Wells pushed in the gurney. "Medbay, surgery level."

"Are you saying she'll be all right?" Ekatya asked as she and Lhyn stepped in. The doors closed, and the lights tinted blue.

"He used a dirty pair of pruning shears; there's almost certainly abdominal contamination." Wells spoke in a clipped, clinical tone. "Fortunately, he was limited by the blade length. Based on the upward angle of the wound, he was targeting her liver. Plenty of blood to attract the *Resilere* and a good entry point for acid to liquefy her internal organs. But he didn't take into account the denser musculature of Alseans. Or the fact that they'd help instead of hurting her." She inhaled sharply and added, "It could have been much worse."

The tremor in her voice was slight, but for Ekatya, it was a startling shift from her earlier ferocity. She rested a reassuring hand on her shoulder. "Good thing she has the best surgeon in Fleet to knit her back together."

Dr. Wells did not acknowledge the touch or the sentiment, instead staring fixedly at the doors.

"She has what she needs," Lhyn said quietly.

At those words, some of the tension seeped from Dr. Wells's shoulders.

Ekatya had no idea why.

36

ICEFLAME

There was a time when Ekatya could pull double shifts and still be alert and ready for her normal shift the next day. As she stood in the lift, slumped against the wall and rubbing her tired eyes, she acknowledged that those days had vanished somewhere along with her commander's bars.

Not that captains were supposed to be working double shifts; that was why Fleet gave them staff. But on days like today, it was unavoidable.

The lift doors opened onto a silent corridor. She stepped across and through the doors of her quarters, finding them equally silent. After a difficult two hours of waiting through Rahel's surgery, Lhyn had gone to the labs, where she and Kade Jalta were no doubt hip deep in data and loving every minute of it.

"Phoenix," she said, stripping off her uniform jacket, "show me the bow view."

Where a blank wall had stretched from the door to the kitchen, she now saw a brilliant starscape reaching to infinity. The *Tutnuken* was already far behind them, its ghostly corridors no longer her problem. A repair crew had arrived under armed escort, and she had spent most of her second shift working with them until the destroyer captain waved her off. She suspected he was enjoying the chance to flex his situational authority over her, but if he thought it got under her skin, he didn't know her at all.

She had happily given the command to set course for Enkara, heard her surf engines come online, and felt the knot in her chest unwind.

Phoenix was free and flying once more.

A quick shower rejuvenated her, and she slipped into comfortable clothing that set her as far apart from the captain as she could get while still on her ship. Then she gathered a few supplies, walked into the lift, and stepped out in the medbay.

The last time she had been here, a crowd of medical staff had waited to whisk Rahel into surgery. Now she stood unnoticed in the spacious lobby and marveled at how peaceful it seemed.

Beneath a ceiling that soared two decks high, a ring of treatment rooms was arranged around a central desk. A curved corridor departed from one side of the lobby, ran behind the ring of rooms, and returned to the other side, giving access to a second set of treatment rooms used for long-term cases and those in need of more privacy.

The second-floor offices looked down onto the lobby, the lower halves of their walls flourishing with a hanging garden that removed all antiseptic odors and gave the medbay the same woodsy scent as the corridors. It was the Pulsar scent, and one Ekatya had never smelled on a smaller ship no matter how good their botanists were.

"Good evening, Captain," a nurse said as she approached the central desk. "Here to check on First Guard Sayana?"

"Among other people. How is she?"

"Awake and resting comfortably in room nine." He pointed the way. "Something of a medical miracle, that was. The whole staff is waiting for Dr. Wells's report on that sealant."

"Don't tell me she's writing that up now."

He looked up at the brightly lit windows of Wells's office, directly across from the main entrance. "I'll be amazed if she isn't."

She thanked him and crossed the lobby to Rahel's treatment room. After giving a light tap for warning, she opened the door and smiled at its occupant. "I hear you're a medical miracle."

"Captain!" Rahel tried to push herself into a more upright position. Her auburn hair was loose and her face pale, making her facial ridges more obvious, but otherwise she looked surprisingly normal.

"Oh, no." Ekatya lifted a hand. "Don't do anything to mess up Dr. Wells's handiwork, or we'll both suffer. How are you feeling?"

"Stupid." With a disgruntled look, she settled back against the raised head of her bed.

"Not quite what I was expecting." Ekatya rolled a stool over and sat down. "Why?"

She gestured at her abdomen. "He stabbed me like I was a sack of grain. I should have sensed him the moment he came in range."

"You were a little occupied at the time. Didn't Dr. Wells explain the effects of an altered state of consciousness?"

The tiny flinch could have been from her injury, but the speed at which it was erased said otherwise. "I haven't talked to her yet. But I've had two doctors and four nurses in here since I woke up, so I'm not feeling neglected." She offered a quick smile, remarkable for its insincerity.

"I'm sure she'll come when she can." Ekatya had no idea why Wells would delegate that, but it seemed that Rahel both knew and was eager to excuse it. "I can't remember the details, but the short version is that you weren't in control of your senses. Any of them. No one's holding you accountable for something your brain wasn't capable of doing."

Though Rahel didn't move, her demeanor seemed much less guarded. "Thank you. Lhyn said the same thing, but . . . it helps to hear it from you."

"She wouldn't lie to make you feel better."

"I don't think she knows how to lie. But you're my oath holder here. Your opinion is the one that matters."

Fleet training hadn't prepared her for this, she thought ruefully. "My opinion is that your performance today was above any reasonable expectations. You showed exemplary courage and selflessness, and you saved lives while working as an integral member of the crew. I think we can count your first patrol an unqualified success."

Rahel stared, her amber eyes wide with surprise. Then her forehead ridges crinkled. "Selflessness?"

"It couldn't have been easy, sharing those memories with so many of us."

She sympathized as Rahel broke eye contact. Had she been forced to reveal such private memories to half the section chiefs in her early career, she'd have put in for a transfer right afterward. Rahel didn't have that option.

"The chiefs will keep it confidential," she promised. "It won't go beyond those of us who were on the link."

"That doesn't mean they'll forget."

"No. But you've earned their respect. And mine."

Rahel looked up, startled once again. "Thank you, Captain. I didn't expect that." She sank back against her pillows, visibly more at ease. "Lhyn said when she and Commander Jalta write up their articles, they'll strip out the emotional truth and hide it under a pile of polysyllabic scientific words."

"That sounds like her. Trust a linguist to say exactly what she wants to."

"What she did took more courage than what I did."

An obvious diversion, but also an honest belief. That Rahel had honored Lhyn's courage on an open com link went a long way in Ekatya's estimation. "She was impressive, wasn't she? Thank you for helping her. You're a good friend to her."

"She's been a good friend to me." She hesitated. "I've been thinking about what happened. It feels like one of Fahla's jokes that you asked me to keep her safe, and in the end, she helped save me."

"I'm not enjoying the irony," Ekatya said flatly. "Our security was breached, and I have to apologize for that. Commander Cox is conducting a full investigation. As soon as we know exactly what happened, I'll share it with you. But I'm appalled. We've been telling you that you're part of a greater whole, yet we failed you. That shouldn't have happened. I'll take steps to make sure it never happens again."

"You feel guilty." Rahel tilted her head, reading her. "Captain, you shouldn't—" She stopped with a wince. "I'm sorry. I didn't mean to make you uncomfortable."

"I'm still getting used to being transparent." *To a subordinate*, she didn't add. She had just about come to terms with Andira and Salomen seeing through her, and to a lesser extent, Lanaril. She wasn't sure she'd ever get there with a crew member. "I appreciate that you don't blame me, but the fact is, I'm responsible. That's my job."

Rahel made no answer, her brows drawing together as she thought. "I've never had real backup before," she said slowly. "The last time I was injured on duty, I was alone in the middle of a forest. I tied a tourniquet around my leg and drove myself to the nearest healing center. They said if

I'd been ten minutes later, I would have died." She gestured at the treatment room. "I don't think having a team means no one ever makes a mistake. I think it means your team is there for you when you need them."

Ekatya looked at her new officer, who had just taught her a lesson, and wondered how the Hades she was supposed to respond to that. At last she held out her forearm and said, "I'm glad to have you, First Guard."

Rahel lit up as she accepted the Alsean warrior gesture. "I'm glad to be here. Well, not *here* . . ."

They both chuckled, and the atmosphere suddenly seemed lighter.

"Do you know what else is different about having a team?" Rahel asked. "When I was in that healing center getting my leg fixed, no one came to see me. No one knew I was there. But Lhyn's been here twice already. Roris brought the whole weapons team, and they're each buying me a drink in the Blue Rocket when I get out. Commander Jalta came by with Commander Zeppy. And Commander Shigeo brought me that." She pointed to her bedside table, which housed a bonsai that looked like an ancient, gnarled pine tree. "I've never seen anything like it. He told me how it's done and offered to teach me, so I'm going to learn. I want to make a tree like that for Salomen."

Ekatya walked around the bed to examine the bonsai more closely. "Beautiful. What a perfect idea for Salomen." She held up the colorful socks that were lying next to the bonsai. "Is there some meaning?"

She had never seen Rahel look playful before. "It's a joke. Between me and Katsu—um, Commander Lokomorra. He says they're to keep my feet warm while I'm in here."

"With lips," Ekatya drawled. "I'm not sure if I want to know the joke or not."

Rahel's smile was positively wicked. "You might, but he wouldn't."

Ekatya laughed as she returned the socks to their resting place. "Now I'm sure I want to know. I'm also sure you won't tell me." She turned to the display on the far wall, currently showing a feed from the *Resilere* tanks. "They're cute, aren't they?"

"Cute? They're adorable. I want to hold a double handful of them."

"Judging by how many people are watching this feed, half the crew agrees with you. Commander Kenji says it's more popular than the latest movie package." She watched a baby *Resilere* swim into view, settle onto a mineral block, and begin sparkling with bioluminescence. "Quite a journey from terrifying monster to crew mascot."

"Lhyn said something like that. She said people respond well to babies of most species, and this is a special case because we saved them."

"She told me it helps that they're tiny and sparkly."

Rahel chuckled and then grimaced. "I keep forgetting it hurts to laugh."

The *Resilere* hatchlings were a safe, non-humorous topic, enabling Ekatya to spend a few minutes in simple conversation until a nurse came and shooed her out.

One down, one to go, she thought as she jogged up the stairs. She'd count herself lucky if the second visit was only twice as difficult as the first.

On the second floor of the medbay, Ekatya found the chief surgeon's office door firmly shut. She rang the chime and waited.

"I thought I told—oh," Dr. Wells said as the door finished sliding open. "Captain. What can I do for you?"

Ekatya shouldered past her and stopped in the center of the room. "You can keep your promise. You said you'd tell me a story when it was all over."

Wells gestured toward her desk. "It's not over, I still have to finish—"

"Phoenix," Ekatya interrupted. "Log Chief Surgeon Wells off duty effective immediately, captain's authorization." She smiled at the dumbfounded doctor. "There. Now it's over."

The expected irritation washed over Wells's face. "That was high-handed and uncalled for."

"I might give you high-handed. But it was definitely called for. Two shifts is already too long." She opened the bag she had brought with her and thunked a bottle onto the cluttered desk. "Iceflame, as promised." Two short glasses joined the bottle. "I was planning to go to your quarters, but you weren't there."

"Captain, I can't. Rahel's wound was filthy; she needs regular checks for infection—"

"For which you have highly trained nursing staff. One of whom was just checking her." Ekatya plopped into a guest chair and waved a hand down her body. "See the civilian clothing? I'm not on duty, and we're friends. Call me Ekatya."

That was the winning move, she noted with some satisfaction. After several seconds of stunned silence, Wells drifted over, taking off her uniform jacket as she walked. It was tossed into her chair, and the two carved wooden sticks holding her hair twist in place clattered onto the desk. She brushed her fingers through her loose hair and sat in the other guest chair.

"Pour me a drink," she said.

Iceflame was two liquors, one hot and one cold, which never stayed blended for long. Ekatya shook the bottle vigorously, mixing the red and clear liquors, and poured two shots.

Wells held hers aloft. "My name," she said solemnly, "is Alejandra."

"It's a beautiful name. I'm happy to use it." They tapped their glasses together.

Iceflame was cold going in and hot going down. Ekatya closed her eyes, savoring the burn. "Oh, I needed that," she muttered.

"It's been a sewage sump of a week," Alejandra agreed.

"And then some. But it ended well."

"If you call nearly losing Rahel ending well, then yes, I'll give you that."

"We have two tanks full of happy *Resilere* who show no sign of wanting to go anywhere else. My ship is out of quarantine. The *Tutnuken* isn't our problem anymore. I was able to schedule Murray's memorial without worrying about creating an alien buffet. Lhyn and Kade Jalta are going out of their minds with the data we've collected. And Rahel is downstairs, awake and talking, with a new pair of lip socks that made her very happy."

"Lip socks?"

"A gift from Lokomorra. They're already such good friends that they have inside jokes with each other. She's had quite the parade of visitors, I hear."

Alejandra's expression hardened. She capped and shook the bottle, poured two new shots, and said, "Ask."

"Ask what?"

"Don't play innocent."

Ekatya leaned back, resting the glass on her thigh. "Why haven't you spoken to her?"

Alejandra drained the shot and stared at her glass. She opened her mouth, closed it, shook her head, and poured another shot. It followed the first without fanfare.

Ekatya was impressed. Two shots in a row should have had her coughing.

She lifted her own glass to her lips just as Alejandra said, "I had a child."

Spluttering, Ekatya hurriedly set the glass down and pressed her sleeve against her mouth. "Give a little warning next time."

Looking cheerier, Alejandra shook the bottle and refilled both glasses. "Fair warning, then. I had a son. His name was Josue. He died before his third birthday." She raised her glass and waited.

Ekatya's mind was racing. She had thoroughly vetted the candidates for chief surgeon and knew Alejandra's Fleet record backward and forward. It included her short-lived marriage, but there was not one iota of information regarding a child.

Which meant she had never wanted anyone in Fleet to know.

"To Josue," she said simply, and tapped their glasses together.

Alejandra's eyes reddened. She tossed back the drink, rubbed her eyes, and said, "Damn, that burns."

"I should think so, that's your fourth one." Ekatya let her have the excuse. "Tell me about Josue."

It was a horrifying, tragic story, and her heart hurt by the time it was finished. But it filled in a few blanks about what drove Alejandra in her work.

"It's a recently terraformed planet," Alejandra said, staring into the bottom of her glass. "Like Lhyn's. I was raised with the belief that our greatest calling in life was to stabilize our community. For me, that meant two things—improving our crops, and having children. I was pregnant before my eighteenth birthday."

Lhyn had told Ekatya about the pressure she lived under on her own planet. As a healthy young woman with a genius intellect, she had been expected to pass on her genes, ideally to a whole basket of children. But where she had fled those expectations, Alejandra had embraced them.

"I should have waited a few years. My body wasn't ready. Josue was delivered surgically." Alejandra looked up with a smile so humorless that Ekatya suppressed a shiver. "There were complications. Isn't that a perfect word? So clean, and it covers so much devastation. The damage to my uterus—"

When it became clear that she would not finish the sentence, Ekatya silently filled their glasses. "Irrevocable?" she asked.

Alejandra threw back the shot and closed her eyes as she swallowed. "He was my one chance. You want to hear the irony? I know how to prevent it now." She set the glass on her desk. "I don't often get the opportunity to deliver a baby. But I'll tell you this. No woman under my care will ever have that happen to her."

"I'm so sorry for your losses." For once, Ekatya found herself wishing for an empathic connection. The words were so inadequate.

"Thank you. I'm . . ." Alejandra glanced out the window, then met her eyes. "I'm glad you know."

"I'm honored that you told me."

"It's easier the second time. And you're wondering what this has to do with not talking to Rahel."

"I wasn't going to press."

"There's a first," she said with a hint of her usual sarcasm. "That awful day during Rahel's second week with us—the day I realized what a shitty job I was doing as the first Fleet doctor to care for an Alsean—that was when I found I could stop her signaling loop by touching her. The way I used to touch Josue. He'd snuggle on my lap and I'd run my fingers over his face and through his hair, and it would put him to sleep in two minutes." She slid lower in the chair, a far cry from the straight-backed posture she normally kept on duty. "She knew. She thought I had a daughter."

"So you told her."

"I needed her to trust me. She thought she was all alone, fighting prejudice and expectations and I—" She heaved a great sigh. "I didn't do her any favors by losing my temper the day she was bullied. She hid her symptoms because she didn't trust me not to use them against her. Yes, I told her about Josue. And it worked. It worked perfectly."

When she went silent, Ekatya picked up the bottle and raised her eyebrows. At the nod, she shook and poured two more shots. "I'm sensing a 'but' coming."

Alejandra gave a derisive laugh. "A big one." She downed her shot and coughed. "I've had two lives, Ekatya." She paused. "That sounded strange. I've never said your name before."

"I'm still getting used to Alejandra."

"I'm still getting used to hearing it from you."

"I have to say, Wells is easier."

This time, her laugh was real. "You can call me Wells if it's better for your poor, overtaxed brain."

"There's no need to be insulting about it." Ekatya drained her glass and thunked it back to the desk. "I like Wells," she decided. "But I reserve the right to use either."

"Fair enough, if I get to call you Serrado when I feel like it."

"Whichever you prefer," Ekatya said magnanimously.

"Then we're agreed." She looked at her glass. "I think I'm drunk."

"I think we both are. You said you had two lives."

Alejandra set the glass next to hers. "Two very separate lives. My name was the dividing line. Remember when I met Lhyn and she asked if I went by Aleja?"

"Mm-hm. You said never, because you were honoring your grandmother—wait. That grandmother? The one who taught you herbalism?"

She nodded. "I was Aleja until she died and I lost Josue. When I registered into the medical program, I became Alejandra. I wanted her strength. Her dignity. Probably fell short on the dignity part."

"I think you're very dignified," Ekatya said. "When you're not yelling at me."

"I only yell at people when they deserve it." Alejandra lifted a finger. "You hardly ever do."

Ekatya choked on her laughter. "Thanks. That's a compliment, coming from you."

Alejandra chuckled with her before the brief moment of humor faded. "I left my old life behind with my old name. It worked just fine for my entire Fleet career, right up until a few weeks ago."

"Telling Rahel ripped it open," Ekatya guessed.

"Wide open. When I lost Josue . . . it broke me. It broke my heart and I couldn't live that way, so I buried that dead piece of my heart with him. I've lived without it all this time. I never imagined it could come back. I never *wanted* it back."

"Because if you had it back, you could be hurt that way again."

"How the fuck did you know that? It took me until today to figure that out!"

Ekatya shrugged. "Psychology is part of the job, remember?"

"That's truly annoying." She ran a hand down her face and slumped even further into the chair. "Rahel got into my heart."

"She does that, I've heard."

"Where?"

"I met her mother at the oath ceremony. She said Rahel collected adoptive parents all over Whitesun after she ran away. She's still close to them, especially Sharro. Then she managed to get the Lead Templar of Blacksun invested in her. Lanaril told me she walked in planning to stabilize Rahel and hand her off to a mental healer. Ten minutes later, she knew she wouldn't let anyone else take that case."

"So I'm the latest in a long line. I'll bet none of them ran away."

Ekatya said nothing, waiting for the rest to come out.

"She did the unforgivable last night. She told me the truth." Alejandra looked up with an expression that said she was expecting judgment, then gave a tiny nod and continued. "We ended up in a new position, with her head in my lap. Stars above, it was so *familiar*. I let it feel good—and then she summarily informed me that I have maternal feelings for her."

Rahel, Ekatya decided, was missing a basic sense of self-preservation.

"I couldn't believe she said that. It was like a slap in the face. I was furious. So I lashed out, and then I walked out."

"Alsean honesty does take some getting used to," Ekatya said diplomatically.

"Voice of experience?"

"Oh, yes. It drove me crazy in the beginning, but I've come to appreciate it. Most of the time," she amended. "I don't have to be anything but me with Andira or Salomen. They won't *let* me be anything but me."

"That sounds terrifying," Alejandra grumbled.

"It was, at first. It helped when I realized the other side of it. While I was getting used to Alsean honesty, they were having to get used to Gaian dishonesty. They can tell each other half-truths or lies of omission, but actual lying? It's not easy."

Alejandra stared at her. "Sainted Shippers. That's why she was so shocked."

"Rahel?"

"She said I could lie to myself, but I couldn't lie to her. She's not used to self-deception, is she? No wonder." Her eyes reddened again. "I rejected her because she told me the truth, and she nearly died today thinking I was still angry. She wouldn't look at me all day."

"And you found out that denying your heart doesn't save you from hurting."

"I can't decide if I appreciate not having to explain it, or if I hate that you already know when it's been torture for me to put it together." She frowned. "Both, I think."

"That's fair." Ekatya kicked off her shoes and pulled her feet up onto the chair. "Is that why you haven't talked to her? Because you don't know what to say?"

"If I didn't know what to say before, it's worse now. Do you know how I got the *Resilere* to back off?"

"No, but given how many shots of iceflame it's taken you to get to this point, I can't wait to find out."

"I had Lhyn tell them I was her mother."

Ekatya was glad she wasn't trying to swallow anything. Alejandra watched with an expression that dared her to say a word.

Then it all fell into place.

"Brilliant." Ekatya's admiration was probably a little too effusive, but she'd had a lot to drink and couldn't be bothered to care. "You hit on the one word we could say that they'd trust, especially with their eggs hatching. But the sound pattern alone wouldn't have worked. You had to convince them."

"I thought she was bleeding out. I thought she was slipping out of my grasp, and my only chance to save her was to reclaim what I buried and *feel* it. All of it, without hiding."

For several seconds, Ekatya stared at her in silence. Then she shook the bottle, poured two shots, and held hers up. "That's the bravest damn thing I've ever seen."

Alejandra let out a sound that was halfway between a laugh and a sob. She tapped their glasses together, threw her drink back, and said, "Now I'm officially drunk. If I were brave, I'd have spoken to Rahel by now."

"You went from a lifetime of denial to full acceptance in about one minute. In a life-or-death crisis. That's brave. Accept it, Wells. You have the heart of a star, and now you have *all* of it."

"Wonderful. Now I just need to know what to do with it."

"Want my advice?"

Alejandra gave her a sideways look. "I don't know. You're drunk. How good can it be?"

"At least half as good as if I were sober."

She considered it. "Might be worthwhile. Go ahead."

"Enjoy it. Rahel won't judge you." Lhyn had told her what little she knew, so she felt safe making that guarantee. "She's known since the beginning, hasn't she? Did she ever give the impression that it made her uncomfortable?"

"She said . . ." Alejandra trailed off. "She'd feel uncomfortable if I was uncomfortable. Stars above, I need to apologize to her. I just don't know how."

Ekatya snorted. "With your temper? You've got to be an expert by now."

"I'm reconsidering being your friend."

"Too late."

37

HARMONIES

"Oh good, you're awake." Lhyn came into the treatment room with a speaker in one hand and excitement sparking off her skin. "I just got this from Commander Kenji. You won't believe it."

Rahel set aside her book, already smiling in anticipation. "Anything that makes you feel like that must be good."

Lhyn sat on the stool, her legs folding up like a gangly insect, and immediately stood up again. "Who used this last, a child?"

Rahel burst into laughter as Lhyn pulled the seat into a higher position. "Ouch, ouch, shekking Mother. Don't do that." She pressed a hand above her wound and tried to stop the chuckles. "It was Captain Serrado. Can I tell her you said that?"

"Oh, stars." Lhyn sat again, knees now at a normal level, and laughed as well. "Please don't. I'll never hear the end of it."

"All right. I'll keep it for blackmail material later."

"This is how I know you used to be a spy." Lhyn held up the speaker. "I'll make you a deal. You never mention that to Ekatya, and I'll play this for you."

"How do I know it's a good deal when I haven't heard it yet?"

"You'll just have to trust me."

"I do," Rahel said seriously.

Lhyn smiled. "Thank you. It'll be worth it, I promise. Remember when I said the *Resilere* were singing? I was right. Commander Kenji jacked up the frequencies to match the Gaian hearing range. Ready?"

"Yes!"

Lhyn set the speaker on the bedside table and pulled out her pad. "I call it the Song of Life."

A chorus of pure voices sang five soaring, lingering notes. After a beat of silence, they repeated the series of notes in a different pitch. Another pause, and they repeated it in a third pitch.

They returned to the first, but with a longer and more intricate melody. Another pause, and it was repeated in the second pitch. Then the third.

In this pause, Lhyn lifted a finger, her eyes shining.

The voices burst into glorious harmony, singing three complex parts that interwove into a beautiful, alien opus. Rahel listened intently, blinking away the moisture in her eyes. This was the other half of her experience, the song behind that loving voice. She had heard the intent but not the words, not the spell-binding artistry that tied it all together.

"Incredible," she murmured.

"Isn't it? I cried the first time I heard it. Just sat there and wiped tears. It's indescribably beautiful. It makes my heart hurt in a good way."

"Mine too. What a way to begin your life."

"Doesn't it make you wonder what other songs they have? Maybe what I thought was speech when Rez was waiting for Rez-Two wasn't talking at all. I'll separate that out tomorrow and see what Kenji can do with it."

They sat in silence then, giving their attention to the sublime opera that filled the room. Rahel closed her eyes, remembering her personal universe and how she would have followed that voice anywhere. Working together, the *Resilere* were as powerful as Salomen. There was a touch of the divine in this, she thought.

An emotional signature registered on her senses, separating itself from the background and growing stronger with every heartbeat. She opened her eyes to see Dr. Wells standing in the doorway, hair down and uniform jacket missing. Her emotions felt heavy, burdened with grief and shame, but the anger was quieter.

"It's the song of the *Resilere*," Lhyn said softly. "Sit with us and listen?"

Without a word, Dr. Wells rolled the second stool to the plexan wall facing the lobby and sat. She leaned her head against the plexan, closed her eyes, and gradually relaxed.

Rahel had not known how much time she spent in that wondrous universe, but she didn't think it was as long as this song. They had been listening for at least five minutes before Dr. Wells came in and fifteen more after. She wanted to ask Lhyn about it, but was reluctant to speak aloud and break the spell that had settled on the room.

Then the song changed. Not the harmonies, but the number of voices singing them.

Lhyn met her eyes. "This is when Helkenn stabbed you. Two *Resilere* went to help you, and four more went to protect their hatchlings. They divided themselves so the song wouldn't be disrupted."

"Three harmonies, four voices each," Rahel said. "In the beginning, I mean. And now two voices each."

"Fascinating, isn't it? Have you figured out the best part?"

"Um, no?"

"Three harmonies. Their hatching song needs a minimum of three singers. Their family units aren't based on pairs. You kept saying how cooperative they were—there were twelve parents all working together to hatch these eggs. This might be four families of three each, or two families of six, or they might all be one large family."

"To quote you," Rahel said, "Wow."

Lhyn laughed. "Yes! Makes me want to set up hydrophones all over Enkara. Are there bigger community groups? Are these twelve all there were in their group, or did that cargo crew break a bigger one? The only other group that's been observed was thought to have between twenty and twenty-four members. Imagine this song being sung by twice as many voices. Or three times."

Rahel could easily picture it. Then she wondered if her imagination was affecting her hearing. There were more voices.

Lhyn nodded at her questioning look. "The four who went after Helkenn are back in the song."

She could hardly believe how little time had elapsed. At this point in the song, Lhyn and Dr. Wells were already lifting her to the gurney. That they had responded so quickly—and then only after Captain Serrado and Commander Cox had already run in to assess the danger—left her awed and humbled.

Two more voices swelled the chorus to its prior level. The crisis was over and the *Resilere* were fully focused on their hatchlings again.

They listened for another ten minutes before the song changed, becoming simpler in its arrangement. The voices softened, their soaring melodies altering to something hushed and gentle.

"The last egg hatched," Lhyn said. "The adults who were in the crates with them are coming down the ramps. They're all together."

With a final, descending series of notes that reminded Rahel of drops falling into water, the song ended.

No one spoke.

Dr. Wells did not open her eyes.

"You were right," Rahel said at last. "It was worth it. Can you put that to a video file? So I can see what was happening in the tanks? I missed so much of it."

"I'd be happy to." Lhyn reached for her hand and squeezed it. "You'll have it tomorrow. I'm going to go see how Ekatya is doing. She said something about how kastrophenol isn't fully effective after a certain amount of alcohol."

"Captain Serrado got drunk?" That was a novel concept.

Amusement hit her senses, and she saw Dr. Wells's lips curve into a tiny smile.

"Roaring. I think she deserved it after this week. It's a good thing the lift is right across the corridor from our door." She rose from the stool and made Rahel laugh by lowering the seat as far as it would go.

"Ouch, stop! You did that on purpose."

"Always leave things as you found them," Lhyn said primly. "Good night. Good night, Alejandra."

"Sleep well." Dr. Wells lifted a hand and watched her go. She was far more relaxed than when she had entered, but anxiety was coming back into the foreground.

"May I apologize now?" Rahel asked.

Dr. Wells dropped her head, then stood up, pulled her stool over to the bed, and sat within arm's reach. "No. I'm the one who needs to apologize."

"But you're still angry with me."

Surprise flickered across her emotional signature like a small bolt of lightning, followed by a low rumble of understanding. "Your senses are fallible. I've been angry with myself, not you."

That wasn't as great a relief as she would have thought. "I shouldn't have said what I did."

Dr. Wells watched her for a long moment. "Why did you?"

"I was tired and . . . grumpy, I guess. My head hurt and I was upset about making you come to me in the middle of a crisis. And making myself useless. I knew I shouldn't have said it."

"In other words, you've been sitting on the truth all this time and it only came out because you were in pain and mad at yourself." With a soft chuckle, Dr. Wells added, "Sounds like me."

She didn't dare speak, too nervous about breaking this tenuous connection.

"I envy you," Dr. Wells said at last. "You have such a clear vision into your own heart. You're not afraid of it. I haven't seen mine clearly for a lifetime. I didn't want to. I was angry last night because you forced me to look."

Rahel thought she'd only begun seeing her heart clearly again when Lanaril counseled her, but now wasn't the time to say so.

"Do you . . ." She hesitated. Ironic, that Captain Serrado would commend her courage when she could hardly get these words out for fear of the answer. "Do you still think I betrayed your trust?"

"Did you tell anyone besides me?"

She shook her head. "No, of course not."

"Then you didn't betray me. I'm sorry, Rahel. There's not much else I can say except that I hope you'll forgive me."

The relief was so intense that it constricted her throat. She cleared it and said hoarsely, "Of course I do. I'm just glad you're here now."

The words dramatically diminished Dr. Wells's anxiety, but its remnants still hovered over her shame like oil on dirty water. "You've been in the medbay for hours," she said. "The emotional pressure has to be building. Would you like a treatment, or have I ruined that for us?"

That had been too much to hope for. Rahel could not stop the silly grin as she blurted, "I'd love it."

Dr. Wells's answering smile was nearly as broad.

The first touch of gentle fingers on her face had a shockingly strong effect. Though she screwed her eyes shut, a tear managed to escape.

Dr. Wells silently wiped it away and went on with her treatment. Regret was strong in her touch, but the anxiety had vanished. In its place was a calm determination.

"Thank you for saving my life," Rahel ventured.

"Thank you for giving me the means to do it."

She didn't understand that at all. But she felt too good to ask.

38

ON THE TEAM

Rahel felt much better by the middle of the next day, but Dr. Wells still wouldn't let her walk on her own two feet. It was embarrassing, having to use a chair, but at least she had the consolation of firing it out of the lift at top speed. She chuckled at the sound of Dr. Wells and Lhyn jogging behind her.

"You should have sabotaged the wheels," Lhyn grumbled as they hustled toward the *Resilere* tanks.

"I didn't think she'd have enough time to be obnoxious," Dr. Wells huffed.

"Warriors always have enough time for that."

Rahel slowed before reaching a point where she might frighten any *Resilere* who happened to be looking out this side of the nearest tank. "What a lot of complaining from two people who aren't stuck in a chair."

After spending twenty-four hours cooped up in a treatment room, it was pure joy to be in this soaring space with the constant patter of rain on water and the rich, organic scent of thousands of plants. And they were the only ones here. The botanics staff were all working elsewhere in the ship until the *Resilere* returned home.

She turned her chair and began moving slowly alongside the tank. A baby *Resilere* was attached to the side, giving her a good view of its silvery underside. Wrinkles radiated outward from a small indentation in the exact center, indicating the location of its mouth. Up on top, its eye stalks weren't even the length of her smallest fingernail.

"Oh, my stars," Lhyn said. "Look at it! They're twice as cute in real life as they are in the footage."

The little *Resilere* watched them move past, appearing intrigued but not afraid. Rahel couldn't sense it, though she felt a background buzz of interest and contentment from the hatchlings as a group. *Resilere* apparently did not pop out of the egg in possession of their full empathic abilities.

She stopped when an adult swam over and attached to the tank's side, then rippled upward. Its arms spread along the top edge, flexing smoothly as its body broke the water surface. Reflective violet eyes on fully extended stalks focused on her.

Mouse was standing at the window, looking out at the red glow staining the night sky as the ship burned. "Where have you been?" he demanded.

"Well met, Rez," she said. "I'm all right, thanks to you." She projected her happiness, an emotion she didn't think Rez could miss given how wonderful she felt. Being here and seeing for herself that it had all turned out so well was the best possible medicine.

Her thanks had already been given yesterday, right before she blacked out.

She leaned forward to rest both hands on the edge of the tank, smiling when Rez gently felt them with two arms. Another arm hovered in the air in front of Dr. Wells, and she saw the memory of her mother inspecting a block of metal, preparing to start her next sculpture.

"You made quite an impression on them," she said. "Rez recognizes you."

Teetering between embarrassment and wonder, Dr. Wells tentatively held out her hand and allowed contact. "Oh—it's so soft!"

Rez looped its arm around her wrist and halfway up her forearm, then smoothly released her.

"What did you see?" Dr. Wells asked, watching the arm retreat from hers.

"Um. I'll just say that you were very convincing in your assertion of maternal rights."

"I'm never going to live that down, am I?" It was said lightly, but Dr. Wells kept her gaze on Rez. What she had spoken of last night, in a soft mood after their reconciliation, was unwelcome now that she was in uniform and on duty.

"Are you kidding?" Lhyn spoke up from Rahel's other side. "I'm hoping you're accepting applications for adoption. If I'm ever in trouble, I want you breathing fire to get me out of it."

Dr. Wells flushed, but her amusement was breaking up the crystalline embarrassment. "I suppose breathing fire is one of my specialties."

"I'm glad I talked to Lanaril last night." Rahel redirected the conversation, not wanting her to be uncomfortable. "So I could come here today without feeling guilty."

"I didn't know you called her," Dr. Wells said.

"I couldn't sleep. She made me swear I'd call whenever I needed to, and . . . I needed to last night."

"Because of Helkenn?" Lhyn asked.

She traced her fingertips over Rez's nearest arm. "Because I thought the worst when Rez climbed onto me. Then it told me it was helping, and I felt terrible that I made such an awful judgment."

"You weren't the only one who made it," Dr. Wells said darkly. "And you had a much better excuse, considering that you were in shock."

"Lanaril said that, too. About being in shock. But she said something else that helped even more. She reminded me that the worst of my nightmares are about someone I trust turning into an enemy."

"A nightmare come to life," Lhyn said.

Rahel nodded. "Getting stabbed was minor compared to thinking Rez would kill me. It really helps to know that there was a reason I thought that. I didn't fail at the last step."

"Fail, right," Lhyn snorted. "I'm not going to dignify that. Is a nightmare the reason you couldn't sleep?"

There was a time when Rahel would never have admitted it. That choice had cost her and the people she loved far too much heartache. "It was the worst one," she said. "And now I know why I had it. Before I called Lanaril, I was, um, upset. I hadn't had any nightmares since boarding the *Phoenix*. I thought they were over."

Lhyn's hand joined theirs in touching Rez. "Shippers, it *is* soft." She stroked as much of the arm as she could reach before saying nonchalantly, "I still have nightmares sometimes. If you ever need to talk and Lanaril's not around, you could call me."

Rahel turned to look at her. After a moment, Lhyn met her eyes and offered a smile.

"Only if you'll do the same, if Captain Serrado can't help."

"Deal."

She watched their hands on Rez's skin. Lhyn's were larger, with long and delicate fingers. Dr. Wells had smaller hands, but Rahel knew from experience how dexterous and soft they were. Her own were mid-sized and calloused from a lifetime of stave practice.

Rez accepted them all, offering no hint as to whether it felt the differences.

"When I was seventeen," she said quietly, "Prime Warrior Shantu offered me the chance of a lifetime. My service for his sponsorship, and I wouldn't even have to give up my independence. I could stay outside the system and work alone. It was a dream come true."

She didn't have to look up to sense how intently they were listening.

"I never knew what I was missing. All of this—" She gestured around them. "Nobody could do this by themselves. I couldn't have saved the *Resilere* by myself. Yesterday, Captain Serrado and Commander Cox put themselves at risk for me. The only reason you two didn't is because the captain wouldn't allow it until she knew it was safe." She met Lhyn's gaze. "I loved Shantu, but he would never have risked himself for me. That's not what an oath holder does. It's backward."

"Not for Ekatya."

She nodded and turned to Dr. Wells. "I thought you were still angry with me yesterday. When we were listening to the song of the *Resilere*, before we talked—I realized that it wouldn't have mattered if you were or not. You'd have come for me regardless."

Dr. Wells smiled. "It's what I do."

"That's what you said the day I broke down in the medbay. I didn't understand it then. I think I do now. I'm on a team." She looked back at Rez and added, "A shekking amazing team."

Lhyn laid a long arm across her shoulders. "What do you think, doc? Shall we let her stay on the team?"

"I think she'll do fine. Now that we've knocked off some of those sharp warrior edges."

Rahel laughed. "You'll never get rid of those."

She looked around the enormous bay, half advanced technology and half garden, and smiled to herself. This ship was starting to feel like home.

39

STRATEGIES

"*Captain.*" Lokomorra's voice spoke quietly in her com. "*We're in the system. We'll reach Enkara in two hours.*"

"Acknowledged. Get any more calls?"

A groan sounded in her ear. "*Eight. Either they don't talk to each other, or they all think they're the ones who know the magic words.*"

Along with Commander Jalta, Lokomorra was in charge of communications between the *Phoenix* and the researchers who insisted they needed to be present for the release of the *Resilere*. Ekatya had delegated that task upon realizing that the researchers came from institutes all over the Protectorate and had no overarching authority she could speak to. This was the xenobiology event of the decade; everyone wanted access.

No one was going to get it. Handing off the job of repeating that to multiple callers was one of the benefits of being captain.

"Look on the bright side," she said, not bothering to keep the amusement from her voice. "I'm sure you'll only get ten or twelve more in the next two hours. After that, they'll stop trying."

"*That's very encouraging, thank you,*" he said dryly.

She closed the call and returned to reading the latest communication from Command Dome regarding the *Resilere* tissue sealant.

Alejandra's report had indicated that it was biologically inert and more effective than any wound sealer the Protectorate had developed. Based on the breakdown rate she was still observing with a sample in Enkara seawater, its rate of dissolution was likely timed to the average rate of tissue healing in a *Resilere*. In Rahel's case, it had indeed stopped all bleeding and provided a protective barrier between the wound and outside sources of infection.

Alejandra had feared that removal might be a sticky nightmare, but like the defensive cement, the sealant had different physical properties in air than in Enkara seawater. In the water, the molecules were less attracted to each other than to the tissues they touched, making it adhesive to the wound. In air, however, they were more attracted to each other. She had been able to peel it off as she repaired the damage. Two days after the stabbing, Rahel was fully mobile and back on light duty.

If Fleet could create a synthetic version of this, they would have a lifesaving addition to the medkits of first responders. Judging by the file on Ekatya's display, Fleet Medical was already salivating over the prospect.

Ironic, she thought as she closed the file. No one could have known the *Resilere* would survive both vacuum and sterilizing radiation, yet it had been her reputation on the line when her ship was overrun with destructive aliens that melted infrastructure and ate brains. Now, though she'd personally had little to do with the breakthrough in *Resilere* communication or the discovery of this sealant, it was her reputation that shone.

As her grandfather always said, a captain was only as good as her crew.

Her entry chime rang right on time. She blanked the display, tapped her deskpad to open the door, and was stepping out from behind her desk when Commander Cox came in with his distinctive bowlegged walk.

"Join me for a drink?" She led him to the small conference table across the room. It was surrounded by four comfortable armchairs and made a more congenial place to meet than on opposite sides of her desk.

"What's on offer?" he asked.

"Alsean shannel. Lhyn's been sending me on duty with a thermal flask of it every morning. I'm hopelessly spoiled now." She opened the door of a recessed cupboard and pulled out the flask and two small cups.

"You've never offered that before." He stood behind his chair, waiting for her to sit first.

"It's taken me this long to decide I'm ready to share."

"In that case, yes, I'd love to join you."

She set the cups on the table, popped the lid off the flask, and took an appreciative sniff. "Ahh. A gift from Fahla. That's the Alsean goddess," she added as she filled the cups. "Take a seat, Commander."

He sat a second after she did and lifted the cup to his nose. "It *does* smell good. A little bit like mulled wine, but it looks like coffee."

"I should probably warn you that it'll burn going down." She took a sip and sighed blissfully. "Oh, I needed this."

His eyes widened as he swallowed. "Whoa."

She chuckled. "That's what they all say their first time."

He held the cup out, examined the liquid more closely, then took a larger gulp and grinned. "Nice. I can see why you didn't want to share. Are we drinking on duty?"

"It's not alcoholic. In fact, it clears your mind and makes you more alert. And it's healthy."

"It's healthy? Why isn't this being exported off Alsea by the shipload? Never mind, nanoscrubbers," he answered himself. "But once the Alseans get their space elevator built?"

"I don't know. It's a global addiction for them. They drink as much as they produce."

"They're no fools." He gave his shannel a long, slow sniff, looking like a man having a religious experience. "This is a good perk of shuttling down there every time we're in orbit."

"No, it's a perk of Lancer Tal giving me a dispenser. You can't just bring up cases of it. There's a production process at the last step."

"You get all the best toys," he said, making her laugh.

"There have to be some compensations for the responsibility." She settled back in her chair and took another sip. "All right, tell me the bad news. How did he get through our net?"

Cox had notified her earlier that he had completed his investigation on Helkenn's escape, ending the call with a warning that she wouldn't like the results. Now he leaned forward and rested his elbows on the table, the cup in his hands. "I'll tell you the good news first. He didn't manage to override the lift lockdown."

"Then how did he get to hydroponics so quickly?"

"Straight down a brace shaft. Then he strolled down the corridor easy as you please and took a chase to get into the bay. I had the report of his escape six minutes after it happened. He was inside hydroponics in five."

"Lovely. Not only did he know exactly where to go, he stole someone's access code to get there. Don't tell me he had someone on the inside."

His hesitation made the hair on the back of her neck stand up. "Not the way you're thinking. He knew where to go because my staff needed a lesson on discretion around prisoners. But he got there using the repair code."

"The repair—" She bolted upright and smacked her cup on the table. "Sholokhov."

He nodded unhappily. "It makes the most sense. Helkenn wouldn't have had access to it through his duties. I've questioned the people he worked with; no one reported him asking or even being with them when they went in the chases. Given the right tools and enough time, he could have broken the code earlier, but I've checked the access records and it hasn't been used since he boarded. Not until his escape. What I can't figure out is why the Director of Protectorate Security would put our security at risk."

She took such a large gulp that it was a wonder steam didn't shoot from her nostrils. "I assume you've already changed our repair code?"

"Of course."

"Good." She shook her head. "That torquat did it again."

"Did what?" he asked in frustration. "What was his game?"

"To win. No matter how it turned out." She held up one hand and looked at it. "Helkenn fails. Sholokhov has the information he wants and gets rid of a resource that has no value. All loose ends neatly tied." She turned to her other hand. "Helkenn succeeds but gets caught. Same results as before. Or, he succeeds and manages to escape, probably by stealing a shuttle and jamming open the exit tunnel with another conveniently provided code. Now Sholokhov has the information he wanted *and* a resource that has suddenly proven very capable." Wrapping her hands around her cup, she added, "He had nothing to lose and something to gain in every permutation."

"Did he want to torpedo your reputation, too? Losing the first Alsean officer on her very first patrol and then letting the assassin escape in a stolen shuttle—our next stop would have been Command Dome for the inquest."

She thought back to her call with Sholokhov and shook her head. "No. He and I have had our differences, but I think he has a grudging sort of respect for me. He gave me a . . . gift, for lack of a better term. An assurance I needed that he had no reason to provide. It didn't gain him anything. I think he gave it as a reward for not letting him take me down." Even though she hadn't done a damned thing. Rahel had saved herself.

"That's abhorrent," he snapped. "He's playing games with lives and giving *rewards* for being a good player?"

"It's not a game. It's just numbers. We're all numbers to him." She lifted the cup.

"Not you."

With a hurried swallow, she set the cup down. "I'm no exception. He would have thrown me into the furnace without a second thought."

"But he gave you a gift." Cox leaned forward, fixing her with an intent gaze. "I've read up on Sholokhov. The man is a psychopath. People like that don't do anything unless it benefits them or their goals in some way. Giving you a reward doesn't do either, does it? You're not just a number to him."

"That doesn't make me feel better. In fact, it makes my skin crawl."

"Yeah, I get that." He sniffed his cup. "I also get how this could turn into a global addiction." After a swallow and an appreciative sound, he was all business again. "I propose we rotate the repair code on a monthly basis and forget to send that detail in our reports. I also think I should go through the crew records and confirm them independently. We could have caught Helkenn that way. His Fleet records don't hold up under a bright light. A bright, non-Fleet light."

"You're saying we can't trust our own system?"

"I'm saying we can't trust Sholokhov, and he has his fingers in our system. We already know there's at least one person on this ship spying for him."

She nodded. "Whoever delivered the orders to Helkenn. Probably the same person who delivered my orders to Dr. Wells, back during our shakedown cruise."

"I don't know about you, but the idea of someone pulling strings on my ship makes my pants itch."

That surprised a chuckle out of her. "I wouldn't put it that way, but now that you mention it . . ."

"Yeah." He held up his cup. "Then I have your approval?"

"You have it." She tapped her cup to his and drained it. "On a much happier topic, are you comfortable with Rahel going on Enkara?"

He grinned. "I've never seen anyone so motivated to get through envirosuit training. She's ready."

"Good, because I didn't know how we were going to do this without her."

"We couldn't have done any of this without her. Does it make you think there might be other empathic species and we never knew?"

"Oh, yes. I think Jalta is losing sleep over it."

He looked into his cup, the skin around his eyes tightening. "How did Dr. Wells really get past the *Resilere*?"

She should have known he wouldn't let that go.

"I believe she explained it at the section chief meeting," she said in a tone of voice that told him to back off.

He met her gaze evenly. "You can tell me it's classified and I don't need to know. That would at least be honest. As your chief of security, I think I deserve more than the lie Dr. Wells told everyone else. She didn't just give the emotional component they were missing from the sound pattern. If it were that easy, they would have let Dr. Rivers through. She's more Rahel's friend than Dr. Wells is. And what she said about responsibility—that's not friendship."

Ekatya tapped her fingers on the side of her cup as she assessed her options. He was right. Other than Commander Lokomorra, Cox was the one person who truly did need to know everything in order to do his job.

Or almost everything.

"She took a chance," she said at last. "Doctors assume responsibility for their patients. The best doctors find a way to do that without walling off their own hearts. I know you don't get along with Dr. Wells, but you can't argue that she is a doctor with heart."

He offered a slight smile. "No one has a temper like that without having a heart."

"That's what she used. We had the sound pattern for a familial association. She told Lhyn to play it and focused on her own feelings of responsibility for Rahel, hoping the *Resilere* would interpret it as a familial emotion. And they did."

"A familial association?" His slight frown evened out. "Are you talking about the sound patterns when Rez was waiting for Rez-Two to rehydrate?

Or the second solid one?" Sitting back in his chair with a thump, he let out a short laugh. "She told them they were *partners*?"

If that was the assumption he drew, she would let him. "That does not leave this room," she said sternly.

His amusement vanished. "No, of course not. I was only—" He stopped, lips pursed in thought. "That was strategic."

"You don't think Dr. Wells can be strategic?"

"I . . . huh." He stared off into space. "I'll have to rethink my assessment."

Biting back a laugh, she lifted her cup and said, "You do that."

40

ENKARA

It was Commander Jalta's idea to send a shuttle to the release site and return with a shallow container of rocks, seaweed, and real Enkara seawater. Rahel and Lhyn wheeled it into hydroponics and up against the midpoint of the two tanks, giving equal access to the adults in both.

The first *Resilere* to approach—Rahel always assumed it was Rez—slipped a curious arm into the water and wrapped the tip around a bit of blue seaweed. Then it became tall and ruffled, its arms coiling, extending, and coiling again as blue and green bioluminescence played over its skin.

Every other adult from both tanks rushed up. It was the first time Rahel had been in close proximity to all twelve of them, but they paid little attention to her. Their arms were sliding against each other, all vying for the opportunity to reach into the container and touch its contents—or perhaps smell or taste, as Jalta had suggested.

Lhyn played the sound pattern for *home*, and Rahel envisioned herself on Dock One. She called up the memory of the ships tied at their docks, cables creaking as they pulled at them—and started when the bells of Whitesun Temple tolled directly behind her, so close and loud that her ears rang from the onslaught. She spun around, almost tripping over an uneven board on the dock. How could the temple be here on the bayfront when it was supposed to be in the center of the city? But there it was, looming before her, its stately dome brushing the sunrise-pink clouds.

The roar of a cresting wave made her turn back in time to see foaming water pour over the boards. It lapped at her boots before draining away.

A stranded fish flopped frantically, its body slapping against the wood and reflecting the early morning light in shades of green, blue, and red . . .

"Whoa! What happened?"

Rahel was off balance, her knees bent while Lhyn's arms were wrapped around her chest, keeping her from falling. With a twist that wouldn't have been possible two days ago, she regained her feet and stood upright, sucking in air. "Fahla, that was intense."

"It must have been. You jumped about a meter in the air and spun around like something bit you." Lhyn stepped back, giving her room to recover.

"No biting, but . . . I don't know how to describe that. It wasn't a memory." The crisp sea air was still in her nostrils, and she was hit with a staggering wave of homesickness. She wasn't sure how much was hers and how much came from the *Resilere*.

"You mean Rez communicated directly?"

After what she had just experienced, the excited anticipation coming from Lhyn was too strong. A headache stirred behind her eyes, sending out exploratory tendrils, and she willed it away. She could not raise her blocks right now.

"I don't think it was just Rez. I think it might have been all of them. It felt like they turned my memories into a dream." She described it as best she could, but mere words were a poor substitute for the depth of that experience.

"Fascinating," Lhyn breathed. She turned to watch the *Resilere* still crowded around the container, her smooth forehead furrowed in thought. "It was home for you, but bigger and brighter."

"And louder."

"Right. And the fish's skin was reflecting the sun in the same colors as their bioluminescence."

It clicked then. "They put themselves into the vision."

Lhyn nodded. "When they asked for help before, they used a memory. Or your brain interpreted it that way. This was much more direct." She met Rahel's eyes. "Maybe they're not asking for help. Maybe they're telling you they know you're helping to get them home."

"Let's hope so."

The *Resilere* began to move away, each taking a rock or bit of seaweed with it. By the time the last one retreated, the container held nothing but water.

"Are we ready?" Commander Zeppy asked from his position inside the closed lift.

"It's time," Rahel said.

In all the hours she had spent here, sitting with the *Resilere* as the ship hurtled toward Enkara, the sound of rain hitting water had been her constant companion. Now it stopped, abruptly and with no fanfare. It felt wrong.

Working together, she and Lhyn upended the container, emptying the Enkara seawater into the tanks with a great splash and spilling some into the narrow space between them. The standpipes briefly gurgled, and then the system was silent.

Hydroponics seemed larger and emptier already.

Lhyn played the sound patterns for *friend* and *home*, the same words they had used before rolling the *Resilere* out of the brace shaft. Rahel projected *safe* with all her might, but she didn't think it was necessary this time. The *Resilere* weren't nervous. They were . . . expectant. Hopeful.

"Preparing to seal the tanks," Zeppy said. *"Is it all right?"*

"I think they know," Rahel answered. "They're ready."

"No arms over the edges of the tanks?"

"Everyone's inside."

"Acknowledged. Sealing in three . . . two . . . one . . ."

With a small popping sound, two bars hurtled toward them from the backs of the tanks and snapped in place over the front edges. They were the weighted leaders of thin, acid-proof screens that had unrolled from cylinders in the back and now covered each tank. Captain Serrado had insisted on the design before they brought in the eggs, a precaution against hatchlings or possibly adults deciding to go for a walk. Part of Rahel's duties for the past two days had been to ensure that the *Resilere* stayed put, but when she wasn't there, other crew members had kept watch via the cams.

The lift doors opened, disgorging Zeppy and three of his staff. This was the moment Rahel was most worried about. She crouched in front of the tanks, watching and sensing for any disturbance as the four newcomers picked up the first of the lids stored against the nearest bulkhead. Each person held a corner of the unwieldy square and carefully walked it to the tank on Rahel's right.

"They're all right," Rahel said, her voice startlingly loud in the new silence of the bay. "No one is afraid of what we're doing."

"Gently, then," Zeppy told his staff. With a few grunts of effort and careful maneuvering, they slid the lid atop the tank and pressed it down. He stepped back, brushing his hands on his trousers. "Still good?"

"Still good."

While the process was repeated on the other tank, a *Resilere* that she thought must be Rez swam up to the front and flattened an arm tip against the transparent material. Rahel pressed her hand against the same point and thought of lying on the couch with her head in Sharro's lap.

Safety and comfort. Home.

With the second lid in place, Zeppy pressed a control to remotely seal the standpipes at both ends. Then he squatted beside her, watching as Rez peeled away and retreated into the interior. "You're going to miss them, aren't you?"

She nodded, still holding her hand against the tank. "This might sound odd. But in some ways, they're more familiar to me than you are. I mean, you Gaians."

His amusement tickled across her senses. "I figured you didn't mean me personally." He used her shoulder to help push himself upright before holding out a hand. "Time to let them go, First Guard."

She accepted the help, despite no longer needing it. "I know."

In another example of Zeppy's forethought, the tanks had been set up on cargo movers. It was a mere press of a button to gently raise the platforms, lifting the tanks with them, and another button to start them moving toward the lift.

Rahel walked beside them, projecting *safe*, while Lhyn repeated the sound patterns for *friend* and *home*. The *Resilere* were moving around with some agitation, but it was born of excitement.

She stepped into the lift with Zeppy and the first tank. "Shuttle bay," she said, and watched the doors close on hydroponics.

Lhyn would accompany the second tank, ready to reassure the *Resilere* with her limited vocabulary should it become necessary.

They rolled out into the shuttle bay, even higher and more cavernous than hydroponics, but filled with the sharp scents of machinery and lubricants. Before they were halfway to the waiting cargo shuttle, she heard the lift doors open again and turned to see Lhyn's affirming nod as she walked out ahead of her tank.

The shuttle's rear hatch was open, but no ramp stretched from it to the deck. Zeppy led her up a short flight of steps instead.

She had been in this shuttle once before, when the captain conducted her tour. The pilot and passenger area up front was separated by an airlock from the open space that made up the rest. Loaders and movers and gadgetry Rahel hadn't yet learned about were attached to the ceiling and rear hatch, currently stowed in their resting positions. Up by the airlock, equipment lockers lined the forward bulkhead. Fold-out seats were stowed in the bulkheads to the sides, and the deck was clean and bare.

Just inside the hatch, Zeppy opened a panel and danced his fingers over the controls behind it. A kind of secondary cockpit whirred as it unfolded itself from the shuttle's hull. It consisted of a chair inside a protective frame, with an intimidating array of switches, controls, and what looked like two large, open gloves.

He stepped out of the hatch and settled into the chair, eyes crinkling as he smiled. "The captain didn't show you this, eh?"

She shook her head. "What is it?"

"Wait and see. And don't move a step from where you are."

Humming to himself, he flipped switches and slid his fingers down a lit pad. The metal arms attaching the chair to the hull extended, leaving it suspended above the deck and a body length from the shuttle. Then Zeppy put his hands inside the gloves. "Here we go!" he called.

Rahel nearly jumped out of the hatch when the loader that had been resting against the ceiling suddenly came to life. It swung down and smoothly moved past her, its wide arms pressed together until it passed through the hatch. With a grace she would not have believed possible for such a large piece of machinery, the arms opened up, slid around the sides of the heavy tank, and lifted it off the cargo mover.

"Coming in," Zeppy announced, fluidly reversing the loader.

What was most surprising, Rahel thought as the tank moved past her at knee level, was how quiet this equipment was. Numerous joints and servos were in motion, and it was handling a great weight, yet all she heard was a soft purr.

The loader slid along the shuttle's ceiling, carrying the *Resilere* deeper inside, then set the tank down so gently that the water barely rippled. She turned to see how Zeppy had managed that and jerked her head back at finding him right next to her. He had propelled the control chair into the hatch, watching the tank as he manipulated the loader.

"Still think you want to go into security?" he asked. "Operations has better toys."

"I'm reconsidering. How long does it take to learn to use that?"

"To use it? Couple of hours. To use it like me? Years." He swung away, the loader following him out like a massive mechanical pet.

The second tank was brought inside with equal ease. While Zeppy returned the loader and control chair to their stowed positions, his staff locked the tanks in place with a complicated web of straps. Rahel went from one to the other, projecting her assurance and confidence until the *Resilere* fluffed back out from their flattened positions. They hadn't enjoyed the ride into the shuttle.

Lhyn crouched beside her, having come inside with the rest of the staff. "I'm playing their calming words. They look a bit rough."

"I think this might remind them of when they were taken," Rahel said. "The machinery and being moved around like this."

Zeppy squatted on her other side. "I'll eat my insignia if I didn't make that ten times smoother than a bunch of illegal miners."

"They *were* cargo crew," Lhyn pointed out. "I'm sure they knew how to operate loaders."

"Not like me. And they thought they were moving rocks." Once again, he used Rahel's shoulder to help propel himself upright. "Time for you to go up front, Dr. Rivers."

Lhyn rested a hand on Rahel's leg. "I hate to go," she said softly.

"I know." Intellectual excitement hadn't been Lhyn's only driving force these last few days. Her sadness at this separation was thick and sticky.

"Right. Well, we shouldn't keep them trapped any longer than we have to. Take care of yourselves," she said to the *Resilere*. "I'm sorry my species was such a bunch of assheads. At least now you know some of us are better than that. I hope we can meet again someday, when I've learned your language." She touched the tank, but no *Resilere* came to match her position. With a disappointed sigh, she unfolded her long legs and walked toward the open airlock.

"You too," Zeppy said. "You'll be more comfortable for the first part of the trip up front. Come back here and get suited up after we've cleared the ship."

She followed Lhyn through the airlock into the much smaller passenger compartment. Up ahead, she saw a familiar head bent over the pilot's controls, the stripes burned into his hair follicles making him instantly recognizable. "Commander Lokomorra! I didn't know you were flying us."

He spun the seat around and grinned, both dimples denting his cheeks. "Captain Serrado said I needed to have some fun. You and Lhyn got to run all over the ship and play with the *Resilere*. Half the section chiefs were there with you. All I got to do was sit up on the bridge. Do you know how boring it is to sit on the bridge when the *Phoenix* isn't doing anything?"

Lhyn chuckled as she took the copilot's seat. "You might not want to get any more promotions. Ekatya says she had much more fun as a commander, back when they let her off the ship now and again."

"Yeah, but as a captain she can shove things off on her overworked exec. I took *sixteen* more calls from Enkara researchers!"

"Shit rolls downhill." Lhyn's head was down as she attached her harness, but Rahel could have felt her amusement from the other side of the shuttle bay.

"See? When you're captain, you're on top of the hill."

"You also make the biggest target," Rahel said absently, looking for her own harness straps in the seat behind Lokomorra. She paused, then met their stares. "What? It's true."

Lhyn shook her head. "You really do think like a warrior."

"I *am* a warrior."

"The hatch is sealed," Zeppy said over the com. *"We're good to go."*

With everyone strapped in and launch permission received, Lokomorra lifted the craft off the deck and nosed into the exit tunnel. Guidance lights flashed down its length, and to the left Rahel could see the large window of the control room. She wondered if the same crew members were inside now as when she had been there with the captain.

The bay doors were already open, a square of deepest black against the brightly lit tunnel. She was fascinated by the way the atmospheric force field passed over their shuttle, a perfect white line following the contours of the craft before they reached the doors. During her tour, she had asked Captain Serrado why the force field wasn't flush with the *Phoenix*'s hull.

"So we can repair it without exposing the whole tunnel to vacuum and sending crew out in envirosuits," was the answer.

One of the biggest surprises of her first patrol was how practical the Gaians were. With their advanced technology, she had expected things to be more magical. It was a relief that they weren't. Magical aliens would have been hard to live up to. Practical people who solved problems in ways that made sense to her—these were people she could work with.

The last of the tunnel slid past, and they emerged into the vastness of space. Rahel tried to imprint the view on her memory, but found it too much to take in. Millions of stars everywhere she looked, stretching into infinity . . . she didn't think anyone could be unchanged by a sight like this.

Then they passed over the *Phoenix*'s engine cradle and turned, and the previous view paled by comparison.

Ahead was an alien world, almost entirely ocean but for the mountains that marched across its surface in narrow, criss-crossing bands. They looked like bumpy little lines from here, but Lhyn had said yesterday that they were twice as tall as anything on Alsea—five times, if you counted the part underwater.

And behind Enkara, bigger than anything Rahel could have imagined, was the gas giant Sisifenach. It seemed blurry, with no sharp outlines, making her want to rub her eyes and look again. The bands of red, orange, and yellow that encircled it were interrupted by vortices of a red so dark as to be nearly purple. They were massive storms with phenomenal wind speeds, and each could fit three or four Alseas. The numbers were a struggle to wrap her brain around, but looking at it now, with her own eyes, she understood. *This* was the magic of the Gaians: their ability to travel among such wonders.

"Did I tell you what Sisifenach means?" Lhyn asked.

Rahel shook her head. "I thought it was a sneeze."

Lokomorra chuckled, and Lhyn stared at her in open-mouthed disbelief.

"A *sneeze*?"

She shrugged, holding back a smile. "Sounded like it."

Lhyn's brows drew together. "It *means*," she said in a deliberate manner, "queen of storms."

"Which is apt, don't you think?" Lokomorra asked. "The stormiest people I know are all women."

"Oh, for the—I can't believe you said that!"

"Two words," he said. "Dr. Wells."

"You're giving me a data set of one? Worse than useless."

"My mother. There's two."

"Now we know why you never went into science."

Rahel gave up on the smile. "He's playing you, and you're letting him."

"Hey! Don't spoil it."

"Sayana," Zeppy said over the com. *"It's time."*

Lhyn didn't allow her envy or longing to show on her face. "Be safe."

"I will. Don't let him yank you off."

As she opened the airlock, she heard Lokomorra asking, "Does yanking off mean what I think it means?"

"No," Lhyn said flatly, and Rahel laughed to herself before shutting the door behind her.

Zeppy and his crew were already in envirosuits, sitting in the fold-out seats along the bulkhead and holding their helmets in their laps. He pointed to the locker closest to the airlock.

Inside was an envirosuit in the size that Commander Cox had determined fit her best. She had checked it before sending it aboard, but mindful of her recent training, she checked it again to be sure. Though Enkara had a thin atmosphere, its extremely low levels of oxygen meant that any faults in this suit would result in rapid asphyxiation.

Satisfied with her inspection, she carried the bulky suit over to the tanks.

Dr. Wells had been the one to point out that if the *Resilere* couldn't distinguish between most Gaians, they might consider Gaians in envirosuits to be an entirely different species. The best solution was to have Rahel suit up in front of them, allowing them to see the change.

Rez came to the side of the tank, plastering itself to the material. She had another vision of Mouse asking where she had been and realized she shouldn't have stayed up front. Right now, she was their only guarantor of safety. Though surely within their empathic range, her absence had made them nervous.

"I'm sorry," she said, projecting her regret. "We should have known. But I'm here now."

She stripped off her Bondlancer's Guard uniform and folded it carefully, setting the jacket and trousers atop her polished boots.

Rez watched with interest, rumpling its skin. To its thinking, she had probably just discarded a shell.

Slowly, she drew on the envirosuit's legs, leaving the upper part hanging while she pushed her feet into the thick boots and sealed the connections. Each lit with a green line, indicating a proper seal.

Getting her arms in place was more awkward, but once they were in, she closed the front without difficulty. When that seal lit up with its own green line, she pulled on the gloves and set those seals. Before taking the final step, she squatted down and rested a gloved hand against the tank wall, covering one of Rez's armtips. It curled up and down again, acknowledging their connection.

She picked up the heavy helmet and set it in place, giving the quarter-turn that closed the final seal. The near silence that suddenly pressed on her ears was the one thing she disliked about this suit. It felt claustrophobic.

The helmet display activated, informing her of the condition of all seals, the suit's internal and external temperatures, and the operational health of the built-in carbon dioxide scrubbers. A colored cylinder, mostly green with a red base, indicated the current amount of oxygen available to the scrubbers.

Every breath she exhaled was full of unused oxygen along with the carbon dioxide. The scrubbers extracted the carbon dioxide, added a bit of fresh oxygen, and returned the mix to her suit.

Beside the green cylinder, in large, shifting digits, was the all-important time remaining readout. Without external oxygen packs, these suits were good for six hours.

Now fully encased, she set her gloved hand against the tank again, thinking of warmrons and lying on the couch with Sharro.

Rez's violet eyes roamed up and down her new shell—a word she could now use literally—and its skin smoothed out.

"Sayana to Dr. Rivers," she said. "You can tell Dr. Wells that it was a good idea. Rez knows it's still me inside this suit."

"She'll be glad to hear it. Everything is green?"

"I did go through the training. Don't worry."

"One thing you need to know about me. I always worry about my friends."

She watched Rez move away and said, "Commander Cox wouldn't let me go if he wasn't sure I'd be safe. He has a healthy respect for Captain Serrado's status as my oath holder. And Dr. Well's status as my protector."

Lhyn's smile was audible in her voice. *"Good. That should keep him in line."*

She carried her uniform back to the locker, then unsealed her helmet and took a relieved breath as she sat next to Zeppy.

"All set?" he asked, taking her helmet so she could strap in.

"All set." Gaians had far too many ways to say *I'm ready.*

Lhyn was lucky, being able to sit up front with the full view of where they were going. Rahel wished she could see Enkara's oceans and mountains zooming up as they passed through the thin atmosphere and descended. Then again, Lhyn certainly wished she could watch the release of the *Resilere.* She would be seeing it through the shuttle's external cams, the tank cams, and Rahel's own helmet cam, but that wasn't the same.

Of the two options, she'd take being with the *Resilere.*

Lokomorra kept them apprised of their progress on the com link that would remain open for all team members until the end of the mission. She felt the change when their angle of descent lessened. When it leveled out altogether, Zeppy gave the order for everyone to put on their helmets and check their readouts.

"The tide's already gone out from where the shuttle landed last time," Lokomorra said. *"We're landing a kilometer further on."*

Commander Jalta had told them to expect that. They were chasing the tide out, which was better than running from it coming in, considering the speed at which it rose. It would have been ideal to release the *Resilere* at high tide, in that brief window when it was neither rising nor falling, but the only way to do that would have been to release them at a location a quarter of the way around the moon—or wait in orbit far longer than Captain Serrado had time for.

Lokomorra set them down with hardly a jar. Once the cargo bay had equalized its pressure with the outside, Zeppy opened the hatch onto Rahel's first alien world.

She stood in the opening, staring in wonder.

The sky was a dark violet-blue, and lapping at their landing struts was water of a similar color, stretching to a range of impossibly high mountains. They lacked snow, trees, or any vegetation that she could see above the high tide line. That line was made obvious by a thin coating of blue and purple that she knew to be seaweed, covering the rocks to the current sea level.

Above that line, the rugged geology was exposed. Bands of pink and silver gleamed against the black rock that composed the majority of the sharp-edged peaks.

Looming over the mountains was the one thing that made this truly alien: the massive bulk of Sisifenach, lit from the side. She could even make out some of the storm systems.

"Sayana, get down the stairs and gawk from there," Zeppy said. *"We need to get these tanks out."*

"Sorry." She walked down the steps and stepped carefully into the shallow water, testing her footing. The substrate was made up of black rocks rounded by eons of wave action—not the easiest thing to walk on even if they weren't coated with slippery patches of blue seaweed. Interspersed throughout the cobbles were occasional crystals of pink or silver, all beneath water so clear that she could count every grain of sand between the rocks.

As Zeppy extended the control chair, she turned to look past the shuttle and was awed a second time. They had landed at the foot of another mountain range, and at this close distance she couldn't make out its peaks. It wasn't that they were obscured in clouds—there were no clouds—but that she simply couldn't see that far.

"Great Goddess above," she murmured.

"Shekking amazing, isn't it?" Lhyn said.

"Oh, yes. I wonder if Fahla comes here."

A small wave rolled in, surging past her and tumbling over the rocks beyond the shuttle's nose. She wished she could hear it without the dampening effect of her helmet.

"Hurry up!" Zeppy said impatiently. *"You should have had those straps off already!"*

A chorus of apologies came through her com. Within a minute, Rahel saw the loader descend from the shuttle's ceiling. It vanished from her sight, then reappeared holding one of the tanks. Zeppy's chair swung to the side, and the loader emerged. She watched it extend half the length of the shuttle before gently placing the tank on the rocks.

Zeppy did his best to keep the tank level, but the rocks weren't, and it tilted toward the ocean. The adult Resilere were frantic, swimming round and round their confined space and bumping up against the lid. Rahel splashed out toward them, the water rising higher on her legs with every step. She slipped, nearly fell on her backside, and finally made it to the tank as the loader vanished into the shuttle again.

"Hold on," she said, trying to project assurance. "Just a bit longer!"

Small waves rolled past the tank, swamping the front and sliding up its lid to splash over the sides. Getting that lid off was going to be much harder here than in hydroponics.

With a delicate touch that Rahel was now recognizing as highly skilled, Zeppy brought out the second tank and set it next to the first. His crew scrambled down the stairs and waded out, with him close behind. When they arrived, Rahel had already pushed up one corner of the closest tank. She stepped back and let them take over.

The moment the lid came off and the screen was rolled back, every adult *Resilere* boiled up and over the front, meeting a wave as it rolled in and vanishing into it. Zeppy and his crew were carrying the lid back to the shuttle, but Rahel forgot their existence as the memory hit.

She was in the detention cell, collapsed and sobbing in her mother's arms. In the space of minutes, she had gone from trapped and lost to having both her dreams and her freedom returned to her.

"Thank you," she choked out.

With a sigh, her mother pressed a kiss into her hair. "It's a little late," she said softly. "But we got there, didn't we?"

Water surged against her legs and arm, bringing her back to reality. She had lost her balance again, and somehow caught herself with one hand on the rocks.

"Rahel? Are you all right?" Lhyn asked.

She pushed herself upright and waded to the tank, gripping its edge for more stability. "I'm fine. Just a blast of memory. They're . . ." She let out a sound that could have passed for a laugh. "They're very, very grateful."

"There are still hatchlings in the tank," Lhyn said. *"They're getting stirred up by the waves coming in. Some of them are hiding in the corners, like they don't know what to do. All of the adults are gone."*

Zeppy and the others had thrown the lid into the shuttle and were returning.

"Do you hear any communication from the adults?"

"None." She sounded concerned. *"Would you pull one of the hydrophones and stick it to the outside?"*

"Doing it now." As Zeppy's crew gathered around the second tank, she waded to the front corner, popped the hydrophone off, and reattached it just before an incoming wave would have rolled over her helmet. "It's in place."

"I see it, thank you."

The lid came off the second tank, and one of the crew flinched as a *Resilere* used him for a rebound point, leaping from the tank to him and then to the water.

This time Rahel was prepared for the memory, and when it passed she was still upright, holding tightly to the tank.

"We're slinging this lid inside and going back in," Zeppy said. *"I'll stay at the bottom of the steps in case you need anything."*

"Thank you, Commander."

"And stay away from the fronts of those tanks. They're heavy enough that the waves shouldn't shift them, but if they do, they'll move forward."

"Understood." She scanned the area ahead of the tanks, hoping for a glimpse of the *Resilere*. The constantly swirling water and thin layer of foam made visibility difficult, and she swallowed her sharp disappointment at the idea of such an anticlimactic farewell. What did she expect, that they would all come back for a warmron?

Joyous anticipation flooded her senses, tearing apart the threads of her dismay.

"Oh my fucking stars," Lhyn said.

"What? What is it?"

Her voice was hushed. *"They're singing."*

Rahel ducked down to look in the tank, trying to keep still despite the buffeting of the water. "Hoi," she whispered. "Look at that! Do you see them?"

"I do."

Inside the tank, every hatchling was moving toward the front—and they were afire with blue, green, and red bioluminescence. The waves rolled in, shifting the rocks and seaweed the adults had carried in earlier, but the hatchlings held fast to the tank floor and walls. They seemed united in purpose, all rippling along at the same speed.

The first ones were already climbing the front wall, and Rahel crept forward to watch. Frustrated at not being able to see well enough, she finally went down to her hands and knees and ducked her helmet underwater.

Much better. Now she could see through the tank walls to the ocean beyond. And there they were, just past the tanks: all twelve adult *Resilere,* lined up and playing matching patterns of bioluminescence. She didn't know if it was the same as their hatching song, but the voice was already murmuring to her.

"Ah! Fantastic," Lhyn said. *"Can you hold that position?"*

"I can. The waves aren't that strong."

It wasn't really a lie. The waves weren't strong coming in, but they had significant suction going out. Still, she wasn't about to move from this perfect spot.

The murmur in her mind gradually rose in volume and intensity, filling her with exhilaration and a sense of perfect belonging. Life began here, and all she had to do was leave this place and follow. The voice would take her home.

She wanted to go home.

Her body floated, weightless, and she let the next wave take her as it retreated, pulling her home—

She was brought up abruptly, hands under her arms yanking her backward and a harsh voice shouting in her ear. It sounded nothing like the loving voice beckoning her forward. She fought the hold, but her body was not responding as it should. It was wrapped in too many layers, unable to properly move. She lifted her hands, finding a helmet trapping her head, and began to undo it.

The voices multiplied, drowning her in confusion until one rang out above the rest.

"First Guard Sayana, settle! That is an order!"

She stopped at the barked command in High Alsean. "Captain?"

"Rahel." Captain Serrado sounded more relieved than Rahel had ever heard her. *"Stand still and let Commander Przepyszny reset your helmet."*

"Yes, Captain."

Water droplets were still running down her faceplate, making it obvious when it shifted in place. She had not noticed the hiss of escaping air until it stopped, leaving her in silence once more. From behind, Zeppy's worry and the sharp remnants of fear pierced her senses.

"It's sealed, Captain," he said.

"Rahel, what is your time remaining?"

She had to concentrate to pull her focus back to the digital readout. "It's . . . thirty-six minutes." It had been five hours and twelve minutes the last time she had glanced at it. Beside the timer, the green cylinder showing available oxygen for the scrubbers had dropped to a level barely above its red base.

"Do you know where you are?"

"On Enkara. I'm sorry, I didn't mean to—" She stopped. In truth, she *had* meant to join the *Resilere*.

"I know. It's all right, Commander Przepyszny stopped you before you got far. Let him take you back to the shuttle."

"Captain—"

"The hatchlings are all out. It's time to come home."

The word stopped her cold. She looked out at the water, already shallower as the tide continued to retreat. This was not her home.

"Yes, Captain." With a hard swallow, she turned.

A *Resilere* surged out of the water at her side, arms reaching out. She dropped to her knees, overjoyed that she had one more chance. "Rez!"

It coiled its arms around her gloved wrists, and she was—

Lying on the sofa, her head resting on Sharro's lap while her legs were across her mother's. After more than eight moons in lonely exile or a form of incarceration, this felt like a dream. She reached for her mother's hand and said, "I thought there was no magic left in the world."

Sharro's fingertips drifted down her jaw. "The best explorers were the ones who wanted to come back home."

The memory faded, replaced by a vision. She knelt on Dock One, but there was no storm and no danger. Beneath a cloudless sky, docked ships rose and fell on the breath of the bay, their quiet movement told in soft clangs and creaks.

A wave rose from the flat water and surged across the boards, leaving behind a fish that calmly settled upright on its fins. It looked up at her with intelligence in its violet eyes, its scales reflecting the blue of the sky.

Then it gave a twitch of its tail and launched into a graceful arc, clearing the dock to vanish in the bay.

The boards beneath her knees became rounded rocks, and the creaks and clangs faded to the quiet cocoon of her helmet.

Rez released her wrists, skin sparkling blue, and slipped beneath the water.

She refused to sniff on an open com. Instead, she took a deep, measured breath and said, "Safe journey. May Fahla guide and protect you."

41

RESILIENCE

Alejandra Wells stood back and made a sweeping gesture into her quarters. "Come on in."

"Thank you." Ekatya stepped through and looked around with interest. She had never been here before and was intrigued by the signs of a hidden private life.

Senior officer quarters were all constructed on the same general floor plan and furnished the same way, until the officers moved in and arranged things to their personal tastes.

Alejandra had gotten rid of the standard L-shaped sofa across from the entry and replaced it with a long workbench illuminated with custom lights. It was covered with at least thirty small paint jars in racks, a profusion of delicate paintbrushes, cloths bearing colorful stains, and other artistic paraphernalia. A tall stool was tucked beneath.

The bulkhead above had been stripped of the standard tile art; large watercolors hung there instead. It sported the usual alcoves full of plants, but where Ekatya's alcoves held the standard species that she had neither time nor desire to care for, these were filled with exotics she didn't recognize. Obviously, Alejandra was not one of those officers who gave the botany section entry permission to care for her plants.

Alejandra followed her gaze. "I've had some of those for twenty-five years. The two over there are from my home world. The rest I picked up on various stations."

"They're beautiful."

"Thank you. I walked away from crop genetics, but I never stopped loving plants."

There was a book's worth of history in that statement. Ekatya looked forward to learning it.

She noted the individual chairs set around the room and how none of them were arranged for company or conversation. Even the dining table seemed unused to guests, covered as it was by spillover from the workbench.

The sound of water drew her attention to the wall display, which showed small waves washing onto a steeply sloped, cobbled shore. As each wave retreated, the cobbles rolled with a rumbling clatter. In the distance, two immense mountain ranges intersected, their craggy peaks spiking into a sky of cloudless violet-blue. Alejandra had paired the Enkara program with soft, haunting piano music that emphasized the loneliness of the landscape.

"I see Lhyn gave you her new scenic program," Ekatya said.

"I figured it was the closest I'd ever get. It's beautiful, in an austere way. I like to think of the *Resilere* singing under there." Alejandra set one hand on her hip. "And not trying to kill Rahel again."

"They didn't *try* to kill her."

"Pretty damned effective for not trying." With her free hand, she pointed at the bottle in Ekatya's hand. "That's not iceflame."

"After last time? I'm going to need a few weeks before I'm ready to drink that again. Or a few months." She carried the bottle to the dining table, where the clutter was stacked up to clear enough space for two small dishes and a plate of finger foods. "What do you do when we go through a base space transition? Doesn't this end up everywhere?"

Alejandra was in the kitchen, pulling wine glasses from the rack. "I clean up just before. It all reappears within hours. I think it's some sort of energy-based alien living in my quarters and office." She carried the glasses over and added, "Maybe we should get Rahel to look for it."

"Maybe we should. She's the reason I have this." Ekatya held up the bottle for examination. "Valkinon. The finest wine produced on Alsea. I can tell you from experience that it's divine." She pulled the tab and let the blue vapor trickle over her hand.

"Why is she the reason you have it?" Alejandra watched her pour.

"Because this was a gift from the Bondlancer of Alsea." She lifted her glass, enjoying the play of light in its sapphire depths. "Who told me, at the oath ceremony, that she expected me to return Rahel whole and unharmed. Which I've mostly managed to do. Salomen said I couldn't open the bottle until the end of the first patrol. So—to a successful patrol and a mostly intact First Guard."

Alejandra chuckled. "She's fully intact. I made sure of it. But it certainly wasn't for lack of effort. Sainted Shippers, that girl gets in a lot of trouble." She tapped her glass against Ekatya's and drank, eyes sliding half-shut with pleasure. "You weren't exaggerating. This *is* divine." After another sip, she pulled out one of the chairs and sat, pointing at the other in an unspoken command.

"How are you doing with that?" Ekatya asked as she took her own seat.

"With what?"

"How much trouble she got herself into."

"Eh. It all worked out."

Ekatya raised her eyebrows.

"Oh, don't start. I'm fine, Ekatya. I'm not going to suddenly revert back to a grief-stricken parent. Though I do have enormous sympathy for her mother. That poor woman must have gone through Tartarus raising her."

"It can't have been easy opening that part of your heart for the first time and then watching her on Enkara."

"I'm *fine*." She paused. "But I'm damned glad you got her attention."

Ekatya was beginning to understand that Alejandra Wells never wanted anyone to see her vulnerable points. That she had revealed them the night of Rahel's surgery was very much out of the ordinary—and if tonight was any indication, it probably wouldn't be repeated any time soon.

"I spoke with Lancer Tal this afternoon," she said, abandoning the effort. "Told her the whole story. She said you were right—the *Resilere* must be extremely powerful empaths, given how easily Rez overwhelmed Rahel while trying to communicate. That's also why they could pick up on her projections, even though she's a mid empath and never learned to do it." She watched a wave pull itself back down the cobbles, a peaceful scene far removed from that singular moment of fear. "She thinks there are only four people in the universe who could have broken through the *Resilere*'s song at that point. Her mother, Sharro, Salomen . . . and me."

"Because you're her oath holder?" Alejandra looked entirely too satisfied. "And how are you doing with that?"

"Well, it's—" Ekatya stopped. "You're a shit."

A gleeful chortle escaped as Alejandra picked up her glass and tipped it in Ekatya's direction. "I give as good as I get."

"You didn't give me anything! All I got was a deflection."

"You didn't wait long enough to ask. If you want that from me, you're better off waiting until this bottle is empty."

"Are you telling me to get you drunk before I ask how you're feeling?"

"Yes."

"For the love of flight." Ekatya seized the bottle and filled her friend's glass to the brim. "There. Drink up."

Alejandra really did have a nice laugh when she let it go.

"In the interests of modeling the behavior I'd like to see," Ekatya said primly, "I'm a little spooked about having that kind of power over a member of my crew. They didn't cover this in Fleet training. I knew I had Rahel's loyalty, but this is something different."

Alejandra leaned down and sipped from her glass where it sat on the table. With the liquid at a safer level, she picked it up and examined its color. "You're only her second oath holder. Third, after Bondlancer Opah, but you're kind of co-oath holders." She looked over the top of the glass. "I read through Rahel's records again, when I knew her better and could understand what they meant. She would have gone to prison to defend the honor of her first oath holder *after* he was dead. If she thinks you're worthy of her loyalty, you have it for life."

"Was that supposed to make me feel less spooked?"

"Nope. Just . . . informed." She sipped her wine. "Stars above, this is good. Can I put in an order for more when you go down there on leave?"

"No, but you can get it yourself."

"We're allowing full shore leave now? What changed the tiny minds of those admirals?"

"Rahel. Though I don't think they changed their minds so much as they couldn't justify keeping a lid on shore leave when we have an Alsean warrior serving with us. Having her first patrol turn out so well took away their best argument."

"Well, it's about time. Alsea's been open to us for six months already." Alejandra set her drink aside, then pulled up a foot and wrapped her arms around the bent leg. "That'll help with crew rotation. I'm tired of losing three-quarters of my staff every time we hit a space station."

"It took a whole patrol for the crew to get used to a single mid empath. A planet full of them? And some of them high empaths? I don't think we'll see a stampede to the shuttles."

"Then they're fools. I'd rather see Alsea than the inside of another space can. I'm going down."

"Good. You've been invited to the State House."

The raised leg slid to the floor as she sat up straight. "I—why?"

"Lancer Tal has a mystery she'd like to solve." Ekatya smiled in anticipation; she was about to hand Alejandra a scientist's dream come true. "They have ten pairs of divine tyrees now, and no explanation as to why they've suddenly reappeared after so long. The High Council voted to keep it all under wraps, so they haven't let the scholar caste in on it. The only ones studying it are templars."

"They gave a medical mystery to religious scholars?"

"That's the problem. It's perceived as a religious mystery, not a medical one. Lancer Tal sees it differently. I mentioned that my chief surgeon is the best in Fleet and might be open to a personal project."

"A *personal* project," Alejandra repeated.

"Lancer Tal is willing to let you study her divine tyree bond with Salomen, including Sharings. You'll be the first Gaian doctor given access."

Alejandra's eyes widened.

"You can imagine how hot that data will be," Ekatya continued. "And how much Sholokhov would love to get his hands on it."

"Ugh. I don't want to think about what makes that man happy."

"Unfortunately, I have to. If he somehow finds out what you're doing, there can't be any data for him to access. You can't keep it on the ship's computers. I'll have Kenji set up an isolated medpad for you, with any programs you need. But that's why this has to be a personal project. You'll have to do it on your own time."

Alejandra took a thoughtful drink and stared past her shoulder. After several seconds of silence, she met Ekatya's eyes and said, "Just to see if I have this in order. First you march into my office and throw your rank around to pull me off duty because you say I work too much. Then you volunteer me to the Lancer of Alsea for a project I'm supposed to do in *addition* to my work."

Ekatya tried not to show her dismay. "Er . . . yes? I thought it was something that would appeal to you."

"And if I say no, you'll have to go back and admit that you promised more than you could deliver."

"I didn't *promise* . . ."

"But you already got me an invitation from the Lancer herself."

Ekatya winced.

"And access to Sharings between her and Bondlancer Opah," Alejandra went on implacably. "The one thing Lhyn couldn't study because she doesn't have the tools for it." At Ekatya's nod, she set her jaw. "My shiny ass you didn't promise. You've already made the arrangements and waited until now to ask me."

"I only talked to her this afternoon! And nothing is set—" She stopped when she saw Alejandra's delighted smile.

"You are the *best* of friends. Can we get to Alsea any faster?"

"You enjoyed that," she accused.

"Hugely. You looked so worried!" Alejandra snickered. "I only wish I could have gotten a picture."

Ekatya held up two fingers pressed together in a gesture she had learned from Andira. "If you're going to spend any time on Alsea, you should know what this means."

"Hm. Not the number two, I assume."

She shifted the gesture to a more familiar version and smiled at the explosion of laughter. "I'm glad you understand."

"I understand that when my captain tells me to fuck off, we've entered a new phase of friendship."

"That's the truth and a half." She sobered. "You're really all right with the fact that I volunteered you?"

"Yes, yes." Alejandra waved her glass in a dismissive motion, coming alarmingly close to spilling. "It was high-handed, but I'm learning to expect that from you."

"Now, wait a minute—"

"You thought I'd jump at this and you were right. I already have some ideas about where to go with it. I'll need comparators. I can't just study a divine tyree bond; I need access to a normal tyree bond and a pair of Alseans who are bonded but not tyrees. Preferably a few pairs of each." She hummed thoughtfully. "I wonder if Rahel would be willing to introduce me to her mother and Sharro. That could be fun."

"For you. Probably not for her." Ekatya hid a smile behind her glass. "But I can give you access to another few Sharings that may or may not be useful to you. Lhyn said you gave her a clean bill of health."

Alejandra instantly snapped back to her professional demeanor. "The last tests were clear, yes. Her neurotransmitter regulation has finally normalized. But that only means she's physically recovered. Mentally—"

"You've held her back long enough. You've held *us* back."

"She had a panic attack on this patrol, Ekatya."

"The first one in three months! I think she had a good reason, don't you? And she controlled it."

"But it does show that she's still vulnerable," Alejandra argued. "Putting her in a Sharing—we have no idea what that does to the Gaian brain. It's a risk."

"It's a risk she wants to take. That's her right."

"We couldn't reproduce your telepathic connection even under perfect laboratory conditions. We know her brain has lasting—"

"Do not say that word."

Her harsh tone startled them both. She took a gulp of her wine and studied its dark blue depths.

"I can't stop you," Alejandra said quietly. "But please consider that Lhyn's experience means she's not the same as she was during your first Sharings. You have no way of knowing how she'll be affected now."

"I do know. So does she." She looked up. "I asked you once to take a leap of faith. We saved Lhyn because you did."

Alejandra gave a resigned nod. "Is this another leap?"

"Sharing won't hurt Lhyn. On the contrary, she needs it." She saw the skepticism and added, "The way a person who's been hurt needs to go home. It's a comfort. A connection that helps heal the psyche."

"You make it sound like a cup of hot chocolate." Alejandra exhaled as she ran a hand through her loose hair. "All right. But you're not doing it without me there."

Ekatya refrained from pointing out that she had already offered. "Done. You can scan us all you want to."

"Oh, I plan to. Exhaustively. Let's hope this is the most uneventful Sharing ever experienced on Alsea."

"That sounds like a toast." She raised her glass. "May our leave be as boring as a box of rocks."

Alejandra sat up straight with a look of mock horror. "Now you've cursed us! Remember the last box of rocks we came in contact with? Aliens, quarantine . . . ?"

"Oh. Right." She cast around for an alternative. "May Fahla smile upon us?"

"You're terrible at this." Alejandra retrieved her glass, still a little too full. "A toast to the comforts of home. We brought the *Resilere* home, now we're bringing Lhyn and Rahel."

"To the comforts of home." Ekatya held the wine on her tongue, savoring the changing flavors that burst on her taste buds in a subtle, ordered parade before she swallowed and asked, "Where is home for you?"

"Right here." Alejandra glanced around her quarters with a smile. "Home is where my work is. Lately, though . . . I'm starting to think there might be more here."

"Can I take credit for that?"

She had meant it as a tease, but Alejandra looked at her seriously. "You can take credit for quite a bit of it. A ship takes on the personality of its captain. Have you worn those bars so long that you've forgotten?"

Startled by the unexpected compliment, Ekatya stumbled over her answer. "I, er, never actually considered—"

"Your decisions," Alejandra interrupted. "Your command style. Everyone takes their cues from you. How many captains do you think would have ordered their crews to help the *Resilere*? We could have solved our infestation problem by sitting and waiting for them to solidify. It would have been the safest option. Zero risk to the crew."

"The safest option isn't always the right one."

"You just proved my point. And last night, Rahel told me the *Phoenix* is starting to feel like home to her. I think you can take a lot of credit for that, too."

"No, that one's on you. I still make her nervous."

"Do you think she'd feel at home so soon if you hadn't ordered the section chiefs to treat her like a VIP? She has no idea that new officers don't normally get hours of one-on-one time with us. You could have turned her over to Cox from day one. Left her to settle in the section she wants. It would have been easier for everyone." She leaned forward, her expression earnest and open as it rarely was. "We can do easy and safe and convenient. Or we can do what's right. You know why I feel there might be more here? Because I know which decision you'll make, every time. You'll do what's right."

Ekatya shook her head, thinking of her stupidity in the lift shaft. "Not always."

"When it counts."

"Not always," she repeated. "I didn't do the right thing on Alsea. Not until it was almost too late. If Andira hadn't outmaneuvered both me and my exec with the self-destruct, we'd have lost the *Caphenon* and thousands would have died in Blacksun Basin." Andira might not have lived through that battle, not with three hundred ground pounders landing intact. The thought still haunted her.

Alejandra picked a cracker off the plate, loaded with colorful slices of fruit and cheese. "Don't make me eat all of these myself. That was more than two and a half years ago. Are you the same person now that you were then?"

"No." Ekatya tried a cracker and found its salty-sweet combination of flavors a good complement to the wine. "Alsea changed me. A tour of duty under Sholokhov's thumb changed me. Being a tyree has changed me. I'm not the same person at all."

"I'm not the same person I was at the start of this patrol. And I didn't know that other Ekatya. I know this one. She's a friend."

"I knew the other Alejandra," Ekatya said. "The one before this patrol. She was a pain in my ass."

Alejandra's surprised sputter turned into a laugh. "And you think this one won't be?"

"I have no doubt she will." Ekatya grinned at her and crunched another cracker.

Alejandra held one between forefinger and thumb. "While I was making these, I was thinking about the *Resilere*. About how perfectly they're named. Medically speaking, they're one of the most resilient species I've ever heard of. They can almost literally come back from death. Solidifying means a complete cessation of normal body processes. I can't begin to guess how they do it." She popped the cracker in her mouth and lifted her wine.

Ekatya sipped her own and waited. She was beginning to learn the signs of when her friend was opening up.

"It occurred to me," Alejandra continued, "that we're pretty resilient ourselves. Rahel says she's had three lives: the life she lived before her best friend died, the life between that moment and when she took Bondlancer Opah hostage, and the life since then. She's lost parts of herself and been reborn."

"The way you have."

She nodded. "I've been around long enough that I could be thinking about retirement. I never imagined I'd be thinking in terms of rebirth. But that's what it feels like. I've hurt for Josue more in the last few weeks than I did for the last two decades. But it's different. It's more . . . peaceful. A hurt I can live with instead of one that tears me apart. I feel more *alive*, if that makes any sense."

"It does."

"And you. You're not the same person you were before Alsea. Another rebirth."

Ekatya stared at her, the sudden realization making her skin prickle. "I've thought so often about what we lost when Lhyn was tortured. But it's not really about loss, is it? Or it's not only about that. She's changed, too. She was strong before, but now . . ."

"She's stronger."

"Shippers, yes. She won't let fear stop her. She won't even let it slow her down."

"Resilience." Alejandra raised her glass. "It's the difference between surviving and truly living. I'd rather live."

"Resilience," Ekatya said, tapping their glasses together. As she drank, her gaze went to the display, where a wave crested and crashed onto the cobbles. Somewhere beneath those pristine waters, the *Resilere* and their hatchlings were home.

She wondered if they were singing.

Published by Heartsome Publishing
Staffordshire
United Kingdom
www.heartsomebooks.com

Available in ebook and paperback.
ISBN: 978-1-912684-03-8
First Heartsome edition: October 2018

This is a work of fiction. Names, places and incidents are either products of the author's imagination or used fictitiously. Any resemblance to actual persons, living or dead (except for satirical purposes), is entirely coincidental.
Fletcher DeLancey asserts the moral right to be identified as the author of this work.

ABOUT THE AUTHOR

Fletcher DeLancey is an Oregon expatriate who left her beloved state when she met a Portuguese woman and had to choose between home and heart. She chose heart. Now she lives in the beautiful sunny Algarve, where she writes full-time, teaches Pilates, tries to learn the local birds and plants, and samples every Portuguese dish she can get her hands on. (There are many. It's going to take a while.)

She is best known for her science fiction/fantasy series Chronicles of Alsea, which has collected an Independent Publisher's Award, a Golden Crown Literary Society Award, a Rainbow Award, and been shortlisted for a Lambda Literary Award.

Fletcher believes that women need far more representation in science fiction and fantasy, and takes great pleasure in writing complex stories with women heading up the action. Her day is made every time another reader says, "I didn't think I liked science fiction, but then I read yours."

All about Alsea: alseaworld.com
Facebook: facebook.com/fletcherdelanceyauthor
Twitter: @AlseaAuthor

ALSO BY FLETCHER DELANCEY

The Chronicles of Alsea series:

The Caphenon

Without A Front: The Producer's Challenge

Without A Front: The Warrior's Challenge

Catalyst

Vellmar the Blade

Outcaste

Resilience

Now available worldwide in paperback and ebook.

Coming Soon

Uprising

CPSIA information can be obtained
at www.ICGtesting.com
Printed in the USA
LVHW112306120319
610461LV00001B/84/P